Readers love *Love Can't Conquer* by KIM FIELDING

"Author Kim Fielding once again gives us a gorgeous story of love and healing—of quiet determination and strength and does so with the greatest of skill."
　　　　—Joyfully Jay

"Kim Fielding's writing is superb with this one. Fantastic!"
　　　　—The Novel Approach

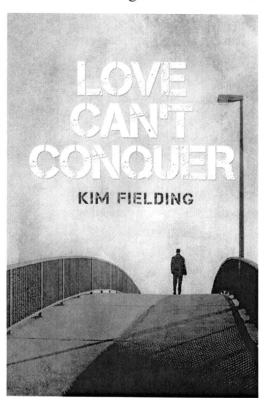

"Kim Fielding's *Love Can't Conquer* is a beautifully written story about two very imperfect, flawed men who find one another when they need each other the most."
　　　　—Diverse Reader

"The story was gripping and emotional and I had a hard time putting it down…"
　　　　—Two Chicks Obsessed

By KIM FIELDING

Alaska
Anyplace Else
Animal Magnetism
(Dreamspinner Anthology)
Astounding!
The Border
Brute
Don't Try This at Home
(Dreamspinner Anthology)
Grateful
A Great Miracle Happened There
Grown-up
Housekeeping
Motel. Pool.
Night Shift
Once Upon a Time in the Weird
West (Multiple Author Anthology)
Pilgrimage
The Pillar
Phoenix
Rattlesnake
With Venona Keyes: Running
Blind
Saint Martin's Day
Snow on the Roof (Dreamspinner
Anthology)
Speechless • The Gig
Steamed Up (Dreamspinner
Anthology)
The Tin Box
Venetian Masks
Violet's Present

BONES
Good Bones
Buried Bones
The Gig
Bone Dry

GOTHIKA
Stitch (Multiple Author
Anthology)
Bones (Multiple Author
Anthology)
Claw (Multiple Author
Anthology)
Spirit (Multiple Author
Anthology)
Contact (Multiple Author
Anthology)

LOVE CAN'T
Love Can't Conquer
Love Is Heartless

Published by DREAMSPINNER PRESS
www.dreamspinnerpress.com

LOVE
IS
HEARTLESS

KIM FIELDING

Published by

DREAMSPINNER PRESS

5032 Capital Circle SW, Suite 2, PMB# 279, Tallahassee, FL 32305-7886 USA
www.dreamspinnerpress.com

Love Is Heartless
© 2017 Kim Fielding.

Cover Art
© 2017 Brooke Albrecht.
http://brookealbrechtstudio.com
Cover content is for illustrative purposes only and any person depicted on the cover is a model.

ISBN: 978-1-63533-213-1
Digital ISBN: 978-1-63533-214-8
Library of Congress Control Number: 2016914560
Published January 2017
v. 1.0

Printed in the United States of America
∞
This paper meets the requirements of
ANSI/NISO Z39.48-1992 (Permanence of Paper).

Thank you to the incomparable Amy Lane,
who gave me part of the name of a certain punk band.

PROLOGUE

September 1997

THE HANDCUFFS fucking hurt. That bitch of a cop could've used a zip tie, but she'd slapped cuffs on Nevin instead and ratcheted them tight enough to trap his small wrists. The knuckles of his right hand throbbed where they had connected with Prick's face. Nevin kicked hard at the inside of the squad car, but he only managed to hurt his foot, so he settled into a deep scowl instead.

The cop kept him waiting as she took her sweet time talking to Nevin's foster father. The guy's name was Price, but Nevin called him Prick instead—because he was one. Like right now, Prick stood in his driveway with the sun glaring off his bald spot, and he waved his hands in what looked like a dramatic retelling of the afternoon's events. Dramatic and full of fucking lies, no doubt.

Nevin Ng snarled as he watched. Prick's nose had swelled, and drying blood splattered his polo shirt. That was good.

The cop finished her conversation with Prick and then spent a long time talking to someone on her radio. When she finally plopped down into the front seat of the squad car, she slammed the door and sighed. She didn't say anything for such a long time that Nevin began to fidget.

"C'mon," he finally growled. "Juvie's waiting."

She twisted around to look at him through the metal grille. "How old are you, Nevin?"

"Fifteen." He looked younger. On the rare occasions he'd gone to a restaurant with any of his foster parents, the restaurant staff automatically handed him the children's menu and crayons. He fucking hated that.

"Pretty soon you'll be too old for juvie," the cop said.

"So?"

"So what do you think is going to happen when a pretty little thing like you ends up in jail?"

He bared his teeth. "Any of those assholes come near me, I'll rip their balls off." He would, too. He could beat the shit out of guys twice his size.

The cop snorted a laugh. "You're a tough little twerp, aren't you?" Her expression softened a bit as she looked at him. "Tell you what. Let's go get something to eat and have us a little chat."

"You're gonna give me a burger before hauling me in?"

"I was thinking something better than burgers. And if we have a good talk, maybe I won't have to haul you in."

Nevin narrowed his eyes. "You're just saying that to keep me calm. I know Prick's gonna press charges."

"Prick—um, Mr. Price—has no choice in the matter. I decide whether to arrest you, not him. And if I do, someone in the juvenile unit at the DA's office decides whether to file a petition." She faced forward, put on her seat belt, and started the engine.

Nevin's wrists still hurt, but now he had something else to think about while the car rumbled through traffic. He didn't know if she was telling him the truth about pressing charges, and he had no idea what her angle might be. What the fuck did she want from him? He considered various possibilities, but nothing made sense.

The car turned onto Macadam, which surprised him. He'd expected her to take I-5 over the river into Northeast, where the juvenile facility was. Instead she pulled into a small strip mall and parked. Then she got out, opened his door, and looked down at him.

"If I take those cuffs off, will you behave?"

"I can't eat with them on, lady."

"Not unless I spoon-feed you like a baby bird. But I'm not that maternal. Okay, I'll take them off, but I warn you—if you make a run for it, I *will* catch you. And then you'll be eating your dinner at Donald E. Long instead."

"They have shitty food."

She grinned. "So don't run."

As she unlocked the cuffs, he considered taking off. But although he was fast, this cop had long legs and looked athletic. Besides, this wasn't the kind of neighborhood where he could easily hide. And he was hungry. He followed her across the lot.

The restaurant turned out to be a Mexican place with an emphasis on healthy foods, which was weird. But they had enchiladas, and the cop let him order chips and guacamole. He dug in as soon as his food arrived, but she held her spoon and looked at him over her plate of rice and beans.

"For a little guy, you can really chow down."

He glared. "Look, lady—"

"Officer Pender to you, kid. Or ma'am."

Nevin rolled his eyes before shoving another forkful of enchilada into his mouth. Officer Pender was pretty. Really old—at least thirty—but with smooth sepia skin and closely shorn black hair. Maybe he should drop the attitude and try for a little flirting instead. She might buy that, even if she was a cop.

But before he could turn on the charm, she pointed her spoon at him. "How come you decked Price?"

He smiled slightly, remembering the satisfying feel of his fist connecting with Prick's nose. But when Officer Pender raised her eyebrows, he frowned. "You didn't read me my rights."

"That's because you're not in custody and I'm not interrogating you."

"Then why are you asking?"

"Because I think Mr. Price lied to me."

That surprised him, and he paused as he reached for his Coke. "Yeah? Why's that?"

"He told me he was trying to get you to do your homework, and instead you called him a name and punched him. But I gotta tell you, kid, my bullshit detector's top-notch, and I think he's full of it. Plus I talked to your social worker. She told me that you have problems with authority, but even when you get bumped around from school to school, you earn straight As."

He shrugged. His classwork came easy to him. Maybe he enjoyed it because it was something to concentrate on besides his crappy life.

"So why did you hit him?" Officer Pender asked.

"You won't believe me."

"Try me."

He pushed away his empty plate and crossed his arms. He knew the drill. He'd spill, but the only thing the cop would see was a runty kid who'd been in so many foster and group homes he couldn't remember them all—an unwanted mutt who'd end up in prison soon enough. That's what everyone else had seen when he tried to tell them about Prick. Officer Pender was going to take him to juvie—or somewhere else with locks on the doors—so Nevin's days in the Price household were thankfully over. Which would have been just peachy, except it left Becka with Prick and nobody to look out for her.

Fuck. Nevin had to at least *try*.

"Prick has another foster kid," he said. "Becka. She's... dunno. Eleven or twelve, I guess. But she thinks more like a preschooler. She doesn't even know her ABCs. She's sweet, though." She couldn't pronounce Nevin's name—she called him Nin instead—and she insisted he watch cartoons with her after school. In the mornings she'd hand him several plastic flower barrettes and wait patiently while he tackled the knots in her curly blonde hair.

Officer Pender's warm brown eyes had gone icy. "What about her?"

"Prick is.... Becka told me he touched her. She doesn't know the right words, so I don't know exactly what he...." Nevin shook his head impatiently. "She didn't like it. I know that much."

"Did you report this to anyone?"

"I tried. I told my social worker. She said I was making shit up 'cause Prick's too strict and I wanted another placement." Nevin hadn't expected that bitch to listen to him. A couple of years earlier, when another pearl of a foster father had taken to slapping him around, she hadn't believed Nevin because he didn't have bruises to show for it.

The officer's mouth thinned. "So what did you do?"

"I tried talking to Mrs. Prick, but she wouldn't even let me get the words out. That twat doesn't care about anything but herself."

"Watch the language. A young man's gotta learn to respect women."

"How'm I supposed to respect anyone who knows her husband's a skeeze and does nothing about it? Anyway, when she shot me down, I told Prick that if he touched Becka again, I'd cut off his dick while he was sleeping. He tried to grab me and I belted him."

"You hit him pretty hard." The corner of her mouth twitched. "Small but mighty."

Unsure what to make of her reaction, Nevin slurped his Coke.

Officer Pender silently ate her meal, seemingly oblivious to the way he toyed with his straw and jiggled his legs. When she was finished, she wiped her lips on a paper napkin and gave him a piercing look. "You care about Becka."

"Yeah, I guess so."

"You've only known her a few months."

"So?"

"Why defend her?"

He looked away. A few tables over, three women in their early twenties laughed as they sat down. They seemed so fucking happy. It wasn't fair. Years ago, he used to dream of someday being happy too. He used to think that even if he didn't land with a decent foster placement, at least someday he would grow up and create a loving family of his own. Now he knew better—and those kind of dreams were for dumbshits.

"She's just a little kid," Nevin said quietly. "I don't know what the hell happened to her family, but nobody's looking out for her."

"Nobody but you."

Nevin twitched his shoulders.

Officer Pender sat up straight and brushed an imaginary crumb from her uniform. If he had a nice uniform like that, he'd keep it clean too.

"You're at a crossroads, Nevin Ng," she said.

He glanced out the window toward the parking lot. "Huh?"

"Metaphorical. Look, life dealt you a shitty hand. That sucks. You can wallow in that shit until it covers you, kid. Until it *becomes* you. Then, I don't care what a tough cookie you are, you're going to end up rotting in prison or just plain dead."

"So?" he demanded, his jaw clenched.

"So you don't *have* to go that way, little man. If you're such a badass, you can beat that shit. Rise above it. Instead of wasting your life, you can use it to help some of the Beckas of the world. Because there's a lot of them, aren't there? Believe me, I know."

His throat was tight. "I can't do nothing for nobody."

"Bullshit. Today—right now—you can do something for yourself. That's where you got to start. Won't be so hard if some folks give you a hand. And I might know where to find those folks. And when you get a few more years on you—and maybe a few more inches—*then* you go out and save the world." She grinned and polished her badge with the heel of her hand. "Cape and tights optional."

Nevin glowered at her, but all she did was smile serenely back. And the damnedest thing happened—he looked at her and saw nothing but the truth. She believed that stuff she'd just told him. Maybe even… believed in him, just a little.

He leaned forward and sighed. "So who are these folks you're talking about?"

CHAPTER ONE

June 2015

CLUTCHING A cardboard coffee cup, Nevin stood on the small porch and watched the rain. Welcome to June in Oregon. A uniformed officer cut across the tidy front lawn and clomped up the stairs. He would have gone tromping right inside if Nevin hadn't stopped him with an upraised hand.

"Wipe your feet first, fuckwad."

The guy opened his mouth as if to protest but then clearly thought better of it and carefully scraped his shoes on the doormat.

"You gorillas just about done in there?" Nevin asked.

The uniformed officers were used to the way Nevin addressed them. Hell, they could treat uniforms the same way if they ever managed to move up the ranks.

This one shook his head. "We're gonna be a while."

"Fuck. Well, send out the landlord. I want to chat with him."

The landlord emerged a minute or two later, his denim-blue eyes wide in his pale face. He'd clearly been running his fingers through his hair, working the strands free of product and into a wavy, sand-colored tangle. He tugged at his polka-dot bow tie, which was a bit crooked. "You wanted to talk to me, Officer?"

"Detective. Nevin Ng. And yeah."

"Colin Westwood." The landlord held out a neatly manicured hand, which Nevin shook. Westwood's palm felt clammy, a good match for his green-tinged pallor. He looked like the type who'd shriek if he found a spider in his bathtub, but Nevin had to give him at least some credit. According to the first officers on the scene, Westwood had waited until emergency personnel arrived before rushing outside to puke into the rhododendrons. It was good of him to tend to the victim and not foul the crime scene.

The porch was bare except for the mat and a pair of empty flowerpots, and Nevin was tired of standing. "Follow me." He led the way down the sidewalk to his car.

Despite the seriousness of the situation, Westwood smiled. "I didn't realize the Portland Police Bureau got so creative with its cop cars."

Nevin stroked the hood, disrupting some of the raindrops that glistened like jewels. "She's all mine. A 1967 with a 400 V-8 and 335 horses under her hood."

"It's… purple."

"Factory original color. Plum mist. Her name's Julie."

Westwood blinked. "Why Julie?"

"Name of the first girl I fucked. Get inside before we drown." Nevin followed his own advice, slipping into the comfortable driver's seat. He didn't bother to tell Westwood that his previous car—a far less showy but perfectly serviceable '08 Camaro—had been named Luis, the first *boy* Nevin had fucked.

After Westwood sat down in the passenger seat and closed the door, he stroked the wood-covered console between them. "Is the interior original too?"

"Some of it. The leather's not a stock color, but I like charcoal gray. Most of the rest is restored or replaced to factory specs."

"Wow. I, uh, don't know anything about cars."

That didn't surprise Nevin. That soulless BMW parked in the driveway undoubtedly belonged to Colin. "I didn't bring you in to talk about cars. Tell me what happened here today, Mr. Westwood."

"Colin. And I already told—"

"Humor me."

"Okay." Colin gave a shaky sigh. "I was coming over to take a look at the toilet. Mrs. Ruskin called yesterday and said it was broken."

"It took you a day to fix a little old lady's toilet?"

Colin rolled his eyes. "It was in the guest bath—she has another. And anyway, she calls just about every week to get me to repair something. It's never a big deal. Last week she said her window was broken, but it turned out the cord for the blinds was so tangled she couldn't reach it. She's really just looking for a little company."

"No family?"

"A niece, but she's in, um, Delaware."

Nevin pulled a notebook and pen from his pocket, opened to a fresh page, and scribbled a few words. "Somebody's going to have to notify the niece."

"I already did. Mrs. Ruskin gave me her contact info years ago."

"I'll need that name and number."

Colin patted his shirt pocket and then frowned. "Darn. I left my phone inside." He reached for the car door, but Nevin grabbed his arm.

"Not yet," Nevin said. "You can get it later. The niece is it?"

"Pretty much. Mrs. Ruskin has a few friends, but they're all around her age. Most of them don't drive anymore, so they don't see each other much. I've been telling her she should consider moving into one of those assisted living places."

"You want to get rid of her so you can jack the rent. Or tear the place down and cram in a couple of fucking town houses."

Colin had one of those faces that broadcasted every emotion, and now he looked injured. "No. I thought she'd be less lonely. And safer."

Nevin jumped on that immediately. "You knew she was in danger?"

"Not from… this." Colin shuddered. "Just, at her age, she could fall or something."

"Or something."

In his lap, Colin's hands squeezed together tightly enough to turn the knuckles white, and he gave Nevin a beseeching look. "Is she going to be okay, Detective Ng?"

Something inside Nevin softened at the man's obvious distress. "Nevin. And I don't know." That stretched the truth. Although Nevin hadn't arrived at the scene until after the ambulance took Mrs. Ruskin away, he'd seen the faces of the first responders, and he didn't think the lady was ever going to return to see the mud tracked into her house by careless cops. Not that it meant the assholes shouldn't stop to wipe their goddamn feet.

Colin exhaled loudly. "She's a nice lady. I come over to fix things that don't really need fixing, and I'm pretty sure she schedules her housecleaning around me, so her place will be tidy when I arrive. We drink tea. We talk about movies and theater, mostly. She used to be a makeup artist. She met a lot of famous people." He gave a weak smile.

Rain traced complex patterns on the windshield and drummed on the roof, making Nevin drowsy. He would need a good run when he was done here. Maybe he'd call Jeremy and see if he was up to it. Jeremy the brawny outdoorsman didn't care about the weather. Hell, he was a tall enough guy he probably produced his own microclimate.

"So you came to fix Mrs. Ruskin's toilet and fangirl over Rodgers and Hammerstein. What happened when you got here?"

"The front door was unlocked. She does that when she knows I'm coming. Saves her from having to get up if she's comfortable in the living room. It's... it's hard for her to stand up, sometimes." He swallowed audibly.

"So you just stepped inside?"

"I rang the doorbell first. I always do, so she knows I'm there. Then... I saw her." His face turned more pallid.

"You better not barf in my car!"

Lips clenched, Colin shook his head. Nevin gave him a few moments to compose himself. It wasn't like most people stepped into a crime scene on a daily basis, and Colin looked like the delicate type. Yellow plaid shirt, coordinating bow tie, and a pretty schoolboy face even though he was probably pushing thirty. He carried a little muscle on his slender frame—a lot of hours spent in the gym, Nevin guessed—and probably had only three or four inches on Nevin's five foot four. He had a soft voice too. Nevin would have bet Julie that Colin spent his teen years hanging out with the drama club and getting bullied by most of the kids in his private high school.

"Sorry," Colin whispered. He picked at one of the dried blood spatters on his shirt.

"Don't do that. They're going to want your clothes as evidence."

Colin gave him a stricken look. "Evidence?"

"Yeah." Nevin made a mental note to make sure somebody gave Colin something clean and decent to change into. Mrs. Ruskin's dresses weren't going to work. "What did you do when you saw her?"

"I... I ran to her. At first I thought she was dead, b-but I saw her breathing. I tried first aid, but it's been a long time since I learned that and they didn't really teach us...."

Nevin nodded. High school health classes weren't usually all that big on how to treat elderly victims of a beating. "You're the one who called 911?"

"Yes."

"When you pulled up to the house, did you see anyone else? Anything unusual?"

After a moment of thought, Colin shook his head. "No. But I wasn't paying much attention. I was distracted."

"By what?"

Colin shot him a sour look. "My boyfriend dumped me last night." He tensed slightly, maybe anticipating a homophobic put-down.

But Nevin shrugged. "This just ain't your week, dude."

"God, it really isn't." He leaned back into the plush leather and closed his eyes.

Nevin sketched a castle in his notebook. A modest one, but sturdy. He imagined it inhabited by a minor prince who wanted to keep his family safe while he went about documenting the history of three rare species of dragon. After he drew the final turret—topped by a tiny flag— Nevin hummed a tune.

Colin turned his head to look at him. "Is that Neil Sedaka?" he asked incredulously.

"Breaking up *is* hard to do."

"That's…." Colin huffed. "You're not what I would have expected in a detective."

"Why not?"

"Well, there's the car for starters. And your suit! I figured detectives wore off-the-rack black polyester. Yours is way nicer than that."

"Off-the-rack doesn't fit me." He'd actually had department store salespeople outrageously suggest he try the boys' department. So he'd found a Hong Kong tailor who occasionally came to Portland to do fittings. He'd measure Nevin up and discuss fabrics, colors, and styles. A month or two later, Nevin would receive a package with his new suits and dress shirts, and everything would look damn good on him.

Unexpectedly, Colin chuckled. "God. Show tunes and fashion. Now we can discuss interior design or hairdressing, and you can give me a medal for being the gayest guy you've talked to this week."

Nevin thought about the hot twink he'd hooked up with a few days earlier. "Sorry, Colin. You're not even in the running."

"You mean I can't even win at being gay this week?" Colin shook his head. "Too bad. I'm usually pretty good at that."

"You can head over to the Silverado when we're done here. That'll restore your cred."

This time Colin snorted. "Is that what you do after a breakup? Go to a strip club?"

"I've never broken up with anyone."

"Seriously?"

Nevin wasn't exactly sure why he was discussing his sex life when he was supposed to be questioning a witness, but whatever. It beat standing in the rain. "I love 'em and leave 'em. Sometimes they demand seconds, but that's all they get." He grinned. "Always leave 'em wanting more. That's my motto." Well, that and *Don't hand your heart to someone who's going to stomp on it.* Maybe some guys wanted relationships—True Love and fucking rainbow sparkles—but he'd seen what that wanting did to them. Jeremy still hadn't recovered from his last ugly disaster, even though that had been years ago and the ex was a douchecanoe.

Colin shook his head. "Not me. I'm... what's the opposite of a commitmentphobe? Back in grade school, I spent hours planning my future wedding even though everybody back then told me I couldn't get married. I am going to wear a white tuxedo with a black bow tie, and Etta James's 'At Last' will play when I walk down the aisle. My groom will wear a black tux with a white bow tie. And we'll have chocolate-dipped strawberries, Bowie, and the B-52s at the reception."

"Invite me," Nevin said. "I like to dance."

"Done. As soon as I find someone to marry me." Colin's smile disappeared. "I probably shouldn't be talking about this stuff when Mrs. Ruskin...."

"Screw the shouldn't be. Life goes on."

"She's a nice lady. We're friends, I think."

It was time to get back to business. "Do you know of any reason why someone would want to hurt her?"

Colin scrunched up his face. "You mean, like, enemies? I doubt it. She's a nice old lady. She has a collection of spoons from every state, and until her knees gave out, she used to like to garden."

"No exes?" Nevin asked, not really expecting a yes.

"Her husband died in the Korean War. No kids, and she never remarried. She told me not too long ago that she was always kind of into girls instead of boys but never had the guts to do anything about it. I told her eighty-three wasn't too old to give it a try."

"You're a genuine goddamn romantic, aren't you?"

"I guess."

Nevin wanted to hate Colin Westwood, with his stupid bow tie, his rental properties, his ex-boyfriend, his fucking German sedan. The guy apparently had an inner life peopled with cherubs, chorus boys, and rainbow-hued wedding planners. But it was hard to hate a man who had weekly teas with an octogenarian and who was so clearly upset over her attack.

Nevin slapped the notebook shut and tucked it away. "Let's go get that niece's information, okay?"

"COMEBUCKET!" NEVIN followed the expletive with a complex series of hand gestures, none of which were visible to the bus driver who'd just cut him off. It wasn't often he longed for the old days—driving one of the bureau's Crown Vics and handing out traffic citations—but now was one of those times. He'd have fucking loved to pull over that asswipe and write him a ticket big enough to make him puke. Instead he snarled at the bus as it lumbered up the street.

He was still growling under his breath as he pulled into his building's parking garage. He was goddamn ravenous. After finishing with Colin, he'd intended to swing by Providence Medical Center with the slim hope of getting a statement from Mrs. Ruskin and then go for a run with Jeremy. Afterward Nevin was going to grab some tacos, shower, and try for a quick hookup. But when he got to Providence, the doctors told him Mrs. Ruskin hadn't made it. No statement from her since he didn't own a fucking Ouija board. He'd gotten tied up forever with Frankl and Blake from Homicide, both of whom decided Nevin should be the one to notify the niece of Mrs. Ruskin's death since he'd caught the case first. Assholes. And the niece? She seemed more annoyed at having to make burial arrangements than torn up over losing her aunt.

Now it was too late and too dark for a run, Nevin's stomach was threatening to consume his other internal organs, and he didn't have the energy even for takeout. Screw it. His freezer must contain something he could nuke.

His fourth-floor apartment boasted one bedroom, a galley kitchen, and a view of the slightly weedy courtyard. He'd chosen this place because it was handy to freeways and downtown, had a secure parking spot for Julie, and housed a fitness center that was a decent substitute when he didn't have time to get to a real gym. A few of his least lame drawings hung on the living room walls, while thank-you cards from victims he'd helped in the past clung to the refrigerator door with advertising magnets saved from junk mail.

He paused long enough to fling his suit jacket over a living room chair before he strode into the kitchen in search of dinner. What he found was an ice-entombed box of General Tso's chicken.

"About as authentically Chinese as me," he muttered as he threw the tray into the microwave.

By the time the appliance beeped, he'd changed into a T-shirt and sweatpants. He dumped his faux Asian food into a bowl, grabbed a fork from the drawer, and uncapped a bottle of Full Sail. Then he plopped down into his usual chair—the one directly facing the TV—and dug in.

Half the food was hot enough to scald, while the other half was still chilly. It made for an interesting eating experience, a sort of Russian roulette of a meal. He didn't care. It tasted like dog shit anyway. And even though he normally enjoyed this brand of beer, tonight it was like swilling piss. He kept flashing on images of Colin Westwood in his bloodstained plaid shirt and the reality of an old lady dying from a beating with nobody to mourn her but her landlord.

Fuck.

He was way too young to be burned out. On days like this, he sometimes contemplated quitting the bureau. But then what would he do? He'd wanted to be a cop since he was fifteen. It was the only job he'd ever envisioned for himself—unless you counted his even earlier aspirations to be a thug. He'd majored in criminal justice, and being a cop was his only marketable skill. His only talent.

Just as he was poking morosely at the remains of General Tso, Nevin's phone buzzed.

I'll be there in 15. Dress code = punk. The text was from Ford Ott, the closest thing he had to family.

Not tonight, Nevin sent back, even though he knew resistance was futile.

Non-negotiable.

Fuck you and the horse you rode in on.

15 mins.

He considered throwing the phone against the wall, but that wouldn't save him from Ford. He tried a different tactic instead. *I don't own anything punk.* Wasn't like he had combat boots and studded leather pants tucked away in his closet.

Just wear black.

Skank.

But Nevin set aside the bowl and empty beer bottle and trudged to his bedroom in search of something black.

"YOU LOOK like hell," Ford said as soon as Nevin got into his truck.

"You told me to wear black."

"I don't mean the clothes, man. Although I gotta say, you look more FBI than NOFX."

Nevin flipped him off. "We can always stop along the way and get an anarchy symbol tattooed on my forehead."

"Too extreme. You might look cool with a Mohawk, though." Ford reached over and mussed Nevin's hair.

Nevin responded by punching Ford's bicep. "I'd've hit you harder if you weren't driving, fuckface."

"Yeah, yeah. Always talking tough." Ford pulled away from the curb and into traffic. He wore his usual: boots, faded jeans, and a worn T-shirt emblazoned with what Nevin presumed was a heavy metal band. Ford's scalp gleamed; as soon as he'd noticed an incipient bald spot, he'd taken to shaving his head completely. As always, his pickup smelled slightly of fertilizer and soil, but apart from a few stray fast-food wrappers, the cab was reasonably clean.

Even though it was far too late to do any good, Nevin launched a final protest. "I'm not in the mood to go out tonight."

"Bummer."

"Ford—"

"I'm in the mood for some feminine companionship, Nev, and we both know we pull better as a team. So shut your yap and forget about whatever crapstorm hit you at work today. You're going to get drunk, we're both going to dance, and if we're lucky, we'll find some temporary company."

Nevin sulked.

Ford took them to a dive bar way out on Division. The hipsters hadn't discovered the place yet—or if they had, they'd cleverly disguised themselves in torn leather jackets and creative facial piercings. The crowd was mostly younger than Nevin and Ford, although a few of the customers might have long ago owned the Ramones on vinyl.

While a band warmed up, Nevin downed a beer and scoped the place out. Ford stuck to drinking Coke—his biological parents had both been hardcore alcoholics, so he avoided the stuff entirely. Which was convenient for Nevin, who, knowing he had a pet designated driver, could get as sloshed as he wanted.

Nevin gestured with his bottle toward the small stage. "What's the name of this band?"

"Dick Zipper and the Jizz Parade."

"Yeah? I like it. Catchy and refined."

"Nobody knows refinement like you, little bro."

As it turned out, Dick Zipper sucked ass. But they played loud and fast enough that it didn't matter. After another beer, Nevin squeezed onto the crowded dance floor and joined the other writhing, sweating bodies. He stopped now and then for enough beer to keep his buzz going. He didn't feel good, exactly. But he was alive, and fucking hallelujah for that!

Eventually his energy flagged. He found Ford dancing with a bleached blonde, grabbed his arm, and dragged him to a relatively quiet part of the bar.

"I have to work in the morning," Nevin yelled over the din. It was past midnight.

"You call that work? I'm the one's gotta transplant rosebushes at dawn."

"Suck on a rosebush, Four-door. I'll catch a cab."

But Ford followed him out of the bar and into the ringing quiet of the parking lot. "I'm hungry," Ford announced. He pointed at the chain restaurant across the street. "C'mon. I'm buying."

Nevin would have refused, but he decided maybe it would be a good idea to soak up the alcohol with some food. On unsteady legs, he crossed the street in Ford's wake.

Nevin had never been to this particular location of the franchise, yet it smelled familiar: coffee, sausage, fake maple syrup. Being a cop meant he'd spent a lot of time in places like this, especially back when he pulled night shifts. The predictable assortment of customers filled about a quarter of the tables. Truck drivers, stoners, college kids, people who'd worked late somewhere else. There was also a healthy scattering of patrons from the club. They were easy to spot with their intentionally torn clothing and creatively gelled hair.

Their waitress was a tired-looking young woman with long hair pulled into a ponytail. She filled their coffee cups as soon as they sat down, earning a thankful smile from Nevin.

"Do you think they have cooks here?" Nevin asked as he perused the menu. "Or does it all come from the same prepackaged mix? They just press a button on a machine to say whether they want waffles or scrambled eggs."

"You're drunk."

"So? Wasn't that your plan?"

Ford opened his mouth to answer, then started waving at someone near the door. Nevin turned around to see. It was the blonde, accompanied by a slightly plump, pretty woman whose straight hair was the color of a fire engine. The women waved back and approached the table. Ford scooted over—the blonde immediately sat next to him—so Nevin did the same, prompting a grin from the redhead.

Apparently deciding introductions were in order, Ford waved a hand. "Nevin, this is Cat and, uh…."

"Riley," said the redhead.

"Ladies, this is my little brother, Nevin."

"Brother?" Riley asked, gaze darting between them.

"Close enough."

That seemed to satisfy her, which was good. Nevin was in no mood to explain, and she didn't need to know, that he and Ford had been in the same foster-home placement for two years until Ford aged out of the system. Nevin had aged out a few months later, and they'd shared a shithole apartment while Nevin went to the community college and they both worked a variety of sucktastic jobs.

The waitress came by, poured coffee for the newcomers, and took food orders. While Ford chose one of those enormous skillet things and the women both wanted blueberry pancakes, Nevin just asked for toast and fruit.

After the waitress left, Riley turned to look at Nevin. "So where are you from?" she asked brightly. She smelled like clove cigarettes.

"Portland."

"No, I mean *before* that."

Oh, Christ. One of those. Nevin sighed. "I was born right here at Good Sam."

She scrunched up her pert little nose and nodded. "What are you?"

Sometimes he had clever retorts for that question. Sometimes he just made shit up, like when he told people his parents were Mongolian yak herders who'd traded him to missionaries for a washing machine. But tonight he didn't have the energy for any of that, so he told the truth. "Half Chinese. The rest, who the fuck knows?" If his mother had any clue who his father was, she hadn't disclosed that little factoid on his birth certificate. And she'd dumped Nevin and disappeared long before he was old enough to ask her.

"I'm Irish, Scottish, German, and French," Riley informed him. "And also one-sixteenth Cherokee."

"That's interesting," he lied.

She slid closer, until her warm thigh pressed against his. "What do you do for a living?"

He rarely told people he was a cop because that knowledge either scared them away or activated bad porn scenarios in their heads. Not that he was opposed to porn, but he liked the good stuff, and the whole man-in-uniform trope never appealed to him. Too close to home. Now, on the other hand, lonely cowboys or naughty doctors....

Nevin smiled. "I'm a professional kung fu fighter." Was there such a thing?

While Riley oohed, Ford landed a solid kick on Nevin's shin. Nevin swallowed a yelp and promised himself that Ford would pay for that later.

The food arrived promptly, and while everyone ate, Riley regaled Nevin with tales of her corgi named Jimbo, her job at a bicycle repair shop, and every band she'd seen in the past three years. But she was funny, and once he got past his initial aversion to her, he realized she was also very sweet. He felt bad about lying to her—but not bad enough to hand her the truth.

The waitress kept bringing coffee, and when Nevin glanced at his phone, it was nearing two. "Shit. I have a buttload of paperwork to do tomorrow."

"Kung fu masters do paperwork?"

He shrugged. "Uh, yeah. Tournament reports."

She snuggled into him. "Too bad. I wanted to introduce you to Jimbo. I bet he'd like you."

Nevin glanced over at Ford, who waggled his eyebrows in return and gave Cat a squeeze around the shoulders. By the looks of things, Ford was going to be driving Cat home instead of him.

"You know what?" Nevin said, hoping he sounded more excited than he felt. "I'd love to meet Jimbo. You have a car here?"

CHAPTER TWO

July 2015

COLIN LAY naked on his bed, sweltering. Considering the cost of his loft apartment, he would have expected the air-conditioning to be in proper order. It wasn't, though, and when he'd called repair places, they'd all said they'd be happy to come take a look. Next month. Apparently when the late July heat wave hit, everyone in the city had turned on their cooling and discovered it was on the fritz. He would have complained to the landlord, but that was him.

He reached into the little bowl on his nightstand, fished out an ice cube, and set it on his belly. It gave him a delicious little shiver as it began to melt.

It wasn't absolutely necessary for him to torture himself by staying in the apartment. He could have gone to his office, even though it was a Saturday. He had plenty of work to do. He could have gone to a movie, a shopping center, a nicely chilled café. He could have gone to his parents' big house in the West Hills, where the AC wouldn't dare give his mother any problems. But none of these options were open to his cat, Legolas, so Colin stayed home in solidarity. Not that Leg seemed to notice—he was currently napping in the bathroom sink.

Nothing was left of the cube but a warming puddle on Colin's skin. The water slid off his waist as he twisted and reached for another chunk of ice, which he placed higher up, midway between his nipples. It settled into the scar there, sending a miniature river down the long groove. He imagined a tiny boat sailing down his body, the captain calling out for his helmsman to beware of the intermittent chest hairs. Captain Hook. No, Captain Jack Sparrow.

Colin sang a few *yo ho*s, but lack of energy made him stop. "Ahoy!" he said through a yawn. He gave his cock a few strokes but gave up before his body showed interest. Despite his friends' attempts to throw him back into the dating pool—and despite not one but *two* matchmaking efforts by his mother—he'd remained solo and celibate since Trent dumped him six weeks earlier. It was just too *hot* to jack off. Maybe he ought to follow Leg's lead and have a nice nap instead.

Just as his eyelids were drifting closed, however, his ringtone sounded. He fumbled for the phone, knocked it onto the floor, and retrieved it barely before it went to voice mail. "Hello?"

"Hey, Colin, it's Manuel. Are you in the mood to do me a great big huge favor?" He sounded flustered, but then Manuel Ceja always sounded like he was waving his hands around in a tizzy. He ran Bright Hope, a nonprofit serving elderly and ill LGBT people, and although he ran it well, Colin worried Manuel was going to work himself into an early grave.

"Anything for you," Colin replied in a calming tone.

"*You* are a peach, Colin baby. So Debbie was scheduled to visit Roger Grey today but she just called to tell me her car broke down on the way home from Lincoln City and there's no way she's going to make it on time and I know usually you see him on Tuesdays but I'm worried about Roger 'cause it's so hot today so if you could go there I'd really appreciate it."

After inhaling in empathy for Manuel's overtaxed lungs, Colin said, "Sure. No problem." Even if Roger lived way the hell out near 122nd and Halsey.

"You're a prince."

"She picks up groceries for him, doesn't she?"

"Uh-huh. I'll message you a list. If you don't mind paying, I'll reimburse you as soon—"

"It's on me. Consider it an extra donation to Bright Hope."

Manuel hummed a few bars of "God Save the Queen," then laughed. "You've just been promoted from prince to monarch."

"Excellent. I've always wanted a crown."

It took genuine force of will to make himself put on clothing. Knowing that most of Bright Hope's clients had few visitors, Colin usually dressed up a little. It helped make the clients feel special. Besides, as more than one of them had pointed out, they got extra enjoyment out of attention from some young eye candy. But although Colin generally tried to look nice, today all he could manage was a pair of fairly skimpy shorts and a tank top. He was going to give the people at Safeway an eyeful.

Legolas meowed sleepily when Colin said good-bye, but the cat didn't bother getting out of the sink. Maybe Colin should get a dog instead. Dogs *appreciated* their people. On the other hand, Leg used to take dumps in Trent's shoes whenever Trent spent the night, and in retrospect, Colin was pleased by that.

The interior of Colin's car was approximately ten degrees hotter than the surface of the sun. He turned on the air full blast as he wiped stinging sweat from his eyes and waited for the steering wheel to cool. He realized he was scowling—not at the roaring heat but at the car itself. He'd never given much thought to vehicles. His parents had given him a sensible sedan as soon as he got his license, and after he'd joined his father's business, he'd been supplied with a stream of BMWs. His dad said it was important to convey class and success to clients. Which might have been true, but at the moment, Colin felt envious of the purple car owned by that detective. Nevin Ng.

Colin's frown disappeared, chased away by a wistful smile. Detective Ng had been an interesting man. And in the shock and distress of Mrs. Ruskin's attack, Colin had found Ng oddly comforting.

The drive was endless, the entire city seemingly stuck in slow motion. But Safeway was heaven. Especially the refrigerated aisles. Colin hung out there for so long that he was in danger of developing permanent gooseflesh and earned suspicious stares from a pimply-faced employee wielding a broom.

"Can I help you?" the kid finally asked.

"I'm, uh, just admiring the yogurt."

Well, that got rid of the kid pretty quick.

Of course, during the time Colin spent in the store, his car had reached thermonuclear meltdown temperatures. It didn't cool at all in the few blocks to Roger Grey's house, and by the time Colin knocked on the apartment door, he was dripping sweat.

"You're not Debbie," Roger said when he opened the door.

"Disappointed?"

"Not in the least. Debbie's a nice young woman, but you, my boy, are a feast for ancient eyes."

Colin hefted the grocery bags slightly. "Can I put this feast away?"

"Of course."

Roger's studio apartment was about the size of a largish hotel room, with a Murphy bed, a kitchenette, a tiny table with two metal-and-vinyl chairs, and one overstuffed armchair. Colin suspected Roger slept in the armchair more often than the bed. A bookshelf—double- and triple-stacked with paperbacks and hardcovers—dominated the remaining space, while newspapers and magazines littered most of the horizontal surfaces.

As small as the kitchen cupboards were, their interiors were nearly bare, and the tiny refrigerator was almost empty. As he put away the groceries, Colin made a mental note to ask Manuel whether someone ought to be restocking Roger's larder more often. "I brought a rotisserie chicken," Colin said to Roger, who'd settled into his armchair. "And some mashed potatoes and gravy. What kind of veggie would you like? Packaged salad or this green-bean stuff?" He held up a plastic deli container.

"You don't have to fix my dinner."

"But I'd like to. Usually I only get to prepare meals for my cat, and he doesn't like green beans."

Roger had a raspy laugh. "Then by all means, go ahead. I wouldn't want to deprive you of the pleasure."

While Colin got everything ready, he told Roger about Debbie's mishap on the way home from the coast. That prompted a risqué, nostalgic tale from Roger about a time he and five friends had rented a house near Cannon Beach and engaged in a weeklong orgy. "They're all dead now," Roger said, staring at the food on his TV tray. "AIDS. Except Emmett. He committed suicide back in eighty-nine, right after his partner died."

Colin turned one of the kitchen chairs to face Roger and sat down. "Was that the first time you guys partied like that?" he asked gently.

So Roger told him more wild stories—which might or might not have been true—and although Colin listened appreciatively, part of his mind was elsewhere. He'd been lying around absorbed in self-pity over Trent, but look what Roger and his contemporaries had been through! Roger had lost his parents and siblings decades ago, when they refused to accept his homosexuality. He'd had to watch as his friends died, as his lover died, and although Roger himself had survived being HIV-positive for over twenty years now, the virus and the treatments had taken a toll on his health and bank accounts. He was frail for a man in his early seventies, alone in a shoebox apartment, relying on charity for food and company.

"I suppose things are different nowadays," Roger said wistfully, cutting into Colin's reverie. "Apps and latex and all that."

"I guess. I'm not really into the scene."

"But didn't you tell me you're single?"

"Yeah." Colin stood and cleared away the dirty dishes, which he took to the sink to wash.

"And you're a very handsome young man. I don't think standards on male beauty have changed so much since my day."

Colin shot him a grin. "Thanks. I've seen your old photos, though—you were a whole lot better-looking than me."

"I was a heartbreaker. But that's not my point. What keeps you from properly enjoying your youth?"

The thing was, Colin wasn't sure he'd ever had a youth, at least not in the way Roger meant. Sometimes he felt as if he'd been born middle-aged. "I guess I'm just the picket-fence type. And I haven't found the right guy."

"If you can't find Mr. Right, settle for Mr. Right Now," Roger said with a leer. Then he shook his head. "It's so strange, all this marriage equality."

"Would you and Frank have gotten married if it was legal?"

"I don't know. We loved each other, that's for certain. But this kind of thing you're talking about, this… *normality*. We never envisioned it. I don't know if we'd have embraced it."

Colin nodded and finished cleaning up. When he turned back around, Roger was regarding him thoughtfully. "You've only recently begun volunteering for Bright Hope, correct?"

"Just a few weeks ago." It had been a way to get his mind off Trent. But he'd also thought of it as a small way to pay tribute to Mrs. Ruskin's memory. She would have been tickled to know Colin was paying visits to aging gay men.

"Why are you spending time with decrepit dinosaurs like me instead of boys your own age?"

"I like spending time with you," Colin answered truthfully. "You're interesting."

Roger chuckled. "And youth is wasted on the young." He waved a hand. "Go. On an evening like this, shirtless, pulchritudinous young men no doubt populate every park and byway in town. Go find some. Ogle them for me."

Colin wiped his hands on a dish towel and hung it on a hook under the cabinet. He looked around to make sure the food was all put away and the apartment was in no more disorder than when he'd arrived. Then an idea struck him. "How about if you ogle them yourself? We could go for a drive, maybe head down to the river or something."

"That would be delightful, but I'm afraid I must refuse. My energy reserves...." He shrugged.

But Colin wouldn't be put off so easily. He'd seen the spark of interest in Roger's eyes. "Tomorrow, then. It's supposed to be slightly cooler. I'll grab some food and we'll have a picnic lunch somewhere. Anywhere you want."

"Maybe... the Rose Test Garden? Frank and I used to go there often. He was quite a gardener, you know. I haven't been in years." His gaze turned hazy and faraway.

"That's a great idea. Pick you up at eleven?"

"You must have something better to do!"

"I honestly don't," Colin said with a laugh.

"Then I shall be ready at eleven. May I pretend it's a date?"

Colin winked at him. "Who said it's pretending?"

WHEN COLIN got home, he fed Legolas, took a quick shower—his second of the day—and changed into something that made him look a little less like a rent boy. Then he apologized to the cat for the serial abandonment before heading back out into the heat. This time he walked, but only a few blocks to one of his favorite restaurants, a Lebanese place. He wasn't especially hungry, so he ordered small servings of tabbouleh and baba ghanouj. The owners knew him and didn't mind that, long after they'd cleared his plates away, he nursed his mint tea and enjoyed the air-conditioning and the view of pedestrians strolling by the window.

By the time he began to wander home, the sun had long since set and the temperatures were becoming more bearable. His loft might not even be too bad with some open windows and strategically placed fans.

His phone began to play a familiar tune, and he groaned before answering. "Hi, Mom."

"Your father says the AC's still out in your building. Why didn't you come here?"

"I was busy." A bald-faced lie—which she undoubtedly knew.

"Sweetheart, excessive heat isn't healthy."

He barely suppressed a whine. "I'm fine. I sweated, I stayed hydrated, and I didn't drop dead."

Paula Westwood made her trademark click of annoyance but changed topics. "Are you out somewhere? I hear traffic."

"Just walking home from dinner."

"Who did you go with?"

"Solo."

"On a Saturday night? You know, Laura Dalrymple—you remember her? From the Art Institute board?—well, her son is an orthodontist, and he—"

"I swear to God, Mom. If you set me up on another blind date, I will show up wearing yoga pants and a fishnet tank top, and I will spend every minute talking about my dead ferret."

"You never had a ferret." She sighed theatrically. "Fine. But you need to at least try putting yourself out there."

Waiting at the corner for the light to turn, Colin tried to feel grateful. Hell, Roger Grey would have fallen to his knees in thanks for a mother comfortable enough with his homosexuality to act as matchmaker. "Mom, I *don't* need to put myself anywhere. I'm good. I don't need a boyfriend to complete me. I have a decent job, some great friends, and a fulfilling volunteer life." That reminded him of something, and he sprouted a fairly evil smile. "And I won't be there tomorrow, by the way."

It was a family tradition dating back to his toddler years. On the third Sunday of every month, everyone got together for brunch. The location varied depending on which restaurant his parents wanted to try, but the other details remained the same. His mother would drink mimosas, and his father would complain that the food wasn't as good as at that *other* place he liked. Colin's sister, Miranda, would argue politics with their father, while her husband bickered with Hannah, their thirteen-year-old daughter, who pouted over the no-phones-at-brunch rule. Colin mostly sat back and grinned, because he loved his family even when they were being pains in the ass.

Still, he wasn't sorry for an excuse to miss a month, especially when his mother was in full Cupid mode.

"Why won't you be there?" she demanded.

"I'm taking a Bright Hope client on a picnic. He doesn't get out much." Or at all, except for doctors' appointments.

"Oh. Well, that's sweet of you. We'll miss you, though. Maybe join us for dinner sometime next week?"

"Sure. That sounds nice." And that was true. He enjoyed his parents' company—most of the time.

The call ended just as he arrived home. *Saturday night*, he thought as he rode the elevator to his loft. Time for nudity, ice cream, and some *Firefly* binge-watching. Because he was happy, dammit.

THE MORNING proved sunny but several degrees cooler than Saturday, just as promised. Colin whistled as he showered and shaved and tamed his hair, and then he dressed in a pair of khaki shorts and his "I solemnly swear that I am up to no good" T-shirt. He gave Legolas a final pat—this time the cat lay in a pool of sunlight next to the couch—grabbed the cooler he'd packed with ice, and headed downstairs.

He stopped at Elephants Deli and bought way too much: sandwiches, chips, a few different salads, a chocolate tart and a lemon one, and an assortment of waters and juices. Whatever was left over from lunch would add to Roger's meager food supply. The deli gave him paper plates and plastic cutlery.

There was thankfully not much traffic on a Sunday morning. Colin sang along with his playlist as he sailed down the Banfield. Maybe he should take a road trip this summer. He could probably find a friend or two to go with him, and his sister and niece would take care of Legolas. He could head up to Vancouver for a little while, maybe with a few days in Victoria. Or he could head south instead, taking the slow scenic route along the coastline to San Francisco. He hadn't been on vacation in a long time. Trent always claimed to be too busy to escape from work and not interested in going anywhere nearby. Well, screw him. Colin was free!

Even the parking lot of Roger's dumpy apartment complex looked bright and cheerful, with birds twittering and two little kids kicking a ball across the adjacent lawn. Colin left the food in the car and practically skipped up the walkway. He gave the door a few solid raps.

Nobody answered.

He tried again, more loudly. Maybe Roger was becoming hard of hearing. Or maybe he was in the bathroom. But despite Colin's pounding and a few minutes of waiting, the door remained resolutely shut.

Colin pictured Roger collapsed amid his clutter of print materials.

The manager lived just three doors down, and at least he answered Colin's knock right away. He was a tall man of indeterminate age, thinning hair hanging to his shoulders, skinny except for a round belly that looked as if he'd swallowed a volleyball. His jean shorts were falling off his narrow hips, and his grayish T-shirt sported a sentimental remembrance of his last several meals.

"Yeah?" he asked, peering at Colin through red-tinged eyes.

"I'm here to visit Roger Grey. I'm a volunteer with Bright Hope?" Colin wasn't sure whether Shaggy knew about the organization. "We were supposed to go somewhere today, but he's not answering."

Shaggy frowned and scratched the stubble on his cheek. "He never goes anywhere, man."

"I know. That's why I'm worried. Can you unlock his door?"

"Uh…." Shaggy thought about it for several moments. "Yeah, I guess so. But I need to stay with you for, like, security."

Colin figured that Legolas would provide better security than this guy, but he didn't argue. "That's fine. Can you hurry?"

No, Shaggy couldn't. Various banging and crashing noises came from inside his place as he searched for the master key and a pair of shoes. In the end, he found the key but apparently only one flip-flop. He wore it to accompany Colin to Roger's, the rubber sole thwacking against the concrete as he walked.

He fumbled with Roger's lock forever, and Colin stuffed his own hands in his pockets to keep from shaking him. All Colin could picture was Roger sprawled on the floor, bright blood pooling beneath him. Or maybe an empty pill bottle near his hand, or a knife, because Roger had casually mentioned suicide two weeks earlier.

The lock finally clicked open, the door swung with a slight creak, and Colin briefly closed his eyes, preparing himself for the worst.

"Huh," Shaggy said. "I guess the dude's not home."

CHAPTER THREE

PERHAPS COLIN had watched too many cop shows, because he'd been certain the police would refuse to do anything until Roger had been missing at least twenty-four hours. Luckily those TV programs had misled him, or perhaps Manuel Ceja possessed a golden tongue. A few minutes after Colin got off the phone with Manuel, the Bright Hope director called him back. "They're sending someone right now," he said. His voice was tight with nerves, but Colin understood, considering that his own stomach was doing gymnastics. "Stay put."

"I wasn't planning to leave," Colin said.

"I know, I know. I'm sorry."

"Don't be. You're just worried because you care. I'll keep you updated, okay?"

"Thanks, Colin sweetie."

Shaggy sat on the curb, smoking a cigarette and looking unconcerned. But then, a zombie attack probably wouldn't be enough to get through the haze in his brain. He'd left Roger's door wide open, and even from the doorway it was clear Roger wasn't home. Colin could even see into the bathroom, where grab bars had been crookedly installed in the shower and next to the toilet. The apartment didn't seem any more or less disorderly than usual. Blankets covered Roger's armchair, and a single green mug sat atop the kitchenette counter, the tag from a tea bag hanging over its edge.

Colin paced the walkway.

A purple GTO pulled into the parking lot, and both panic and excitement flared in Colin's head, making him a little dizzy.

The word that came to mind as he watched Detective Ng walk toward him was *tight*. Yeah, Nevin was gorgeous, with warm brown skin, full lips, and cheekbones any starlet would kill for. And even though it was a hot day, he wore a closely tailored charcoal suit with a tangerine-colored button-down open at the neck. He would have looked at home on a fashion runway, even if he was too short to be a model. But his beauty and attire weren't the most significant things about him—more important was the way he held himself, as if every muscle were poised to leap. He was like a coiled spring, like a finger beginning to depress a trigger. Not menacing, exactly, but *ready*. And sharp. When he smiled, Colin half expected Nevin's teeth to be as pointed as a shark's. They weren't—but they were very white.

"Oh, God. Is Roger dead?"

Nevin blinked at him. "You tell me. I just got here. And where's your bow tie?"

Colin looked down and realized that his "up to no good" T-shirt had turned out to be a poor choice under the circumstances. "If Roger's not dead, how come you're here?"

"Because somebody called the fucking cops, numbnuts." A look of comprehension dawned. "Shit. You think I'm Homicide, don't you? Don't worry—I'm not one of those goddamn stiffs."

"But—"

"Don't tell me you own this dump too. What are you? Slumlord to the masses?"

"I don't own this place. I was just visiting. I volunteer with Bright Hope, this group that—"

"I know about Bright Hope." Nevin looked him up and down. "Tell you what, kid. Why don't we start from scratch. Who's that?" He pointed at Shaggy, who was staring off into oblivion.

"The apartment manager. When Roger didn't answer the door, I got the manager to let me in."

"And I'm guessing that unless I want to bum a gram of Maui Wowie, he's not going to prove especially helpful."

Colin choked on a nervous laugh. "Um, I don't think so."

"You stay right here, Bow Tie. Let me have a few words with him, and then you and I will have ourselves a nice parley."

Simultaneously apprehensive and pleased at the prospect, Colin nodded. He looked for a place to sit. He rejected the curb because he didn't want to inhale Shaggy's cigarette smoke, then rejected the lawn because he didn't want grass stains on his shorts. He ended up perched on the hood of his car, the metal warming his ass even through the fabric of his clothes. He watched as Nevin spoke to Shaggy and wrote things in his notebook. In his long sleeves and suit coat, Nevin must have been uncomfortable, but he didn't seem hurried. Thorough, Colin thought. A good detective.

After a few minutes, Nevin made a quick phone call. He had just tucked away his notebook and started toward Colin when several cars pulled into the lot: three marked squad cars and one plain white car, the same model as the others. A bunch of uniformed men and women got out and headed toward Nevin. It was interesting. Even though they were all taller and bigger than Nevin—even the women—it was clear that Nevin was in charge. And not just because of his fancy suit. Everyone's body language said that Nevin was going to tell them what to do and they were going to obey.

Eventually the uniformed cops entered Roger's apartment and Nevin strode toward Colin, who hopped off the car and walked around the back. He popped the trunk just as Nevin joined him.

"It's a good thing you're not a suspect," Nevin said.

"Why?"

"If you were, I'd have just shot you dead, nimrod."

Colin had been reaching into the trunk, but now he froze. "Huh?"

"I got one dead old lady and one missing old man. How do I know you're not going for a gun?" He sounded annoyed but not alarmed.

"It's just an ice chest."

Nevin huffed. "I bet you've never been accused of anything, have you, white boy? You just flash those big baby blues and nobody suspects a thing."

"Hey!" Colin would have been more offended, except Nevin was pretty much right. Not that Colin had ever done anything too awful, but when he'd been late with homework as a kid, he could always convince the teachers to buy his lame excuses. And that time in high school when he and his friend Jay skipped class and went downtown instead. A security guard had found them lurking in an alley—both of them stoned off a joint Jay had stolen from his older sister—but had believed Colin's ridiculous story about losing a set of keys. That was the one and only time Colin tried recreational drugs, though. Not because he was afraid of being arrested, but because he kept picturing his parents' reaction if he was caught.

Scowling, Colin removed the lid from the cooler and took out a bottle of water. "I was just going to offer you something to drink. Because you look hot."

Ignoring the offered bottle, Nevin snorted and pushed in beside him. "I *always* look hot." He peered inside. "You catered?"

"Roger and I were supposed to go on a picnic."

Nevin gave him a look, then grabbed the water. "Exactly how many people did you invite to this picnic?" He uncapped the bottle and took a long slug.

Colin tried not to look at Nevin's lips wrapped around the bottle's rim. "Uh, just him. He doesn't eat very well, so I guess I was trying to tempt him. I figured he could use the leftovers later." His stomach growled at the thought of food. "I'm pretty hungry, actually. Is it okay if I eat one of these sandwiches?"

"Sure. If I can have one too. I'm gonna let the gorillas look for evidence, and you and I can eat while we talk."

"Look for evidence. Does that mean—"

"It means that between what you and the manager have told me, I have enough info to call this a crime scene. That's all. We'll see if the boys in blue dig anything up."

Relieved that the police were acting so quickly, Colin handed Nevin a paper-wrapped sandwich before taking one for himself. He snagged a water too. Then he followed Nevin down a narrow sidewalk that ran alongside the building. An identical building stood behind Roger's, but in between was a grassy space with a rudimentary playground and a concrete picnic table. The buildings cast the area in shade. Nevin sat on one side of the table and gestured Colin to the other.

"How'd you know this was here?" Colin asked as Nevin unwrapped his food.

"I'm a detective, remember?"

"Who specializes in investigating alfresco lunch spots?"

"Who's bright enough to ask the manager where there's a cool place to sit."

They both ate a few bites, and Colin tried with limited success not to stare at the handsome man across from him. Nevin seemed either preoccupied with the ingredients in his sandwich or lost in thought. A baby cried somewhere and then stopped.

"Okay," Nevin said, still chewing as he produced his notebook and a pen. "Let's start at the very beginning."

"A very good place to start," Colin sang back.

Nevin stared, then shook his head. "You're here because you volunteer for Bright Hope?"

"Yeah. I started a few weeks back."

"After Mrs. Ruskin died?"

"Yes." Colin frowned. "Do you have any idea who did it?"

"Not my case. I told you—I'm not Homicide."

"Then what are you?" That came out more stridently than Colin intended, but Nevin had a way of getting under his skin.

"Family Services Division. Vulnerable Adult and Elder Crimes Unit."

"That's… sort of a mouthful. You investigate crimes against old people?"

Nevin tapped his pen on his notebook. "And other adults who are at risk, like the mentally disabled."

"That's… wow. That's really cool." Colin hadn't realized the police had special protections for those people. Clearly he was woefully ignorant about law enforcement practices.

Nevin shrugged. "It's a job," he said, but Colin didn't believe his nonchalance. "And you're trying to distract me, Colin. We were talking about you and Bright Hope and Roger Grey, and the intersection thereof."

Colin briefly explained his reasons for volunteering, his previous interactions with Roger, and the content of yesterday's visit. Nevin asked a few questions, but mainly he took notes. When Colin was finished, Nevin tapped the pen again. "Does Roger have signs of dementia?"

"Not that I can tell. He's super smart, actually."

"But he's been poz for a long time, right? Sometimes that can aggravate mental problems. Memory. Depression. How did his mood seem last night?"

Colin thought about it before answering. "I don't know him all that well, but he seemed okay, I think. I mean, his life circumstances kind of stink. He's so alone."

"Not everyone minds being alone," Nevin said with an edge to his voice.

"Yeah, but it's one thing if it's by choice. It's something else if all your friends and family either die or abandon you."

"My question is, how does *he* feel about it?"

Not understanding Nevin's barely contained anger, Colin dropped his voice. "I don't know. I think he's… sad. A couple of weeks ago he said something about suicide."

"Yeah? And you didn't think that was worth mentioning a little sooner?"

"He said he wouldn't do it. He told me that he's kicked death's ass this long, and there's no way he's giving the bastard such an easy win."

To Colin's surprise, Nevin gave a loud laugh. "I think I like Roger Grey. Okay. Is there anything else you can tell me?"

"Nothing I can think of. Just…." He cleared his throat. "We were going to the rose gardens today because he used to go there with his partner. And he used to have all these orgies and he got arrested in protest marches and I think he was sort of wild, in a really cool way, and now…." He stopped, shocked at the tears prickling his eyes. He didn't even know Roger that well.

Nevin was quiet for a moment. Then he clicked his pen closed and shut the notebook. "I don't know him, but he's important to me," he said carefully. "And I treat every case like the victim matters, because they do."

"Thank you."

After making sure Colin had his contact information, just in case, Nevin gathered the sandwich wrappers and his nearly empty bottle. "Gotta check on the gorillas," he said as he walked away.

CHAPTER FOUR

WHEN THERE was no sign of Roger Grey by Monday morning, Nevin knew the cause was lost. Roger's brain broke and he wandered off. Or despite his ballsy words to Colin, the old guy had decided to off himself and hadn't wanted to do it at home—either because his postage-stamp apartment was too fucking depressing or because he wanted to spare Colin from finding him dead. Either way, his corpse would show up eventually under a freeway overpass or floating in a river.

Shit.

"Hey! Slow down!"

Nevin looked over his shoulder and saw that Jeremy trailed several paces behind. "Hurry up, old man. You're the one with the goddamn Paul Bunyan stride." But Nevin *did* slow down his run, just a little, because his thigh muscles were beginning to burn.

When Jeremy caught up, he walloped Nevin's shoulder with one of his paws. "Can't... run away... from your problems," he huffed. Jeremy was in great shape, but he had ten years on Nevin and at least twice the body mass to haul around.

"Not running from anything, Germy."

Jeremy whacked him again. "Don't lie to me." Then he pulled ahead with a burst of speed.

Dawn hadn't yet broken when they reached Jeremy's apartment building. The spa on the first floor hadn't opened yet, and the second-floor offices remained empty. That meant they could thunder up the stairs to Jeremy's loft as loudly as they wanted, shouting insults at each other the entire way. Jeremy got to the door first—mostly because he pushed Nevin on the second-floor landing—and Nevin flipped him off. "Nice cheating, Boy Scout."

"I never took that oath." Jeremy unlocked the door and ushered him in with a ridiculous bow.

They both headed for the bathroom, stripping off their running gear as they went.

Jeremy was drop-dead gorgeous, a corn-fed slab of muscle topped off with a square chin, storm-cloud eyes, and golden blond hair. He was sweet as cherry pie too—when he wasn't racing Nevin—and had a heart as big as the whole fucking Midwest. He was out and proud, even back when he worked for the police bureau, where being queer wasn't always easy.

Although Nevin was not at all picky about his sex partners, he and Jeremy had never fucked, mainly because they were friends and Nevin didn't want to screw that up. But neither of them minded being buck naked in front of the other. Nevin tended to throw in some gratuitous ogling for good measure, but Jeremy just rolled his eyes.

Jeremy's bathroom was bigger than some of Nevin's first apartments, and the two of them fit easily into the shower for a quick rinse-off.

Jeremy got out first and tossed Nevin a towel. "C'mon. Caffeine's awaiting."

While Nevin put on the suit he'd stashed at Jeremy's before their run, Jeremy dressed in his green park-ranger uniform. As chief ranger, he could have chosen to wear a suit, but he wasn't the type. Besides, he looked damn good in that uniform, as he undoubtedly knew.

After they left Jeremy's place, they walked a half block to where Julie was parked. Nevin closed his gym bag in the trunk, and they sauntered the couple of blocks to P-Town, Jeremy's favorite coffeehouse. Even this early the place was bustling. But despite the commotion, Ptolemy, the gender-fluid barista—dressed today in a blue button-down, black vest, and jeans—gave them a wide smile. "The early bird gets the criminal?"

"And the park vagrants," Jeremy agreed. "Hey, did you ever get your car fixed?"

Ptolemy made a sour face. "Car's dead. I'm doomed to public transportation."

"Only until you finish your PhD and conquer the world."

"And *then* I'll travel everywhere in one of those obnoxious SUV limos." Ptolemy winked.

Because he came to P-Town often and was good friends with the owner, Jeremy had his own personal mug. It was as oversized as he was. Ptolemy filled it to the brim, then gave Nevin his usual double espresso.

Whatever part of the gender spectrum Ptolemy expressed on a particular day, they were fascinating—brilliant and quirky and funny as hell. Shortly after they'd met, Nevin had hit on Ptolemy hard.

"You just want to see what I have between my legs," Ptolemy had said.

"Darling, I'm sure whatever you have between your legs is goddamn delightful, but it's what's in your head that's turning me on. Besides, I'm looking for sex, not satisfying my curiosity."

They had never hooked up, but after that, Ptolemy had taken a shine to him. Jeremy later informed Nevin that it was because Nevin truly didn't care about Ptolemy's gender or think of them as a freak. Maybe so, but it was weird—Nevin wasn't exactly renowned for his sensitivity.

After Nevin and Jeremy paid and received their pastries, Jeremy led the way to a table near the window.

"What did you catch?" Jeremy asked after a few minutes of silence.

"Don't want to talk about it."

One massive shoulder shrugged. "Okay."

And then, as Pink Martini sang something French over the café sound system, Jeremy wolfed his breakfast while Nevin picked at his and watched a cute brunette jog by the window. "Missing persons case."

"Alzheimer's or autism?"

"No. HIV-positive for, like, twenty-something years. He outlived his friends, and his family dumped him decades ago."

Jeremy tsked, then sipped his coffee. "You have a photo?"

"Nothing recent."

"Well, send me what you have. I'll tell my rangers to keep an eye out."

Nevin nodded his thanks and took out his phone, messaging Jeremy the information. "He could have made it to Rocky Butte if he was feeling sprightly."

"I'll take a look there this morning. I have a nine o'clock at Laurelhurst Park, but it shouldn't take too long."

"Thanks, Germy." Nevin didn't hold any hope that Jeremy would find Roger Grey, but he still found comfort in knowing Jeremy was on the job. Jeremy had a quiet confidence that he could save the whole world, given a chance, and although Nevin knew that plenty of people were past saving, Jeremy made a valuable ally.

"Hey, Nev? You don't have to do this to yourself. Maybe the job's taking its toll."

"So I should become a park ranger? I look shitty in green."

Jeremy rumbled a laugh. "And I honestly can't picture you traipsing through Forest Park. You might get your suit dirty. But there are plenty of other ways for you to help people."

"Yeah, right. I could volunteer for Bright Hope, like the poor schmuck who reported Grey missing. Kid's all broken up over it too." He sighed. "And he's the delicate type."

"Not hard as old shoe leather, like you."

"Fuck you," Nevin said without heat as Jeremy grinned.

"I'M SO sorry about the mess," said Manuel Ceja, looking around for someplace to put the cardboard box he held.

"You're getting ready to move?" asked Nevin. Open boxes crammed the office, each of them labeled in green Sharpie.

Manuel sighed and set the box back on the chair he'd taken it from. "I love working downtown, but they've raised the rent again. Our grants only stretch so far, you know? I don't pay Crystal enough, and she and her boyfriend want to get married, buy a house, have kids. You know." He waved toward Bright Hope's only other full-time employee, who glanced briefly at Nevin over her computer screen. She didn't smile, but that didn't surprise Nevin. She always looked angry about something. Maybe she had a grudge against cops.

"Where are you moving to?" Nevin asked Manuel.

"Beaverton." Judging by Manuel's tone, it might as well have been the depths of hell. "My husband's cousin gave us a deal on some office space. It's not as convenient, since most of our clients are here in Portland, and some of the volunteers aren't thrilled either, but we've managed under worse conditions."

That was true. Manuel had established Bright Hope a few years earlier, when the agency's budget came entirely out of his own pocket. He'd worked from home and without a salary. Gradually he'd been able to bring in some grants and donations, and he organized an annual fundraiser. Nevin had attended—and contributed—over the past three years. Nowadays Manuel was able to draw some modest pay, and he'd hired Crystal to handle most of his paperwork, but he clearly still operated on a shoestring.

"I need to ask some questions about Roger Grey," Nevin said.

Manuel's eyes went watery. "Of course, of course. I'm sorry about...." He waved his hands vaguely.

"How about if we head over to Peet's?" Not only could he get some coffee—the double espresso from P-Town had only minimally lightened his fatigue—and sit without displacing boxes, but he'd avoid Crystal's disapproving looks.

"Okay, sweetheart, sure. Crystal, can you hold down the fort? I'll bring you back an iced latte."

She waved, apparently in acquiescence.

Manuel was a short, pear-shaped man with thinning dark hair and a penchant for LGBTQ-themed T-shirts. Today's celebrated marriage equality. During the short walk, he talked about the logistics of the move. The topic clearly agitated him, and Nevin knew Manuel wasn't comfortable with change.

"Do you need some muscle?" Nevin asked. "I have a buddy with brawn to spare, plus he's got a ginormous SUV." He didn't feel guilty about volunteering Jeremy, who lived for all kinds of helping crap. He was always spending his weekends and evenings collecting supplies for the homeless or creating community gardens or tutoring kids who lived in group homes.

Manuel brightened. "Really? I'd love if you could come help out. We're moving a week from Saturday."

Nevin hadn't actually intended to volunteer *himself*, but he couldn't back out without looking like a huge asshole. "Sure."

The early morning rush had passed, and Peet's was quiet. Most of the customers wore name tags on lanyards around their necks— conventioneers from the Marriott next door. They were mostly middle-aged men in suits, and as he took his seat, Nevin wondered what their gig was. Sales of some kind maybe.

He took out his notebook and pen and waited until Manuel had a few slurps of iced tea. Nevin had ordered another double espresso, which probably wouldn't be his last for the day. "What can you tell me about Roger Grey?" he asked.

Manuel had more information than Colin, but little of it would likely prove useful. Roger had earned a graduate degree—Manuel didn't know the field—but had put most of his youthful energy into activism and partying. He'd worked at a bookstore until his health became poor. Although the meds managed the HIV fairly well, he had other problems— heart disease, a fucked-up liver, some other things Manuel didn't know the details of. But as far as Manuel knew, Roger's mind was clear.

"And you don't know about anyone he might have gone away with?" Nevin asked. He'd sketched Julie and a spreading oak tree but hadn't taken many notes.

"Nobody."

Frowning, Nevin told himself not to be such a pussy. *He* had people. Ford was his brother. And he had friends too—Jeremy and a few others. Guys he worked out with. Sometimes they watched basketball together. Anyway, he was solitary by *choice*, goddammit. As long as he got his rocks off now and then, he didn't need anybody else.

"Detective? Is something wrong?"

"Just thinking." He leaned back in his chair. "Tell me about Colin Westwood."

Manuel's eyes widened and he clapped his hands to his chest. "Colin? I'm sure he didn't do anything to Mr. Grey."

"He's not a suspect at this point. But as far as I know, he was the last person to see the victim. That makes him a person of interest." Nevin didn't mention Mrs. Ruskin.

"Well, I've known him for a couple of years. Some of my clients have rented homes from his company. And his company has given us some generous donations."

Sure, Nevin thought. *Nice tax write-off for him.* "But he also volunteers."

"That's more recent."

"What does he do?"

"Nothing fancy. He just visits with a couple of our clients. Mr. Grey on Tuesdays and, um… Bob and Ivan Thomas on Thursdays. He chats with them a little, makes sure they're eating well and taking their meds. Mostly just gives them some company and brightens their day."

"But he went to Roger's house the day before yesterday, and that was Saturday," Nevin pointed out.

"Another volunteer usually has Saturdays. She picks up his groceries too. But her car broke down, so I called Colin and asked him to take over."

That was interesting—Colin had apparently not planned ahead to see Roger Saturday evening. And he was doing so little on a Sunday that he could drop everything and sit around with an old guy. Didn't rich kids do things on weekends? Clubbing? Gambling away their trust funds?

"Colin said he and Roger were going on a picnic yesterday. Was that usual?"

Manuel shook his head and gave a small smile. "No. I didn't ask him to do that. I think he offered it to be nice."

Or to do something nefarious. Thing was, Nevin had no idea what that evil deed might be. And if Colin had done something to Roger, why would he call to report Roger's disappearance? Like a lot of good cops, Nevin had a solid gut instinct. And while Colin might be a spoiled rich kid and the type to faint at a good old slap of reality, Nevin's gut told him Colin wasn't dangerous.

He wouldn't hurt anyone.

Nevin had no more questions, and he and Manuel were simply nursing their drinks when Nevin's phone buzzed. He glanced at the text from his captain. An elderly man had just been admitted to the VA hospital with bruising and broken bones. Hospital personnel suspected abuse. Well, fan-fucking-tastic.

Nevin tucked away his notebook and pen and slid one of his business cards across the table. "Take this in case my contact info is lost in one of those packing boxes. Give me a buzz if you learn anything I should know."

"You bet. Thanks for your hard work, sweetie. I know you'll do your best for Mr. Grey. Maybe he just met some hot young thing and is having one last fling." Manuel clearly didn't believe that any more than Nevin did, but Nevin let it go.

"Sorry, gotta run. Another call."

"Of course. We'll see you and your friend a week from Saturday, bright and early!"

Nevin inwardly groaned.

CHAPTER FIVE

TUESDAY BROUGHT no additional news of Roger Grey. It did, however, deliver a nice clean bust of the fuckwad elder-abuser of the day before. The battered father was being treated at the hospital but would survive, and the fuckwad adult son was cooling his heels in jail, probably still boohooing how nobody understood what an asshole dear old dad was. Probably the old guy *was* an asshole, Nevin thought as he sat in front of the TV that night. This time he'd managed to stop for takeout noodles, so at least he wasn't forcing down General Tso. But even if the father was the world's biggest son of a bitch, that didn't make it okay for Junior to use him as a punching bag.

Not for the first time in his career, Nevin wondered whether the old man had slapped his son around when the son was a kid. Most of the time, abusive pricks learned their tricks at their parents' feet. If so, it was too bad the father never did time in jail for it—but it didn't excuse what the son had done today.

That was one of the worst things about his job. Even when everything went like clockwork, happy endings were few and far between. People died. Families disintegrated. Beat-up little kids grew up and ended up in prison for beating somebody else.

On Wednesday, still no word on Grey. Nevin tracked down anything he could find on the guy. Some minor arrests in the sixties and seventies, mostly for antiwar and gay rights protests. A bust for public indecency that was the result of a bathhouse raid—not that a bathhouse was very public, but the cops hadn't cared. A DUI in the early eighties and a fine for possession of a couple of grams of weed in the midnineties. Nevin wondered whether the pot had been recreational or a way of medicating some of the HIV symptoms. In any case, while Roger's rap sheet told an interesting story, it didn't shed light on his disappearance. Nevin did the paperwork to pull in some other details, like phone records and insurance info, but he wasn't optimistic that he'd learn anything useful.

Other cases came and went over the following days. He filled out his usual mountain of paperwork. At home he watched some old

Westerns, the stupid ones where the stoic good guys wore white hats, the women were hardworking and virtuous, and the savage Indians wore feathers and talked mainly in grunts. He cringed at the stereotypes, yet something about these movies comforted him. Their simplicity, maybe. And the white hats always won.

He did some drawing. Nothing serious, because he wasn't very good. But he sketched a couple of cityscapes and a scene from P-Town, with Ptolemy in a floaty sleeveless blouse and her favorite ethnic earrings, finessing the espresso machine.

And Nevin thought about solitude. As far as he could tell, Roger Grey had been vital and fascinating, yet he ended up alone, relying on charity for food and companionship.

And what about Jeremy Cox? Jesus, Jeremy was anyone's wet dream of a man: buff, handsome, smart, kind. Maybe he was never a Boy Scout, but he was certainly the embodiment of their motto. It had been several years since he'd gotten rid of his douchecanoe boyfriend, yet here he was, alone. Nevin suspected Jeremy hooked up with men now and then, but if he did, the sex didn't seem to make him happier and he never talked about it.

Then there was Colin Westwood. He was cute. Didn't seem like an airhead. He had money. So how come he hadn't found anyone to split his wedding cake with?

If men like Jeremy and Colin were doomed to remain single, it was a good thing Nevin wasn't in the market for a relationship. He just felt sorry for those other guys. That was all.

ON FRIDAY night Ford parked his truck near Nevin's apartment and they took the light-rail downtown. They visited several bars, and while Ford drank Coke, Nevin got increasingly wasted. They ran into Katie, a girl Ford used to date. She must not have harbored a grudge, because she took him back to her place. Nevin didn't mind—he and Ford had a noninterference agreement under those circumstances. No cockblocking allowed. He knew that Ford would show up to reclaim his truck eventually, either later that night or sometime in the morning.

Remaining at the bar, Nevin dug out his phone and tapped on Grindr. Less than an hour later, he was in a room at the Benson Hotel, getting blown by a bear from Cleveland. The guy wasn't all that talented at it, but Nevin was too drunk to care. He caught a taxi home.

His phone woke him up on Saturday morning. He wouldn't have answered it, but he thought it might be Ford wanting to be buzzed in to the building. It ended up being Jeremy.

"How about a run?" Jeremy asked, sounding so fucking chipper that Nevin wanted to shoot him. "Or some time at the gym?"

The thought of moving even as far as the bathroom made Nevin ill. He groaned. "Not today."

There was a pause. "You sound hungover," Jeremy boomed. "How much did you drink last night?"

"Fuck yourself with a cactus," said Nevin. Then he felt slightly guilty because Jeremy's ex was a drunk, which naturally made the big guy sensitive about the issue.

Jeremy was quiet for a moment. "Do you want me to leave you alone to feel miserable in peace?"

"Yeah. I…." Nevin rubbed his face with his free hand, which didn't help his headache and nausea but did at least demonstrate he had some fine motor control. The motion jostled a thought loose too. "We're helping Bright Hope move shop a week from today."

"Shoot, Nevin. I can't. I've got this hike scheduled. Maybe I could reschedule, but—"

"Never mind. It's my bad. Should've asked you first. We can manage without you."

"You sure?"

Jeremy sounded distressed, and Nevin imagined him sitting in his loft, upset with himself for not being able to meet a commitment he'd been clueless about. Such a softhearted twit of a man. He'd spent years dealing with some of the foulest messes humankind could shit out, and yet he still believed he could make the world smell like roses.

"Go take a hike, Germy," Nevin said gruffly.

Jeremy laughed. "And you go take some ibuprofen with a lot of water."

BY EVENING Nevin felt better. When he called Ford later to see if he wanted to go out, Ford said no. "Katie from last night? We're doing dinner and a movie."

"That's ass-backwards," Nevin said. "It's supposed to be dinner and movie first, then fucking."

"We mostly talked and caught up, actually. She's pretty cool." That was high praise from Ford. Jesus, maybe he was going over to the dark side too, and pretty soon he'd be like Colin, planning the menu for his wedding reception.

"Have fun."

"I'll catch you later, little bro."

Feeling too restless to stay home, Nevin remembered a female EMT he ran into occasionally at work. They'd slept together once, and although she wasn't into dating, she said she wouldn't mind a rerun. He found her number in his contacts and gave her a ring. They caught some burgers at a brewpub, then went to her tidy little house for a quick screw.

"You're good," she said, holding out his car keys as he buttoned his shirt.

He shrugged. "Thanks."

"I heard you play for both teams."

"I'll play on any team that'll take me," he answered with a grin. "'Cause it beats playing with myself."

"But which do you like better? I mean, if you *had* to pick just boys or just girls, what would you do?"

"I'd feel like I was being cheated."

She pulled on her T-shirt. "I stay unattached because there's no way I'm going to let anyone tell me what to do. I'm my own woman—no compromises. But you—are you single because you don't want to settle on just one or the other?"

His headache returned in a rush. "Just because I'm bi doesn't mean I can't be faithful. If I did have a thing with a girl, I wouldn't cheat on her just because I missed cock. And vice versa. If I had a thing with a person, they'd be all I wanted."

"But you don't. Have a thing, I mean."

He faked a leer and stuck his groin forward. "You've *seen* my thing, baby."

"You know what I mean."

"Look. I don't do relationship talks, okay? I'm the goddamn Lone Ranger. No Tonto either. I ride into town, I give the folks what they need, and then I ride off into the sunset." He tipped an imaginary hat forward.

"And it's way past sunset now." He turned on his heel and headed home to find more ibuprofen.

ANOTHER MONDAY rolled around with a fresh stack of reports to write and papers to file. Nevin was in a foul mood and snarled at everyone, and it wasn't until lunchtime that he remembered why: he'd dreamed about Colin Westwood the previous night.

The dream had been set in what was supposed to be Rocky Butte Park, even though it looked nothing like the real one. It was Colin's wedding, and he wore a white tuxedo with a yellow plaid shirt and a bow tie. He was dancing around, making sure all the decorations and food items were perfect. Jeremy and all his green-uniformed park rangers were there, and so were Manuel Ceja and Ford and Roger Grey's stoner apartment manager and the bear from Cleveland.

Dream-Nevin had stopped Colin. "Who's the other groom?" Nevin asked.

Colin gave him a pitying look. "What does it matter to you? You're not invited."

Then a bunch of police officers in blue appeared, guns drawn, forcing Nevin away from the wedding and backward toward a cliff.

Nevin teetered on the edge, an impossibly long drop beneath him. "You said I could come, asshole!" he shouted at Colin. "You said!"

Then the other groom showed up—in a black tux and a bow tie that matched Colin's—and gave Nevin an evil grin. Nevin recognized the guy: Dwayne Price, the foster father he'd punched in the nose all those years ago. "You don't matter, Nevin, and nobody will miss you when you're gone."

Then Nevin fell.

So it was little wonder that he was unhappy today. He did his best to stay in his office with his paperwork and lots of coffee, but occasionally he had to poke his head out and interact. One of these interactions happened on his way out of the building to grab some lunch from a food truck.

"Why the ever-living fuck don't I have Roger Grey's phone and banking records yet?" he barked at one of the uniforms. "The subpoena went out a week ago. Did somebody have to travel to Outer Mongolia to get the fucking things?"

The officer shook his head. "I'll check into it."

"Fuck you very much," Nevin snarled and pushed by him. He might apologize later, but right now he didn't have it in him.

He stomped several blocks to a pod of food carts, where he bought a bowl of lamb tagine and took it to a wooden picnic table. He'd had the stuff before and knew it was good, but today the spices tasted off and the texture was weird. He ate only a few bites before tossing it away. He wasn't really hungry anyway.

With a little time on his hands, he walked around downtown for a while and then sat on a bench in the South Park Blocks, wishing he knew how to meditate. He really would have liked to empty his mind, at least temporarily.

The foster mother he'd had when he was six or seven had spent a lot of time in court. Nevin didn't know why and wasn't sure whether it had anything to do with him. Hell, he didn't even remember her name. She was nice, though, if overwhelmed by life. It must have been summer, because the weather was nice and Nevin wasn't in school. While the lady was in court, she'd park Nevin in the hallway with her teenage daughter and promise them both ice cream if they behaved. Nevin sat quietly on the hard floor and read or drew. When the foster mother was done in court, she'd take Nevin and her daughter to McDonald's for soft-serve cones and then walk them to the Park Blocks to watch the pigeons.

One day his social worker turned up at the house, told Nevin to put his things in a plastic bag, and took him away. He never saw the lady or her daughter again. Maybe a part of him believed he'd run into them if he sat in the park long enough.

Oh, for fuck's sake.

Back at the office, the uniform greeted him with a smile. "Got the banking records."

It took Nevin only a few minutes to learn that Roger Grey didn't have much money—and didn't spend much either, except on the basics of life. But an interesting pattern emerged, beginning a couple of months earlier. Roger had started making regular withdrawals at an ATM not far from his house. His already small account had dwindled rapidly.

And the last withdrawal was at 9:17 on the morning he'd disappeared.

Nevin sent the uniform to the bank to ask for surveillance footage. And maybe Nevin's earlier tantrum lit a fire somewhere, because when he got to work on Tuesday morning, the footage awaited him. As did an audience—Frankl and Blake from Homicide, looking rumpled and tired, coffee cups in hand.

"Rough night?" Nevin asked.

"Shooting on Northeast Alberta," Frankl said. "Victim's going to live, but half the neighborhood was sprayed with gunfire."

"Gang?"

"Probably."

Nevin sighed. "So why don't you go home and get some rest? This is my case."

"Missing persons—that's us too," said Blake. He always looked as though he'd had his hair cut by a blind barber.

Deciding it was less hassle to let them play along, Nevin cued up the video. It was handy to know the exact time he was looking for—no need to watch endless hours of nothing. The quality wasn't great, in part because of the morning sun's glare, but he could easily see a man approaching the camera.

"Is that him?" asked Frankl.

Nevin paused the recording and looked closely at the screen. The man had sparse gray hair and wore glasses and a long-sleeved shirt. Nevin hadn't been able to find a recent photo of Roger Grey, but he thought he recognized the man's narrow face and slightly knobby chin. "Yeah, I'm pretty sure." He tried to analyze Roger's expression. Not a happy one, but then most people didn't look ecstatic while doing a cash withdrawal. Was he frightened or stressed? The image wasn't clear enough to tell.

When Nevin restarted the video, Roger took a wallet from his back pocket, pulled out a card, and replaced the wallet. When he reached forward, probably to touch the ATM screen, his hand appeared slightly shaky. Age and ill health or fear?

After a moment Roger reached forward again, then turned and walked away. Nevin waited to see if anything else relevant would appear. When it didn't, he stopped the video.

"He didn't put the cash in his wallet," Nevin said thoughtfully. "Or in a pocket. His card either." When he took money out of a machine, Nevin always tucked it away immediately, unless someone else was waiting their turn. Nobody had visited the machine until long after Roger was gone.

"Maybe he was going to buy something right away," Blake suggested. "There's a grocery store right there, and it's open Sunday mornings."

Maybe. Except Colin had just brought Roger groceries the evening before. Had Roger wanted to contribute something to the picnic? Possibly, but if so, it made more sense that he'd wait until Colin arrived and then have Colin drive him to the store. From what Manuel had said, Roger tired easily, and he wouldn't likely have been eager to walk several blocks right before a major outing.

Something niggled at Nevin—something from the video. He rewound it to the point when Roger appeared and watched again. And again. He was on his fifth repeat when he caught it. "Wait!" he said, quickly hitting Pause.

Frankl had walked away to toss his empty coffee cup in the trash. Now he returned to peer over Nevin's shoulder at the screen. "What?"

"Watch carefully. On the left." Nevin rewound again, but only for a few seconds. Then he inched the video forward, frame by frame. "There!"

"Yeah, something's there," said Frankl, bending closer. Blake pushed in, too, sandwiching Nevin between them. They both towered over him. He fucking hated that.

But now wasn't the time to be a diva. Nevin flicked through the next couple of frames until a bit more of the object lay within the camera's view. "That's somebody's arm," he said. It was the area right around the bend of the elbow, and judging by the amount of dark hair, the arm's owner was male. Nevin realized, with more relief than he wanted to admit, that it couldn't be Colin, whose arms were covered in fine blond hairs.

"Any idea who that is?" asked Frankl.

"None." Well, he could rule out *one* potential suspect. He shook his head. "Too bad the bureau doesn't keep elbow mug shots."

They watched the video several more times without gleaning any additional information. It was frustrating as hell, like hearing an important conversation you couldn't quite make out. And it was troubling, because it confirmed Nevin's belief that Roger hadn't simply wandered off. Somebody had waited for him to withdraw money—perhaps had even driven him to the ATM in the first place—and then left when Roger did.

Nevin gave the other detectives a bleak look. "Someone's going to have to get the surveillance video from his previous ATM visits and see if Mystery Arm Man shows up there too. Don't suppose you bitches want to volunteer."

Blake clapped him hard on the back. "Nope. Wouldn't want to interfere in your case, Ng."

"Dickwads."

Frankl had the grace to look a little chagrined, but Blake just gave a cheery smile. Nevin flipped them both off and reached for his notebook.

CHAPTER SIX

SOMEHOW COLIN had let slip his plans for Saturday, and his mother had spent the better part of the week trying to talk him out of helping with the Bright Hope move, even going so far as to drag his father into the battle. "Your mother says you've had too much stress lately," his dad said over the phone on Friday afternoon, sounding more weary than warrior-like.

"For God's sake, Dad. This isn't stressful, and I'm not going to drop dead. And if I do, Mom can have 'I told you so' inscribed on my tombstone."

"Don't make that joke where she can hear it. She won't think it's funny."

"No, probably not." Legolas was curled up in Colin's lap, and Colin stroked him a few times to calm himself. "Look. I'm thirty, I'm of sound mind, and I'm capable of running my own life and making my own decisions. If Mom can't learn to back off, I'm going to move away."

"Colin—"

"I'm serious. I know you love me, but I'm an adult man and you guys are suffocating me. There's nothing really tying me to Portland except work, and I can find a job somewhere else." He'd been thinking for a long time about giving this little speech but hadn't intended to deliver it over the phone. Although it might be a better choice than over Sunday brunch at Salty's, he would have preferred that his mother hear his declarations firsthand. And he *was* serious. He liked Portland and didn't want to leave, but he was willing to do so if it was the only way to gain his independence.

His father was silent for a moment. "You're right, Colin. I'll talk to her. But you're going to need to have a conversation with her yourself."

"I know. Maybe soften her up for me first?"

"Deal."

After Colin ended the call, he remained on his couch, silently petting Legolas. It was time, perhaps, for a pre-midlife crisis. He wasn't miserable, and by almost anyone's standards, he had things pretty good. Nice apartment, decent car, parents who loved him, job he didn't hate.

Friends who were fun to hang out with. And a cat who was currently purring like a motorboat.

"I'm stagnant," Colin informed Legolas.

He'd spent most of his life going with the flow. When he was a kid, his mother told people he was a fighter, but that wasn't true. *She* was the soldier; he just followed in her wake. He'd attended college at Lewis & Clark instead of going somewhere far away, and then he earned an MBA at Portland State because it seemed like the thing to do, especially after his mother—who was an attorney—convinced him he didn't have the temperament for law. He'd worked for his father's firm. He'd moved into a loft in one of the firm's buildings. He'd dated a little before getting serious with Trent, whose parents belonged to the same club as Colin's. And Colin had never questioned any of it.

But being dumped by Trent had thrown him for a loop, and he'd been a mess right afterward. Now that he'd had a few weeks' perspective, Colin wondered if breaking up hadn't been for the best. He'd liked Trent, a lot. Maybe loved him. Trent was comfortable, predictable, safe. But they hadn't shared a passion for each other. Even their sex life had been... humdrum. A little fooling around at Colin's place on Friday and Saturday nights, each of them knowing which motions would get the other off with a minimum of fuss. Trent usually spent the night after, which was nice.

"Excitement in a relationship is overrated," Colin said to Legolas. "And it never lasts. Even if Trent and I had been all hot and heavy to begin with, those hormones would have settled eventually."

Legolas made a chirpy sound and rolled onto his back, daring Colin to rub his soft tummy. Colin took the dare.

While years of instruction had told Colin it was bad to get his blood rushing, now he wasn't so sure. He thought about Mrs. Ruskin sitting alone in her house, making up excuses just so she'd have a visitor now and then. And Roger Grey alone in *his* apartment—and now seemingly vanished. How many years of solitary life would either of them have traded for one more chance to make their hearts race with joy and exhilaration?

Colin didn't want to end up like that.

But after three decades of hesitation, he had no idea how to leap.

SATURDAY WAS the first day of August, and Colin woke up longing for winter. Although it was well before nine, his loft had already heated uncomfortably. Legolas grumbled when Colin removed him from the bathroom sink in order to brush his teeth. Then Colin dressed in the same skimpy shorts and lightweight tank he'd worn the last time he saw Roger, and for the same reason—he couldn't stand the thought of too much fabric covering his skin. With the voice in his head reminding him not to get dehydrated—the voice sounded remarkably like his mother—he filled a large water bottle before leaving the house.

Since the traffic was light, he made it downtown in a few minutes and arrived at the Bright Hope office well ahead of schedule. But he gasped when he saw the vehicle squarely in the middle of the no-parking zone in front of Bright Hope's door: a purple muscle car that had lately become quite familiar.

Colin momentarily considered turning around and going home. But he'd promised Manuel he'd help with the move. Besides, if Colin did leave, he might die from curiosity. What was Detective Ng doing here? Oh God. Had someone else disappeared?

Colin parked his car—legally—and went inside the building. When it was immediately clear that nobody looked stressed, his worry about mayhem was replaced with happiness over his decision to stay. He didn't know which was more gratifying: Nevin looking astonished to see him, or seeing the detective in a pair of shorts as skimpy as but tighter than his own. Nevin wore a T-shirt instead of a tank top, but it fitted him snugly and showed off his trim waist and compactly muscled torso.

"What the fuck?" Nevin exclaimed, still staring at him. "What are you doing here?"

"Helping Manuel move. You?"

"*You*'re gonna lug boxes, Bow Tie? Don't you have servants to do that shit for you?"

Colin rolled his eyes. "I give them a half day off on Saturdays, if they're very, very good."

Before Nevin could answer—likely with a swearword—Manuel entered from the adjacent room, a computer monitor in his arms. "Colin baby! I'm so glad you're here!"

"Happy to help. What do you want with me?"

"Oh, honey, don't give me *ideas*. I'm a married man, remember?"

Colin ignored Nevin's snort and winked at Manuel. "Just 'cause you're married doesn't mean you can't look, right?" He shot his hips to the side and made a muscle with his right arm.

"Jesus Christ," Nevin said. "Will you two nancies knock it off? You're turning my stomach."

Colin whirled to glare at him. "Are you *homophobic?*" He hadn't gotten that vibe from Nevin during their previous meetings. Nevin hadn't batted an eye when Colin mentioned breaking up with his boyfriend, and he also hadn't seemed to care that Roger was gay. But maybe that was a neutral mask Nevin wore when investigating a crime.

For some reason Manuel began to giggle. Nevin just rolled his eyes. "Untwist your panties. I don't give a flying fuck who or what you like to sleep with. Just stop with the flirting—it makes me gag."

"What's wrong with flirting?" Not that Colin was especially adept at the art himself, nor did he do it often, except when he was kidding around. But he figured it was generally harmless and maybe even fun.

"It's a goddamn waste of time. Either you want to fuck someone or you don't—and vice versa. If you're both on board, go for it. If not, stop playing around." He cocked his thumb at Manuel. "Manny here has a ball and chain wrapped so tight around his dick he can barely move. And *you*, princess, are up in your ivory tower waiting for fucking Prince Charming to whisk you away. So no way you two are gonna screw each other."

"You're mixing your stories. Ivory towers are for academics, not princesses. Rapunzel was in an ordinary stone tower. And Prince Charming, I'm pretty sure, was from *Snow White*. Rapunzel got Flynn Rider in the Disney version. I don't know who the Grimms gave her."

Nevin was gaping at him again. "Holy shit. That is the gayest speech I've ever heard—and I've heard guys begging their 'daddies'"— he made air quotes for the daddies part—"to stuff their big cocks in their hot little holes."

"Knowing about fairy tales makes me gay?"

"It does if you're not a six-year-old girl. I bet you can sing the entire *Frozen* soundtrack."

Although Colin momentarily considered bursting into song, he decided to, well, let it go. This was a really stupid conversation anyway. He turned his back on Nevin and addressed Manuel. "What do you want me to do?"

"I rented a truck. Why don't you guys schlepp things out while I finish boxing this up? Just don't carry anything too heavy until more help arrives."

Nevin looked as thrilled to be working with Colin as Colin felt, but they couldn't really refuse Manuel's request. So Colin lifted the nearest box—it was heavy—and walked to the door.

When he'd initially arrived at the office, he'd been so preoccupied with Nevin's car that he hadn't noticed the small rental moving van parked at the curb. Kayla—the volunteer who trained newbies—leaned up against it. She waved when she saw him. "Hi, Colin!"

The back of the truck was open, so he dumped the box inside. "Hey. Manuel recruited you too, huh?"

"Yep. I'm in charge of security and transportation." She thumped the side of the truck. "I'd help you guys with the boxes, but my balance sucks."

He nodded. When she'd given his volunteer orientation for Bright Hope, she'd mentioned she had MS. "That's cool. Security and transportation are important jobs. But you're okay in this heat?"

"The truck's got AC. I'll hop in the cab and blast it if I need to cool off." She looked as if she was about to say something else, but then she saw something behind Colin and her expression shifted to surprise. "Nevin!"

The box Nevin carried was nearly as big as he was, yet he didn't seem to strain much as he heaved it into the truck. He turned to Kayla and gave her a big hug. "Didn't expect to see you today," he said after they broke apart. "I thought you worked on Saturdays."

"My shifts changed. I get weekends off now."

"Nice." Then he leered. "How's that boyfriend thing working out for you? 'Cause, you know, all this could still be yours." He gestured at himself like Vanna White showing off an especially nice prize.

Kayla gave him a playful push on the shoulder. "Been there, done that, remember?" she said.

"How could I forget? And how could you settle for anyone else?"

"Settle is the operative term here, Nevin. Larry and I moved in together."

"Your loss," he said with a grin. "But congratulations."

Colin had been frozen in place as he watched the little drama, but now he stalked back to the building, pretty much side by side with Nevin. "I thought you were opposed to flirting," Colin said.

Nevin shot him a look. "This is an exception. Kayla and I slept together. Twice." He said the last word as if it were a true accomplishment.

That was interesting. Colin would have guessed that Nevin's bed partners were attractive young girls, the type who dressed stylishly and liked to party. But Kayla was probably in her late thirties, and there was nothing especially stylish about the jeans and T-shirts she seemed to favor.

"Why did you sleep with Kayla?" Colin blurted out.

Pausing in the doorway, Nevin gave him a disgusted look. "She's nice and she was willing."

"That's it?"

"It's sex, Bow Tie. You and the other person can stand each other and you have a couple hours of fun together. That's all."

Colin wasn't sure whether Nevin's attitude was supremely cynical or just practical. "I don't get it."

"Well, that's why I'm a detective and you're the rich boy with rental houses. Oh, and another thing, Sherlock." Nevin pointed a finger at him. "If I'm homophobic, what the fuck am I doing spending my day off hauling shit for Bright Hope?" He stomped inside.

Two more men and a woman arrived shortly afterward, all of them ready to help, and Colin managed to mostly avoid Nevin as they carried things out to the truck. One of the men was enormous, with hair well past his shoulders and an impressively bushy beard. Colin had to choke back laughter when he learned the guy's name was Harry. He looked like a Viking war god and had a disconcerting habit of clapping everyone on the back, and he could lug a lot of boxes.

There was plenty to carry. Manuel had accumulated a lot of papers and office supplies, but he also had a substantial collection of books to lend to clients. Two rooms held items—most of them donated—for clients in need: nonperishable food, clothing, household articles, small pieces of furniture, and various medical supplies. Soon the truck was packed full. Kayla and two other volunteers drove off to unload at the new location in Beaverton, while everyone else stuffed as much as they could into their cars.

"Could've used Germy's tank," Nevin grumbled as Colin walked by. Nevin was trying to fit one more box into his trunk.

Since Colin was burdenless at the moment, he lent a hand, shifting another box slightly to make room. "Germy's tank?" he asked, confused.

"Never mind." Nevin leaned in to adjust a box that was blocking the trunk's hinge. Then he looked at Colin over his shoulder. "And stop ogling my ass."

"You think just because I'm gay I'm going to check you out? I'm tired of straight guys who think they're so irresistible to us." He sounded overly self-righteous even to his own ears. Probably because he actually *had* been ogling Nevin's ass. He couldn't help it. It was a superb ass—

the thin fabric of Nevin's shorts stretched tightly over rounded muscle—and it was almost within reach.

Nevin straightened up, slammed the trunk closed, and gave Colin an amused look. When he sauntered toward the building, he definitely put some extra wiggle in his walk.

"Jerk," Colin muttered to himself.

The Saturday morning traffic on Sunset Highway must have been light, because the empty truck returned less than an hour and a half after leaving. This time they filled it primarily with bulky furniture, leaving only a handful of items in the old office. Manuel gave the remaining boxes a considering look. "I can get all that tomorrow. Let's head to the new place and unpack."

Everyone got in their cars and formed an uneven convoy that snaked toward the suburbs.

BRIGHT HOPE'S new home was a little gray bungalow in downtown Beaverton, and Manuel gave them a quick tour before they finished unloading the vehicles. The house had been converted to office space at some point, but most of the original kitchen remained. It had three decent-sized rooms downstairs and three more on the second floor, with a bathroom on each level. It had more square footage than the old place in Portland. The property also boasted a detached garage and a neat little backyard with a patio and mature trees.

Colin looked things over quickly but with a practiced eye. "The place is in decent shape," he assured Manuel. "Nothing's new, but it looks in good repair."

Manuel nodded. "Good, good. I'm going to miss my favorite restaurants, but the rent is dirt cheap. I might want to do something about the walls, though. White is so boring."

"Let me know if you do. I know a good painter."

One thing the house lacked was air-conditioning—not that it would have helped much, since the door was propped open for carrying things inside. But Colin frowned, thinking of Manuel roasting through the summer while trying to work. And when Kayla mentioned something about lunch—it was past noon—Colin had an idea. "I can go pick up lunch for everyone," he volunteered.

Manuel clapped him on the back. "That's great. We'll unpack while you're gone. But someone should go with you to help." He turned to Nevin, who was helping another volunteer maneuver a bookshelf into place. "Nevin, go with him."

"Why me?" Nevin asked sourly.

"You know Beaverton. Go."

Still looking reluctant, Nevin followed Colin outside, then surprised Colin by not complaining when they walked to Colin's car instead of Nevin's. He got into the passenger seat and looked around curiously. "This is a boring car," he announced.

"I don't think BMWs come in purple."

"It's boring inside and out. I'd expect your ride to have more personality."

"I'm sorry it's not fabulous enough for your expectations," said Colin as he pulled away from the curb. "It's a company car."

"But it's your company. You can do whatever the hell you want with it."

"It's my father's company, actually, and no I can't. Dad's not real big on whimsy or innovation."

"Oh," said Nevin, as if some theory had just been confirmed.

They stopped at a light, and Colin glanced at him. "Do you really know Beaverton?"

"Guess so. It's outside my jurisdiction, but sometimes we have to cooperate with the Beaverton PD. Why?"

"I want to buy an AC unit for Bright Hope. I thought I'd pick one up before we got lunch. Do you know a place?"

Nevin remained quiet a moment. "Yeah." Then he began giving directions.

They ended up at Fred Meyer, which wasn't far away. Colin chose the most powerful window air conditioner. But after Nevin helped him lift the box into their cart, Colin stared thoughtfully at the display.

"What?" Nevin demanded.

"I'm trying to figure out whether two of these will fit in my car."

"One's gonna be enough for that little house."

"I know. But the central air in my place crapped out, and there's no sign it's getting fixed soon. It makes it hard to sleep." He made a decision and reached for another box. "I think this one can go in my backseat."

"Two of these are gonna set you back almost a grand."

Colin glanced at the price tag and nodded. "Almost."

"Must be nice to have enough money to throw around like that."

Totally fed up with Nevin's string of snide comments, Colin glared. "Yeah, I have some extra cash. So what? I don't actually throw it around—not that it's any of your business. I spend it on stuff that's worthwhile. A comfortable working environment for Manuel and a decent night's sleep for me are worthwhile."

A woman shot them a worried look and hugged the opposite side of the aisle as she walked by. She was probably wondering why two men in skimpy shorts were having an argument in the housewares section of Freddy's. Nevin, however, didn't look the least bit ashamed. Colin wondered if he was even capable of embarrassment. "You're cute when you're having a hissy fit," Nevin said.

"Oh, for God's sake!"

That just made Nevin grin wider. But he helped Colin wrestle the second box into the cart, and he whistled happily as they navigated to the checkout lines.

After they fit both boxes into the BMW, Colin and Nevin sat in the car with the engine and AC running, saying nothing. Colin was about to remind him that everyone at Bright Hope was waiting for lunch, but Nevin spoke first, his voice uncharacteristically subdued. "Roger Grey is dead."

Colin's stomach clenched. "You... found him?"

"No. But if he was alive, he'd have showed up somewhere by now."

"I'm, um, the last person to have seen him." Colin shifted in his seat.

"No, you're not. And in case you're wondering, you're not a suspect."

Actually, that thought hadn't occurred to Colin. Now that Nevin mentioned it—even in negation—Colin felt slightly dizzy. "Why would I want to do anything bad to Roger?"

Nevin sighed. "I dunno. People come up with all kinds of reasons to fuck over other people. Greed. Anger. Revenge. Jealousy. Just plain old cocksucking evil." He leaned back against the headrest, his eyes closed, and Colin wondered what kinds of horrible things he'd seen in his career.

"People do good things for each other too," Colin insisted.

"Thank you, Miss Molly Optimist." Nevin didn't even open his eyes.

"It's true. Not everyone, not all the time. But look at Manuel, for instance. He could be doing lots of other things with his life—things that pay better and don't require an office in Beaverton—but here he is."

When Nevin didn't reply, Colin softened his voice. "Look at you, then. Lugging office supplies around on your day off."

This time Nevin did look at him, although his expression was unreadable. After a long moment, he said, "I'm fucking hungry."

He directed Colin to a nearby strip mall containing a Vietnamese sandwich place, where they chose an assortment of banh mi along with some fruit drinks and bubble teas and, because they looked so good, some pastries. Colin pulled out his wallet to pay, but Nevin shouldered him out of the way and handed his credit card to the kid behind the counter.

When they returned to Bright Hope, the other volunteers greeted them like conquering heroes and fell ravenously upon the food.

"These are great," Harry boomed as he polished off his third sandwich. "Maybe Beaverton's not such a hellhole after all."

Manuel rolled his eyes. "Beaverton is not a hellhole, sweetheart. It's a suburb." He sounded resigned, as if they'd had this conversation before.

"Same diff. But at least I talked you out of taking that place in Vancouver."

"The rent was a steal."

"Because it's in Van*couv*er. I'd've quit if you tried to drag my ass over the river."

Manuel reached up to pinch Harry's cheek. "You can't quit, darling. You're slave labor, remember?"

"Yeah, yeah, yeah. I work my buns off and nobody pays me what I'm worth."

"But they're nice buns." Manuel winked at him.

After lunch was over, Colin and Nevin dragged one of the air conditioners into the house. Manuel looked perilously close to breaking down in tears. "You guys are the best," he sniffed, wrapping an arm around each of them.

Nevin extricated himself from the hug. "*Colin's* the best. It was his idea and his money."

"And you navigated, and carried things, and bought lunch," Colin pointed out, but Nevin just scowled.

By the time everyone had set the furniture in place, unpacked the boxes, and put everything away, dinnertime had arrived and the crew was hungry again. They ordered pizzas this time—Manuel paid—and munched their slices while standing in the house's biggest room. Thanks to the AC, the air was comfortably cool.

"I'm in the mood for celebrating, after I change out of these sweaty clothes," Manuel said, wiping his hands on a napkin. "How about we all meet up at JayJay's in a couple of hours? First round of drinks is on my husband, since he couldn't help us move today."

Usually Colin liked JayJay's, and he would have enjoyed an evening with this crowd. But he suddenly felt tired and over-peopled. "I'm going to have to call it a night. I have some work to do," he lied.

Manuel tsked and Kayla looked sad, but Colin waved, gave Manuel another hug, and walked out to his car. Before he could start the engine, Nevin appeared. Colin rolled down the driver's side window. "Yeah?"

"You don't have work to do tonight."

Colin rolled his eyes. "Thanks, Detective. Are you planning to run surveillance on me?" If so, Nevin was in for a night of disappointment, because Colin planned an evening of petting Legolas and watching old movies. He was in a Cary Grant mood.

"Do you have hired muscle at home?"

"Um, no." Did Nevin think he needed a bodyguard?

"Then how do you plan to get the air conditioner inside?"

Oh. Colin hadn't thought of that. The unit was too heavy for one person, especially since he'd have to carry it from the parking lot across the street, through the building lobby, and then down the hall from the elevator. "I'll find someone to help."

Nevin gave him that look again—the one that said Colin was the most idiotic human being he'd ever encountered. "What's your address?" he asked.

"Why?"

"'Cause it's easier to ask you than to run your plates, genius."

"But why do you need my address?"

"So I can meet you there and give you a hand with the fucking AC." Nevin shook his head. "I have your address in my notebook from our chat at Mrs. Ruskin's. I could get it from there."

Colin was tempted to refuse to tell him anything, just because Nevin was so infuriating. But, well, he really did need help. And he was fairly certain that if he didn't cough up his address, Nevin would follow through on his threat to just look it up.

"Fine," Colin said and gave him the information.

EVEN THOUGH Colin had a head start, when he arrived at his building, the purple GTO was already there. In the fire lane. Colin generally stuck pretty close to the speed limit; Nevin, he suspected, did not. Colin pulled alongside Nevin's car and lowered the passenger window. "You can't park there," he said loudly.

Nevin sat behind the wheel, tapping his fingers impatiently. "Nowhere else to park in your fucking neighborhood, is there? Not for the rabble, anyway." He nodded toward the gated entrance to Colin's lot.

"But it's a red zone."

"And every goddamn meter maid and gorilla in blue knows Julie. I'm not getting ticketed."

Okay, so being a cop brought privileges. "What if there's a fire?"

"Then your building goes up in flames, hundreds die, and you get to blame me. Satisfied?"

Colin had never been so tempted to wrap his hands around another person's neck. It was lucky he couldn't reach Nevin at the moment. "Fine. Meet me at my car." He pulled away and into the lot.

Without exchanging more than a few grunts, they wrestled the heavy box across the street and up to Colin's apartment. They had to put it down while Colin got out his keys and unlocked the door. "Don't let Legolas out," he warned as he turned the knob.

"Who?"

"My cat."

They got the box inside, and Nevin kicked the door closed. "What kind of name is Legolas?"

"You know, the elf." They set the AC down. "From Tolkien. Orlando Bloom was one of my first crushes."

Nevin clearly had no idea what he was talking about.

"*Lord of the Rings*," Colin explained.

"Never seen it."

"You should. It wouldn't wound your masculinity. It's not Disney, there's no singing, and no princesses." He paused and thought for a moment. "Okay, there sort of is one. She's an elf too. But mostly there's a lot of fighting. Manly fighting." He decided to omit the homoerotic undertones of Frodo and Sam's relationship.

"I don't watch that shit."

"What *do* you watch? Car chases and explosions?"

Nevin shrugged. Then, instead of leaving, he ripped the flaps of the box open. "Gimme a hand."

They knew from Bright Hope that getting the unit out of the box was slightly tricky. They managed it, though, and soon plastic wrapping and bits of packing foam lay scattered on the floor as the air conditioner did its best to combat the oppressive heat. But Nevin still didn't head for the door, and Colin felt rude and ungrateful.

"You want something cold to drink?" he offered.

"Hell yes."

Nevin trailed him into the open kitchen, then waited through Colin's recitation as he peered into the fridge. "Water? Beer? Diet Coke? Iced tea?"

"You got a whole convenience store tucked away in there?" Nevin shook his head. "Iced tea's good."

Colin handed him a bottle and took one for himself. He unscrewed the top and took a few long swallows, watching as Nevin gave himself a slow tour of the loft. Nevin glanced at the TV and sound system and looked briefly at the corner Colin used as a home office, but he seemed most interested in the shelving units. "You have a lot of books. And DVDs."

"I suppose so." Colin had been collecting movies and books since he was a kid, and he could rarely bring himself to get rid of any. Sometimes he made a stab at organizing them, although he kept changing his mind about which scheme to use. Genre? Chronology? Author or director? Title? And sometimes he just set them in piles until Leg threatened to topple the stacks.

Nevin mostly looked, but sometimes he pulled a book or movie from the shelf and read the back before replacing it. He obviously wasn't in a hurry. Colin liked the way he moved, his motions graceful yet economical, his slow stride self-assured. And God, he was beautiful. So well-made. But there was also a certain set to his shoulders that Colin thought he recognized. Was Nevin lonely?

"Are you going to JayJay's?" Colin blurted. When Nevin turned to look at him in surprise, the words flowed out of Colin's mouth as if he'd accidentally turned on the stupidity faucet. "Because maybe you are, or maybe you have other plans. It's Saturday night after all. But, you know, you could hang out here if you wanted. We could watch a movie or something. I was going to do *The Philadelphia Story*, but we don't have to. We could watch something else. Like *An American in Paris*. Or *West Side Story*. If you want. And I won't molest you or anything, because I'm not the type who loses it over straight guys." He pressed his lips together before things got worse.

To his surprise, Nevin didn't make fun of him and didn't refuse. Instead he stared. Then his mouth twitched into a small smile. "Who says I'm straight?"

"You told me yourself that you slept with Kayla."

"I've slept with a lot of girls. And a lot of boys. I've never seen any good reason to limit my opportunities."

Colin gaped. Then he narrowed his eyes. "You're teasing me."

"Whattaya want? A testimonial from my last several fuck buddies?" Nevin held up his right hand, making the oath gesture. "I swear on a stack of Corbin Fisher discs that I like dick as much as pussy, and when it comes to ass, well, I'm an equal-opportunity kind of guy."

He seemed sincere, at least as far as Colin could tell, and Colin couldn't think of a good reason for him to lie. "Okay. You could have mentioned this back when I was accusing you of being a homophobe."

"Where would've been the fun in that?"

"Does Manuel know?"

"Yep."

Well, that explained Manuel's amusement that morning. Manuel could have said something, but maybe he figured it wasn't his place to out Nevin if, for whatever reason, Nevin chose to keep his bisexuality to himself. Colin sighed. "Do you want to stay and watch a movie or not?"

"I get to choose it."

And now a new emotion made itself known inside Colin—excitement. God. He *wanted* Nevin to stay. "Take your time. I'm feeling kind of rank, so I'm going to take a quick shower, okay?"

Nevin looked down at himself. "Me too." He rolled his eyes. "After you're *done*, Bow Tie. Just 'cause I play for your team doesn't mean I think you're irresistible." He smirked a little, no doubt pleased with himself for throwing Colin's earlier accusations back at him.

Deciding to be a gentleman over the whole thing, Colin waved a hand toward the bathroom. "You first."

The loft's bed-and-bath area was separated from the main space by a partial wall that came nowhere close to the high ceiling. A small water closet offered the toilet complete privacy, but the sink and oversized shower were open to the bedroom. It was an arrangement that worked perfectly for Colin because he lived alone. It had never been a big deal when Trent came over either. But it felt a bit awkward with Nevin.

Colin grabbed a towel and washcloth from the closet and handed them over. "Um, everything else is in there." He waved at the shower.

"I bet you have bodywash instead of soap. And a half-dozen kinds of hair product."

Okay, so Nevin wasn't mocking him because Colin was gay—he was mocking him because Nevin was kind of a jerk. No. Not a jerk. Just... prickly? Maybe he treated even close friends that way. Colin smiled sweetly. "Only three, but you're welcome to try them all." Then he walked away.

Thanks to the loft's acoustics and lack of interior walls, he heard the shower running even when he was in the kitchen feeding Leg. The sound led to thoughts of Nevin *in* the shower. Naked, running soapy hands over his slick body. Knowing Nevin was into guys somehow made Colin feel less guilty about such thoughts. But the naughtiness would need to stay in his imagination. Sure, Nevin liked him enough to want to spend a couple of hours with him. And by Nevin's own description, that meant he'd likely be willing to sleep with Colin. But it would be nothing but a one-night stand, and Colin didn't do those.

Right?

"Hey! Collie!" Nevin's shout carried well, especially now that the water had stopped. But... *Collie*?

"What?"

"Come here!"

Nevin sounded so urgent that Colin almost ran—only to come to a screeching halt when he saw Nevin standing in the middle of the bedroom without a stitch of clothing on.

"Uh," said Colin.

Ignoring him, Nevin toweled his hair dry, walked back near the shower, and hung the towel on a hook. Then he toed at his clothes, which lay in a little pile on the floor. "These fucking reek. Can I borrow something?"

Since Colin's tongue didn't seem to be working, he just nodded. It was a relief to turn away and paw through his dresser. He pulled out some things nearly at random—a Han Solo T-shirt, a pair of boxer briefs, and thin gray sweatpants. But when he spun back around, Nevin was still naked, still right *there*, a few droplets of water shining on his warm brown skin. His body was sleek and nearly hairless, every inch of him so perfect that Colin's mouth went dry.

"Here," Colin said, pushing the clothing at him. "Um, they should fit."

Clearly amused, Nevin took them. But instead of putting them on, he held them to his chest and sauntered toward the bedroom exit. He paused at the opening. "I'm gonna grab another iced tea, okay?"

"Uh, help yourself."

Nevin walked away. Colin's hands shook slightly as he stripped off his own clothes and turned on the spray. But by the time he stood under the downpour, he'd made a decision.

CHAPTER SEVEN

WHEN NEVIN reached for the refrigerator door, he caught the cat watching him. It was a handsome animal, with a triangular face like a Siamese, blue eyes verging on violet, and pale orange coloring on the tips of its fur. "Hello, Legolas," Nevin said. The cat looked as scandalized by Nevin's nudity as Colin had.

Nevin hadn't actually intended to shock or provoke Colin. After all, he was used to wearing his birthday suit around men he had no intention of fucking. Gay, straight, or otherwise, none of the guys at the gym gave nudity much thought. Okay, that wasn't quite true. Sometimes some of them checked each other out. But none of them ever looked as stunned as Colin just had.

"Your boy doesn't get much action, does he?" Nevin said to the cat. And since the cat still looked disapproving, Nevin set the bottle of iced tea on the counter and pulled on the borrowed underwear and tee. He didn't bother with the sweats because it was too hot, and anyway, the boxer briefs offered just as much coverage as the shorts he'd been wearing all day. That should be enough to calm Colin.

As he wandered toward the bookshelves, he asked himself what in high holy hell he was doing. Sure, Colin was cute and, it turned out, a little more multifaceted than Nevin had thought. While Nevin had expected a spoiled rich kid, Colin had worked as hard as anyone else that day, never once bitching about the heat or heavy labor. He hadn't seemed to be craving attention or appreciation—hell, he hadn't even asked Manuel for a tax receipt for the AC donation. He'd been unexpectedly fun to work with. And he was sweet, which was all the more reason for Nevin to get his ass out of here. Colin didn't want what Nevin had to offer, and he likely deserved a hell of a lot more.

And yet. Here Nevin was, wearing Colin's goddamn underwear and trying to choose between *Up* and *The Lion King*.

Fuck.

"Hakuna matata."

Nevin startled so violently he nearly dropped the DVD. "What the fuck?"

Colin smiled at him. He'd put on a clean T-shirt—it had a drawing of a superhero Nevin didn't recognize—and a clean pair of running shorts, and although it looked as if he'd tried to tame his hair with a comb, the damp locks were escaping into waves. He smelled good, like exotic spices. "It means no worries," Colin said.

"Huh?"

Colin reached over and tapped the DVD case. "It's from the movie."

"What are you, part cat? You fucking snuck up on me. You're lucky I wasn't carrying."

"You don't really have anyplace *to* carry at the moment." Colin looked him up and down. "Um, am I overdressed?"

"Too hot for sweats."

Seemingly satisfied with that explanation, Colin snatched *The Lion King*, pranced across the room, and stuck the disc into the player. Then he waved at the couch. "Have a seat. I'll join you in a sec."

Bemused, Nevin obeyed. It was a comfortable couch, and Colin had angled the AC to blow air that way. While Nevin settled in, Colin rustled in cupboards, then stuck a bag of popcorn in the microwave. It was funny—earlier in the day, Nevin had accused Colin of ogling his ass, but now Nevin was doing the ogling. For good reason, because Colin had a really nice one, round and meaty. The type a guy could really hang on to.

Except Nevin wasn't going to hang on to anything, remember?

Colin bounced over, settled a bowl of popcorn in Nevin's lap, and plopped down on the couch beside him. Closer than Nevin had expected, actually.

"Now," Colin said, picking up the remote, "you are welcome to sing along."

"I don't know the words."

"Not to any of the songs?"

"I've never seen this movie," Nevin admitted.

"Never?" Colin looked as if Nevin had just told him he'd never used indoor plumbing. "I mean, I get it. Nowadays you're the big bad cop. But what about when you were a kid?"

Nevin managed not to flinch. "I didn't watch movies then."

Colin gave him an odd look, then shrugged and grabbed some popcorn. "Fine. I will sing along all by myself. Maybe you can pick up the chorus." He pressed Play.

He did sing, and well. And of course it was just a dopy kids' cartoon, but Colin obviously enjoyed it, and Nevin found he enjoyed sitting next to him, hearing him laugh. Somehow the space between them gradually vanished, so eventually they sat hip-to-hip, the fine hairs on Colin's thighs faintly tickling Nevin. Nevin wasn't usually the touchy-feely type, but he didn't mind the contact.

Then, just when Simba was chatting with his father's ghost, Colin's phone rang on the end table beside him. He glanced at it and frowned. "Crap. Sorry, gotta take this." He picked up the phone in one hand and paused the movie with his other. "Hi, Mom," he said into the phone. Giving Nevin an apologetic smile, he stood and walked into the kitchen.

"Yeah, I'm sorry. I was busy all day. It was a lot of work. ... But I *didn't* drop dead. ... Mom, I'm not going to check in with you every time you worry. That would be, like, all the time. You're listed as my next of kin. If I keel over, you'll be the first to know. ... Yeah, yeah, I'm sorry. ... I'm busy right now. I have a friend over and we're watching a movie. I'll call you tomorrow, when I'm still not dead. Okay? ... Love you too. Good night."

While Colin was in the kitchen, the cat appeared out of nowhere and stood at Nevin's feet, looking up at him expectantly. As soon as Nevin set aside the popcorn bowl, Legolas hopped up, landing lightly in his lap, and settled into a purring little lump. The fur behind his ears was incredibly soft.

"Want anything?" Colin called.

"I'm good."

Colin was sipping from a bottle of beer when he returned to the couch. "Sorry about the interruption."

"You're kinda old to be checking in with the parents, aren't you?"

With a frustrated sound, Colin sat and tipped his head onto the back of the couch. "Way too old. Mom's just... overprotective, you know? And mostly it's easier to humor her than make a fuss."

"Just tell her you're a big boy and she needs to take a fucking hike."

Colin laughed. "Can't really picture using those words with her." He turned his head to look at Nevin. "Would you tell your mom that?"

"Yes," Nevin answered tightly. In the unlikely event the bitch was still alive and he ever saw her again, he'd have a hell of a lot to say.

"Hmm." Colin picked up the remote but didn't turn the movie back on. Instead he jerked his chin toward Nevin's lap. "You should consider yourself honored. Leg doesn't like too many people other than me."

As if in agreement, the cat made a quiet chirrup and rolled over, exposing his soft belly for rubs. Nevin had never had a pet and rarely gave animals much thought, although he had seen what a positive effect they could have on people. He'd witnessed more than one distressed victim calmed by the presence of a dog or cat.

Hell, he felt pretty peaceful himself at the moment, as if he could finally relax just a bit. Maybe Legolas was the cause. Or maybe it was Colin's loft, with its exposed brick and warm woods. It was a big improvement over the series of generic apartments Nevin had called home. Undoubtedly well out of his price range too, even though it wasn't as huge or high-end as he'd expected. The furniture, while obviously good quality, was comfortable and well-used. Colin hadn't cluttered the place with froufrou knickknacks either. A few framed old-movie posters hung on the wall.

So for now he'd enjoy the pleasant surroundings and the pettable cat. And the company of a nice and handsome man.

Colin reached over and stroked under Legolas's chin. "That was nice of you to help out today," he said.

"Manny and I go back a few years. I've referred some victims to him. Sometimes when I'm worried about someone—someone like Roger Grey—Manny will come out and talk to them, let them know about Bright Hope."

"That makes sense." Both men continued to stroke the cat, and Legolas purred vigorously enough for Nevin to feel the vibration. "What made you decide to be a cop?"

Sometimes Nevin gave simple answers to that question. It paid fairly well. It was interesting. He wasn't stuck behind a desk all day. It could be exciting. He didn't have a supervisor breathing down his neck very often. He got to boss people around. All of those things were accurate. But somehow he found himself telling Colin the real truth. "I wanted to rise above the shit."

Colin didn't laugh at him or tell him his answer was stupid. He didn't even ask for an explanation. He gave Nevin a long look, something raw in his expression, and finally nodded. "Good for you, Detective Ng."

A tight muscle in Nevin's back loosened, just a little. He sighed. "There are a lot of people out there who have nobody to look out for them. Nobody's got their backs. You… you have a mother who tracks your every move, which kind of sucks, but I bet if you needed help, she'd be there in a split second."

"She was," Colin agreed but didn't seem eager to explain what he meant.

"She doesn't care that you're queer?"

"None of my family does. It's always been a nonissue for us. Not like Roger, huh?"

"There are a lot of Rogers. And Mrs. Ruskins too. Family dies off or turns their back for lame-ass reasons. Or maybe the people who are supposed to take care of them have their heads so far up their own rectums that they can't even take care of themselves." He paused, marveling at how much easier it was to share confidences when you were both petting the same cat. "I can't help all of them. Not even most of them. But I can help *some*. So I do."

Colin's smile was so warm and beautiful, Nevin had to look away.

"Why'd you end up helping today?" Nevin asked roughly. "Aren't you supposed to play golf or some kind of shit like that on your days off?"

"I don't golf," Colin replied with a chuckle. "Dad does, though. A lot. He's talked me into going with him a few times, but it bores the heck out of me, and the clothes make my eyes bleed. Anyway, Crystal called the other day and asked if I could help out."

"*Crystal* called you?"

"Sure. Why the surprise?"

Nevin shook his head. "I don't think she's ever said more than three words to me. She hates my fucking guts."

Colin stilled his hand and drew back a little. "Really? Why?"

"No idea. And no, I haven't sworn at her, hit on her, or insulted her."

"I believe you use your weapons with care. But that's weird. She's really nice to me." He scrunched up his face thoughtfully. "Maybe she doesn't like the police."

Nevin considered that for a moment. Plenty of people had a grudge against the bureau, either from bad personal experiences or on general principle. Although many of his colleagues were great, Christ knew there were enough assholes to give them all a bad name. "Plausible," he concluded.

"Well, if so, it's too bad she can't see past the badge. You're kind of amazing."

And before Nevin could recover from his surprise at that announcement, Colin swooped in for a kiss.

A lot of things zoomed through Nevin's mind. *What the ever-living fuck?* was among them. So were *He tastes like popcorn and beer*, and *He has really soft lips*, and *He's gonna squish the goddamn cat*. Predominant, however, was *Oh God, yes!* because Colin was an excellent kisser, firm but not pushy, and some part of Nevin sang from Colin's touch.

Some part? His dick, obviously.

Nevin gently pushed Colin away.

"Oh no. God, I'm sorry." Colin started to retreat, but Nevin grabbed his arm to stop him.

"You do not need to apologize for that kiss," Nevin said. "Ten out of ten."

"I promised not to molest you."

"I've beat the shit out of guys twice your size and ten times as mean. If I hadn't wanted that, believe me, I'd have let you know."

Although Colin looked slightly relieved, he was far from happy. "But you stopped me."

"Confusion, Collie, not discontent. Why don't you tell me what the fuck's going through that pretty head of yours?"

"I…." Colin bit his lip. "You said you don't like flirting, and I'm not very good at, um, seduction. So I tried the direct route."

"Okay. That's the what but not the why. What made you decide sticking your tongue down my throat was a good idea?"

Colin tugged his arm out of Nevin's grip, stood, and walked to the edge of the room. He turned to face Nevin. "I wanted to have sex with you. I thought it was a good first step."

"Why did you want to have sex with me?"

In a preschool-teacher voice, Colin replied, "Well, when two men like each other in a very special way, the two of them get together and the blood flows—"

"Not what I mean." Nevin shooed Legolas off his lap and prowled across the floor. Colin backed up until he was against the wall, but Nevin kept going until they were almost touching. "What I *mean* is why do you want to fuck *me*?"

Although Colin's eyes were wide, he wasn't afraid. Nevin had seen fear plenty of times, and this wasn't it. That wasn't the emotion making his own heart pound either. "I like you," Colin said tightly. "You're funny and smart and… real. And God, Nevin, you look so—"

"If you say *exotic* I'm gonna fucking blow a gasket." That adjective had been flung at him far too many times, by men and women both.

But Colin shook his head and frowned. "I was going to say handsome. And… firm." He huffed at Nevin's raised eyebrows. "I'm not talking about your penis. I meant all of you. I can look at myself in a mirror and find a hundred little things I'd like to change. My stupid hair. My skin, which freckles and burns if I even think about sun. My arms look scrawny even if I work on them a lot. I have weird-shaped little toes. But you! Every inch of you is perfect."

"I'm not—"

"If I was an artist who drew me, I'd still be doing a lot of erasing. If I drew *you*, I'd be done." He held his arms wide.

A slight flush colored Colin's cheeks, and for a moment, Nevin forgot why the hell he was dragging his feet. This man was fucking delicious, he was right at hand, and he was practically begging Nevin to fall into bed with him. And shit, no complications, because Colin was single, and—

And there was the rub.

"We can't do this," Nevin said, falling back a step.

Colin's face fell. "Because I'm a suspect?"

"Jesus, no! If you were a suspect, would I have spent the last couple of hours sitting on your couch watching goddamn cartoons with you?"

"Maybe you're… investigating me."

"For fuck's sake! I'd name myself as the perp before I named you." And that was true. Nevin was usually careful not to screw up evidence, and getting personally involved with a potential witness was a little sloppy of him. But he doubted Colin had much to offer in either the Ruskin or the Grey case, and anyway, the Ruskin case wasn't even Nevin's anymore.

"If you're not going to arrest me, why won't you sleep with me?"

"You want to know why?" Nevin surged forward, and this time he initiated the kiss, deep and urgent, pouring all of his lust into it. He would have sworn he felt fucking sparks pass between their skin.

They broke apart after a moment, both of them panting. "That… doesn't really explain things," Colin said. He grasped Nevin's arms, and Nevin didn't resist when Colin turned them around and sandwiched him between Colin's body and the wall. "Succumb to my pelvic sorcery," Colin whispered into his ear.

"What?"

"Never mind." Colin sagged slightly against him. "I just don't understand you."

With Colin in contact with so much of his body, Nevin had trouble finding words. He marshalled his resources as best as he could. "You felt it when we kissed, right? Electricity."

"God, yes."

"If we fucked, we'd see goddamn fireworks."

"Still not—"

"And then I walk away. Because I'm not your Prince Charming."

Colin licked along his jawline, making Nevin shiver. "Good. Fine."

"I'm serious. I'm not going to be your boyfriend. I won't date you. I sure as hell won't make any commitments."

Another slow swipe of Colin's tongue, followed by a gentle nibble of Nevin's earlobe. Nevin felt his resistance draining away. He had to clench his hands into fists and grind them into the bricks behind him to stop from clutching the back of Colin's shirt.

"I don't want any of that," Colin purred. "I want to see you naked again, and this time I want to touch too. And taste." A third lick made Nevin's breath hitch.

Nevin didn't have a particularly active fantasy life—he was a practical guy—and he would never have imagined this scenario. Or predicted how much he'd like it when Colin went all assertive and butch. Jesus, he liked it a *lot*. But he'd have to live with himself in the morning, wouldn't he?

"You told me yourself, Bow Tie. You don't play around."

"*Didn't* play around." Colin tipped Nevin's chin up so their gazes locked. "You know what? My whole life people have been telling me who I am and what I need. I usually go with the flow. I'm usually careful. Not tonight, Nevin. Not if you want me too. I promise, this is just sex. No strings attached, no promises or expectations. Just this." He nuzzled Nevin's neck and pressed his groin to Nevin's, giving evidence of a hard and substantial bulge.

Nevin was only human. He grabbed handfuls of that tempting ass, making their contact even tighter, and tipped his head to give Colin better access. "Yes," Nevin breathed as Colin bit lightly at the cord of his neck. "Goddammit, yes."

Apparently Colin was dead serious about the nudity thing, because next he tore Nevin's T-shirt right down the middle. "You wrecked your shirt," Nevin said.

"Don't care. Always wanted to do that." Colin ran a hand down the center of Nevin's chest and belly, stopping just above the waistband of the boxer briefs. No calluses on his fingers, but his palm was scorching against Nevin's skin, a wide line of fire that made Nevin grunt and buck his hips. Perhaps taking that as encouragement—and rightfully so—Colin bent and began to suck on Nevin's nipple.

If Nevin had planned this scene ahead of time, he would not have pictured himself gasping and goddamn mewling helplessly while Colin Westwood—he of the natty bow ties and classic musicals—fucking ravished him. And that would have been a pity, because he couldn't remember an occasion when his libido had gone from zero to a hundred so quickly. His engine was running faster than Julie's, and if the bricks dug into his back after Colin tugged the ruined shirt away, Nevin didn't notice and he wouldn't have cared.

Colin didn't rip Nevin's borrowed underwear, but he did tug them to his ankles and then help Nevin balance while he removed them entirely. Since Colin was already on his knees, he took advantage of the position by tonguing the indentation of Nevin's navel and laying painless little bites along the edge of Nevin's hip bones. It was sexy as hell, Nevin naked as the day he was born and Colin still wearing clothes. Colin ignored Nevin's cock, which was both frustrating and a relief. Nevin was already locked and loaded—and he didn't want to shoot too soon.

In fact, that gave him a thought. "Lube?" he panted. "Rubbers?" He usually carried both, just in case, but hadn't come prepared today. He never was a Boy Scout.

"Bedroom," Colin replied, apparently also reduced to nothing but nouns.

They stumbled toward the bedroom, groping and kissing as they went, never quite separating. It was a small miracle they made it without injuring themselves, and when they arrived, Colin gently pushed Nevin onto the mattress and then fell on top of him, continuing his delicious torture with mouth and fingers.

Nevin worked his hands underneath Colin's shorts, discovered he was going commando, and squeezed his ass. Touching wasn't enough, though. Like Colin, he wanted to engage as many of his senses as possible. "Undress," he ordered.

After a moment's hesitation, Colin stood and pulled off his shirt. Nevin liked what he saw—not rock-hard abs but pale skin over nice muscles. Pink nipples stood at attention, surrounded by a sprinkling of russet hairs, and a long scar, faded but still slightly puckered, stretched down Colin's sternum. A narrow treasure trail ran down his belly, disappearing under the waistband of his shorts. Which, Nevin couldn't help but notice, were impressively tented.

"What exactly are you packing there, Col?"

"I should have known you'd make gun analogies." Colin played uncertainly with the elastic.

"I'll stow the analogies and I'll keep my big trap shut if you'll just strip and get back here."

Colin made a *here goes nothing* face and pulled the shorts down. He might have tossed them aside, but Nevin didn't notice.

"Sweet mother of God," Nevin breathed.

"It's just a dick."

"And Everest is just a pile of rocks."

"I thought you were going to shut your trap."

Nevin grinned and made a zipping motion over his mouth. Then he gestured, waving Colin forward. Now, in Nevin's experience, guys with cocks that big liked to use them. Instead Colin knelt on the mattress between Nevin's legs and began licking Nevin's smaller but still perfectly respectable cock.

Just when Nevin was about to tell him to stop, Colin dragged himself up Nevin's body and kissed him, now tasting more of salt than of beer. "What do you want?" Colin whispered when his mouth was free.

"You're doing just fine calling the shots. You choose." Nevin was as all-embracing about sexual positions and activities as he was about his partners. And honestly, he was convinced that anything with Colin was going to be good. Hell, he'd happily just make out some more while they frotted—that would get him off pretty quickly all by itself.

Apparently Colin had other ideas, however. He reached for the bedside table, opened a drawer, and rummaged blindly inside, all while licking Nevin's neck. Then he made a small celebratory noise and tossed something onto Nevin's chest. "Open it."

One-handed, Nevin popped the cap on the bottle of lube. He was trying to decide what to do next when Colin took it from him and squeezed a healthy amount onto Nevin's fingers. The liquid dripped down Nevin's skin, cool against his own heat. Colin took Nevin's wrist and guided it to his ass. "It's been a while. Go slow."

"I'll do my best." But that wasn't easy, because Colin's body opened up to his slick fingers, drawing him into silky tightness, making Nevin want more. Colin undulated on top of him, inhaling raggedly with every digital thrust but lifting his hips to urge Nevin's fingers more deeply inside. His tiny moans were a symphony to Nevin's ears, and his hair tickled Nevin's shoulder and cheek.

"It's been a *while*," Colin repeated, only this time Nevin thought it was an explanation for a short fuse rather than a reason to be gentle. Colin gave Nevin's lips a quick brush with his own before grabbing his arms and rolling them both over so Nevin landed on top. Nevin didn't mind. As much as he admired Colin's ass, it was even better to look at his flushed face with the wild hair and dilated pupils.

Colin reached between them and began to stroke Nevin's aching cock. He played his other hand down Nevin's spine, over the curve of his butt, then back up again before settling on the lower back. It had *not* been a while for Nevin—he'd had sex just a couple of days earlier. But that didn't seem to matter, as Colin's touch made him burn, made his body tighten with need. When he reached his lubed fingers down behind Colin's balls, Colin spread his legs wider and lifted his hips.

"Yes," Colin said. "Please."

It was good—Nevin thrusting into Colin's fist while Colin writhed against the penetrating fingers. Good but could be better. Nevin stilled, found the wrapped condom on the nightstand, and opened it with slippery fingers that shook with urgency. As he rolled it on, he realized that it must have originally been intended for someone else, because although it fit him well, it wouldn't have worked on Colin. That ex-boyfriend, probably. At the thought, Nevin pushed away a twinge of jealousy. He didn't *do* jealousy. Wasn't in his repertoire.

Colin shuddered and guided Nevin's cock closer to his ass. "Get in," Colin said, and Nevin grinned. Nothing he liked better than a pushy bottom. He might have teased awhile longer, but he was as eager as

Colin. They rearranged themselves somewhat, Nevin sticking a pillow under Colin's ass and Colin bending his knees and resting his calves on Nevin's shoulders. Then, with more care than he thought himself capable of, Nevin slid inside.

Colin was ready for him. His face registered no discomfort at the intrusion, and in fact, he wiggled a bit, urging Nevin deeper. And shit, the feeling of Colin's body welcoming him, clenching him tight, was almost enough to end him right there.

"Are you going to move?" Colin asked, voice tight but lips quirked into a grin.

"Jack yourself. I want to see you work that meat."

Colin's eyes widened slightly, but he didn't hesitate to grab his thick shaft and start wanking. Nevin remained still for several moments, watching with fascination as Colin's foreskin covered and then revealed the shiny red glans. God, what would it feel like to have that monster inside of him, stretching him wide and probably rearranging his internal organs to boot? Just thinking about it made his balls tingle.

Time to move.

He thrust deep and hard, grunting with effort. He and Colin were noisy together—groans and huffs of air, skin slapping against skin, bedsprings creaking, and the headboard banging against the brick wall. Colin's fist flew up and down while his other hand clutched the bedding and his pink-tinged skin beaded with sweat. But his gaze stayed focused on Nevin, sharp and bright as a knife-edge.

Heat gathered in Nevin's core and his body felt full and heavy, his skin too tight, his lungs overworked, his head not too solidly connected to the rest of him. Colin emitted a long, low cry and tightened around him. Pearly ropes of come shot onto Colin's chest. Nevin let go, and for one sublime moment, he was lost.

CHAPTER EIGHT

NOT EVEN Nevin had the courage to do the walk of shame naked. His fumbling around in the predawn darkness, looking for his clothes, woke Colin. "They're in the dryer," Colin said through a yawn.

Nevin turned to look at him. "What?"

"Your clothes. I washed them last night, and now they're in the dryer. Which is hidden in that closet near the fridge."

"Oh." Nevin ran a hand through his hair. "I was going to sneak out."

"Yeah, I got that."

"You're not pissed off?"

Sighing, Colin sat up and rubbed his face. "I promised you no strings and I meant it. Heck, I was pleasantly surprised when you fell asleep with me." He'd expected Nevin to clean up, maybe thank him for a nice fuck, and roar off into the night. When he'd collapsed next to Colin instead, his breathing soon turning deep and even, Colin had remained awake for some time, treasuring the unforeseen gift.

Nevin was silent for a few seconds. "It's kind of a douchey thing to do—sneaking out at oh-fuck-hundred in the morning, I mean."

"Then come back to bed for a couple of hours. Wait until it's a more human hour and I'll even make you breakfast before you take off. I have an espresso machine."

"Of course you do," Nevin grumbled, but he climbed back into bed and pulled the covers over them both.

Neither of them went back to sleep. They breathed in tandem for a while; then Legolas appeared from one of his many napping spots and hopped onto the bed to curl up beside Nevin, which made Colin smile. Nevin stroked the cat for a time—Colin heard the purring—then rolled onto his side to face Colin. A streetlight shone just enough brightness through the window for Colin to see his thoughtful expression.

"What's this from?" Nevin asked, running a finger the length of the scar on Colin's chest.

Colin turned his head away. "It's old."

After a pause Nevin moved his fingertip lower, dipping it briefly into Colin's belly button and down his abdomen—still crusty from last night's activities—pushing the blanket out of the way as he went. Nevin's touch made him shiver.

"Cold?" Nevin asked.

"No." The loft was still warm.

When Nevin got to Colin's soft dick, his finger continued its journey, tracing lightly down the length of the shaft. Then Nevin cradled the entire organ in his hand, hefting it as if assessing its weight. Like the rest of Colin, his cock grew more awake.

"You could be a porn star with this thing," said Nevin.

"It's nice to know that property developer isn't my only career option."

"I thought you were a real estate tycoon."

Colin chuckled. "Nope, that's my dad. He buys 'em. Nowadays he's spending a lot of time playing golf, so I do most of the day-to-day operations."

"Hmm," Nevin said and gave Colin's cock a little squeeze. "Well, even if you're not going to make a fortune off your schlong, you should post a couple dick pics on your hookup app of choice. The boys will be pounding on your door."

"Great." Colin had no intention of signing up for any hookup apps. He was glad he'd gone to bed with Nevin—the sex had been amazing— but now he found a new little shard in his heart. Another jagged piece of frustrated longing. The night had been worth it, but he didn't think he could survive any more sharp bits inside him.

They stopped talking as Nevin's stroking became more serious. Annoyed with the thrashing and moans, Legolas meowed, hopped off the mattress, and stalked away. Colin wasn't sure what to do with his hands at first, but then he buried his fingers in Nevin's hair, which was straight and thick and very soft. There wasn't enough light for him to discern the mink-brown color of it, so he closed his eyes and let his other senses rule.

The previous night, Colin had explored much of Nevin's body. This morning Nevin had apparently concluded that turnabout was fair play. He tickled, fondled, and tweaked, and sometimes he nibbled with sharp teeth. Eventually, though, he focused all his attention on Colin's cock and balls. When he slid his mouth over the glans, Colin gasped. "I can—"

Nevin freed his mouth to interrupt. "You just lie back and take it like a man, baby." Then he went back to work.

Colin hadn't had many sex partners, and none of them had been able to take all of him in their mouths. Nevin couldn't either, although he gave it his best effort and wrapped his fist around the base. He used his other hand to play with Colin's balls and rub the tender skin behind them, and then he inserted one finger into the passage still slightly slick from last night's lube.

That stuff Nevin said about fireworks? Absolutely true, because colored sparks exploded inside Colin's eyelids. For the first time in ages, he worried about his heart. But then Nevin did something clever with his tongue and Colin decided that if he had to kick the bucket, there was no better way than this.

"G-gonna come," he warned.

Nevin redoubled his efforts and slid a second finger inside, and that was enough. Colin roared.

And when his skin had become too sensitive for further touching, Colin watched as Nevin knelt upright, gave his own hard cock a few brutal tugs, and spurted all over Colin's groin and abdomen. It was a little kinky, a little dirty, and it was the sexiest thing Colin had ever seen.

Nevin collapsed beside him with a noisy *oomph*. "*That* was a challenge, Collie."

"You seemed up for it."

"Maybe with practice I—" Nevin cut himself off abruptly.

Daylight had begun to seep through the windows, allowing Colin to see Nevin's thick eyelashes dark against his skin and a tiny divot of a scar above an eyebrow. Stubble dusted his chin and upper lip, and when Colin reached over to stroke the sandpaper and silk of his face, Nevin drew Colin's thumb into his mouth and lightly sucked.

"Your mouth should be a registered weapon," said Colin.

"I've been told that before."

Colin believed it. Those lips. That wicked tongue. Those white teeth.

Heaving a sigh, Colin patted Nevin's cheek. "Omelet?"

"Yeah, sure. Can I shower first?"

"Of course."

Colin was the first one out of bed. He peed and washed up, then laughed as Nevin ogled him pulling on clean underwear and a plain blue

T-shirt. He put an extra swish in his hips when he left the bedroom to fetch Nevin's clothes.

While Nevin was in the shower, Colin fed Legolas, stuck some refrigerated biscuits in the oven, and snipped some herbs from the planter box in one of his windows. He stirred the herbs into the egg mixture, then chopped some mushrooms and grated a bit of cheese.

"Christ on toast, that smells good," Nevin announced as he sat on one of the breakfast stools.

"No Christ, no toast. Eggs and biscuits." Colin grinned and set a plate in front of Nevin. After walking to the espresso machine, he turned back. "What's your poison?"

Nevin eyed the machine, large and sleek and able to produce almost anything with the touch of a few buttons. "Double espresso, straight up."

"Done."

Nevin downed his coffee in two swallows, not waiting for it to cool. Colin winced a little as he watched, sipping his own decaf cappuccino. He was afraid to make conversation because every topic he could think of was inane—or hinted at a future he and Nevin didn't share. It was odd to have sex with someone, to sleep with him, to have sex with him again, and then eat eggs together, knowing you'd probably never see each other again.

"I bet you didn't want to be a property developer when you were growing up," Nevin said. He stuck out the tip of his tongue and licked a bit of jam from the corner of his mouth.

"I didn't really think about it that much."

"Bullshit. You had a dream tucked away somewhere."

Colin looked outside. It was going to be another scorcher, and already joggers and dog-walkers hurried down the sidewalks, trying to get their exercise in before the heat became unbearable. The street was Sunday-morning quiet, though. "I kind of wanted to act," he admitted quietly.

Nevin laughed but not meanly. "I should have guessed that. School plays?"

"Sometimes." When he was well enough to attend.

"You sing well. Even if it's just shit from a cartoon about lions."

"Thanks."

"So did you ever do anything about this dream?"

"No."

"Why not?" Nevin persisted as if he were interrogating a suspect.

"It's stupid. Unrealistic." That's what his parents had said the one time he'd mentioned it. And they were right. Plus, his mother pointed out, the stress and unreliability of an actor's life would be bad for his health.

Nevin pointed a fork at him. "That's why they're called dreams. So, what? You went to school and majored in boring instead?"

"Political science." That was his mother's suggestion. He winced. "And then I got an MBA." His father's idea.

"Can't picture you sitting there getting hard over spreadsheets or whatever the fuck it is they talk about in business school." Nevin slid off the stool, grabbed his plate and Colin's, and carried them to the sink. He seemed to consider for a moment whether to wash them or put them in the dishwasher, but in the end he just left them on the counter. He bent to pat Leg, who'd found a patch of sunlight on the floor, then sauntered back to Colin.

"You're a good guy," Nevin said, his head slightly cocked and gaze bright. "And I know the good guys from the bad. This thing we did, that was terrific, right?"

"Yeah."

"And it happened because you grew a set and decided to tell the *ought-to*s to fuck off. You should try that more often, Bow Tie."

Colin smiled thinly. "You think I should quit my job and run off to Hollywood?"

"I think Los Angeles would eat you alive." He stood for a few seconds before returning to Leg for more scritches behind the ear. "I like cats. They do whatever the fuck they want to."

"I like cats too. But I think I'm more of a dog. You know, the faithful hound?"

Nevin snorted and shook his head. His shoes were by the door, where he'd left them the night before, the unwashed socks still stuffed into them. Nevin put the shoes on his bare feet and balled the socks into one hand. Then he just stood there. Colin didn't budge from his stool, as if doing so would break some spell. The refrigerator hummed and somewhere a car horn honked once.

"We had sex twice," Nevin finally said, not meeting Colin's eyes. "That's my limit."

"So you told me."

Nevin glanced at him and nodded. "Stay out of trouble, Bow Tie." And then he left.

CHAPTER NINE

September 2015

THE BITCH was lying through her teeth, but Nevin nodded like he bought every word.

"She wasn't supposed to go anywhere *near* the stove," said Molly Gillett. "She knew that. Told her a thousand times." She took a long drag from her cigarette before stubbing it out in a glass ashtray somebody had stolen from an Embassy Suites. The house smelled like smoke, and Nevin wondered if he'd be able to get the reek out of his clothes.

"But she went anyway?" he prompted her.

"I guess so. I went to use the restroom—wasn't in there more than a minute before I heard her screaming. I rushed right back out to find her there on the floor, holding her face. But I've *said* this already, Officer. Said the whole thing to those other officers."

"Detective. And please tell me again. Sometimes they don't get the details right."

She huffed impatiently and fumbled another cigarette out of the pack. Most mothers under these circumstances would be clamoring to get to the hospital, to the bedside of the daughter with the third-degree burns. But not Molly Gillett, who looked impatient to get back to the talk show blaring on the TV in the next room. Well, just because a woman gave birth didn't mean she qualified as a mother; Nevin certainly knew that.

"What were you cooking?" he asked.

"I was gonna make her macaroni and cheese. That's just about the only thing she'll eat. That and SpaghettiOs and bananas. Give her anything else for lunch and she just throws a huge fit, kicking and screaming and carrying on. So I was making her mac and cheese."

That was interesting, because there were no boxes waiting on the kitchen counter. It was possible Mrs. Gillett was waiting for the water to boil before taking the box out of the cupboard, but nothing else seemed ready either. Nothing to drain the noodles with after they were cooked, no spoon, no bowl to put the food in. Just a pot on the floor in a puddle of water.

"So what do you think happened while you were in the bathroom, Mrs. Gillett?"

"I think Jeanie grabbed the pot handle and splashed hot water all over herself. Even though she wasn't supposed to be near the stove."

The ambulance was long gone, as were most of the gorillas in blue. Nevin had no idea how Jeanie was faring, although one of the responding officers told him she was burned pretty bad. Even if she recovered, she wouldn't be able to tell them much about what had happened in the kitchen. She was in her twenties but had a severe intellectual disability that made her nearly nonverbal.

He decided to change his tactics slightly. "Does she do that a lot—disobey the rules?"

"All the time. She pretends like she's too dumb to know what I'm talking about, but when she likes what I'm saying, that girl hears me just fine."

"It must be exhausting to care for her."

She blew out a cloud of smoke. "It is. Like having a baby that won't never grow up. Except this baby's as big as I am, so when she's being naughty I can't just give her a swat on the behind and carry her up to her room."

Maybe Jeanie Gillett never had much hope for a good life. But maybe if she'd been born into a different family, she'd have been mentally fine. Or even if she wasn't, maybe she'd have been loved and cared for, given every opportunity to do the best she could, and when her caregivers felt overwhelmed, they'd have found somewhere to turn for backup. But she lived here, where the walls and curtains were stained yellow, where he saw no sign of suitable toys or books, where her mother—with badly dyed hair and dead eyes—sat in the kitchen and smoked. Fate was a goddamn cunt.

"Was Jeanie especially difficult today?" he asked, feigning empathy.

Mrs. Gillett shook her head. "You don't know the half of it."

By the time Nevin left the Gillett home, he had several pages of incriminating statements from Molly Gillett, whom he'd placed under arrest. He drafted one of the officers to haul her to jail in a squad car, while another stayed behind to oversee the evidence techs and wait for Mr. Gillett to make an appearance. But Nevin didn't feel especially satisfied. Even if the DA threw something heavy at her, this perp would plead it out. And Jeanie would be left with the agony of facial burns, assuming she survived at all.

A hint of crispness colored the air as he walked down the cracked pavement to Julie. She was a little dusty. He'd get her washed over the weekend. For now, though, he wanted caffeine and a break from the evils of the world. But he couldn't have either, because hours' more work awaited him.

The smell of cigarettes on his clothing overwhelmed him after he got into the car. So before heading to the hospital, he stopped at home to change. As happened every time he'd stepped into his apartment over the past several weeks, he mentally compared it to Colin's loft. There was nothing wrong with his place, but aside from his stupid drawings, it lacked character and warmth. Maybe he should get a cat.

He stopped at the hospital, but the nurse told him Jeanie was in surgery. It would be at least a day or two before he could even try to get information from her. "Probably longer," said the nurse solemnly. "The burns are extensive."

"Fuck."

She nodded in agreement.

He was in a foul mood when he arrived at the jail, and his temper worsened when he learned that Mrs. Gillett had already lawyered up. It was probably just as well he wasn't going to be in a room with her right now, but he would have liked to find more ways for her to put her foot in her mouth.

A call came in as he was leaving the jail, informing him Mr. Gillett had been contacted and was on his way to the hospital. So Nevin returned there and spent nearly two hours trying to get coherent statements out of a man in the midst of falling apart. Deciding that he could wait until the next day to talk to the EMTs and the hospital staff, Nevin grabbed a drive-through burger, which he took back to his office.

He was in the middle of a mound of paperwork when Frankl knocked on his open door. Frankl looked tired and old, his hound-dog eyes sagging more than usual. "Rough one?"

Nevin squinted at him. "Mom poured boiling water over her mentally disabled daughter."

It took a lot to shake a homicide cop, but Frankl flinched. "Kid gonna be okay?"

"She'll probably live. But she might lose an eye, and she's looking at months of skin grafts and that kind of shit." Not to mention a fuckload of pain and no real ability to understand why. And who was going to comfort her? The bitch who hurt her and was now locked up tight? Or the father who looked three seconds from a nervous breakdown?

"I have news for you, but maybe tonight's not—"

"Spill, dickwad."

"We found Roger Grey's body."

Nevin had been certain the corpse would turn up eventually, but still, Frankl's words made his heart sink. His chair squeaked when he leaned back. "Where?"

"Out near Sandy. Hunters found him near the edge of a field." Frankl shook his head wryly. It was well-known that a homicide detective's biggest friends were hunters and dogs, who managed to find bodies ditched in the most remote places.

"Sure it's him?"

"Body's in bad shape, parts kinda scattered, but his wallet was there. We're checking dental records now, just to make sure. Mandible's missing, but we have the rest of the skull."

"Cause of death?"

"Dunno."

Nevin sighed. After two months of hot weather, there might not be much left but bones. "Roger sure as fuck didn't walk to Sandy."

"He's not that far from a road, but he didn't have a car, right?"

"Didn't drive."

"Okay. I'll keep you in the loop."

Nevin waved his thanks and turned his attention back to the Gillett case.

At a little after nine o'clock, his phone buzzed. He rolled his shoulders to unkink the muscles and glanced at the screen.

Drinks. Now.

He sent a quick reply to Ford: *Working.*

Bad guys will still be there in the morning.

Ford did have a point. Besides, Nevin's vision was beginning to swim and he was probably typing mostly nonsense at this point. As he considered an answer, another text came through. *You downtown? I'll pick you up.*

Sure. Why not. *Gimme 30.*

He finished the paragraph he was writing, hit Save, and powered down his computer. Then he thought about his clothing options—either the suit he was wearing or the spare set of exercise clothes he kept at the office.

Neither was ideal, but he chose the suit, leaving his tie over the back of the chair. He would have left the suit jacket too, but he needed something to cover his holster. Portland wasn't enough Wild West anymore to welcome a guy open carrying in a bar, even if he was a cop.

Ford grinned as Nevin climbed into the truck. "Don't we look snazzy tonight."

"Just be happy I don't smell like a fucking ashtray. No punk tonight, okay?" An incipient headache throbbed at his temple.

"Nah, bro. We'll do classy and refined."

One of the nice things about Ford was that he didn't interrogate Nevin about his work. He listened when Nevin felt like talking, but otherwise he chose different topics. Tonight he complained about a client. "The moron wants a cactus garden. I been trying to tell him this is Portland, not Phoenix, but he won't listen."

"What are you going to do?"

"Dunno, man."

"Dump him. If you're short on cash, I can—"

Ford gave Nevin's shoulder a gentle push. "I'm paying the bills on time."

Money was a bit of a touchy subject between them. Nevin's pay was fairly generous, and aside from rent, he had nothing much to spend it on besides clothes and Julie. Ford, on the other hand, had an unpredictable income, with more work than he could handle in the spring and summer and almost nothing during the winter months. But he was also really proud of his business, and he wasn't the type to put in plantings he knew would fail.

Just a couple of blocks later, Ford pulled into a hotel parking garage. Then he and Nevin headed to the bar, which turned out to be busy for a Thursday night. Most of the men wore clothes like Nevin's, but Ford wasn't out of place in nice jeans and a plain white tee that showed off his sleeve tats. They sat side by side at the bar and ordered—beer for Nevin, Coke for Ford.

When he went out with Ford, Nevin usually cruised women instead of men. Ford didn't care—he'd experimented with men a few times himself before deciding women were more fun—but the crowds at the places they went to were primarily straight. Besides, even when there were some potentially interested men present, Nevin apparently didn't trip their gaydar. Maybe his indeterminate ethnicity jarred the gaydar settings, or maybe it was his cop face. Whatever the reason, he almost always ended up with women, which was fine.

Tonight, though, the bartender held Nevin's gaze a beat or two longer than a straight guy would, and he seemed awfully eager to offer Nevin a refill. By the time Nevin was on his third beer, Ford was deep in conversation with the woman sitting next to him and the bartender had parked himself in front of Nevin, pretending to wipe the counter.

"Are you staying at the hotel?" the guy asked. His name tag said Troy. He wasn't especially handsome, although his green eyes were striking with his light brown skin and dark hair. His smile was nice too. Nevin guessed he was in his midtwenties.

Nevin thought about telling Troy that yes, he was a nuclear scientist visiting from Bismarck, but he didn't have the energy to lie. "No, I'm a local. Name's Nevin."

"Hi, Nevin. Just out with a friend tonight?" Troy's gaze shifted briefly toward Ford.

"Yeah. Decompressing after a rough day at work."

"What do you do?"

"I'm a cop."

Troy's eyes widened and he leaned forward. "Really? Cool! Horse patrol? When I was a kid, I loved seeing those guys."

"No," Nevin said with a chuckle. He'd never ridden a horse and had no desire to try. "Family Services."

Troy clearly didn't know what that meant—few people did—but he nodded. "It's probably real stressful. I mean, working here, that can be hectic too. Weekends get hopping, and sometimes everyone wants stuff all at once. Or somebody gets drunk and acts like an asshole. But it's not dangerous."

"I'm not generally ducking bullets either."

"Sure." Troy gave the clean counter a few more swipes. "So, uh, my place is just a couple blocks from here." He licked his lips slowly.

"Don't you have to work?"

"We're overstaffed. I can leave early." He must have known how cute his smile was, because he turned it on full force. "I have beer at my apartment, too, and you can drink that for free."

"Yeah, okay." Nevin slapped down enough cash to cover his tab and the tip. If he stayed late at Troy's place, he could always just head straight to the office from there. No real reason to stop back at home—

nobody was waiting for him—and he could shower in the locker room at work. He even had clean underwear at the office, although he'd be stuck in today's shirt. Unless he wore his workout tee with the suit. Yeah, that might work. He could pretend he was doing a *Miami Vice* retrospective, minus the pastel colors.

Grabbing the money, Troy beamed at him, tossed the towel off to the side, and had a hurried conversation with a coworker. Meanwhile, Nevin slid off his stool and thumped Ford's back.

Ford looked away from the pretty girl he'd been chatting up. "The bartender?"

"Yeah. You okay?"

"I think I'll splurge and stay here tonight. Always wondered what the rooms look like." He leaned in close to Nevin and whispered, "Or maybe I'll get to share someone else's room." He didn't ask about Nevin's plans, but they both knew that if Nevin wanted to go home, he could take the light-rail or a taxi.

A few minutes later, Troy joined Nevin near the door. After Troy waved a good-bye to another coworker, they walked outside. A definite hint of chill had settled into the night. Nevin would have been cold if not for his jacket. Few other pedestrians walked the sidewalks, and traffic was light, but the streetlights and signs kept the streets brightly lit.

Troy wrapped his arm around Nevin's. He was short—although taller than Nevin—and slightly built, with a bounce to his steps that reminded Nevin of a young child. "God, I love living downtown," Troy said. "It's so great to be able to walk everywhere. I don't even own a car."

Nevin thought of Julie, tucked away in the parking garage at work. "I guess public transportation works."

"Sure, plus I have a bicycle. I like to bike on my days off. You?"

"I prefer four wheels."

"That's cool."

They didn't say anything for the remaining couple of blocks. What was there to say? They probably had nothing in common and would never see each other again. Each of them knew what he wanted from the other. Conversation was unnecessary. Overrated. It was like spending a couple of hours sitting on a couch and watching lions and hyenas sing, when all anyone wanted was a nice orgasm or two.

Just like that.

Troy lived in a studio apartment that smelled like herbal tea. Apparently he slept on a futon couch that could open flat. His bicycle and a big-screen TV with several gaming consoles took up much of the remaining space.

"Can I get you a beer?" he asked, waving toward the dorm-sized fridge.

Nevin wasn't thirsty and didn't want to drink anymore. He shook his head, took Troy's arm, and drew him close for a kiss.

Troy wore cologne with a nice musk and spice scent, and his cheeks were smooth. He tasted minty—Tic Tacs or gum, Nevin supposed. Nevin didn't have to crane his neck too far upward or tug Troy too far down. And Troy gave in to the kiss beautifully, parting his lips and wrapping his arms around Nevin's waist. It was a nice kiss.

With a deep sigh, Nevin drew back. "This was a mistake."

"What did I do?"

"Nothing." Nevin gave Troy's cheek a quick stroke. "You're sweet and perky and fucking adorable. And you taste good."

"You're not into guys?" Troy looked distressed despite the reassurances.

"I'm into guys. I'm sorry I made you leave work early. I'm sorry if I'm disappointing you. I just... I gotta go."

"I know this place is kind of a dump. We can go to yours if you want. Or we can—"

"It's not a dump. Believe me, I've lived in worse." That was true, but the next part was a stretch. "I need to head home, kid. Rough day at work and I have an early morning." This time he patted Troy's cheek. "But thanks for inviting me. Maybe another time."

Looking disappointed but not devastated, Troy walked him the short distance to the door. "Well, you know where I work. Wednesday through Sunday nights. So when you're in the mood...."

"You bet. Thanks." Feeling like a complete douche, Nevin made his way back to the street.

His office was nearly a mile away, so the walk gave him time to think. Why had he bailed on poor Troy? The guy was good-looking enough and hadn't done anything to annoy him. He was exactly the type Nevin would enjoy for a quick poke. It might have taken the edge off a bad day, and it had been over a week since he'd hooked up with anyone. But Nevin wasn't interested. Why the hell not? What was wrong with him?

He didn't have any answers by the time he got into Julie and drove across the river to his apartment.

He fell asleep almost as soon as his head hit the pillow. But he kept waking up from unsettling dreams, most of which he couldn't remember. One of them, though… that one shoved him right out of slumber and left him sitting bolt upright in bed, his heart hammering and the sheets sticking to him from sweat.

He'd dreamed of Becka, the girl who'd shared a foster home with him twenty years ago. A sweet girl with crooked teeth, who liked to color and play with Barbies, and who begged Nevin to comb her frizzy yellow hair because only he could manage it without tugging too much. He'd never seen her again after Officer Pender drove him away from Prick's house, and as far as he knew, Prick never faced charges for molesting Becka. But Officer Pender did visit Nevin a few months later at his new—and much improved—foster placement, and she'd assured him that Becka was out of Prick's grasp and somewhere safe.

In the dream, though, Becka stood in the Gilletts' kitchen, her hair in wild snarls. She held her palms over her face. When Nevin gently pulled her hands away, he saw nothing but a grimacing skull. "Nevin did it!" Becka screamed with her fleshless mouth. "Nevin burned my face away!"

Back in the here and now, he glanced at his phone and then got out of bed. Four thirty. Not too early for a morning run.

CHAPTER TEN

JEREMY CRADLED his oversized coffee mug in his hands as he gazed steadily at Nevin. "You're off your game."

"I was running slow for your sake, geezer."

"Yeah, right. And you've hardly sworn at me at all today."

"Fuck you, you motherfucking fucker. How's that?" Nevin's espresso cup was empty, but he still had a glass of fresh-squeezed OJ and an almond pastry. He picked at the food. He'd spent the past week up to his neck in the Gillett case and hadn't been eating well, but he wasn't hungry. Not even after a long Saturday morning run with Jeremy.

Jeremy was grinning at him. "Lacking in style and originality. You can do better than that, my friend."

Nevin flipped him off, making Jeremy boom out a laugh.

P-Town Café bustled this morning, almost all of the tables occupied and the baristas zooming around. Ptolemy must have been in a grunge mood this morning. He wore a knit beanie, baggy jeans and tee, and a plaid shirt tied around his waist. A lot of the customers were on phones, tablets, or laptops, while many of the others just chatted and a few read books or newspapers. Nevin recognized a couple seated a few tables away—the blond man played guitar at the café sometimes and the brunet with the eyepatch was obviously his boyfriend. They made such disgustingly lovey-dovey faces at each other that Nevin almost gagged. He angled his chair so he didn't have to look at them.

"I'm going to Cape Lookout tomorrow," said Jeremy. "Want to come? It's just a little baby hike. Even you could handle it."

This time Nevin flipped him the bird with both hands, but his heart wasn't really in it. "Got plans. I'm going to spend all day tomorrow in bed, watching porn and thumping the pump."

"Thanks for the visual."

"Any time."

It was good to see Jeremy smile. He'd been off his game lately too. Nothing Nevin could put his finger on—just a sense of melancholy. Loneliness had a good deal to do with it. Quick hookups didn't seem to help the settling-down types much. Jeremy's first boyfriend hadn't lasted past college, and the second one was a complete fucking disaster. Luckily that guy had been out of the picture for five or six years now, but Jeremy hadn't made a love connection since then.

For a fleeting moment, Nevin considered setting Jeremy up with Colin Westwood. They were both good guys who were looking for commitment. But he immediately pushed the idea away. He told himself it was the fifteen-year age difference that made him reject it, but that wasn't the truth.

"How's tricks in the parks department?" Nevin asked after a couple of minutes. "I assume you've been rounding up all the evil people who don't clean up their dog shit."

"That is evil and yes I have. But I've had one or two other tasks too. We're planning a new community garden up north of Albina. The lot'll need clearing first, come spring. Think your brother will give us a deal?" Jeremy smiled endearingly. Nevin had never met anyone so good at wheedling favors from people. Not even Manuel.

"I'll ask him. He'd probably be willing if you promise him a Blazers ticket."

"I'll see what I can do. And I've been talking to the folks at Patty's Place about a summer work program next year. I'm thinking if we can get those kids out in the parks, it'd be a win-win."

"So they can clean up the dog shit instead of you?"

"That's a good place to start."

Nevin had visited Patty's Place a few times and liked what he saw. It operated as a group home for runaways and foster kids but also had programs for nonresident kids. Almost all the kids at Patty's fell somewhere along the LGBTQ spectrum, and a lot of them had been kicked out of their homes by parents who couldn't accept their children's gender or sexual identities. Patty's had saved a lot of lives—and, Nevin hoped, helped make sure those kids never faced Roger's fate of ending up alone.

As if reading Nevin's mind, Jeremy said, "What have you been cleaning up at work?"

"Same as you—shit." Nevin shook his head. "I've got a girl in the hospital with burns and her mother in jail."

"Damn."

Quietly Nevin said, "Did you hear they found Roger Grey's body?"

Jeremy's face turned grave. "Your missing senior?"

"My murdered senior, most likely. They found him twenty miles from home."

"Any leads?"

"Nope. I think someone had been shaking him down for money. But who and why, I don't have a fucking clue. Coulda been you for all I know. And it's not like he had much dough to begin with. Who the fuck strong-arms some poor old bastard who's got nothing but a bunch of books?" Realizing he'd raised his voice, he shut his mouth and rubbed his temple.

Jeremy stood and snatched Nevin's espresso cup off the table. "Do you want more innocent pastry to assault too?"

Nevin looked down at the remains of his breakfast. "Nah. Just hit me with more caffeine."

A line snaked from the counter almost to the door, but of course Jeremy stood patiently, striking up a conversation with the middle-aged woman in front of him. As Nevin idly scanned the room, he couldn't help noticing that irritating couple at the nearby table. The man with the eye patch was telling some kind of story, his hands gesturing so wildly he almost knocked over his coffee cup. His partner didn't appear to be saying a word, but he laughed and moved the cup safely out of range.

It hurt to look at them. A physical ache grew somewhere deep in Nevin's chest and made him want to turn away. But he couldn't. The blond made some kind of gesture—Nevin didn't quite catch it—and the brunet guffawed, then reached across the table to quickly stroke the other man's cheek. Nobody would ever look at Nevin the way the blond looked at his partner—as if he was the most amazing creature ever to walk the earth.

Yeah, that devotion was dandy for now. But what would happen when the eye-patched man fucked some guy he met at work, or the blond woke up one night and realized that the other dude's snoring was driving him batshit? Broken fucking hearts, that was what would happen. Misery. Better not to go there at all. Better to keep everything short, sweet, and meaningless.

Better.

Nevin pulled out his phone and brought up the contacts list, then scrolled to the *W*s. He'd put Colin's phone number in there after meeting him at Mrs. Ruskin's house—in case Colin was needed as a witness. But he wouldn't be, because Homicide hadn't made any progress at all in that case. Colin's number was still there, though. Maybe eventually he'd be needed for the Grey case.

Nevin stared at the screen until it went blank.

When Jeremy returned to the table, carrying fresh coffee for them both, he was accompanied by Rhoda, the café's owner. She dyed her hair unnatural shades of red and enjoyed outfits that looked like a rainbow had exploded all over her. Today she wore a sparkling purple paisley tunic with chartreuse leggings and a matching chartreuse sweater.

"Nevin, honey! Where have you been hiding?"

"I'd never hide from you."

She laughed and swatted his shoulder. He'd once propositioned her. Why not? She was funny and widowed, and she had really great boobs. She'd laughed herself into hysterics when she realized he was serious, then cited the twenty years between them as a reason to decline.

"Doesn't bother me," he'd said honestly. "Besides, isn't the whole cougar thing the latest fashion?"

"Darling, I'm no cougar, and I like my men with a little more mileage. But thanks for thinking of me."

In retrospect, it was probably best she'd shot him down. P-Town was Jeremy's favorite hangout, and it might have been awkward for Nevin to join him there ever again after fucking Rhoda. Sometimes she pinched his cheek or winked at him, though, letting Nevin know she hadn't forgotten. Now she pulled a chair over and sat between him and Jeremy, mostly blocking his view of the nauseating couple.

"It wasn't good?" she asked, pointing at Nevin's mangled pastry.

"It's fine. Just not hungry."

"Wouldn't it be great if we could transfer hunger from one person to another? Or maybe just the calories?"

"I'm sure the top scientists are working on it," he said.

"Good. So you boys had a good run this morning?"

"Nevin was slow," Jeremy said, like a brother ratting out his sibling.

"I told you. I was waiting on your big fucking carcass."

Rhoda ignored their squabbling, as she usually did. "Last time I had a checkup, I told my doctor how many steps I get each day on my Fitbit, and then I asked her if I should take up jogging instead. She asked me whether I wanted to, and I said hell no. She said, then don't. I've never understood the appeal, frankly."

"It comes in handy now and then in our lines of work," Jeremy pointed out.

"I suppose so."

The conversation shifted to Rhoda's son, Parker, who lived in Seattle but had been talking about moving back to Portland. "What about his job?" Jeremy asked.

She sighed. "He switches jobs more often than I switch bras. He's such a smart boy, but he has no direction. No idea what he wants to be when he grows up. Right now he's working at a coffeehouse, which is silly because after all the hours he put in here, he swore he'd never do it again." She made a face. "And he's working at Starbucks."

Nevin gasped and held a hand to his chest. "No! Not that!" She swatted him again, and that was good.

Rhoda gave Nevin a look. "If he does come back here, will you take him out to a couple of clubs?"

"You want me to date your son?"

"Good God, no! Just get him out of the house a little, show him some fun. I'd ask Jeremy, but he never goes anywhere fun."

"Hey!" Jeremy protested, but without much vigor because he knew damned well it was true. He spent far more time tromping up mountains or finding new winter coats for homeless people than he did cruising bars.

"I'll be happy to," Nevin said. "You could join us, though."

She laughed. "Right. Because every young man wants his mother along when he's trying to pick up other men. He'd end up in therapy for years!"

Actually, Nevin could picture her in a club, confidently setting up Parker with the most eligible guy in the place. If the guy was hesitant, she might bribe him with free coffee and pastries. And that made Nevin think that maybe he should ask Rhoda to play matchmaker for him—but then he remembered he didn't want a fucking match.

"Dickwad," he mumbled.

"Pardon me?" said Rhoda, eyebrows raised.

"Nothing. I just remembered what an idiot I am."

A few minutes later, Rhoda left them to give her baristas a hand. That cleared Nevin's view of the couple a few tables over. At first he was relieved to see them occupied—the blond reading a book and the brunet looking at something on his phone. But then Nevin realized they were both grinning slightly while playing footsie under the table, and that was just too much.

"Gotta go," he said, standing quickly.

"Do you want your running clothes?" asked Jeremy. Nevin had left them at Jeremy's place before they walked to P-Town.

"Another day. I just… I have to go."

Looking troubled, Jeremy nodded. "Okay. If you change your mind about tomorrow's hike, let me know."

Nevin wouldn't change his mind, as they both well knew. He waved to Jeremy, shot a final glare at the lovebirds, and headed to the door.

HE DIDN'T usually go into the office on weekends unless something new cropped up. But shortly after driving home, he got back into Julie and headed downtown. He waded through piles of paper and stared at his computer screen until his eyes hurt, but nothing popped out at him. He didn't even know why he was bothering, seeing as the Grey case now firmly belonged to Homicide. But he couldn't shake the feeling that there was *something* he was missing, some bit of evidence that would make the rest of the puzzle fall into place and allow him to pin the murder on someone.

He didn't realize until nearly eight in the evening that he'd skipped lunch entirely. In fact, other than a few crumbs of almond pastry and a glass of juice, he hadn't consumed anything except coffee all day. He ought to find some dinner, but nothing appealed. Maybe he'd just go home and excavate his freezer.

But when he pulled out of the parking garage, he found himself heading northwest instead of northeast. "No parking in this fucking neighborhood," he said, even though he didn't *want* to park there. He shouldn't park there. He should go home.

He left Julie in a loading zone, entered the building's lobby, and rang the buzzer marked *Westwood*. Nobody answered, and Nevin cursed himself. Colin was probably out with friends. Maybe he'd found a new boyfriend. Or maybe—

"Yes?"

"It's Detec—Nevin."

The door leading to the elevator clicked as the lock opened.

When Nevin got upstairs, Colin stood barefoot in his doorway with Legolas in his arms. He wore ratty jeans, a T-shirt with a picture of a cartoon plant, and a hoody.

They looked at each other silently for a moment. "You're not coming here to arrest me, are you?" Colin finally asked, smiling.

"I left the handcuffs at home."

Colin stepped aside. "Come in." Once he'd closed the door, he asked, "Want something to drink?"

"Iced tea?" Nevin had drunk enough coffee already.

"Sure." Colin shoved the cat at him, which surprised Nevin but not the cat. Legolas seemed content with the change in attendants, snuggling himself into Nevin's arms and starting to purr. When Colin returned with the bottle of tea, Nevin set Legolas down on the floor. The cat wound around his legs a few times before walking away.

After uncapping the bottle and taking a swig, Nevin looked around. "I'm, uh, not interrupting you?"

"Does it look like it? I was just hanging out." Colin waved toward the TV, where a black-and-white image of an actor in a fedora was frozen onscreen.

"Who's that?"

Colin gave him an incredulous look. "Bogart. Holy cow, don't tell me you don't know Humphrey Bogart."

"I've heard of him. Just never—"

"It's not a cartoon and there's no singing. Heck, Bogart even plays a detective in this one. A private eye, but still."

Nevin shrugged.

"Were you raised by wolves?"

"This was a mistake. Sorry." Nevin set the bottle on a table and started for the door. But Colin rushed over and blocked his way.

"Hey, hey. Hold on. You didn't even tell me what 'this' is. Why'd you come here?"

Nevin could easily have pushed him aside. Instead he shrugged again. "I was in the neighborhood. Thought you might want dinner. It was fucking stupid, okay? I'll just—"

Colin grabbed his arm. "Give me five minutes." He was smiling widely, his eyes sparkling.

So Nevin sipped his tea and stared at Humphrey Bogart while Colin made hurried thumping noises behind the bedroom wall. It took him closer to ten minutes, but when he emerged—his hair tamed into neat waves—he wore a pair of wine-colored skinny jeans and a black tee. He clicked off the television, then laced on black sneakers. "Am I dressed all right?" he asked, holding his arms out.

"Guess so. I didn't have a particular place in mind." Nevin wore his usual Saturday outfit—slacks, a long-sleeved shirt, a light jacket.

Colin grabbed a brown leather jacket from a hook near the door and shrugged it on. "Can I pick a place, then?"

"I guess."

When they got outside, Colin clicked his tongue at Julie and kept walking. "Loading zone," he said.

"And how many deliveries were you expecting on a Saturday night?"

"I wasn't expecting anything, but sometimes surprises show up."

They went to a brewpub, which shouldn't have been a surprise since half the buildings in the neighborhood seemed to boast one. It was crowded, but the hostess seated them right away at a table near a corner. It was so noisy, with everyone's voices bouncing off the hard surfaces, that they stared at the menus instead of talking to each other. The group of people at the next table were waxing enthusiastic about a new gluten-free brewery, and Nevin made a herculean effort not to tell them they sounded like a bunch of douchecanoes.

When the waiter appeared, Colin ordered a porter and some fancy mac and cheese, which reminded Nevin of Jeanie Gillett. Nevin opted for a salmon sandwich and more iced tea.

"No beer?" Colin asked after the waiter left.

"I have to drive home." Did Colin look disappointed at that? It was hard to tell.

After several minutes of silence, Colin leaned forward in his seat. "What kind of name is Nevin?"

That question had come from left field. "Huh?"

"I've never met a Nevin before. Is it your actual name or short for something?"

Nevin tried to think what his name would be short for and came up blank. "It's my actual, legal name. Nevin Ng. No middle."

"Mine's Oscar, which means my initials are COW. My parents didn't think that through very well. And I was named Colin because that was my father's great-uncle's name. Some kind of family thing, I guess. It actually does mean puppy, so when you called me Collie, you were right on." He winced slightly and looked embarrassed, as if he'd said something he hadn't intended.

"I don't know what the fuck Nevin means. It's just a name." He'd looked it up once and discovered it was Irish, although he doubted his mother had known that. He'd always suspected she'd actually meant to name him Kevin or Devin but was too wasted or too stupid to spell it right. But then Colin looked down, and Nevin felt guilty for his sharp tone and softened his voice. "Still volunteering for Bright Hope?"

"Yeah. I have regulars. On Tuesdays it's a lady named Harriet. Well, she prefers Harry. She was a gunnery instructor in the Marines during World War II. She's in a nursing home now, so I go just to visit for a bit. She has some great stories. And on Thursdays I have Bob and Ivan, and they've been together since 1963 and have the same last name. But Ivan says they won't get legally married because he doesn't want to feel tied down." Colin chuckled. "They own a house in Northwest that would be worth a fortune if it wasn't about to fall down. It's way too big for them and they can't manage the stairs. I mentioned maybe they could move to a condo, but they refused. Bob says he's going to die in that house."

Nevin couldn't imagine getting attached like that. Four walls and a roof, right? He'd never even owned a place, just rented. That made it easier to pick up and leave a neighborhood whenever he wanted.

When Nevin didn't say anything, Colin must have felt obligated to keep the conversation alive. "I heard about Roger," he said solemnly.

"Manny told you?"

"Yeah. I'm sorry, Nevin."

"What do you mean, you're sorry? I never even met the guy."

"I know." Colin picked up his fork and stared at the tines, then put it down. "But you were hoping for a better outcome. I could tell."

"There are no good outcomes in my business."

Colin cocked his head. "Really? Aren't there those people whose back you have? The ones who can turn to you when they have nobody else?"

Squirming, Nevin shrugged. Colin was right—those people did exist. A fair number of them, really. But sometimes it was easy to forget them when the Roger Greys and Jeanie Gilletts were crowding his mind.

Their food and drinks arrived shortly. As they ate, Colin chatted about a development project his father had in mind and how a lot of people were opposed because they'd lose a food-truck pod. Not that there weren't endless other pods around the city, but Portlanders did treasure them. Then Colin mentioned that his sister had just separated from her husband, which was causing turmoil within the family. Nevin hadn't known Colin had a sister.

"How about you?" asked Colin. "Sibs?"

As far as Nevin knew, his mother hadn't given birth to anyone else. Maybe she had, though. And fuck only knew who his father was and whether he had other kids. And how to explain Ford without getting bogged down? "A brother. But we're not blood relatives."

Colin blinked, then seemed to take it in stride. "I always wanted a brother. I used to bug my parents about it when I was little. I even asked for one for Christmas when I was six."

Nevin's food had somehow disappeared, and his belly was pleasantly full. He wiped his mouth with the napkin and leaned back. "Easter bunny didn't bring you one either, huh?"

"I think Mom and Dad were afraid to try after me. I, uh, had some health problems."

Remembering the scar on Colin's chest, Nevin nodded.

They ordered dessert—a sticky chocolate cake to share. When their forks collided over the plate, Colin cast a piercing look at him. "Is this a date, Nevin?"

Fuck. "I suppose so."

"Good," Colin replied, grinning. "But why?"

Nevin put his fork down and wished he'd ordered booze. "A fit of insanity? I don't know. I was just thinking… maybe we only fucked once. Because both times happened within less than twenty-four hours."

"Ah. I didn't know there was a time codicil."

"Plus, I blew you, but you didn't even touch me that second time. So it's really one and a half, max."

After pausing to swallow a big bite of cake—then licking the chocolate from the corner of his mouth—Colin gave a slow nod. "So I owe you one half of a fuck. Plus interest would make it a full one, right?"

"You're the MBA—you tell me."

Colin stuck out his tongue to slowly clean the fork, definitely teasing Nevin. Just as Colin no doubt planned, Nevin remembered what that tongue could do to him. He shifted in his chair and regretted the tightness of his pants.

As Colin stared at him, something caught the attention of the patrons near the front of the restaurant. People hurried over to look out the windows, and with a sigh, Nevin stood. "Be right back." With skill built on considerable experience, he pushed his way through the crowd to the big panes of glass and looked outside.

"Oh, for fuck's sake." A guy knelt on the sidewalk, his jeans pushed down to his knees, his hand busily working his dick. Nevin couldn't quite make out what he was shouting, but thought it had something to do with ninjas and TriMet buses. Three guys with manbuns and beards stood nearby, taunting the guy as he bopped the boloney.

As Nevin walked to the door, he took out his phone and dialed 911. "Detective Nevin Ng. Send a car over here." He gave the operator the address. "Public indecency. Don't know whether the dude's tweaking or off his meds, but either way he's giving the Pearl District a show." Then he put the phone away and, ignoring the masturbator, strode over to the heckling hipsters on the sidewalk. "You. Scram."

"Who put you in charge?" demanded one with ginger hair and a potbelly.

Nevin pulled out his badge and flashed it. "Portland Police Bureau, dickwad. Now vamoose."

Ginger looked like he might argue, but Nevin gave him one of his don't-fuck-with-me looks, and Ginger's pals grabbed his arms and towed him away. Several gawkers remained—plus the entire peanut gallery inside the brewpub—but none of them were Nevin's problem. He turned to the kneeling guy. "You want to put that thing away?" he asked calmly.

"They're using the satellites to control our minds! The drivers can hear it all through their radios."

"Okay. We can talk about what to do about that. But you've gotta pull your pants up first."

The man looked down at his crotch and seemed surprised to find himself with dick in hand. "They can't hear our thoughts if we clean the pipes. Gotta clean the pipes." He'd stopped shouting and sounded almost reasonable, as if he were discussing a plumbing issue.

"Sure. Makes sense. I like to keep my pipes clean too. But I'm thinking it's more effective somewhere with a roof overhead. The satellites can see you out here."

The man looked up at the night sky. He was in his early twenties and looked healthy enough. A little overweight and no telltale signs of frequent meth or dope use. Fairly decent clothes, from what Nevin could see. They looked clean. Mental health issue instead of drugs, he concluded. Poor kid.

As a siren neared, Nevin slowly approached him, hand out. "Get dressed, dude. My buddies are gonna be here in a sec, and they'll take you somewhere nice and quiet, with a roof."

Although he looked uncertain, the man staggered to his feet and pulled up his jeans. "The FBI's known about this for years," he said. "And the CIA."

"I bet they have. I never trust the feds."

When the squad car pulled to the curb a moment later, Nevin held up his badge and motioned the goons to stay calm. "My friend here is worried about mind-reading satellites," he informed the officers when they got out of their car. "And the feds are in on it. Can you take him somewhere and get a statement from him?"

The man seemed eager about that idea. "I'll make a report! But you'll have to redact my name. I'm in the witness protection program after I inculpated Governor Kitzhaber for fracking. That's the real reason he resigned."

"We'll make sure Kitzhaber doesn't know a thing," said one of the gorillas soothingly. Nevin had interacted with her before. Couldn't remember her name, but he hadn't gotten the impression that she was a nimrod, so that was good.

Clutching his jeans and muttering about spies, the guy got in the back of the patrol car. The officer managed to smooth-talk him into handcuffs by suggesting the metal might help protect him from spy satellites.

Nevin pulled the other officer aside. "Go easy on him. He's sick, not criminal."

"Yeah, okay." The cop looked around. "Everything else is under control?"

"Of course. I'm here."

The squad car pulled away, its lights and sirens off. Nevin turned back to the restaurant and discovered Colin leaning against the wall next to the door, holding Nevin's jacket.

"That was pretty amazing," he said as he handed the jacket over.

"Did you expect me to shoot the poor bastard instead?"

Colin rolled his eyes. "No, I wasn't expecting gunfire. But that situation could have turned ugly, and you chilled everyone out."

"It wasn't that kid's fault. He's got too much of the wrong chemicals zapping around his brain or something. Bad genes, probably."

"Nobody can help it if they lose the genetic lottery."

An awkward silence fell, but Colin broke it by clearing his throat. "I paid already. You want to go?"

"I asked you. I'm supposed to cover the bill." He slid one foot back and forth on the pavement. "Look, I'm gonna—"

"I have a plan."

"What?"

"The sex I owe you? It's not quite up to one, but it will be by the end of the night. Compounding interest, you know."

Colin was so goddamn adorable that Nevin couldn't stop a grin. "Yeah? So you have an idea of how to keep ourselves busy until payment comes due?"

After a moment of chewing his lower lip, Colin nodded. "You'll have to drive, though."

"You just wanted another chance to get inside Julie."

Colin grinned and they walked the few blocks back to his building.

Nevin liked being inside the car with Colin. It was intimate, like sharing a bed. "Where to?" he asked as he pulled into traffic.

"Hmm. You prefer the Burnside Bridge or Hawthorne?"

"Burnside."

"Then off we go, my good man."

Stopped at the light on Broadway, Nevin shot him a look. "Are you used to having a chauffeur?"

Colin snorted. "No, can't say I am. We're not *that* rich."

"Fancy cars, though."

"I bet Julie's worth more than my Beemer."

Nevin scowled, mostly because Colin had a point. "Private schools," he countered.

"Um, yeah. But my MBA's from Portland State."

Which was where Nevin earned his BA, so he couldn't press that issue too far. "West Hills mansion."

"I don't know that it's a mansion...."

The light turned green, and Nevin hit the gas harder than he needed to. "How many square feet?"

Colin hesitated, then whispered the answer. "Seven thousand."

Satisfied that he'd won the skirmish, Nevin snorted. "I bet you could lose my apartment in one of your closets."

"Maybe, except I don't live there, remember? I haven't since grad school. I mean… yeah, my parents have money. My income's middle-class, though."

"And that loft?"

"Belongs to Dad's company. It's an investment."

"Must be nice."

"Look," Colin said, "if you're going to be an asshole about this, just stop the car and I'll go home. But it's stupid. If I don't care how rich my family is, I don't know why you should."

Nevin pulled into a bus zone and stopped. But when Colin reached for the door handle, Nevin grabbed his other arm. "You don't care because it's never been an issue. You've never gone hungry because there was no food in the house, never stayed up all night worrying how the fuck you were going to pay the bills. Never watched the roaches crawling all over your walls and considered yourself lucky to have someplace to sleep at all."

Shit. He hadn't intended to give a speech. He recovered by making the lecture longer. "You never went to school embarrassed because your shoes were falling apart, wearing hand-me-downs somebody else had stained. When you were in college, you didn't have to choose between buying your textbooks and paying the heating bill. You didn't have to walk two miles to campus because the fucking bus schedule sucked. Didn't struggle to stay awake in your classes because you'd worked all night at a shitass job. I bet you spent all your vacations going on fucking cruises and ski trips and jaunts through Europe."

One hand still on the door handle, Colin stared at him, wide-eyed. "I've never traveled much," he finally said, his voice quiet.

Nevin huffed, let go of him, and fell back against his seat. "I don't know what in fuck I was thinking. We're nothing alike."

"You want me to go?"

"Yes. No. I— Fuck." Fantastic. He was going to have a meltdown right here and now, and over what? He'd been working too hard. He needed more exercise. Maybe he ought to join Jeremy in planting posies or whatever the fuck park rangers did.

Instead of leaving, Colin leaned closer and put a hand on Nevin's shoulder. "Trent—my ex—and I? We're a lot alike. Fancy houses, fancy schools, the whole deal. He really did go on those ski trips. His family owns a cabin in Bend. But I think you're a lot more fun to hang out with than he ever was."

Nevin peered at him. "Even when I'm having a tantrum?"

"Trent's one of those people who gets all quiet when he's unhappy, forcing you to play Twenty Questions to figure out what's wrong. When he told me we were breaking up, it took me totally by surprise and I didn't have a clue *why* he was dumping me."

"Because he's a colossal prick."

Colin giggled. "Actually, he's kind of… small." He held his thumb and forefinger about an inch apart. "Anyway, look. This? It's just one date. That's all. I think we can both survive it despite our socioeconomic differences."

Once they were moving again and over the bridge, Colin directed Nevin down MLK Boulevard, then east on Division. When they got to Twenty-Sixth, Colin grinned. "Do you think you can find a legal parking spot in this neighborhood?"

"Legal spots are for pussies." But Nevin did find one, and when they got out of the car, Colin grabbed his hand and swung it.

"It's only eleven. Let's go have a drink first."

"First?"

Colin just laughed and took him to a bar, where Colin ordered a ridiculous cocktail with gin and beet juice and Nevin had a goddamn beer. He pointed at Colin's drink. "I think bartenders make that shit up just to see what they can get patsies to drink."

"It tastes pretty good," Colin replied mildly.

"It's a contest. Each week, the dude who conned a customer into the most idiotic drink wins a prize."

"A few months ago, I had one with horseradish, jalapeño, and egg-white froth."

Nevin made a face. "Bet that bartender won that week."

At eleven thirty, Colin said it was time to go. Nevin paid the tab and they walked hand in hand for a few blocks. But Nevin stopped when he realized what their destination was. "You've got to be fucking kidding," he said.

"Nope. You ever been?"

"Why the hell would I want to—"

"I wanted to go when I was in high school, but Mom wouldn't let me stay out that late. So I went in college instead. Sometimes I dressed up as a Transylvanian. *You'd* make an amazing Frank-N-Furter. Too bad we didn't have time for costumes."

Colin seemed so enthusiastic that Nevin didn't have the heart to refuse, especially after his little performance in the car. With considerable trepidation—and maybe a tiny bit of shared excitement—Nevin allowed himself to be dragged into *The Rocky Horror Picture Show*.

Chapter Eleven

The entire way back home, Colin belted out tunes from *Rocky Horror* while Nevin drove. Although Nevin looked horrified and made his usual snide comments, a smile kept stealing across his face. He'd smiled during the movie too, and even tossed a few playing cards shared by the girl seated next to him. And he'd leaned against Colin's shoulder, which had been awfully nice.

He even parked in an approved spot when they got back to Colin's building.

Legolas launched himself at both of them as soon as they got inside, explaining with loud meows that he definitely deserved an extra dinner even if the vet said he was getting too pudgy. Colin refused him, though, so Leg had to console himself with chin scratches from Nevin.

Colin hung their jackets by the door. "Want anything?" he asked, gesturing toward the kitchen.

"Just you." Nevin leered dramatically. God, he was so beautiful, so… vibrant.

"I do owe you. With interest."

For the first time that night, they kissed. It was weird, because although they'd had only that one previous night together, the kiss felt familiar. Not in a humdrum way, but like a favorite pair of jeans that fit exactly right and made your ass look fantastic. Nevin melted against him and gripped Colin's hair tightly.

"Bed," Nevin said when they paused to breathe. As he blew lightly into Colin's ear, they both shivered.

In the bedroom, they kissed after removing each item of clothing. Colin discovered that he was even hungrier to taste Nevin than he had been last time. "You're like a brownie with ice cream and caramel sauce," he said, and Nevin laughed against his neck.

While Nevin used the water closet and then washed up, Colin took out the rubbers—both sizes—and lube. He was mostly hard already, just from the kisses and from seeing Nevin's bare body.

Nevin climbed into bed and grinned at him.

"Be right back!" Colin promised before going to pee, wash, and brush his teeth. He considered additional primping but decided against it. He turned toward the bed.

"Hey, Nev—"

Nevin lay curled under the blankets, Legolas resting against his chest. They were both sound asleep, and Nevin looked almost absurdly young and innocent.

Tiptoeing, Colin switched off the lights and climbed carefully into bed. He fell asleep with Nevin's hair tickling his face.

THE NEXT morning Nevin considered him gravely from a few inches away. "That wasn't what I planned." Legolas was behind Nevin's head on the pillow, one leg sticking indelicately into the air while he licked himself.

"Was it bad?"

Nevin shook his head slightly. "No. It was…. We didn't fuck."

"People do that sometimes. Go on dates and even sleep together without having sex."

"I don't."

Colin reached up to stroke his cheekbone. "Well, now you did. Once, at least."

Nevin's gaze was so acute it felt as if he were reading Colin's mind. Maybe that was how he got confessions from bad guys—staring straight into their souls. Oddly enough, the scrutiny didn't make Colin uncomfortable. Usually people examined him only to gauge his medical condition, but this was much better. Yes, it made him feel naked, but then he *was* naked, so that was all right. Nevin was naked, too, his vulnerability clear in those warm brown eyes.

Colin didn't know what would have happened next. But Leg meowed, Colin glanced at him, and then he saw the clock behind him. "Oh, shit!" he exclaimed, sitting up suddenly.

"What?"

"Sunday brunch with the family. I have to be there in less than an hour."

Nevin stretched, perhaps deliberately allowing the blankets to drop and expose more of him. "Blow them off."

"I can't. Not this month. My sister's getting divorced, so things are... fraught." Then he had an idea. "Come with me."

The look of horror on Nevin's face would have been perfect in any slasher flick, and he bolted out of bed so fast that Leg squawked and ran and Nevin nearly tripped over his own feet. "No fucking way."

"It's just brunch, not a torture session. This month we're going to this place my dad likes. It's kind of a pain because it's out near the airport, but he likes the river views. Food's pretty good too."

But Nevin was already stumbling around, grabbing frantically at his clothing. It was the first time Colin had seen him look rattled and uncoordinated.

Colin stood, bemused, hands on hips. "Do you have some kind of aversion to mimosas?"

Nevin nearly fell over as he put his underwear on, and he did an odd dance to pull up his pants. He found one sock near the bed and looked around frantically for the other. Colin decided not to tell him it was outside the bedroom, probably somewhere near the couch, and Nevin apparently decided to give up. He tossed the one sock away and shrugged into his shirt, buttoning it as he hurried toward the door.

But Colin got there first and snatched up Nevin's shoes, holding them far above his head.

"Give me my fucking shoes," Nevin growled.

"Only if you tell me what's going on."

Nevin's jaw worked. "Brunch," he ground out as he buckled a holster over his shoulder.

"Yes?"

"With your parents."

Ah. Ahh! "They're not horrible people. They're actually pretty nice. I mean yeah, Mom's bossy and overprotective and Dad's not very creative, but they're funny and can make good conversation. They'll like you."

"I don't do parents."

Colin would have laughed if Nevin hadn't looked so genuinely distressed. "It's not an engagement brunch, Nevin. It doesn't imply future promises. It's just... eggs. Probably some prime rib."

"I can't."

Relenting, Colin gave him the shoes. He even fetched Nevin's jacket and handed it over. He wanted to ask whether they could have another date soon, and he tried to think of a flippant and witty way to word it so he wouldn't scare Nevin off. But then Nevin surprised him by cradling Colin's face in his palms. "I'm sorry, Collie. I'm just not made that way."

"That's okay."

Something softened and relaxed in Nevin's face. "You mean it, don't you? You're not pissed off at me."

"I get it. It's fine. I'm just sorry I have to go."

Giving a slow nod, Nevin made a thoughtful hum. "I'm going to see if I have the balls to call you soon for another date."

"That would be great," said Colin, beaming. "Or just stop by. I don't mind."

Nevin kissed him fiercely, then left without another word. Colin looked at the closed door for a few moments before padding off to the bathroom to get ready.

COLIN SHOULDN'T have been happy about his sister's separation. But the entire brunch conversation centered around Miranda and what she was going to do now and how she could help her daughter, Hannah, get through the crisis. Hannah wasn't there—she was away on a school-choir trip—which was just as well. Miranda was a wreck. Colin pretty much concentrated on his food, occasionally dropping sympathetic phrases into the conversation.

At length, though, his mother turned her attention on him. "There's a lot of cholesterol and fat in that omelet," she said, pointing at his plate. "You know, you can ask them to make it with egg whites only."

"I can, but then it tastes like crap."

"Colin—"

"Mom, I'm fine. I saw the doctor just a couple of weeks ago and he said I'm doing great, remember?"

For a change, Miranda swooped in to temporarily rescue him. "I've got tickets to see *The Book of Mormon* in January. Now that Russell's not going, want to come with me?"

"Thanks, Miranda. I'd love to." But Colin's thoughts strayed to Nevin as he wondered what he would make of that musical. He'd probably love it—there was a character named General Butt-Fucking Naked. He'd even like the songs.

"You look a million miles away today," his mother said. He could rarely get anything past her.

"Probably just a little tired. I went to *Rocky Horror* last night."

"You haven't done that in years. Did you dress up?"

"No. It was a last-minute kind of thing."

She cocked her head. "Who went with you?"

Uh-oh. He tried to think of a way to turn the conversation. "Hey, Miranda, do you think Hannah would like to go?"

"She's too young. Give it two or three years. Though God knows that crap her father lets her watch on YouTube is ten times worse."

Torn between interrogating Colin and giving parenting advice to Miranda, their mother hesitated. And that was just long enough for their father to make an entry into the conversation. "That movie's at the Clinton Street Theater, right?"

"Yeah, for thirty-something years."

"There are a couple of houses I've been considering near there. Tear-downs, but we can fit at least six townhomes into those lots. I'd like you to come take a look with me this week. Tuesday?"

"Sure." Then Colin remembered something Nevin had said to him when they first met. "You know, Dad, a lot of the houses in that neighborhood have character. A history."

His father peered at him over his coffee cup. "So?"

"So it's a shame when they're replaced by... boring modern stuff."

Judging by his expression, Harold Westwood clearly suspected that his son had been replaced by an alien replicant. He glanced at his wife, but she smiled smugly. She and Harold had discussed the value of old neighborhoods in the past, until finally the arguments had become so heated they'd mutually declared the subject off-limits. She didn't criticize his real estate plans, and he didn't complain when her law firm represented clients fighting developers like him.

"We're running a business, Colin. We could pour a lot of money into those two houses and, at best, end up with a couple of duplexes that still have tons of old-house quirks. Or for roughly the same investment, we demolish them and put up nice new units. Trilevels that'll bring in several times as much as those old heaps."

"But we already have plenty of money, Dad."

"Are you turning communist? Or entering a monastery?"

"Never mind," Colin mumbled.

AFTER RETURNING home, Colin did a few chores. He smiled when he found Nevin's lost sock, and he threw it and its mate into his hamper. Mingling Nevin's laundry with his own made him happy, even though he knew it had only happened because Nevin was in such a panic over brunch.

Colin could understand him freaking out over the thought of meeting the parents. Colin's disclaimers notwithstanding, it was a scary prospect, and not just because it implied a relationship that didn't exist. Nevin had divulged very little about his background, but it was clear he'd grown up much less privileged than Colin. He certainly wasn't poor now—his clothing was expensive and his car probably cost a small fortune—but that didn't mean his past poverty didn't continue to affect him.

When Colin sat on the couch to think about this, Leg jumped into his lap. "You turned out to be a complete slut," Colin informed him, stroking his back. "Not that I blame you. He's amazing." Amazing but also puzzling.

Trent was a simple guy. He came across as a slightly spoiled rich kid, the type who supported the arts but believed that if people suffered economic hardships it was probably their own fault. And when you got to know him better, you learned your initial impression was pretty darn accurate. He wasn't cruel, wasn't even an asshole. He liked to talk about exercise and fashion and whether the locally sourced cheeses they served at his favorite restaurant were better than imported ones. He bought himself a sporty new convertible every two years even though he rarely put the top down. He'd hired a decorator for his luxury condo downtown, and the walls ended up hung with ugly paintings even Trent didn't like but by artists whose careers promised to take off soon. And in the end, Trent hadn't had patience for a boyfriend who had too many medical appointments and not enough ambition.

But Nevin, on the other hand—the more Colin got to know him, the more complicated Nevin turned out to be. He was far more than the good-looking, arrogant, foul-mouthed cop Colin had initially met.

"He's not an onion, Leg. He's a prism. Shine a little light on him and you find a rainbow." But like a rainbow, Nevin's brilliance was intangible. Colin couldn't hold on to either kind of beauty.

What would it be like to be forced to survive the way Nevin once had? Colin couldn't wrap his head around it. He didn't think he'd been a particularly greedy kid; he didn't demand stuff from his parents the way many of his classmates did. But when he needed something, he got it. He'd never thought of himself as rich, yet he'd never worried about how to pay for things. Money was just there, like oxygen. Hell, in his case, occasionally money was more accessible to him than oxygen.

Okay. So Nevin hadn't possessed that safety net when he was younger. Even if he was financially secure now and had done well in his profession, it was hard to shake childhood fears. God, Colin understood that. Sometimes even now he would lie quietly on his back, feeling his heart pump steadily, yet expecting it to falter with the next beat.

As his fingers made transitory patterns in Leg's plush fur, Colin realized Nevin's issues didn't just involve money. They involved family as well.

The thing was, even when they were being enormous pains in the ass, Colin loved his family. And he'd never been anything but completely confident that they loved him. Every one of them had made sacrifices for him, had abandoned their own goals and plans in order to spend hours carting him to doctors' appointments or, worse, sitting by his hospital bed. One of his earliest memories was cuddling Miranda's stuffed unicorn—the one he wasn't normally allowed to touch—while singing along to *The Wizard of Oz* with his mother. His father had hooked up a VCR to the television earlier in the day, which was against hospital rules. The nurses pretended not to notice the violation because Colin was going to have another operation in the morning and he was scared.

Nevin had briefly mentioned a brother unrelated by blood. Stepbrother? And that was it. Maybe Nevin had grown up without a supportive family—an absence even harsher than poverty. A kid who was poor could possibly grow up to earn a good living, but he couldn't manufacture loving parents.

Deep in thought, Colin clutched Legolas hard enough that the cat squeaked a protest and gave him a dirty look. "Sorry, Leg."

If Colin hadn't been blessed with money and family, what would he be now? That was easy—he'd be dead. But even if he'd somehow survived, he'd be nothing. Mediocre looks, no special skills. Maybe he'd have some kind of crappy job and a depressing apartment like Roger Grey's, but he wouldn't even have Roger's solace of good memories.

Nevin, though, had made something of himself despite what seemed to be a rocky start. He had an important career where he helped people, a cool car, a sharp wardrobe, a keen mind. Hell, even Legolas was a fan. Nevin must have been made from some pretty incredible raw material, and he must have fought like a lion to get where he was.

"No wonder he resents me." Maybe resent wasn't quite the right word, but Colin couldn't find a better one. He was aware that a wide gulf stretched between them. Apart from being two single queer men who lived in the same city, they had little in common. Well, good sex. Great sex. And Colin enjoyed Nevin's company, and Nevin seemed to enjoy his as well. But they had no future, and if Colin didn't watch out, he was going to end up with a broken heart. His heart was weak enough already—he shouldn't endanger it further.

CHAPTER TWELVE

NEVIN WASN'T proud of his hasty retreat from Colin's place. He wasn't a coward, not by a long shot. But he would sooner have walked naked into Sureño gang territory with the Norteños' number 14 tattooed on his ass than go to brunch with Colin's parents. Even several hours later, showering off the sweat of a good run, the idea made him shudder.

He'd thrown on clean sweats and was heading for the kitchen in search of lunch when his phone rang. "Hey, Chief," he said after glancing at the screen.

"Chief, huh? No Germy Cox today?"

"Don't have the fucking energy to irritate you."

"Sounds like the apocalypse is nigh." There was a lot of background noise on Jeremy's end of the call, but his deep voice boomed clearly. "Come meet me at P-Town. We'll caffeinate you back to your usual irksome self."

"Thought you took a hike."

"Canceled."

"I'm just going to—"

"I'll drag you here myself if I have to. Pick you up and put you in my pocket."

"You just want me near your dick. Or your ass."

Jeremy guffawed. "It's all I dream about."

With a mixture of reluctance and relief, Nevin drove over to P-Town. The joint was jumping, which was usual for a Sunday afternoon, but Jeremy had scored a good table by the window. He sat there, a mountain of competent calm, while Nevin waited in line.

"How's the dissertation?" Nevin asked Ptolemy when it was his turn.

"Ugh. Maybe I should give it up and spend my life making coffee instead."

"You're good at making coffee. But you'll be better when you get that doctor in front of your name and you're bossing the peons like me around."

Ptolemy laughed and handed over Nevin's coffee, along with a plate containing an oversized cookie.

"I haven't had lunch yet," Nevin protested.

"It's oatmeal raisin, so it's practically health food."

Nevin paid for his coffee, accepted the free cookie with a wink, and wended his way to Jeremy's table.

"Why the ape-man-like threats?" Nevin asked as he sat down. "We just saw each other yesterday. Can't last one more minute without my company?"

"Yep. I was dying, right here." Jeremy slapped a paw over his heart. He flashed his dopy, handsome grin and slurped his coffee. "I had to cancel the hike because of a work emergency this morning. But then I scored some tickets to the Blazers' opening game. Want a couple for you and Ford? They're playing the Pelicans."

It briefly crossed Nevin's mind to ask for three tickets and invite Colin, but he rejected the idea immediately. The game was over a month away, and he'd be long gone from Colin's life by then.

"They're floor seats," Jeremy said, perhaps taking Nevin's pause for hesitancy.

"Who'd you have to blow to get those?"

"Some of us, Nevin, can accomplish things without sexual favors."

"Where's the fun in that?" But then Nevin remembered what it had felt like to wake up cuddled against Colin—a man he had *not* fucked the night before—and a sneaky little smile stole onto his face. "I'll take a pair," he said before he could dissolve into a puddle of mush.

"They're all yours. Want another so you can bring someone?"

Nevin shook his head hard. "Just mine and Ford's."

"Okay. A couple of guys from work will be joining us, plus Amy Lassiter. You know her, right?"

"Sure." She was with the DA's office, and Nevin had testified in a couple of her cases. She was good. "Sounds like you've got quite a shindig planned."

Jeremy shrugged. "I have a bunch of tickets. I asked Rhoda, but she said she can't stand the shoes squeaking on the floor. Huh. I wonder if Parker would drive down from Seattle and join us. A little break might be fun for him."

Nevin snorted. It figured; Jeremy was trying to rescue someone again. It was a real fixation for him. Someday he'd learn he couldn't save the whole damned world. Couldn't save most of it, even.

One of the good things about Jeremy was that he could be quiet. Not that there was anything wrong with his conversation; he was a smart guy who knew a lot of random interesting shit. But he was also perfectly content to keep his trap shut, to sit with someone and just people watch. His presence tended to have a calming influence on Nevin, as if that big body were exerting a special gravitational field.

They sat and drank their coffee, Nevin ate his cookie, and they let everyone else's conversations wash gently over them. At one point they both tensed when it looked like a pair of bicyclists outside were about to beat the crap out of each other over a near-collision. But then one of the cyclists rode away in a huff, and Nevin and Jeremy relaxed.

"Twats," Nevin mumbled.

"Just people. It's easy to get worked up, especially when the adrenaline is flowing."

"*You* never get worked up." When Jeremy had been one of the few openly gay cops in the bureau, his ability to keep his cool even under miserable circumstances had eased his way with colleagues. Even the worst homophobes were grateful to have a serene giant as backup. When the shit went down, where your partner liked to stick his dick was a lot less important than whether he was likely to get you killed. Nevin had always been out too, but in his case, nobody gave him shit because he'd kick their asses if they tried.

"I get angry too, Nevin. I just try not to take it out on anyone else."

Nevin lifted his cup in salute. "Saint Jeremy."

"And you're that little horned devil sitting on everyone's shoulder?"

"Fuck yeah."

When there was a lull at the counter, Jeremy fetched them refills. "Did you get any sleep last night?" he asked a few minutes after retaking his seat.

Nevin thought immediately of Colin's big comfortable bed, the mellow morning light shining in through the windows, Leg's rumbling purr. And Colin, warm and sleeping beside him. "Yeah," he answered defensively.

"I just thought with the Grey case and that burned girl…." As he trailed off, a smile played at the corners of his lips. "Ah. You hooked up with someone."

"Fucking right I did." Jeremy didn't need to know the night had involved dinner, *Rocky Horror*, and a sleepover without sex. He might read too much into what was clearly a fluke.

"Whatever gets you through the night," said Jeremy.

"Isn't that a song? Elton John or someone?"

Jeremy shook his head in mock despair. But he also seemed relieved, and Nevin realized this Kaffeeklatsch had been another of Jeremy's rescue attempts, in this case aimed at Nevin.

"I don't need a goddamn hero, Germy. I can take care of myself."

Jeremy sighed. "You always have, right?"

NORMALLY NEVIN would have had no trouble concentrating on work, where he had more interviews to conduct on the Gillett case as well as piles of paperwork. Other tasks crowded his schedule, too, such as a senior-center talk on avoiding Internet scams and some visits to group homes for developmentally disabled people. But Nevin spent the week trying not to think about Colin, whose image sometimes intruded at damned inconvenient times. Nevin ran long and hard in the mornings and visited the gym in the evenings, but when he ate at all, it was whatever crap he could grab on the fly.

He didn't feel good. Maybe he was coming down with the flu.

On Friday night he worked until well past dark. He got into Julie and nearly steered her over to the Pearl District—and Colin's loft—before pulling over on Broadway and poking at his phone.

"Meet me somewhere," he barked when Ford answered.

"Where?"

"Don't care. Anywhere with booze and women." Because he was thinking that maybe if he had sex with a woman—a voluptuous one with big tits and rounded hips—he'd shake Colin out of his head.

Ford was silent, then cleared his throat. "Um, how about if we go somewhere quieter instead?"

Shit. That sounded foreboding. "Yeah, okay."

They ended up at a diner not far from Nevin's place. That was good on two counts—he could eat for the first time that day and he was across the river from Colin. The Willamette really wasn't much of a barrier since there were plenty of bridges, but it provided psychological distance, at least.

Nevin arrived at the diner first and commandeered a big corner booth. By the time Ford got there, Nevin already had a coffee and had studied the menu. Ford had already eaten and just ordered a Coke, but Nevin asked for a burger and fries.

"You look like shit," Ford observed.

"Fuck you very much."

"I'm serious, bro. You got bags under your eyes, and I swear you've lost weight since I saw you last. What's wrong?"

"Nothing. Just up to my neck in shit at work. You're the one who sounded so fucking ominous when I called. What the hell's going on?"

Ford shifted, making the vinyl seat squeak, and pointed his gaze at one of the entirely unremarkable prints hanging on the wall. His scalp was freshly shaved, and he was sporting a new mustache. It looked good on him. He'd dressed up a bit too, in a white button-down and new-looking jeans. But the fingernails tapping on the tabletop were a landscaper's—ragged and permanently stained from his work in the soil.

Nevin leaned toward him. "If you don't spit it out, I'm going to yank your tongue out of your goddamn mouth."

For some reason the threat appeared to relax Ford a bit. He gave a weak smile. "Got a new tattoo."

"That's what's got your panties twisted? Unless it's my face on your ass, what the fuck do I care?"

Instead of answering, Ford unbuttoned his left cuff and painstakingly rolled up the sleeve. His arms were already heavily inked, but a few blank spaces remained. He pointed to a spot on the underside of his forearm, between a thorny rosebush and some kind of tribal symbol. Nevin peered closely.

"It's a human heart with the letter *K* in it," Nevin said, even though Ford undoubtedly knew that.

"Yep."

"Meaning?"

"Um… remember Katie?"

Nevin did. She was the old flame Ford had been sleeping with recently. "She's the *K*?"

"Yeah, and… she's, uh, my fiancée, actually."

After a moment of gaping, Nevin buried his head in his hands. "You knocked her up. You stupid fuck, we've talked about keeping helmets on our dicks since we were kids, and you—"

"She's not pregnant." Ford looked sheepish when Nevin glanced at him. "We did kinda have a scare. She's on the pill, but we thought…. Well, anyway, she's not pregnant. But for a day or so we thought she *might* be, and that got us talking."

"About what? What fucking idiots you are?"

"We're not idiots!" Ford looked apologetic over his outburst when the waitress arrived with his drink and Nevin's food. She pointedly ignored him and stalked away. He continued in a calmer voice. "The scare got us thinking, is all. And the thing is, we both decided that maybe settling down—even having a kid—wouldn't be such a bad thing."

Nevin poured ketchup onto his burger before taking a vicious bite, chewing, and swallowing. "Having a cold isn't such a bad thing either. Doesn't mean you should go out and fucking get infected."

"Why are you so pissed off about this? You don't know Katie well enough to hate her."

"You don't know her all that well either. You guys broke up ages ago, and now you've been seeing each other for only a few weeks, right? And you're talking till death do you part? And *babies*?" He shuddered.

"Yeah, babies, Nev. I want to be a daddy. I mean, I never learned anything from that shitbag who fathered me, but I really think I can do better."

Ford's voice sounded strained and plaintive, and Nevin scrutinized him. For the first time that night, Nevin managed to get his head out of his ass and think about someone besides himself. What he saw was his brother nearly on the verge of tears, silently pleading for understanding. Nevin took in a deep breath and released it.

"You'll make a fucking amazing father," he said and watched Ford visibly relax. "But are you sure you want this now, with her? It's not your biological clock rattling your balls?"

Ford gave a small smile. "No. Katie… she's amazing. She works at Target now, but she's really into gardening and would love to become my business partner. She works really hard, and she's tougher than anyone I know. Even you. But she's sweet. And when I'm with her, I don't even care if we're doing something stupid like watching reality TV or going grocery shopping, 'cause I'm having fun. She feels like home."

Nevin couldn't help it—he remembered sitting on Colin's couch, petting the cat and listening to Colin sing about being king. Something uncomfortably warm and fuzzy stretched inside him. He stomped on it. But then he managed a grin. "I better be your goddamn best man, asshole."

They grasped hands hard over the table until Nevin pulled away and socked Ford on the arm, causing Ford to knock over his Coke and send cold, sticky liquid everywhere. The waitress rushed over with towels in her hand and murder in her eyes. But Ford couldn't stop laughing, and so Nevin couldn't either.

NEVIN HAD barely settled into his office on Monday morning when Frankl appeared. The homicide detective looked more animated than usual, his hound-dog eyes sparkling with excitement. "Got a lead on the Grey case," he announced, heaving himself into the chair opposite Nevin's desk.

For a split second, Nevin imagined Colin in handcuffs, his kind, handsome face transformed into a mask of hatred. Then Nevin shook himself. "Yeah?" he asked nonchalantly.

"Last week some guy in Boring was doing his yard work when he found a human jawbone in the middle of a flower bed."

"That must have been a nasty surprise."

"Nah. The old codger's so excited to have something interesting happening, you'd have thought he discovered Jimmy Hoffa."

Nevin had met plenty of people like that. "And the jaw was Grey's?"

"Yes indeedy."

Drumming his fingers on the desk, Nevin thought that over for a moment. He knew pieces of Grey's body had been missing, which wasn't that unusual for a corpse left in the open for a couple of months. Animals had a tendency to drag bits away. But the jawbone in Boring was six or seven miles from Sandy, where most of Grey had been found.

"I take it you don't make the codger for Grey's murder," Nevin said.

Frankl snorted. "Nah. But that bone didn't walk itself there. His property adjoins three others, and now we're checking on the neighbors. One of them's got priors—beat up his ex-wife a couple times and dabbled in crank."

Although Nevin nodded, he didn't share Frankl's optimism. Lots of people had skanky neighbors, but this particular one didn't sound like he had any logical connection to Grey. Still, there had to be some explanation for that bone in Boring, and at least this was something. "Think you'll get anywhere on this?"

"Dunno. But it turns out our codger's got surveillance cameras on his property—somebody keeps breaking into his shed, he says—so we're watching the footage. It's gonna take time, though. That jawbone could've showed up anytime over the past two months."

Nevin was heartily grateful not to be stuck watching eight weeks of footage of a garden in Boring. "Good luck with it," he said with a smirk.

Frankl flipped him the bird. "Fuck you very much, Ng."

That made Nevin laugh.

But long after Frankl wandered back to his own office, Nevin sat unmindful of his computer screen and stacks of papers. He was going to blame Roger Grey's ghost for this, but he couldn't get Colin Westwood out of his mind.

By lunchtime Nevin had accomplished almost nothing and was about to go out of his fucking mind. In fact, maybe he had already lost it, because he found himself looking up the address for Westwood Development, which turned out to be less than a mile away, over near Tenth and Morrison. "Fuckwad," Nevin growled as he grabbed his jacket.

It wasn't raining, but the sky was the color of an elephant's hide and the air smelled faintly of moisture. The city trees hung on to their gaudy leaves, waiting to shed them at the first downpour, and pedestrians who hadn't yet abandoned their summer clothing scurried through the growing chill.

Nevin marched, oblivious to traffic sounds and the scents from food carts, and as he entered the building, his jaw was set tightly enough to hurt. After glancing at the directory, he rode the elevator to the twelfth floor. He expected to find a fancy reception area, but instead there was just a glass door painted with the elegant Westwood Development logo and, on the other side, an older lady at a desk in a cubicle. She looked startled to see him. "Can I help you, sir?"

It suddenly occurred to him that they probably didn't get walk-in traffic. He put on his blankest cop face. "I'm here to see Colin Westwood."

She tapped at her computer, a frown pulling her brows into a V. "Did you have an appointment? I can't seem to find—"

"No appointment. Just tell him Detective Ng is here."

She widened her eyes. "Detective! Is everything all right?"

Oh, for fuck's sake. "I need to speak with him."

"Of course." Flustered, she picked up her phone and punched a button. "Colin? There's a Detective Ng here to see you." She called him by his first name. Interesting.

Nevin was still mulling that over—and ignoring the lady's nervous stare—when Colin came loping out of a hallway. He wore dress slacks, a violet shirt, and a patterned yellow bow tie, and fuck if Nevin's heart didn't give a little lurch at the sight of him. Goddamn it.

"Nevin!" Colin came to a screeching halt close enough for Nevin to smell his spicy cologne.

"I need…." Nevin stumbled over the next word. He didn't know what he needed or why he was here. Didn't even know what he intended to demand from Colin.

Instead of getting angry or impatient, Colin seemed to calm a little. The corner of his mouth twitched before he turned to the woman. "We have a meeting. Please make sure nobody interrupts us." Then he faced Nevin. "Right this way, Detective."

Photos of buildings lined the hallway walls. Nevin recognized the one where Colin lived as well as several others he'd seen around town. Most seemed to be condos or townhomes. Colin's office was near the end of the hall. It was a large space with windows commanding a partially obstructed view of the river. The furniture looked expensive and stuffy—not really Colin's style—but the framed movie posters made Nevin smile.

Colin closed the door. Then he surged forward without warning, pushed Nevin back against the oversized desk, and cradled his face in his palms. "I certainly hope you're not here to arrest me."

Before Nevin could answer, they were kissing. Not sweetly and softly. Not teasingly. Ferociously and voraciously, lips pressed tight and tongues tangling, breaths coming in desperate little bursts, deep animal sounds crawling from both of their throats. They separated eventually, but only so they could hang on to each other like two men saved from drowning.

"I've been working here since I was a teenager," Colin said. "And I have never kissed anyone here before."

"Not even Trent?"

"Never."

It was stupid to feel triumphant, but Nevin did. He clung more tightly.

Then Colin choked out a laugh. "In about thirty seconds, we're going to end up having sex here. Which I've also never done. And unfortunately it's a really bad idea."

"No rubbers handy?"

"And the furniture's uncomfortable. I'd suggest the floor, but the walls are thin and my father's office is next door."

Bile burned Nevin's throat and he pulled away. "I need to—"

Colin grabbed him. "No. Why'd you come here, Nevin?"

Maybe it was the kisses that messed up his mouth. When Nevin looked for an answer that was brisk and profane, what came out instead was raw truth. "He's leaving me."

Stunned, Colin gaped and released Nevin's arm. "You have a boyfriend?" he asked in a tiny voice.

"For fuck's sake, no!" Sometimes Nevin believed English had too many words and not enough meanings. This was one of those times. "I don't have a boyfriend. I've never had a boyfriend. Or a girlfriend either, if you want to be thorough. I'm... shit." He rubbed his face.

"Never ever?" Colin asked, stepping close again, speaking softly in Nevin's ear. "Not even, like, a high school crush?"

Nevin smiled despite the pain. "You had a lot of those, didn't you?"

"My first true love was Mark Oshiro, who sat next to me in second grade. He did not share my ardor. But our au pair used to pack me these enormous lunches because—"

"Au pair? You had a fucking au pair?"

"Shut up. I'm sharing here. Her name was Anna and she was Italian. And I was underweight, so she sent me to school with enough lunch to feed an army. Mark's parents were into weird macrobiotic foods or something. I let him gorge on my sliced ham and cake, and he let me tell everyone we were boyfriends."

"Mark Oshiro was easy," Nevin said with a chuckle.

"Yep. And a cheat. During recess one day I caught him doing one of those paper fortune-teller things with Jennifer Blaylock. He broke my heart." Colin clapped a dramatic hand to his chest, but his eyes flashed with real hurt.

"I could look him up for you," Nevin offered. "See if he's got any outstanding warrants and needs a trip to jail."

"Not him. Cheating aside, he was a goody-goody. I'll bet he doesn't even jaywalk."

"Could have traffic follow him around for a while. Fucking *everyone* does something we can cite 'em for."

Colin grinned and gave Nevin's cheek a gentle kiss. "That's gallant of you, but we can let him be. I've moved on."

"Right. You had Trust Fund Trent."

"I've moved on since him too." Colin shook his head. "But we were talking about you. Who left you?"

Now Nevin felt silly for putting it that way. "Nobody," he muttered.

"See, unlike you, I'm unskilled in the third degree. So I'm going to just keep repeating the question. Does that make me the bad cop? Who left you, Nevin?"

Instead of answering, Nevin detached himself from Colin and walked to the window. He could make out the steely glint of the Willamette River, which nearly matched the color of the sky today. He watched the boats working their way upstream and the crawl of traffic across the bridges.

Colin came up behind him. And although Colin didn't say anything, Nevin heard him breathing, felt the warmth of the body just behind him. He had the impression that if he leaned back a little, Colin would wrap his arms around Nevin's middle and hold him tightly. But Nevin moved a few inches closer to the cold window glass instead.

"My brother is getting married," Nevin said to the city of Portland. "He's not really my brother but close enough, and the only fucking family I have. He's always been there, right? If I needed a place to crash or a ride home when I was wasted. If I needed a wingman when I was picking up girls. But now he's got a fiancée and he's all… besotted. Pretty soon it'll be all about mortgages and college funds, and I'll be just…." He groaned. "Fuck. I'll be just a whiny-ass bitch."

It was so fucked-up. On the one hand—and it was a goddamn *big* hand—he was mortified to be that whiny-ass bitch, ashamed that he was anything less than celebratory over his brother's good news, perplexed about why he was spilling his guts to some guy in a bow tie. Yet there was that other hand, and damn if it wasn't open rather than clenched into a fist. On that hand, admitting the truth of his feelings to Colin felt… like relief. As if he'd been carrying around a shit-ton of rocks and someone had finally told him he could set that burden down, at least for a minute. Or maybe that someone was helping him hoist the load.

"I'm so fucked," Nevin muttered, and he wasn't just talking about Ford's engagement.

Colin set a light hand on Nevin's shoulder. "Come with me, okay?"

Nevin didn't like to take orders—a characteristic that had caused grief within the bureau more than once—but now he followed Colin obediently to the door and waited while he slipped on an overcoat. The coat was dove-colored lightweight wool, and Colin looked delicious. It probably would have cost Nevin a month's rent.

Colin paused with his hand on the doorknob. He used his free hand to gently cup Nevin's cheek. "Come with me," he repeated.

And fuck it all if Nevin didn't do just as he was told.

CHAPTER THIRTEEN

COLIN THOUGHT Nevin was going to bolt. He would have held his hand as they walked down the hallway, but Nevin was stronger and could have simply pulled away. But when Colin's father emerged from his office, probably in search of lunch, Colin placed himself smack in the middle of the corridor, blocking Nevin's escape. Nevin's eyes widened, and for a moment Colin honestly thought he was going to get run over—or heck, maybe Nevin would just pull out his gun—but then Nevin squared his shoulders and erased all expression from his face.

"Hi, Dad." Colin would have given everything he owned for the ability to communicate telepathically with his father right then. He tried, staring hard while projecting his thoughts as forcefully as he could: *Be cool. Don't spook him.*

Harold Westwood wasn't psychic, but maybe Colin's body language was strong enough to get through. Harold smiled mildly. "Hi, Col. Heading out?"

"Yeah. Dad, this is Detective Nevin Ng. Detective, this is my father, Harold Westwood."

Nevin shot Colin a look that might have been grateful before shaking Harold's hand.

"Is this about Mr. Grey's murder?" asked Harold.

Now it was Nevin's turn for nonverbal communication. It looked as if he was both pleading with Colin to lie for him and apologizing for it. Colin nodded at both of them. "Yeah. He has some more questions. I figured we might as well deal with it over decent coffee."

"Don't blame you. I hope you're able to make some headway in the case, Detective. It's a terrible thing."

"Thanks," Nevin said.

"Colin told me the family wouldn't have anything to do with Mr. Grey because he was gay."

"Yeah. Fucking asswipes."

Nevin briefly looked like he regretted the words, but then Harold nodded vigorously. "Couldn't agree more. A family's duty is to love and support one another. I can't think of a more important job."

Crap. Colin was going to get misty-eyed if this kept up. "Well, I guess we should—"

"What about you?" Nevin interrupted. "You don't care that your only son is a great big fairy?"

Harold gave Colin a long look, maybe to assess whether Colin was angry over the question or the terminology. But when Colin smiled, Harold simply shrugged. "I think he's more of an elf. His ears are a little pointy."

"Dad!"

Then Harold faced Nevin and deepened his voice. "I love my son. Unconditionally. I care that he's gay, but only because it's a part of him, like his ability to sing or his heart con—"

"Dad!"

Harold sighed. "It's who he is. He's an amazing kid—no, an amazing man. I sure as hell don't wish he was someone different."

After a long pause—unreadable emotions flashing across his face—Nevin nodded curtly. "Good."

The hallway was too small for all the churning emotions, and Colin had used up his store of nonverbal communication. "See you later, Dad!" he announced, then turned and marched away. He was grateful when Nevin followed closely.

Nevin didn't say a word as they left the office suite, and he remained silent in the elevator. He didn't even protest when Colin led them to the BMW.

"I'm sorry," Colin said as he started the engine.

"For what?"

"I, uh… my dad. Sorry you got…." Well, he wasn't sure of the right terminology. Sorry you got *involuntarily subjected* to a parent?

Nevin made an impatient little growl. "I didn't spontaneously combust, Collie. Anyway, I like him. He's not an asshole."

Figuring that was high praise, Colin grinned and shifted the car into reverse.

THE FIRST thing Colin did was head to a favorite sandwich place in Northwest. He was hungry, and although he didn't know whether Nevin had eaten lunch yet, Nevin looked like he could use a decent meal. But after Colin had circled the block for the third time, Nevin growled again. "Just fucking park the thing."

"There aren't any spots."

"Right there." Nevin pointed.

"Fire hydrant. And this isn't your car—they'll tow me."

Nevin made another noise, and Colin had to suppress a laugh. He liked seeing Nevin all prickly and annoyed. It was much better than earlier, when he looked as if his world was falling apart. Other people could look like that but not Detective Nevin Ng, the man who was usually ready to take on the world.

"Just go somewhere else, then," Nevin groused. "Before you make us both fucking dizzy going around and around."

"We're not going to eat inside. I just want to grab stuff to go."

"Then park your ass in the goddamn red zone. I'll stay here and protect your precious piece of German crap from the big, nasty tow-truck men."

That time Colin did laugh. And he followed orders too, even though he felt as if he might get struck by lightning as he pulled to the red-painted curb. He kept the keys in the ignition and didn't ask what Nevin wanted before bounding out of the car.

"You're gonna get towed," said the lushly bearded guy behind the counter.

"My passenger's a cop and swears I won't."

Laughing, the guy took Colin's order. Colin's back was to the windows, so if Nevin did have to fight anyone off, he missed it. When he hurried back outside carrying a paper bag, the car was still there. Nevin grinned at him from the passenger seat.

"Where are we going?" he asked after Colin was back in the car and had placed the deli bag on Nevin's lap.

"Picnic."

"It's fucking fifty degrees outside, Collie. And it's going to rain."

"Car picnic," Colin replied cheerfully.

He could have taken a more direct route, but instead he drove up Vista and then wound through Washington Park, eventually circling back and pulling in to a lot atop the hill. Nevin didn't comment until the engine was off. "Rose gardens?"

"Yep."

"No flowers this time of year, and the view sucks."

He was right. The rosebushes looked forlorn, and there was nothing much to see other than clouds, but Colin didn't care. Heck, he preferred it. On a nice spring or summer day, the gardens would be packed, but now they had the place to themselves. Not that he wanted to mention that intimate fact to Nevin. He pointed at the bag. "One of the sandwiches is roast beef and the other is turkey. Take your pick."

Nevin dug around for a moment before handing a paper-wrapped parcel to Colin and taking one for himself. There were chips in the bag too, and pickle spears, plus two bottles of iced tea.

"There's enough meat on this thing to choke a bear," he said as he eyed his lunch.

"Yeah, they pile it on. They bake their own bread too."

Colin had ended up with the turkey, which was fine with him. But Nevin, after taking a few bites of his own, swapped half of his sandwich for half of Colin's.

"You don't like it?" Colin asked.

"No, it's great," Nevin answered with his mouth full. "Just wanted to try yours too." He stared out the window. "Wonder if Germy will come lumbering along."

"Huh?"

"Friend. He's chief park ranger. Tends to strut around places like this like a fucking action hero, the big jackass." He said it fondly. It was the first time he'd mentioned a friend—mentioned anyone he was close to except his brother.

"Park ranger sounds like an interesting job."

Nevin snorted. "Hugging trees, dancing around with butterflies, shooting the shit with winos. Jeremy thinks he can stomp all over in his size thirteens—you could house a family of four in the man's goddamn boots—and rescue the whole fucking world. Moron."

"Right. 'Cause you're not at all interested in saving people."

Nevin shot him a quick glare.

After a few minutes of chewing and swallowing, Colin asked, "Is Jeremy a close friend?"

"I'm not fucking him."

"I wasn't fishing for your sexual history. I just wondered if he was a good friend."

"Yeah. Guess so. We work out together, go running. Catch a ball game now and then. Drink coffee. He's a good guy—the real deal, you know? You'd like him." Nevin barked a laugh. "I thought about setting you up with him."

Colin twisted in his seat to goggle at him. "Seriously? Why?"

Nevin didn't meet his eyes. "Told you. He's a good guy. Fuck, you'd drool just to look at him. Blond hair, square chin. He's got muscles on his muscles. Looks like Paul fucking Bunyan."

"He doesn't sound like my type."

"Oh, he's got a fancy private college degree too. And he's the settling-down kind. Your type."

Colin wadded up the empty sandwich paper and reached over to put it in the bag near Nevin's feet—which put him conveniently close to Nevin. "I think I prefer my men smaller," Colin purred. "And... thornier." And he was telling the truth, because Nevin's studly park-ranger friend didn't interest him at all. Nevin, though... Nevin interested him a *lot*.

He shifted back into his seat and watched as Nevin neatly folded his wrapper. Rectangle, square, rectangle, square, triangle. Then Nevin tucked the paper into the bag and brushed a few stray crumbs off his dark suit. When he turned to face Colin, Nevin's expression was opaque. "How many men have you fucked?"

"Uh... what?"

"In your life. How many men have you fucked or let fuck you? Let's be expansive in our definition, shall we? Include blowjobs. Hell, include hand jobs too. Include anyone who touched your junk or vice versa."

"Why?" Colin thought that Nevin's brain was a very twisty-turny place, full of secret passageways and hidden alleys.

"Humor me."

While he thought, Colin stared through the windshield at dark green foliage and gray flannel sky. In the summertime, everybody in town came here for wedding photos, but nobody wanted that today. He wondered where people went if they wanted outdoor wedding photos in the fall. And then he considered Nevin's question. "Does it count if we jacked off in front of each other but didn't touch?"

Nevin clicked his tongue in annoyance. "Fine."

"Okay. Then... ten."

"Ten."

"I think so. A couple guys in high school, a few in college, and a few before I met Trent." Did that sound pathetic? He wasn't a virgin by a long shot—he'd just never much wanted to play the field. "Then you," he added, smiling.

"That douche bag dumped you over three months ago. You haven't fucked anyone but me since him?"

"Nope."

Nevin shook his head. "Right, then. Ten. In like, what? Fifteen years? Colin, I usually fuck ten different people in a month."

Colin wasn't surprised by that declaration. He had friends who were that sexually active, and Colin didn't judge any of them as long as they were safe in their behavior and honest with their partners. But still, Nevin's words made his chest ache. "So I'm not experienced enough for you?" Colin spat.

Nevin surprised him by caressing Colin's thigh. "You know that's not my point. Besides, we were fucking amazing together."

"What *is* your point, then? I'm lost."

"My point is, I'm not your type."

Oh. "Are you breaking up with me? I don't think you can do that since we were never really a thing to begin with."

"No." Nevin squeezed his eyes shut, then opened them again. "I like you. Dunno why—haven't even had a real chance to play with that monster cock of yours, so it's not that. You know what? I haven't had sex with anyone since you."

That statement also made Colin's chest ache, but in a totally different way. "Why not?"

"No idea. But here's the thing. I'm never going to be what you want. What you deserve. So we can fool around a little, but—"

"What about what *you* want and deserve?"

Nevin gave his head a quick shake.

While they were talking, raindrops began to patter on the windshield and roof, and the insides of the windows were starting to steam up. Suddenly Colin wanted to be somewhere else. He turned the ignition and waited for the defogger to work.

"You can drop me off at my office," Nevin said wearily.

"No. Not yet."

He took a more direct route out of the park, ending up on Burnside heading toward downtown. But when he continued over the bridge and cut south, Nevin apparently couldn't stand the suspense any longer. "Where?" he demanded.

"Want to show you something."

As they neared the Clinton Street Theater, Nevin made one of his noises. "*Rocky Horror*'s not playing on a Monday afternoon."

"Not where we're going." Colin continued down the street for a few blocks and was happy to discover a vacant spot in front of a pale blue house with a peaked roof.

"What's this?"

"We just bought it. Well, actually we're still in escrow, but it's vacant and I know the code to get inside. Come see."

Although Nevin looked doubtful, he followed Colin up the sidewalk through the badly overgrown yard and onto a broad front porch. The splintery boards creaked ominously under their feet, but nothing gave way before they managed to get inside. Colin had already toured the place before his father made an offer. Now he stood in the front room, where layers of wallpaper hung in strips and everything reeked of cat pee. "Look around."

Nevin raised his eyebrows. Then he shrugged and started to wander. Colin stayed put, tracking Nevin's progress by the footsteps and occasional swearing. He knew what Nevin was seeing—some structural damage, outdated wiring and plumbing, a kitchen last updated in the sixties, bathrooms older than that. Water-damaged floors and ceilings. Cracked windows. Dust and grime and mouse turds....

After exploring the upstairs and then loudly announcing his refusal to go into the basement, Nevin eventually returned to Colin in the front room. "I've seen murder scenes in better condition. In fact, I'm not sure there aren't bodies in the basement. Or in that cabinet near the top of the stairs."

"Yeah," Colin agreed sadly. "It's a mess. Needs a new roof too, and a new furnace. And lead paint removal."

"If you're trying to sell me the place, you're doing a piss-poor job."

Nevin had a smudge of dirt on one cheekbone. Colin smiled and rubbed it away with his thumb. "Not trying to sell it. But what do you think of it?"

"You said yourself. A fucking mess. Location's good, but you'd have to pour in a fuck-ton of money just to make it habitable."

Colin slumped slightly. "Yeah. You're totally right."

But then Nevin grinned. "But shit, did you see that fireplace?" He pointed toward the adjoining room. "Fucking gorgeous, once the tile's cleaned and the mantel's repaired. And the upstairs windows all have leaded glass, plus the claw-foot up there is big enough even Germy could fit in. Or you and me," he added with a leer.

"It's a great tub."

"Good-sized front porch, as long as nobody falls through it. Could invite the whole fucking neighborhood for a party on that porch. And the... the fancy wooden shit around the doors and windows. They don't do that anymore. It's pretty." He turned around slowly, his head tilted to the side. "Yeah, it's a money pit, but it's got character. It'd be nice all fixed up."

Delighted, Colin threw his arms around Nevin, who was so startled he squawked. But Colin only hugged him tighter, moving them both until Nevin was sandwiched between him and the front door.

"Wha—" Nevin began.

Colin silenced him with a kiss.

However surprised Nevin might have been, he got with the program right away, pushing his hands under Colin's coat to grab handfuls of his ass. Nevin was a good kisser. No—a *great* kisser. Trent hadn't really enjoyed making out; he was a quick-peck-on-the-lips type. But Nevin put all his energy into it, as if kissing was as important as sex, as if Colin were the most delicious meal he'd ever tasted.

Then Nevin nibbled on Colin's earlobe—almost hard enough to hurt—and Colin groaned so loudly it echoed in the empty room.

"What was this all about?" asked Nevin, his breathing ragged.

"You saw."

"Saw what?"

"The value in this house. The real value, I mean." Colin let himself slump against Nevin. "Dad wants to tear down this place and the one next door—it's in bad shape too—and put up townhomes. They'll be nice townhomes. He doesn't do cheapy stuff. But they won't be... this."

"So tell him to stuff it. It's your business too, right?"

"Sort of." His father was sole owner and president of the company, but Colin was vice president. Which sounded more impressive than it was. And although Harold had increasingly been handing over the day-to-day operations, he still liked to make the big decisions, such as what property to buy and what to do with it.

"He's not going to disown you for arguing with him, Collie. If it's important to you—I was going to tell you to grow a pair, but hell, I've seen what you've grown. *Use* 'em. Tell Daddy to take a hike."

It wasn't that easy, but Colin wasn't in the mood to argue about it. He clutched Nevin instead. "I'm glad you see what I do in this house. It's not all about money."

"Money's not important when you have plenty of it," Nevin replied. But he sounded tired, not angry, and Colin remembered how lost he'd looked in Colin's office, gazing out bleakly at the gray city.

"You know that conversation we were having at the rose gardens?" Colin asked. "Well, screw it. Forget all that stuff about how many people we've slept with and whether anyone's the right type. Forget tomorrow. I could drop—" He'd almost said the wrong thing. "I could walk out of here and get splatted by a renegade TriMet driver. You're the cop—I don't have to tell you how random death can be."

"So?"

"So let's just worry about right now, right here."

With this kiss, Nevin's head thunked back against the wall, knocking loose a little shower of wallpaper and dust. He didn't seem to notice, though, and soon Colin was focused on nothing but the way Nevin filled all his senses. Touch of course—small hard body against his, strong hands on his ass, soft lips and tongue. And taste, which was a bit oniony from lunch but no less wonderful because of it. The scent of Nevin's soap—nothing fancy or expensive; probably Ivory or something similar, purchased from the grocery store. And the sound of Nevin making sexy little whimpers and sexier full-throated moans. Colin's body vibrated like a tuning fork in response. He even opened his eyes to see what he could focus on at such close range—velvety skin and thick sable hair, both sprinkled with tiny pieces of falling-down house.

If they kissed long enough, Colin might finally understand this fierce, complicated man.

But he gradually became aware that he was pressing his groin rhythmically against Nevin's, Nevin was thrusting right back, and they were both in danger of coming in their pants. Which was a shame when they could have more skin-to-skin contact.

Colin moved his mouth to suck on the tight cord of Nevin's neck, leaving Nevin free to utter breathy pleas. It was funny. Ordinarily Nevin swore more than a Martin Scorsese film. But when he and Colin were having sex, the f-bombs disappeared, replaced by needy gasps. Those noises made Colin feel powerful.

Spurred by hormones and wickedness, Colin took a step back, shrugged out of his coat, and spread it on the floor. He turned back to Nevin. "Strip."

Nevin's eyes went wide. He glanced at the windows, which were covered by thin, ratty curtains. Not the best privacy, he was likely concluding, but at least the house was set back from the street. And the front room was only dimly lit by faint light from the next room.

"We'll ruin your coat," Nevin said, but he was already taking off his own.

"I'll buy another. This one is *so* last year anyway." Colin winked.

It took time for Nevin to peel off his layers of clothing, in part because his hands shook a bit. Eventually he was bare, his cock standing erect and his chest visibly heaving. He was a work of art.

Colin gestured at the coat. "Lie down."

Nevin positioned himself on his back with his legs spread invitingly and his elbows propping his upper body.

"Jesus," Colin breathed. When the realization of his situation hit him, he had to steady himself against a wall. It was early afternoon, and he was in a decrepit house he didn't quite own, ogling a naked police detective.

Nevin grinned up at him. "Yeah. I get that a lot."

Laughter broke enough of the tension for Colin to steady himself. He stripped quickly, throwing his clothing aside and not caring how dirty it got. But when he kicked off one of his shoes, it went flying like a missile and collided with a spindly little table abandoned at the edge of the room. The table fell over with a crash, mostly disintegrating on impact, and Colin started to giggle. He was still chuckling after he'd removed the other shoe—more carefully—and his socks, and then laid himself full-length atop Nevin.

"What's so funny?" Nevin asked as he trailed slender fingers down the crease of Colin's ass.

Colin blew into Nevin's ear before answering. "Buffy."

"What?"

"The first time she and Spike had sex was in an abandoned house, and the sex was so… violently passionate that they destroyed the place."

Nevin was squinting at him. "What are you talking about?"

"*Buffy the Vampire Slayer*. You know, the TV series. You never watched it?"

"No."

Colin made a mental note to introduce Nevin to the singalong episode. Then he forgot all about Buffy, Spike, and anything non-Nevin-related as Nevin kissed him again.

They didn't have rubbers or lube. No problem, because Colin mostly wanted to run his tongue over every inch of Nevin's body. And that's what he did, paying special attention to the hard little nipples and the creases where legs met torso. He sucked on all ten of Nevin's fingers, licked his collarbones, and bent his legs so he could get at the backs of his knees. The results were amazing. Nevin squirmed and begged and grabbed at whatever parts of Colin he could reach. Then Colin scraped his teeth ever so lightly against Nevin's balls and lapped gently at the delicate skin behind them. But when he poked—just a bit—at the puckered opening and began to fist Nevin's hot, hard cock, Nevin *howled*. Seconds later his spend splattered Colin's hand.

Colin's cock was heavy between his legs, untouched and neglected, yet his triumph in making Nevin fall apart was almost as good as an orgasm. Almost. Colin didn't protest when Nevin tugged at him, urging him to scoot up Nevin's body. Using Nevin's come to ease the slide, Colin rocked his hips into the crook of Nevin's hip. There wasn't a lot of friction, but Nevin was playing with his ass again, plus Colin felt Nevin's sticky, softening cock against his hip. Those things, added to Nevin's whispered encouragements—"That's right, baby. Just like that. Feels good."—were enough to tighten Colin's body and send him spinning over the edge.

A few moments later, Colin lay beside him, partly on the coat but mostly on the hard floor. His heated body had begun to cool in the chilly room. He started to laugh again.

"More *Buffy?*" Nevin asked, tousling Colin's hair.

"I was just thinking that this is the messiest sex I've ever had."

"Is that a bad thing?"

"No. Not at all." It was, Colin thought, pretty darn good.

CHAPTER FOURTEEN

THEY WASHED up before they left Colin's wreck of a house, but the effort was mostly futile. The place only had cold running water, and they didn't have so much as a napkin to dry themselves. Shivering and still fairly dirty, they got back into their clothes. Colin had attempted to tame his hair with his fingers, without much success, and his coat was a goner. He hadn't even tried to put his bow tie back on and shoved it in a pocket instead.

But all those lovely postfucking hormones thrummed through Nevin's body, and he didn't want to give Colin up just yet. "Coffee?" he asked as they walked to the door.

Colin couldn't seem to stop grinning. He looked like a naughty schoolboy. "Sure."

"I know a place on Belmont. Take us there."

During the short drive, Nevin had misgivings. Jeremy probably wouldn't be at P-Town, because he was working. But Rhoda likely would, and Nevin wasn't in the mood to explain Colin. Especially since Rhoda was bright enough to know the moment she saw them what they'd been up to. Hell, Colin's fair skin was still flushed, and Nevin's lips felt kiss-swollen. By the time he decided to maybe route them elsewhere, however, Colin had pulled into a spot directly in front of P-Town. Nevin couldn't think of a way to redirect him without being a twat, so he girded his loins and together they walked into the coffeehouse.

Not too many customers, and no sign of the owner. Nevin heaved a tiny sigh of relief.

"Hey, Ptolemy," he said to the barista. "Where's Rhoda?"

Ptolemy was wearing elaborate eye makeup that reminded Nevin of ancient Egypt, but the flannel-and-jeans outfit looked more like nineties grunge. "Parker is having an existential crisis. Again. Rhoda drove up to spend a couple of days with him."

"Sorry to hear that." Which was true despite his relief that he wouldn't be dealing with Rhoda today. "The usual for me. And whatever he's having."

Those Osiris eyes widened. Shock at Nevin showing up with someone who wasn't Jeremy? Surprise at Colin's obvious postcopulatory state? Or interest in Colin himself, who looked good enough to eat with a spoon? Nevin couldn't tell.

Colin had been swiveling his head, taking in the atmosphere and décor. Judging from his grin, he liked P-Town. "Do you have herbal tea?" he asked Ptolemy.

"Of course." Ptolemy handed him a laminated list and waited patiently for Colin to read it.

"Is the peppermint caffeine-free?"

"Yes. Nevin's having enough caffeine for the both of you, huh?"

"Probably."

Once Nevin had his double espresso and Colin had a ceramic pot, large mug, and tea bag, they picked a table in the back, next to the tiny stage.

"You're a regular here?" Colin asked as he sat down.

"Yeah. It's Germy's place, really—he lives a couple blocks away— but I come pretty often." If he was honest, at some point P-Town had become his place too. It was comfortable and quirky, and Rhoda had a knack for cultivating customers who were interesting and… good. Some of the regulars were queer and some weren't. They ranged from teenage to geriatric. A few had bank accounts cushier than Colin's, a few looked like they lived out of shopping carts, and the rest were somewhere in between. A lot of them had skin a lot darker or features a lot less European than Nevin's. And a couple of them—like one of the regular musicians, a beautiful man with long pale hair—were definitely a little… odd. But Rhoda's regulars were all decent people.

And Colin fit right in.

"The artwork here is really interesting," Colin said while he waited for his tea to steep. "I like that one best." He pointed at a painting of a unicorn, Bigfoot, a wolf, and a merman playing cards.

"It's your style," Nevin said.

"What's your style?"

Nevin thought about the bad sketches on his walls at home— castles, cottages, and cars—and shrugged. "Art's not really my thing."

"Huh."

"*Huh*? What's that supposed to mean?"

"Nothing. Except I've seen you drawing in that notebook you carry. And sometimes you trace shapes with your finger on tabletops."

Nevin clenched his treacherous hands into fists and put them on his lap. "I don't—"

"You totally do. You're not the only one who can notice details, Detective."

"Asshole," Nevin muttered, then scowled when Colin laughed. "What?"

"Swearwords are like terms of endearment from you."

Nevin almost cussed at him again but stopped himself with a mouthful of espresso. Looking smug, Colin fished the tea bag from his mug, set it on a saucer, and took a cautious sip. "Mmm."

"Why are you drinking… lawn clippings?"

"Peppermint."

"Yeah, but why?"

Colin lost his grin. "I, uh, try to avoid too much caffeine. I do a morning coffee, sometimes some iced tea, but that's about it."

"Why?"

Instead of answering, Colin took another sip. Then he gazed around the room again, eventually taking a moment to stare at two men sitting several tables away. One of them was reading a paperback, while the other was writing in a notebook. Colin leaned closer and dropped his voice to a whisper. "That guy looks just like Tab Hunter."

"Who?"

"Tab Hunter. The actor."

"Never heard of him."

Sometimes Colin looked at him as if Nevin had just landed from another planet, but right now Colin just seemed sad. "He was big in the fifties. My mom told me he was her first heartthrob. She was, like, eight. Maybe we could watch one of his movies together. *Damn Yankees*, I think."

"Collie, we can't—"

Colin put up a hand. "Don't. I don't know why you've convinced yourself you can't do a relationship, but whatever. I'm not expecting one. I'm not asking you to make any promises. Sleep around if you want— just don't tell me about it. But we have a good time together, right? So why can't we do that? For a little while, at least."

It was an appealing offer. He'd had plenty of good fucks in his life, but none of those people made him feel the way Colin did. Hell, he'd want to hang out with Colin even if they didn't have sex—though Christ almighty, the sex was good. But the more time they spent together, the harder it would be when they stopped.

"You need to move on from Trent the douche and find your One True Love."

"Fuck my one true love!" Colin yelled loud enough to make the movie star guy and his friend turn to look. But he didn't seem to care. "I'd rather have a wild and reckless fling. Or, I don't know. Maybe a friend with benefits. I *like* you, Nevin."

Nobody liked him. Okay, that wasn't true. Jeremy Cox did, but then that ox liked everyone. Ford did, but back when the world was a cruel, empty place, all they'd had was each other. That leaves a mark heavy enough to withstand time and shitheadedness. There were a few other people who could stand Nevin's company for short periods. But here was Colin Westwood with his bow ties and his earnest face and his fucking BMW, and he wanted Nevin's company.

Maybe he was crazy.

Nevin shot back the rest of his espresso and set the cup on the table hard. "Ford? I met him when we were in the same foster home."

"Yeah?" Colin replied carefully.

"It was the last one for both of us because we hit eighteen. Wasn't a bad place. Decent bed and food, and the foster parents stayed out of our hair as long as we did what we were supposed to." He set his jaw but had to loosen it to say the rest. "That was my fifteenth placement." He hadn't known the precise number until a few years earlier, when he'd used his connections to gain access to his old records. He'd spent a weekend going through the files and reading the social workers' notes, and he'd gotten so drunk he had to call in sick to work on Monday.

"What happened to your parents?" asked Colin.

"Father wasn't anything but a sperm donor. Mother…. That bitch left me alone in a shithole apartment when I was three. Probably went to score crack or turn a trick. She must have got lost on the way, 'cause she never came back."

Colin didn't envelop him in a sloppy hug or say he was sorry. He didn't spout platitudes, or get weepy, or ask stupidass questions. What he did was stare for a second or two and then say, "That's fucked-up."

And somehow that was the perfect response. Nevin threw his head back and laughed. "You're all right, Bow Tie. You really are."

"Does that mean we can fling?"

"I suppose it fucking does."

That made Colin leap from his chair and attack Nevin with a bear hug.

NEVIN SPENT Wednesday morning at an adult day care center. In theory he was there to chat with the staff, but he knew that particular facility well and the employees were some of the best he'd seen. What he really did during his visit was play Go Fish with Alzheimer's patients. Then a couple of women with therapy dogs came by, and Nevin stuck around to watch the clients pet golden retrievers. He saw that even the more confused and distressed people relaxed as they stroked the clean fur, and that reminded him of Legolas. Animals were a little magic, sucking away the pain and replacing it with calm. Some people were like that too.

He was about to swing back to the office and maybe stop for lunch along the way when a call came through about an elderly woman in distress. He diverted his route to the address in Northeast, where he was beckoned to the side door of a modest house by a woman in her late twenties. "It's Gram," she said, flustered. "She thinks someone's stealing from her, but nobody is. She's just confused." The woman wore old jeans and a sweatshirt, and her hair was in a messy ponytail.

"I'd like to talk to her, please. What's her name?"

"Shirley Gerhard. But she won't make any sense." She led him through the kitchen and living room, where a toddler was watching TV, and down a dark hallway. The interior of the house was cramped—with old furniture shoved into rooms that were too small—but it was reasonably clean. Toys lay scattered across the floor and the walls looked a bit grubby, but that wasn't unusual in a home with at least one small child. Nevin certainly didn't see anything constituting a health hazard.

Mrs. Gerhard sat in an overstuffed armchair in the master bedroom. Beside her, a plastic-and-metal TV tray held several pill bottles, a remote control, a glass of water, and a pair of eyeglasses; a small television perched on the dresser. She wore a puffy bathrobe and a scarf over her hair. "Who are you?" she demanded, ignoring her granddaughter completely.

"Detective Ng from the Portland Police Bureau."

"You're not a policeman."

He'd been through this before. He wasn't sure what made people question him—his lack of uniform, his height, his ethnicity. Whatever the cause, he knew what to do. He dug out his badge and held it so she could peer at it.

"I called you people hours ago."

"I'm sorry, Mrs. Gerhard. But I'm here now. Can you tell me what your complaint is?" To show he was earnest, he pulled out his notebook and pen.

Mrs. Gerhard waved impatiently at her granddaughter. "You can go now."

The young woman shot Nevin a long-suffering look, then left the room.

"I've been telling her about this for months," said Mrs. Gerhard, "but she doesn't listen. That girl thinks she knows everything. Takes after her father, and he was dumb as a rock and twice as hardheaded."

Nevin nodded, not letting his sympathy for the granddaughter show. It couldn't be easy, caring for an elderly relative as well as a young child. A lot of people wouldn't even try. "What's the problem, ma'am?"

"Someone's been stealing my things. That's the problem!"

He ended up fetching a chair from the kitchen and listening for almost two hours while she told him her theories about people taking her jewelry and other belongings. Mostly she blamed the neighbors and her granddaughter's friends. She gave her opinions on all these people and their habits, devolving often to discuss her long-dead husband, who was apparently the next best thing to a saint.

When she'd exhausted herself enough to run out of words, Nevin closed his notebook and stood. "Thank you for such a thorough report. I'm going to do everything I can to help the situation."

She patted his arm with a shaky hand. "Thank you, Detective. You're a good boy. I bet your mother is very proud of you."

"Yes, ma'am," he lied.

In the kitchen, the granddaughter was chopping vegetables while the toddler played with a set of plastic cups on the floor. "Nobody stole her jewelry," she said wearily. "That stuff was sold years ago."

"I understand."

"And my grandfather? He was a drunk. He used to beat her and my mom." She dropped a handful of sliced carrots into a pot.

"Death and decades smooth over a lot of faults."

She snorted. "I guess so. She used to be this strong, amazing lady, you know? Pretty much raised me. And now...."

"Has she been diagnosed with dementia?"

"No. I mean, she's got a lot of health issues, but this is new."

Nevin pulled some cards from the collection in his pocket and set them on the counter near the cutting board. "Talk to her doctor right away. It could just be a reaction to some of her meds, and if they adjust those, you might see an improvement. One of these cards is for a respite-care group—give them a call. They can find ways to give you a little break now and then."

She didn't stop chopping—a potato this time—but when she glanced at Nevin, she smiled gratefully. "I try really hard."

"I can tell. You're taking good care of your family. But you need to take care of yourself too."

She sniffled and nodded.

"Another thing that group can help you with is finding some companionship for your grandmother. You're really busy, and she's probably a little lonely. Sometimes people just need a new set of ears to listen to them."

"She hardly ever gets out," she said. "And she's outlived her friends."

Nevin briefly thought of Roger Grey. "This group can help. I work with them a lot. I've left you my card too—call me if you need help."

She put down the knife and wiped her hands on a towel. "Thank you, Detective. I know you have lots of really important things to worry about, and—"

"You and your grandmother *are* important. Helping you is my job."

She walked him to the door and then surprised him with a quick hug. "Thank you," she said when she pulled back. She swiped her eyes with the back of her hand. "Really, thank you so much."

"You take care."

Sitting in Julie, he made a few quick notes. Real ones instead of the muscle cars he'd been sketching while Mrs. Gerhard spoke. He'd have to do a little paperwork on this case; maybe he'd phone the granddaughter in a week or so to see how things were going. Police calls like this one could be frustrating, but they kept him going. For a couple of hours, an old lady had received a willing audience, and maybe her restless mind was comforted. Her granddaughter certainly was. If the respite group could help, the whole family would benefit.

But this story wouldn't have a happy ending, no matter what he did. Mrs. Gerhard wasn't going to miraculously return to her tough, active self. Her granddaughter would still be faced with the painful job of caring for her family while watching a loved one fade. That fuckface Mr. Gerhard would rest peacefully in his grave, absolved of effort or blame by the final benefit of death.

Then the thought that was never allowed entered Nevin's head, and this time he couldn't summon the strength to push it away. What would become of him when he grew old? He refused to rot in some institution—he'd sooner put a bullet in his brain. Would he end up like Roger Grey, visited by pitying young charity volunteers, or like Mrs. Ruskin, murdered for fuck knew why? Maybe Colin was right and it would all end much sooner than that, Nevin's brains splattered on the asphalt.

Jesus H. Christ. What kind of life were you living if the best possible ending involved getting flattened under the Number 8 bus?

Growling, Nevin pulled out his phone and began to text.

CHAPTER FIFTEEN

DINNER TONIGHT?

The phone didn't give the identity of the person who'd texted him, so it wasn't anyone in his contacts. It could be a scam or wrong number. But as Colin sat in his office, staring at the screen, his heart did a little dance.

Is this a fling dinner? he texted back.

It's fucking steak and potatoes, Bow Tie. You in?

Colin smiled so widely his face hurt.

A few minutes later, he knocked on his father's door. "Dad?" he called.

"Come in."

His father sat in one of the leather armchairs, a golfing magazine in his lap. "What's up?"

Trying hard not to fidget like a schoolboy, Colin said, "I'm heading out early today."

"Sure. I was thinking of doing the same but haven't gathered the energy. You have plans?"

"Dinner. Um, dinner date, actually."

His dad frowned slightly. "Your mother didn't set you up with someone again, did she?"

"Believe it or not, I found this one by myself. Remember that detective?"

"Really?" his father chuckled. "Police interrogations. There's a way of finding romance I never thought of when I was single."

Remembering what Monday's "interrogation" session had become—his coat was currently at the dry cleaner's—Colin blushed. "Yeah. Nevin is… interesting." Well, that was a lame way to describe a beautiful, complicated man. "But actually, I didn't come here to talk about my love life."

His dad looked relieved. When Colin was nine and started asking questions, his father had been the one to explain the birds and the bees. He'd done so gamely, giving Colin the basics on both straight and gay sex, which Colin had always figured more than fulfilled parental duties.

But those conversations had been awkward, and when Colin became old enough to date, his dad mostly pretended not to notice. He'd done the same with Miranda, so it had nothing to do with Colin's sexual orientation. It was just not a subject he wanted to think about.

Colin took a deep breath. "You know those houses on Twenty-Seventh?"

"Sure."

"I don't think we should tear them down."

"We've talked about—"

"Not really." Colin sat in the other armchair and leaned forward. "I mentioned it, but you didn't listen. I know we'd make a lot bigger profit if we put up townhomes. But Dad, there's a cost. We're killing the character of these neighborhoods."

His father moved his magazine to the armrest, which Colin supposed was a good thing. It meant his father was paying attention. "Two houses won't make a difference," his dad said.

"Two houses here, another one there. How many have we already demolished? And that's just us. I know there are plenty of other companies doing the same."

"Exactly! We're just a drop in the bucket, and we're making sound business decisions."

"Business decisions." Colin stood, walked to the big window, and gazed out. "What about decisions of the heart? What about doing what's right instead of what will make our bank accounts fatter?" Huh. Staring out a window made it easier to say hard things. Nevin had been onto something.

"Colin—"

But Colin spun around to face him. "Really, Dad. What do we need that we don't already have? Most people have way less money than we do, and they manage just fine. I don't need a bigger apartment or a newer car or more... more stuff."

For a moment, his father silently worked his jaw. Everyone said that Colin looked just like him, and now Colin wondered if that was how *he* appeared when he was angry, with a line between his eyebrows and spots of color on his cheeks. Still, his dad's voice was measured when he finally spoke. "What happens when I'm gone, Col?"

Colin blinked. "What?"

"I'm sixty-eight years old. And healthy, or so my doctor says. Maybe I'll live to see a hundred, or maybe I'll wake up one day with cancer eating my pancreas."

Colin winced. His father's best friend had died of pancreatic cancer three years earlier. "I don't—"

"My point is that I'm mortal. And so is your mother, although I'm not sure she'd admit it. I just want to make sure that if something *does* happen to us, you're taken care of."

It was tempting to swear like Nevin, but Colin just shook his head. "I can take care of myself."

"Now, yes. But what if you… if you get sick again? Insurance goes only so far, and Miranda has herself and Hannah to worry about."

"I'm not fragile! And even if I was…." Colin chewed on his lip and tried to find the right words. "Mrs. Ruskin died and they didn't even have a funeral. Roger Grey—well, I don't know what they'll do with his body when they're done with the investigation. And then they're gone and mostly forgotten, and it's pretty much like they've never lived at all."

His dad stood and walked over. Quietly he said, "You're not like them. We love you. A *lot* of people love you."

"I know. But that's not my point. A hundred years from now, do you think anyone's going to be walking around inside their Westwood Development townhome, thinking *I sure am glad they built this house*? Is anyone going to point at one of our places from… from their hover car and say, 'Wow, look at that old beauty!'"

"We're providing homes to people *now*."

"Sure. But there are a lot of ways to do that. I was in one of those houses this week, and I know it's a dump. But for a century, people have been living there. Raising their families there." *Making love there.* "It's like after all of that, the house has grown… a little bit of a soul. There's no soul in those things we build. But this house has one, and with some rehab we could nurture it. Restore it. Keep it alive." His voice cracked on the final word.

His dad regarded him for a long time before setting a hand on Colin's shoulder. "I had no idea this was so important to you."

Colin barked a laugh. "Me either."

"I think I get it. You want to matter."

That was it, more or less. Colin nodded.

"You already do matter, to your mother and me, and to Miranda and Hannah and your friends."

"I know."

It was his father's turn to nod. "But you want something... bigger. More lasting. You want to make a mark in the world. I understand that too." He puffed out a noisy breath. "Tell you what. Get some estimates on those houses. We'll see if we can make it work."

Colin drew him into a hug. "We'll make it work," he promised.

LEGOLAS HAD obviously looked forward to an evening of cuddling on the couch, and he meowed his disapproval when Colin changed into dress pants and a silk floral-patterned shirt instead of comfy sweats.

"Sorry, bud. Sexy cop trumps cat, at least for a few hours. C'mon, you've met him. Do you blame me?" But he poured a little extra kibble into Leg's dish to compensate.

Nevin's restaurant choice was an interesting one. With valet parking, tuxedoed waiters, and a dark wood-and-brick interior, it had been serving meat to Portland's well-heeled since before Colin's father was born. It had been one of his grandfather's favorites, a place the family went to celebrate birthdays and Father's Days. Colin wouldn't have guessed Nevin would pick it—but then Nevin was full of surprises.

Julie was in the parking lot when Colin turned in. In his eagerness to get to Nevin, he practically threw the key at the poor valet. But it turned out his hurry was worthwhile, because Nevin was stunning in a black suit, royal blue shirt, and canary tie.

"Wow," said Colin, unable to tear his gaze away. Nevin tried unsuccessfully to hide a pleased smile.

"Don't look half-bad yourself," Nevin said as Colin took his seat. "But no bow tie."

"I like to mix things up now and then."

They perused the menu in silence. The waiter, who must have been psychic, appeared to take their order at the precise moment they were ready. Then he disappeared.

"Is there an occasion?" Colin asked. On the table, a candle flickered, sending warm light and shadows across Nevin's face.

"I was hungry."

"Well, I have something to celebrate."

"Yeah?"

Colin took a sip of water. "I grew a pair today. Or, well, I used my pair, just like you advised me to. I told Dad we needed to renovate those houses."

"How'd he take it?"

"Well. We're going to give it a go."

Nevin raised his water in a toast. "Way to go, Collie."

They clinked glasses. "But it's more than that. I think I had a genuine epiphany today."

"Did it hurt?"

God, Colin could never get enough of that sharp white smile. "A little. But it hurt so good."

"Know what that's like," Nevin responded, throwing in a leer in case Colin didn't catch his drift. Then Nevin's expression turned more serious. "So what realization was handed to you by the gods?"

"I know what I want to be when I grow up. I want to find houses like the one we visited, and I want to fix them up. Preserve their character. Give them a heartbeat." Jesus, yes. Saying it out loud like that, he knew that was *exactly* what he wanted to do. And sure, maybe it wasn't what he dreamed of when he was a teenager standing on stage and belting out the theme from *Oklahoma!* But that was okay, because he wasn't a teenager anymore.

He leaned over the table and dropped his voice. "I want to take something that nobody's valued properly and make it feel loved."

Colin expected Nevin to go all prickly at that, to sneer and swear and pull away. Instead Nevin's face softened, the sharp planes turning young and his eyes filling with wonder. "You could do that, couldn't you?"

"I could."

Neither of them spoke for a time after that, but it wasn't an uncomfortable silence. Nevin kept staring as if Colin were an amazing discovery, and Colin felt warm and strong.

They'd each ordered a glass of pinot noir, which arrived along with their order of onion rings. Colin's cardiologist would probably have had a coronary if he'd heard Colin order his meal. But red wine was supposed to be good for the heart, right?

"Fuck, these are even better than I remembered," Nevin said after polishing off a couple of the onion rings.

"So… you come here often?"

Nevin snorted. "Smooth, Bow Tie. And no. Haven't been here in years." He ate another two onion rings, pushed the rest in Colin's direction, and wiped his hands on a napkin. "I'd heard about this place somehow. Passed it now and then. But when I was a kid, it was a big fucking deal when I went to Mickey D's. I sure as hell never came in here. I bet you did."

Colin shrugged. "Sometimes."

"Figured. I used to think, *When I can go in there and order their biggest steak, that's when I'll know I've made it.* But I never really expected it to happen. It was a dream, right?"

"Like getting swooped from an ivory tower by Prince Charming," Colin replied, smiling.

"Yeah. So I'd just turned twenty-one, and Ford and I were sharing this skanky apartment out on Powell. We weren't there much, each of us busting our ass at a couple shitty jobs, and me going to community college. I got my associates degree, but it was… I didn't go to the ceremony because Ford had to work, and it wasn't like anyone else gave a fuck. I was feeling sorry for myself, Collie, and that's not a pretty sight."

"I doubt that. I bet you do even self-pity attractively."

Lightening the mood a bit was a good choice, because instead of shutting down, Nevin shook his head in bemusement. But he also continued his story. "Graduation day I had to pull a shift cleaning the machinery at a potato salad plant. Took the bus home, went to Safeway, and bought a case of Coors 'cause it was on sale. I planned to get sloshed." He lifted his wineglass and drained it.

"And?" Colin prompted.

"I walked into our apartment, and there was Ford in a suit and the biggest shit-eating grin you've ever seen. 'Put that on,' he says, and points to another suit hanging over the back of a chair.

"'What the fuck?' I asked, because neither of us owned anything but jeans, and we never needed better than that.

"He tells me we're going out to dinner and won't say anything else. He'd borrowed the suits from some guys at work. Mine didn't fit well, but it wasn't awful. The smug bastard had borrowed someone's car too. He drove us here and made sure I ordered wine, appetizers, fucking half a cow—everything. He'd been saving up two *years* to celebrate my graduation, the son of a bitch."

"Was it a good meal?" asked Colin, pretending not to notice the extra moisture in Nevin's eyes.

"Best fucking meal I'd ever had."

"Your brother loves you."

Nevin managed a grin. "Yeah, he does. Stupid asshole." He toyed with the empty wineglass, spinning the stem between finger and thumb. "I've been able to afford restaurants like this for a while now, but that was the last time I came here."

"I'm glad you invited me."

They stuck with lighter conversation over the rest of the meal. Nevin talked about how he'd found Julie and fallen in love with her, and Colin told him about a local architect who was being featured in all the big-time magazines for his innovative designs. "I wonder if he'd be willing to design townhomes," Colin mused. "When it doesn't involve tearing down old houses, that is."

"Sounds as if you're already changing your job description."

"Just feeling my way around." It felt good, but not as wonderful as the full sensation in his chest every time Nevin smiled at him.

When the food was gone, they lingered over coffee—decaf for Colin—until he took Nevin's hand. "Come over to my place?"

"Yeah. That'd be nice."

Nevin got there first, of course, and Colin grinned to find Julie parked in a respectable, legal spot and Nevin leaning on the wall near the building entrance. "You drive like an old lady," Nevin said.

"Some of us aren't magically immune to tickets."

Legolas ignored Colin and greeted Nevin like a long-lost love, meowing loudly and winding between his legs. "He's getting fur all over your suit," Colin warned.

But Nevin bent down and rubbed behind Leg's ears and under his chin. When he stood up again, he had a weird expression—like a kid who was going to eat lima beans even though he thought it might kill him. "We're not fu—having sex tonight."

"Um, okay. Did I do something wrong?"

"You, Collie, have done everything absolutely fucking right. Which is why tonight we're making like monks."

It took Colin a moment, but then he got it. "You want to try it out. A date with romance, but that's all."

Nevin gave a tight little nod. "I know I can rock your world in the bedroom—"

"Or on the floor."

"—or over the goddamn kitchen counter. Let's see if I can pull off just being a… companion. For a few hours."

Colin already knew Nevin could do that, but he smiled. "You can pick the movie."

Again, Nevin surprised him with his choice. Colin expected he'd opt for something gritty and noir, but instead, after careful consideration, Nevin handed him a musical. *"Singin' in the Rain?"* Colin asked.

"You look a little like him." Nevin pointed to the photo of Gene Kelly on the case.

And Colin couldn't help it—he gave Nevin a kiss on the cheek. Then he moved his head back a little. "Was that okay under tonight's rules?"

Nevin seemed to consider the question carefully. "Yeah. Lips allowed on faces only, and no touching below the waist."

"Wow. Those monks have it tough."

They took off their suit coats and shoes, and Colin brewed an espresso for Nevin and fetched an herbal iced tea for himself. Then they cuddled up on the couch with Leg in Nevin's lap and watched the movie. Afterward they made out a little but never went past first base.

It was the best evening Colin had had in years.

CHAPTER SIXTEEN

IT WAS the best evening Nevin had experienced in years, even though all he and Colin did was eat and snuggle. And pet the damned cat. Nevin badly wanted to spend the night, to feel Colin's bare body against his own, but he knew he'd never keep his vow of celibacy if he did. So when the movie ended, he dislodged Legolas from his lap, stood, and stretched.

Colin walked him to the door and asked, "Are you free this weekend?" He bit his lip as he waited for the answer.

Nevin reached up to smooth the indentation with his thumb. "Yeah." Fuck. He was making a date several days in advance and yet wasn't bleeding from his ears.

"Good. I'll call and we'll figure something out. Thanks for dinner. And for… this." Colin waved toward the couch.

"Guess it's time I grew a pair too."

They kissed sweetly before he left.

On the way home, he caught himself humming the "Good Morning" song from that fucking movie.

His pants and jacket were liberally dusted with orange and white hairs, so when he got home, he stripped and left the suit by the front door and put the rest of his clothes in the hamper. He should have gone straight to sleep because it was getting late and he had plenty of work to do in the morning. But he still had the delicious taste of Colin on his tongue, the scent of him in his nostrils, the feel of him on his fingertips. When he finally went into the bathroom to brush his teeth, he caught sight of himself in the mirror.

He ran a finger down the middle of his chest, tracing the same path as Colin's scar. His nipples tightened immediately, as did all his skin from toes to scalp, and his cock filled so quickly he felt light-headed. In the reflection, he watched his hand move across his chest and imagined it was Colin's hand—bigger, paler, softer.

He startled himself by groaning.

"Screw this," he said and ran, bare-assed, for his phone.

No more monks, he texted. *We've proved the point.*

The answer came quickly. *Oh thank God.*

As a cop, he knew better than to send dick pics to anyone under any circumstances, and he wasn't going to encourage Colin to violate that rule either. Fine. They both had functional imaginations. *Strip.*

Been there done that.

Holy shit. Nevin pictured Colin spread-eagled on his bed, his white skin and sandy hair glowing in the mellow light of the bedside lamp, his porn star cock firm and heavy against his belly. Texting became too difficult for Nevin's trembling hands. He called Colin instead. "Are you in bed?" he asked as soon as the call connected.

"Yes."

"Put your cell on speaker."

While Colin apparently obeyed, Nevin did the same with his. Then, with the bedroom lights off, he set the phone on the nightstand and lay back on his mattress.

"Nev?"

"I'm here." He felt so heavy with need that he wondered whether he could come from the sound of Colin's voice alone. He'd been a horny teenager—no surprise there—sometimes jacking off six or seven times a day. Hell, he still engaged in hand-to-gland combat often, even when he was getting laid regularly. But like a lot of his sex with partners, most of his wanking was just scratching an itch. Not with Colin, though. God, not with Colin. In person or over AT&T's lines, sex with Colin was a religious experience. If Nevin could have melted through Colin's skin, could have wrapped himself around Colin's heart just to feel it beating, he would have.

"What's wrong with me?" Nevin whispered.

"Nevin?" Now Colin sounded alarmed, which is not how Nevin wanted him.

"Just getting myself a little worked up. Where's your hand, Collie?"

"Anywhere you want it."

That was much better. "Play with your nipples. Pinch 'em. Flick your thumb over 'em." As he spoke, Nevin followed his own commands. "How does it feel?"

"Um... good. I've never had phone sex before. I don't think I'm any good—"

"You're doing just fine." Nevin wasn't lying. At this point, though, Colin could be reciting the Criminal Code of Oregon and that would be plenty to get Nevin off. "What're we doing next with our hands?"

After a brief pause, Colin's voice came back a little throatier. "Abs. You have great abs, Nev. Just… feel those muscles."

Nevin did, the ridges hard under smooth skin. Colin was a little softer there. "You feel like warm velvet," Nevin said. His mouth was dry, and he wished he had water within reach.

"Oh, God. I want…. Cup your balls."

"They're heavy." Nevin gently tugged and squeezed the sensitive flesh. He heard Colin breathing, which ironically made it harder for Nevin to work his own lungs. "You've got a free hand. What are you—"

"Nipples. I have really sensitive nipples."

Fuck. Nevin followed suit, but while his right palm continued to roll his ball sack, his left moved down his belly to his dick. He didn't want to leave Colin behind. "Put a hand on your shaft. You ready for that?"

"Definitely ready," Colin replied with a slight hitch.

"Feel how big it is. How solid it feels." Nevin shifted his foreskin up and down over the swollen head. Colin's cock would feel different from his, a little longer and a lot girthier.

"Nev? I can't believe I'm saying this out loud…. I'm going to put two fingers in my mouth and suck on them. Make them nice and wet."

Nevin tried to answer, but nothing came out except an embarrassing whine. He stuck fingers in his mouth to shut himself up. But he heard Colin *slurp*, the most erotic, dirty sound imaginable, and Nevin's cock pulsed in his fist. "Moving along," he managed to choke out.

Colin laughed. That was sexy too, and Nevin almost sobbed with the desire to see him and hold him. When had that happened? Craving not just a fuck, not even physical contact for its own sake, but desiring a particular body. A very *specific* person. And knowing that no other human being on the planet, male or female, would fill his need.

This ain't just physical, said a voice in his head. A cop voice that wouldn't listen to arguments. *Collie Westwood's squirmed into your heart. That heart's not as fucking hard as you pretended, is it?*

A particularly rough tug on his cock shut the voice up. But not, he feared, for long. Fucking. That's what he needed to concentrate on. "Slide those fingers inside yourself," he coaxed. "You feel so tight, baby. So hot."

"God."

Good. Now Colin was whining too.

From that point on, the best either of them could manage were a few garbled syllables and a lot of grunting and panting. "Close," Nevin rasped. His bedsprings squeaked as he pumped his dick and probed himself, and although he knew his body well, he pretended it was Colin's. It was, goddammit. It was all Colin's.

"N-no monks next time."

"Okay," Colin agreed breathlessly.

"N-next time... I want... mmm... want...." His brain was so close to short-circuiting that he could see the fucking sparks. "I want y-you in m-meee."

Colin's answer sounded like agreement.

A few more seconds, a few more strokes, and Nevin was spiraling outward—and Colin was there with him, despite being across the river in his sweet, cozy loft instead of in Nevin's arms. But even as Nevin floated back to reality, his nerves thrumming and his skin sticky, he knew that whatever happened from now on, some part of Colin would always be with him.

"BUSY NIGHT?" Frankl asked as he plopped into a chair across from Nevin's desk on Thursday morning.

Nevin rubbed his face. "Did you walk all the way down the hall just to fuck with me? 'Cause an old bastard like you, I figure you'd just do a phone call instead."

Frankl didn't take the bait, but then he rarely did. Sober as a judge, he was the kind of cop who refused free coffee, even when he worked a beat. Nevin's bullshit bounced right off him. Some of the gorillas called him Saint Frankl behind his back.

"Believe it or not, Detective Ng, I don't spend my waking hours thinking of ways to get under your skin." He tapped the desk with a broad finger. "I worry about catching the bad guys."

"Yeah? Did you catch any today?"

"Sort of."

For the first time, Nevin concentrated fully on Frankl instead of on the report he'd been completing. "Who?"

"Blake and I spent the last three days watching video surveillance footage of a backyard in Boring. It was every bit as thrilling as you imagine."

"Oscar-worthy, huh?"

"Well, we learned how Roger Grey's mandible got there."

Frankl paused and examined his fingernails as if he were considering getting a manicure. Then he leaned back in his chair and gave the sort of smile a man might display when a vending machine gave him two bags of chips instead of one. Nevin scowled, determined to wait Frankl out. But Frankl hummed and pretended to be fascinated by the muscle-car calendar on Nevin's wall.

After briefly considering pulling his Glock, Nevin heaved a sigh. "What did you see? Did you make the neighbor for the murder?"

"No. We gave Clackamas County sheriffs enough to pop him for trespass and burglary, though. Turns out the guy really was breaking into the shed and stealing stuff."

"But the jaw?"

"It fell from the sky." Frankl made a falling missile gesture with one hand.

"C'mon, Frankl. I'm not in the mood."

"And I'm not kidding. It's clear as day on the video—that bone dropped straight out of the sky."

"So… what? Roger Grey was murdered on a fluffy white cloud by an angel?"

Frankl shook his head. "We've talked to some people on this. Made some calls. We even had people watch the video in case we were missing something. And we've all come to the same conclusion. A bird."

"What?"

"A bird dropped the bone. That yard in Boring's less than seven miles from where the rest of the body was found. Some kind of scavenger—our best guess is a turkey vulture—picked up that jaw, carried it away, and released it over our guy's backyard."

Nevin stared at him, but there was no indication Frankl was making shit up. The one decent lead in the case turned out to be a goddamn bird. "Fuck me sideways," Nevin groaned before sinking his head into his arms.

"No, thanks. I'm a married man."

NEVIN SPENT most of Thursday reminding himself that texting Colin would be the act of a needy, pathetic asswipe. The kind of asswipe who claims he doesn't want a commitment but then glues himself to some poor bastard like a leech. At least a dozen times he started to compose a message but deleted it before hitting Send. He almost sobbed with relief when his phone buzzed.

Sleep well last night? Colin asked.

Like a baby. No lie there. After the phone sex, he'd dragged himself out of bed just long enough for a quick cleanup, then collapsed back onto his mattress until his alarm startled him awake. He didn't remember any dreams.

Am I stalking you now?

No. I'm glad you texted. Nevin stopped himself just in time from saying he missed Colin. Fuck. Fuck. Fuck. A change of subject was in order. *Found out the story on Roger's jaw.*

A suspect?

No. A vulture dropped it.

Colin didn't answer immediately—not that Nevin blamed him. It was the kind of news that took some time to digest. When Colin finally did respond, it was with a *wow* emoji, then, *I'm sorry that went nowhere.*

We'll keep looking. Somehow sharing this work-related frustration with someone who wasn't a cop made him feel a little better.

I know you will. I bet Roger would be tickled if he knew about the vulture.

???

It's like he had one last adventure.

Nevin smiled at Colin's insistence on seeing the glass half-full. *He'll be remembered around here, that's for sure.*

That would make him happy too.

After a brief pause, Colin sent another text. *Will I scare you off if I set another date with you already? For Saturday?*

Not tonight? Nevin added a winking smiley face even though he wasn't quite kidding.

I wish. But it's my night to visit Ivan & Bob. Tmrw is dinner with parents. Mom's bday. You could join us if you want.

Nevin shuddered and didn't answer. After a minute—and probably a deep sigh—Colin texted again. *Ok. Sat @8. I'll pick you up.*

After a brief hesitation, Nevin sent his address. Nobody except Ford ever came to his place. Not even Jeremy. But there was no way to refuse without being a twat. Nevin could meet him outside. He followed with another message. *Call if you want tonight. Wouldn't be stalking.*

Colin sent him a sparkling heart emoji.

In retaliation, Nevin texted back with the eggplant emoji and, for good measure, a finger pointing at a cartoon hand doing the "okay" gesture.

LOL, Colin typed. Of course.

"Jesus Christ," Nevin muttered. "We're fourteen-year-old girls." But he couldn't stop grinning.

CHAPTER SEVENTEEN

WHEN BOB AND Ivan Thomas bought their Northwest Portland house in the 1960s, the neighborhood had been in decline. People with money had abandoned the grand Victorians in favor of modern houses in the hills or suburbs, and many of the houses were subdivided into apartments or simply torn down. Bob and Ivan, though, had lavished loving care on their home, painting it in bright colors that emphasized the fancy gingerbread trim and furnishing it with carefully restored antiques. Maybe back then some people had hassled them—two openly gay men living in a time when most were forced to remain closeted—but the Thomases and their house had stood strong.

Now, though, things were very different. While neighboring houses, most of them restored and updated, sold for over a million dollars, the Thomas house sagged and peeled. Bob and Ivan, who were in their eighties, remained mostly confined to a few dusty rooms on the ground floor. Not only were they unable to manage the stairs to the upper floors and basement, but even the steep steps between the front door and the street were too much for them.

Manuel had been trying for years to convince them to move somewhere more accessible, a condo or even assisted living, but they'd flat-out refused. "This is our home," Bob had explained to Colin more than once. "We're here until we die."

Colin didn't argue with them. He understood the wisdom of Manuel's advice but didn't blame the Thomases at all. Over fifty years together under that roof, weathering the kinds of challenges Colin could only imagine, accumulating memories all the time. He'd want to remain there too.

On Thursday evening, Colin circled several times before finding a parking place a few blocks away. Then he dashed through the rain, doing his best to keep the grocery bag dry, and finally reached the protection of the front porch. The doorbell had died at some point in the indeterminate past, so he knocked.

It took a long time for Ivan to answer, but Colin expected that. Eventually the door swung open. "Colin! Come in, my dear boy, before you catch pneumonia."

It was damp but not all that cold outside. Still, Colin stepped into the foyer with a grin. As usual, Ivan was dapper in dark pants, a white shirt, and a velvet-and-satin smoking jacket. Colin had never seen an actual smoking jacket until he met the Thomases. Tall, thin, and mustached, Ivan bore a strong resemblance to an elderly Vincent Price.

"I picked up a few things," Colin said, handing over the grocery bag.

"You didn't have to. You know we get food deliveries."

"Sure. These are just a few treats."

Ivan peeked into the bag. "You scoundrel, you! Our doctors would disapprove completely. And that is why we love you so." He pinched Colin's cheek with his free hand. "Come, come. I'll never hear the end of it if Bob doesn't get to feast his eyes on you fully."

Once upon a time—long before Colin's time—Ivan and Bob had run a jazz club downtown. They'd been active in local theatre too, and sometimes Bob could be persuaded to warble a few tunes. His voice was now weak and hoarse, but Colin loved to listen. Neither Bob nor Ivan had changed their showy, flamboyant mannerisms over the years. And Colin loved that too.

"Darling! I'm so glad you made it." Bob needed a walker when he moved around. But mostly he preferred to remain—as he was right now—in an armchair in the parlor, ruling over his little world as if from a throne. Today he wore striped silk pajamas and had a purple woolen blanket over his lap. He was shorter and rounder than his partner, with the most mobile eyebrows Colin had ever seen.

Colin hurried over to kiss Bob's cheek. "I wouldn't miss a visit with you guys, you know that. I look forward to you all week." That was true.

But Bob waved a hand. "You're silly. A beautiful boy like you should be spending every night dancing to terrible music and making wild, passionate love under the stars."

"I'm a bad dancer and it's raining."

While Bob humphed and Ivan creaked his way to the kitchen with the groceries, Colin removed his coat, hung it on a crowded rack, and sat in his usual spot on a spindly piece of furniture his hosts always called the settee. It was probably constructed before Colin's grandparents were born, and it wasn't comfortable, but at least it held his weight.

"So how have you been?" Colin asked.

"Boring. We are ancient and decrepit and boring as dirt."

"You're none of those. Hey, do you think we could look at some of those photos again?"

Bob smiled widely and clapped his hands. "Of course! And do you know what? Ivan found a new album you haven't seen yet."

In their jazz club days, the Thomases had taken pictures of their club, of performances they were involved in, of parties at their house, of the vacations they'd taken. Colin sometimes even recognized a few celebrities. His hosts seemed delighted to share their collection with him, and Colin genuinely enjoyed it as well.

So today he took turns sitting beside Ivan or kneeling next to Bob, gazing at depictions of people and places long gone. The Thomases had interesting stories about everything, and although almost all their friends and family had passed away, their memories were joyous.

"Now," Ivan said when they were through with the album, "give a pair of old queens a thrill. Tell us what *you* have been doing."

"Nothing all that thrilling." Wait. That wasn't quite true. "Remember those houses I told you about? The ones my dad wants to tear down?"

Ivan and Bob clucked and nodded. Ivan stroked Bob's arm. "Such a terrible shame. You should have seen some of the gorgeous houses that used to stand around here. Now gone, all gone, and nobody to remember them but us."

"I know. But that's the thing. I spoke with my dad yesterday, and I think I've convinced him to let me rehab those houses instead."

"You'll return them to their former glory!" Bob exclaimed.

"I'm not sure if glory's the right word. Those places were never as fancy as yours. But we'll make them nice again." He suddenly felt completely confident about that.

Silence fell as Bob and Ivan exchanged significant glances. Then Bob nodded regally and Ivan turned to Colin. "Dear boy, we want you to know that we've been speaking to our attorney."

"Is everything all right?"

Ivan patted Colin's knee. "Everything is as wonderful as it can be for two quite aged gentlemen. But you see, Bobby and I have been worrying about what will become of our home when we're gone."

"Oh, you're not—"

"Darling," Bob interrupted. "My ninetieth birthday is soon, with Ivan's not far behind. We embraced our mortality some time ago. And frankly, as one's body falls apart, one tends to become less attached to it. So let's accept the inevitable approach of death and discuss the matter frankly, shall we?"

Colin bit his lip and remembered what he'd said to Nevin about TriMet buses. And heck, he'd been living his entire life on borrowed time. "Okay."

"Such a delightful boy," said Ivan with another knee pat—and maybe the hint of a thigh grope. He winked—and so did Bob. "We're not dead *yet*," Ivan added.

Bob continued. "But to return to the matter at hand, we've discussed our home with our attorney. Also… well, not to be indelicate, but our finances have become strained. Neither of us expected to live this long, and we've nearly exhausted our savings. Our attorney suggested that we might sell the house to someone but reserve a life estate for ourselves. I daresay that life estate won't last long."

Although he was no expert in property law, Colin had picked up quite a bit of knowledge on the subject while working in real estate. "That makes sense, I guess."

"It does. And darling, we would like to sell the house to *you*."

"Me?"

"Well, your company, I suppose. We can undoubtedly reach a fair price. Ivan and I haven't any heirs, so our only interest is ensuring we have sufficient funds to spend our final few years in relative comfort."

Like a mirage, a vision of the house flashed through Colin's mind—but in the vision, it was repaired and restored, coddled back to its original beauty. Still, he shook his head. "It's my father's company. I can't guarantee he'll give your house its due." Westwood Development could throw up a whole lot of expensive condos where the Thomas house now stood.

"But we trust you'll do your best," Ivan said. "Because we know you can appreciate this home."

"I can. I do. But—"

"No, that's enough for now. At this point, we shall leave it to the attorneys, while we turn our attention to much *juicier* matters."

Maybe it was the lingering effects of the previous night's phone sex—Colin had *never* come so hard and so satisfyingly while masturbating—or maybe the smoking jacket and silk pajamas had a hypnotizing effect. He felt dizzy. "Juicier?"

"Yes," Ivan said with a wicked grin. "Such as how we are going to get you thoroughly, completely laid. Do you use apps?"

Colin felt the flush warm his face and silently cursed his fair skin. Bob caught on immediately, leaning forward in his throne. "Do tell, Colin. Please. Give us a vicarious thrill—it's all we have left these days. You know, there was a day, oh, only a few decades past, when we would have lured you into our bed and debauched you so utterly that you forgot your own name."

The blush deepened, but Colin laughed. "I can believe that."

"So? Who is the lucky man who landed you lately?"

Telling his father about Nevin hadn't ruined anything, so Colin took a risk. "It's... new. I met him several months ago, actually, but we just lately, uh, graduated."

"To what?"

"I'm actually not sure. He's a great guy. I mean—really, he's incredible. But he had a rough start in life, and he's convinced he doesn't do relationships. I think he *wants* to, though. He's got this hard shell, but then it slips and I get a peek of how sweet and amazing he is."

While Ivan spread a hand over his own chest, Bob's eyebrows danced. "Ah," Bob said. "The rogue with the heart of gold. A type we knew quite well and have found irresistible ourselves."

"He's not a rogue—he's a policeman. A detective."

"Even more alluring! But be careful, my boy. You want to redeem him and make his true nature shine through. That can be a dangerous enterprise. Sometimes in the end, they only make that shell tougher, and you're left—"

"Bobby!" When Ivan interrupted, both Colin and Bob gaped. But Ivan pointed sternly at his partner. "Stop that at once." He faced Colin. "When I met Bobby, he *dazzled* me. I'd never seen such an enchanting creature. But I was still closeted, believe it or not, so much so that even he didn't realize how I felt. It took three *years* before I worked up the courage to approach him."

"One of the happiest days of my life," said Bob, clasping Ivan's hand.

"And mine. And a decision I have never regretted for an instant, not even when, well... things were difficult for us."

Colin looked at their somber faces and wondered whether those difficulties were in their relationship itself or came from outside, from people who couldn't tolerate two men in love. "And you stuck it out," he said.

Ivan nodded. "For sixty years, if you can imagine such a thing! I certainly could not at the beginning. But Colin, it could have been sixty-three. And while I have never been remorseful over a single day spent with Bobby, I still grieve for the thousand days I *didn't* spend with him. So forget what that silly old man was telling you about being careful. Since when does taking care bring joy? If you believe this detective is worth it, then by all means take the risk. Even if it doesn't work out, I promise that when you're ancient, you'll be sorrier if you never even tried."

Colin left the Thomas house with damp eyes, a promise to discuss the house with his father, and a determination to die with a minimum of regrets.

COLIN CALLED Nevin on Thursday night, and they had another round of phone sex. It was just as good as the first time. This time, though, instead of going to sleep right away, they chatted for a while—"like teenage girls," Nevin said with a snort—until Colin was yawning too much to talk. They didn't discuss anything of great importance, but it was nice. Nevin described his colleagues' reactions to the vulture, and then he told a funny story about a time when he and Ford were twenty and got stranded in Council Crest Park in a heavy rain. Colin described his visit with the Thomases, although he omitted the part where they gave him relationship advice.

"They sound interesting," Nevin said, yawning audibly as well.

"Very. You could come with me sometime, if you'd like. They would eat you up."

Nevin chuckled. "Maybe I will. Now get your beauty sleep, princess."

"You too."

Friday morning, Colin called Bright Hope. "Hi, Crystal, this is Colin Westwood. Can I talk to Manuel?"

"He's running some errands for a couple hours. Is it an emergency?"

"No, nothing like that. You know Bob and Ivan Thomas?"

"Sure."

Colin would have preferred to speak directly to Manuel about this, but he figured giving Crystal a summary would stop Manuel from worrying about an unspecified situation. Besides, Crystal would hear about it from Manuel soon enough anyway—she knew everything that went on at Bright Hope. "They want to sell their house to my father's company but still continue to live there. And I want to check that it wouldn't be a conflict of interest or something for me."

"You mean because you're our volunteer? I'm sure it's fine. But I can check with Manuel if you want."

"Thanks. I'd appreciate it."

She called back about fifteen minutes later. "Manuel says no problem. It sounds like a good deal for everyone."

"Well, I hope so."

"That house of theirs is worth about a zillion bucks. If you buy it, they'll get a nice infusion of cash, right?"

"That's the plan."

Shortly after the call ended, Colin sat down with his father to tell him about Bob and Ivan's offer. His dad listened carefully and, when Colin was done, asked, "Do you think it's a wise business decision?"

"If we can negotiate a good price, which I'm pretty sure we can. Fixed up, that house will literally be worth a fortune, and you know how hot that neighborhood is. And you know, a lot of people around town are grumbling about all the new development. Westwood could get a reputation for being the good guys, the company that cares about preserving the character of neighborhoods. In the long run, that could pay off big-time."

His father smiled. "You've thought about this a lot."

"I have."

"All right. I will too. And we'll see if we can get the lawyers to palaver." He shook his head in bemusement. "If this works out, your mother will never let me live it down. She's been trying to convince me for years that I'm evil."

"You take credit for the idea, then. You need the capital with Mom more than I do."

"Maybe we'll share the credit," his dad responded with a wink.

At dinner that night, Colin tried to convince his mother that rehabbing the houses rather than razing them had been his father's plan, but she didn't buy it for a minute. She gave Colin a hug and a smooch on the cheek, then patted Harold's shoulder. "I hope you didn't suddenly start listening to sense just because Colin's male," she teased.

"Nope. It's because he's not a bloodsucking lawyer."

She swatted him harder and everyone laughed. It was a good family get-together.

That night Nevin called—which Colin counted as a major advance—and Colin gave him a rundown of the deal with the Thomases and dinner with the family. He carefully avoided suggesting that Nevin might meet the rest of them one of these days. And Nevin, to his credit, did not freak out.

They didn't have phone sex—didn't even mention sex, apart from Nevin's usual curses and innuendoes. But even those were toned down. He sounded relaxed and comfortable, and Colin seriously considered driving over there now that he had the address. Just to hang out. But he didn't want to push too hard, so he resisted the impulse. "See you tomorrow night," he said.

"Dress code?"

"Casual. I don't have anything too fancy planned. Just, you know. Date stuff."

"Date stuff," Nevin echoed. "All right."

Colin spent Saturday exercising at the gym, cleaning his apartment, and thinking obsessively about Nevin. He kept reminding himself that this whole thing between them was a big old trial balloon, an experiment that might very well crash and burn. "This could be a big mistake," he said to Legolas, who was trying to kill the broom while Colin swept.

Legolas took another swipe at the brush.

"I'm getting myself stuck on a guy who warned me not to. And I've never fallen like this for anyone. Trent was okay, but he wasn't an addiction."

Unimpressed by Colin's dilemma, Leg gnawed on a broom bristle, then made a face when it poked his cheek. Colin pointed at him. "Consider yourself lucky you're neutered, buster."

But then Colin remembered how *good* sex with Nevin felt, and he was extremely thankful he wasn't neutered as well.

When he pulled up to Nevin's building a few minutes before eight, Nevin was waiting for him, shoulders hunched against the drizzle. "Didn't want you to have to fuck with the security gate," he explained. Colin suspected there was more to it than that, but he didn't push. Nevin crushed him in an embrace as soon as he was inside the car, and that was more important than whatever Nevin's apartment issue might be.

Colin had used recreational drugs only once, a little bit of pot. But as he stuck his nose into the crook of Nevin's neck and inhaled, he knew exactly how it must feel to be a junkie getting a hit.

"What are you *doing* to me?" Nevin moaned.

"Sniffing you."

Nevin barked a laugh. "Not what I meant, Collie. You're... I don't get hung up on people like this. I can't."

Colin pulled away to gaze gravely at him. "You're ignoring the evidence, Detective. You can and you do."

"I think about you all the time. You. Not that enormous cock or that tight ass. The nerd with the bow ties and the collection of Julie Andrews DVDs."

"Blame yourself," Colin replied, his heart warm and full. "I was just supposed to have a postbreakup fling. I wasn't supposed to feel feelings for a cop with a show-off car and a mouth that needs washing out with soap."

"My mouth fucking needs *something*," said Nevin, which of course was the prelude to a kiss. An excellent kiss, the kind that made Colin's mind check out and his body sing.

"I do not want to fuck in your BMW," Nevin proclaimed when they stopped to breathe.

"It would be okay if we were in Julie?"

"Only if we protected the leather."

Colin threaded his fingers through Nevin's thick hair. "How about if we have dinner now and try for an actual bed later? I think I still have splinters from Monday."

"Dinner now, dessert later."

Colin took them to a downtown restaurant he liked, a sort of hipster diner with oversized sandwiches and terrific milkshakes.

"Germy likes this place," said Nevin as they entered. "Mostly because they have ogre-sized portions."

"Jeremy is an ogre?"

"Nah. Too fucking pretty for that."

Colin opted for a salmon and gouda scramble, while Nevin had a beet salad with chicken-apple sausage on the side. They ate slowly. "My mom would approve of your meal more than mine," Colin said, pointing his fork tines at Nevin's plate.

"She still has to nag you to eat your veggies?"

Then Colin remembered that Nevin had never had anyone to badger him to eat his broccoli, which made Colin sad. He countered with one of his own painful truths. "I'm supposed to be careful about cholesterol and fat."

Nevin's scrutiny was piercing but not cruel. "Heart, huh?"

Colin lost his appetite. Why on earth had he raised this subject? "Yeah. We can… talk about it later. Okay?"

"Any time you're ready." Which was a kindness from a man accustomed to interrogating people.

After Colin paid for dinner, they strolled hand in hand back to the car. And when they reached the lot, Colin didn't want to let him go. "How about a walk?" he suggested.

Nevin muttered something about sappy princesses, but he continued to hold Colin's hand.

They ended up on the waterfront, which was nearly abandoned due to the dank, chilly weather. Colin might have been a little worried about his safety if he were alone, but he was with a cop. Heck, he was with Nevin, a force who struck terror in bad guys' hearts.

"I think this would be more romantic in summer," Nevin said as they gazed out at the river. Colin's arm was around Nevin's shoulders, but they still shivered a little.

"Do you think we'll still be together by next summer? Jeez, are we together *now*?" Not accusing, but searching for honesty.

After a pause, Nevin answered. "We're together now. I can't promise more than that. Wait, yes I can. I can promise that I won't lie to you. And that as long as we *are* together, it's just you."

"That's… that's actually a pretty big promise," said Colin, his voice shaking. "Thank you. I promise not to ask more of you than you want to give, okay?"

Nevin's laughter sounded bitter, but he nodded. Then they watched the cars go over the Morrison Bridge, headlights and taillights glowing, and Nevin nestled more deeply into the crook of Colin's arm.

"Tetralogy of Fallot," Colin said.

"What?"

"It's a congenital heart defect. Four defects, actually, which is where the tetra part comes in. It's named after some French guy. Nobody seems to know what causes it, although they're pretty sure genetics plays a part."

"Which is why your parents never gave you that baby brother for Christmas."

Colin sighed. "Yeah."

"It's congenital, but you're here now."

"They caught it right after I was born. I was a blue baby. Had a heart murmur too. They did the first surgery when I was just a couple months old."

Nevin went rigid against him. "First?"

"I had a couple more when I was older." The next part was harder to talk about. "And chances are I'll need another in the future."

Nevin tore himself away, took a step back, and turned to stare at him, wide-eyed. "You're sick?" he demanded, voice ragged.

"No! No, no. I'm fine." Colin reached for his arm, but Nevin ducked away. "I see a doctor often, and he says I'm doing well. I can exercise—do pretty much whatever I want to. The odds are that I'll end up at some point with a leaky valve, but they can fix that."

"Huh." Nevin pressed his lips together and turned his face away.

"This… it's a problem for you?" Damn. He shouldn't have said anything. But Nevin had seen the scar and must have already suspected. And he'd already divulged the secret of his own painful childhood; Colin owed him the same.

"How serious is this thing?" Nevin asked tightly.

Honesty. "If I hadn't had the surgery as a baby, I probably wouldn't have lived until kindergarten. Even if I had, I would have had physical problems. Slow growth, stuff like that. But I *did* have the surgery and I survived and I lead a normal life."

"I just found you. I just opened…." Nevin shook his head hard and turned away.

But Colin stepped in front of him and pulled him close. "I can't guarantee I won't drop dead five minutes from now, Nev. But nobody can guarantee that. You're a cop—you could get shot up by a meth addict with an AK-47."

Nevin spoke into Colin's chest. "Tweakers don't use AK-47s."

"Whatever."

"Don't you dare fucking die on me, Colin. I mean it."

"I'll do my best to avoid it."

After a hug so fierce Colin could barely breathe, Nevin loosened his hold. "It's why your mother…."

"Yeah, it's why I'm a mama's boy. I guess you never quite get over watching your kid almost die. God, you should have heard her argue when I was ready to move out of the house. She's a smart lady, but I think in her eyes I'm always going to be a sickly toddler."

"Show her you're a man."

"Working on it."

Nevin tipped his head up to see Colin's eyes. "Yeah. You are."

CHAPTER EIGHTEEN

NEVIN HAD never felt so fucking terrified. Not even when he was a rookie on a domestic violence call during which the loving husband waved a gun at him while the loving wife came after Nevin with a kitchen knife. But now he'd… let someone in. Opened his heart. Only to learn that the someone was distressingly mortal.

And now here he was, trying not to have a complete breakdown on the banks of the Willamette fucking River.

"I have issues," he admitted to Colin's neck.

Colin laughed. "We have quite a collection of them between us. We could keep a couples therapist very, very busy."

Nevin shuddered. "Couples therapist. That is the vilest fucking phrase I've ever heard." He'd needed a psych evaluation as part of the background check for the police bureau; that was enough headshrinking to last him forever.

"We can skip it. Do you want to go have coffee? At P-Town, maybe? I liked that place."

A fresh bolt of fear made Nevin's stomach churn. Rhoda would be at the café tonight, and maybe Jeremy too. Nevin just wasn't ready for them to meet Colin. He decided on a course of action only slightly less scary. "Would you come home with me now, Collie? To my place?"

"God yes." Colin nuzzled his neck. He did that often enough that he'd already spawned a new kink, as if Nevin needed another. But Jesus Christ, those warm lips on his skin made him dizzy with need. Made him want to tear off Colin's clothes and… *possess* him. That was the right word, wasn't it?

"Let's go," he said roughly, pulling away.

When they reached the security gate to Nevin's building, he had second thoughts. Third and fourth thoughts. They could go to Colin's loft instead; the damned cat would be happy to see them both. But he punched in the code to let them in and directed Colin to a guest parking spot.

"You don't own this building, do you?" Nevin asked as they walked to his door.

"Nope. We don't do apartments. We do condos and townhomes, and mostly we sell those."

"What about Mrs. Ruskin?"

"We own some rental houses too. Just a few. Dad started out as a landlord, so we have some long-term tenants like her." He sighed. "They never caught whoever killed her."

"Not yet," Nevin replied with more confidence than he possessed. In reality, Homicide had little evidence and no leads. The best theory was that it had been a burglar, although why the perp ran off without stealing shit was anyone's guess.

He unlocked his apartment and held his breath while Colin looked around.

There wasn't much to see. It was a basic one-bedroom with generic furniture. Nevin kept it neat and clean, and he didn't have enough possessions to create clutter. Even his kitchen tended to be bare because he rarely cooked, and when he did, the meal was basic. A couple of pots and pans sufficed.

"Minimalist" was Colin's comment.

"Never picked up the habit of accumulating crap." When moving from place to place as a kid, he needed to fit all his belongings into a plastic garbage bag. And when he and Ford moved in together, neither of them had the money to buy anything but essentials. Since then, well, what was the point? He didn't need much, and buying things didn't make him feel fulfilled.

Colin stopped to stare at a sketch of a house. Nevin had tacked it to the wall earlier that week, and when he realized what Colin was seeing, he hurried over, intending to tear it down.

But Colin caught his arm. "Don't!"

"It's just a shitty—"

"It's our house. The one where we made—"

"The one where we fucked on the floor. So what?" He folded his arms and hoped his skin was too dark to show his blush.

Colin smiled crookedly. "It's good." He held up a hand to stop any protests, then spent a good ten minutes carefully examining every damn drawing in the room. He asked questions about them and scowled until Nevin answered every one.

"This is why I don't bring people here," Nevin said.

"Get over yourself, Nevin. I like these. I mean, I'm not an art critic or anything, but they seem well-done to me. And they have character. Like this one." He waved at a doodle of Julie with wings.

"They're fucking stupid."

"No, they're not. You don't think so either, not really, or you wouldn't have hung them up. And should I point out that they're all houses or vehicles?"

"You promised we could skip the therapy."

"I guess I did," said Colin, coming closer. He laced his hands behind Nevin's head, and they stood there chest-to-chest, just breathing. Nevin liked that Colin was only a few inches taller than him, but even more, he liked that Colin managed not to loom.

Taking a deep breath, Nevin stretched his palm over Colin's chest. If he pressed gently, he could feel the heart beating, even through the fabric of Colin's shirt.

"See?" Colin whispered. "Still ticking."

"Did you know how bad it was, when you were a kid? Did you know you might die?"

"Yeah. Mom and Dad believed in being straightforward. I mean, they sugarcoated things when I was really little. Nobody wants to scare the crap out of a three-year-old. But they were up-front with me when I got a little older. I would have guessed anyway. You can tell how serious things are by the way the doctors and nurses act."

"You were scared." Nevin remembered his own abrupt journeys in strangers' cars, the feeling of spending the night in a house where he knew nobody, the knowledge that if he fell, he had nobody to catch him. And fuck, the uncertainty and frustration of a life out of his control.

"I'm not scared now." Colin kissed him, sweet and soft at first, just a butterfly brushing of lips. Then harder. He licked Nevin's mouth before entering, and Nevin sighed like an ingénue at her first ball.

And the thing about Colin—well, one thing about Colin—was that Nevin didn't always have to be strong around him. Nevin had built defenses for so long that he didn't remember laying the first stones, and he'd built them carefully. But when Colin was near, Nevin could unlock the gates, could… well, maybe not venture outside, but he could at least allow someone in.

To his immense shock and mortification, a sob escaped from his lungs. Just one.

His eyes remained dry, but Colin kissed his eyelids anyway and nibbled on the shell of his ear. "Will you take off your clothes?" Colin asked.

Yes. Good idea.

Colin shed his coat and tossed it onto the couch. Then he waited, eyebrows raised and the corners of his mouth turned up in a small smile. Apparently he expected Nevin to put on a show. Fine. Doable.

At first Nevin kept his movements slow, unfastening each button with care. But by the time his shirt was on the floor and his shoes and socks lay scattered, he had grown impatient. He skimmed out of his pants and underwear quickly and stood, hands on hips, allowing Colin to inspect him.

"Turn and face the wall," Colin said.

"That's my line."

"Not tonight."

Fuck. The apartment wasn't chilly, yet Nevin's flesh broke out in goose bumps when he placed his palms on the plaster and slightly spread his legs.

Apparently Colin was nothing but patient tonight. He stalked closer—all that time spent with a cat—and stopped near enough for his breath to tickle Nevin's hair. He settled his hands on Nevin's hips and began to lick and nip at Nevin's nape.

Within moments Nevin had to lean against the wall for support, arousal making his breath come in gasps. Colin worked his body with painstaking care, mouthing at shoulder blades, at spine, at ribs. Whenever Nevin tried to turn around and touch him, Colin pinned him in place with one hand on the small of Nevin's back. And yes, Nevin was stronger, and he was trained in fighting techniques. But that one gentle palm was enough to trap him.

Just when Nevin was about to give in and beg, Colin dropped to his knees and started licking the globes of Nevin's ass. He kneaded the heavy muscles as he traced his tongue cleverly, and when Nevin moaned and spread his legs wider, Colin pointed that tongue and stuck it into the crack.

"Jeeesus."

"Do you want this, Nev?"

"God yes. Please." Even though he never pleaded, the words fell easily now. "Please don't stop."

Colin didn't. While Nevin pressed his forehead to the wall and pushed out his ass, Colin licked and nibbled and fingered. Over, around, and then just the smallest bit in. Nevin's position was dirty—naked, desperate, dripping with spit and sweat and precome—with Colin still fully clothed behind him, smoothing with one hand even while he intruded with the fingers of the other.

With his own hands still flat beside his head, Nevin closed his eyes and concentrated on staying upright.

When Colin stood and moved away, Nevin almost cried. Then he heard a series of unmistakable sounds: a zipper opening, a foil packet being torn, a plastic cap being popped. "Oh fuck, yes," he groaned.

Colin was damnably careful. He tongued Nevin's ass until the opening was relaxed and tingling, then used his fingers and so much lube that Nevin could almost taste it. It took Nevin's strongest will not to beg or swear, not to grab his own throbbing cock and start tugging. His patience was rewarded when Colin finally, slowly, pushed his latex-covered cock inside.

Even with all the preparation, it took a few moments for Nevin to adjust to Colin's girth. He was stretched and filled, with just enough zing of pain to keep him grounded. Colin remained still, panting in Nevin's ear, caressing the points of Nevin's hips. He'd done nothing more than shove his jeans and underwear down to his thighs, and Nevin found the sensation of the clothing against his bare skin breathtakingly erotic.

"Move," Nevin rasped.

After wrapping his fist around Nevin's cock, Colin obeyed, first rocking his hips slowly and shallowly, but soon going harder and deeper. Nevin encouraged him by angling his ass even more. And pretty soon Nevin was hanging on for dear life, his senses flooded and his brain completely useless.

"Now," Colin said between grunts. "Close."

Nevin was close too, and he wanted to assure Colin that he was pounding him just right—hitting that sweet spot inside and stroking just hard enough on Nevin's dick. But language eluded him, so he mewled instead. He figured Colin got his drift.

A little faster, a little *more*. Just on the edge of too much but balancing, balancing. Until Colin scraped his teeth along Nevin's shoulder and Nevin fell, hard and fast. Only the wall and Colin's grip kept him from collapsing.

"Oh, fuuuuuck!" Colin howled. For a moment he remained still, as deeply inside Nevin as he could get, and then he sighed and sagged onto

Nevin's back. Both of them dropped in slow motion to the floor, limbs tangled. Colin was no longer inside Nevin, but they held each other until their pulse rates calmed. Colin carefully removed the rubber, and when he seemed at a loss as to what to do with it, Nevin tied it off and tossed it aside.

Colin giggled. "See? My heart holds up just fine."

"But you've picked up my vocabulary. And were you this assertive with douche bag?"

"Trent? No. Our sex life was sort of a paint-by-numbers thing. Uncreative."

That was immensely satisfying. "Yeah? You seem pretty goddamn creative to me."

Colin kissed Nevin's temple. "With you, sure. Trent appreciated my penis size and… when he dumped me, he said I'm a nice guy. Ugh. I think as far as he was concerned, I was easy to deal with and well hung. And to be fair, he was easy for me too. You're not."

"Is that good?"

"I'm bare-assed on a floor with you for the second time this week, Nev. I think that speaks for itself."

"I'm a difficult asswipe, so you boss me around when we fuck?" Nevin knew that wasn't it, yet he had to push, like poking a tongue at a sore tooth.

But Colin kissed him again and ruffled Nevin's hair. "Not difficult, just complicated. And I boss you around when we make love because we both get off on it. I figure when someone's been in charge of himself—in charge of everything—as long as you have, it's nice to give up the driver's seat now and then."

God, it really was. Nevin didn't say so, instead cupping Colin's face and leaning their foreheads together.

Colin ended up spending the night, which nobody but Ford had ever done before. His presence gave Nevin's dull apartment more life, as if his colorful self might rub off on white walls. And speaking of rubbing off on walls, Nevin was going to have to scrub his in the morning. He fell asleep in his queen-size bed, holding Colin and smiling at the thought.

IT WAS startling to wake up with a naked man in his bed, but it was awfully damned pleasant. Sleepy Colin was adorable with pillow-mussed hair and a lazy smile, and when he reached over to poke a finger against the tip of Nevin's nose, Nevin didn't even bite him.

"Legolas is going to be so pissed off at me," Colin said.

"He doesn't like when you do sleepovers?"

"I *never* do sleepovers. And it's past his breakfast time."

"What about when you were dating douche bag?"

Colin sat up, yawned, and stretched. "He'd come over to my place."

"Was he hiding secrets at his?" Nevin narrowed his eyes and imagined how satisfying it would be to throw the douche bag in jail for hurting Colin.

"No, I don't think so. We just always seemed to end up at my loft."

"It was easy."

Colin shrugged. "Guess so." He got out of bed and stretched again—a lovely sight—then started gathering his clothes from the night before. His movements were languid, his face carrying the serene expression of a man who'd had really good sex not too many hours before.

While Colin put on his underwear and jeans, Nevin focused on the pink line bisecting his chest. "Did douche bag dump you because of your heart?"

Pausing with his shirt in hand, Colin gazed at him steadily. "Partly, yeah. Our parents have been friends for years, so he knew about it even before we started dating. But there are some things I have to be careful about. I don't ski. I've never been comfortable at the idea of traveling too far from home—from my doctors, I guess—so I wasn't going to join him at some chalet in the Alps. He felt like I limited him."

"Fuckwad."

"Well, there was more to it than that." Colin slipped into his shirt and began fastening the buttons. "He's vice president in a tech company—"

"You're a veep too. It says so on your office door."

"But Trent doesn't work for his daddy. He's a mover and shaker. I'm not."

Nevin hopped out of bed so he could capture Colin's hips and draw him close. "I think you move and shake damned well."

Colin laughed. "I knew you'd say that. Look, forget about Trent. He's ancient history. And I am so glad he dumped me, because now I have you. For now!" he added hastily. "I'm not implying you have to—"

"I know."

"Anyway, I'd trade a lifetime with Trent for a few months with you."

"Smooth talker. You just want to get in my pants."

Colin slid his palms over Nevin's naked ass. "You're not wearing any."

It was soon after that when Colin's clothing came off again. And across town, Legolas was surely waiting impatiently for his very belated breakfast.

CHAPTER NINETEEN

November 2015

THEY WERE dating. Going steady like a teenage couple in one of Colin's stupid old musicals. Nevin had avoided the terrifying word *boyfriend* and the deadly one, *love*, but by early November, he had to admit that he and Colin were a thing. They spent weekends together—except when Colin had family commitments—and some weeknights as well. And on evenings when they didn't see each other, they called or texted. They had lots of sex and watched movies. Nevin spent countless hours petting the damned cat. They went out to dinner and even spent a day at the coast, watching a storm whip the waves. And one night Colin brought him flowers. Goddamn *flowers*.

It was all warm and wonderful and amazing, and because Nevin looked so happy, people at work were beginning to ask him what was wrong.

And of course he was scared shitless the entire time.

A week into November, on a damp Saturday afternoon, Colin and Nevin were on Colin's couch, riding the waves of postsex bliss. Nevin lay naked atop Colin, with a microfleece throw pulled over them both and Legolas curled near their feet. "If my heart did give out, I'd want it to be like this," Colin said.

"Don't joke about that shit."

"I mean it. This is good, Nevin. Just about as good as it gets."

After a moment Nevin braved the waters. "Just about?"

Colin sighed heavily enough to jostle Nevin. "I haven't met anyone in your life. And you've met hardly anyone in mine."

Over the past weeks, Colin had introduced Nevin to a couple of his friends over pints at a brewpub. That had been pleasant enough, but of course those people weren't family. Colin had told his family about Nevin, and by all accounts, they were eager to meet him—meet him properly, in the case of Colin's father—but the very idea made Nevin panic.

"Sorry," Colin said. "I didn't mean to bring it up. But it has to happen eventually. I mean, if there is an eventually."

Colin deserved far more than the half-assed promises Nevin had made, and Nevin wanted to reassure him. But he couldn't.

Beneath him, Colin stretched. "I have to pee."

"I'm too comfortable to move."

"You won't be very comfortable if I pee on you."

Grumbling and clutching the blanket, Nevin peeled himself off Colin. He got to watch Colin walk away, though, which was always a treat. And when Nevin sat back down, he picked up his phone and sent a hasty text.

"Something up?" Colin asked when he returned. It was a pleasure watching him approach too.

"How about if we shower and get dressed?"

"With a goal in mind?"

"Early dinner."

Judging by Colin's expression, he was aware there was more to it than that. But he was a master at knowing when to push Nevin and when to let things go, so all he did was nod. "Okay."

Colin's shower enclosure was big enough for both of them, and they often shared. Colin liked to joke that they were conserving water, but they usually used quite a bit by the time they were done groping and petting and fooling around. Today was more businesslike, not counting when Colin gave Nevin's ass a few healthy squeezes.

Somehow Nevin had repeatedly left changes of clothing at Colin's place, along with a toothbrush and hairbrush. And Colin never complained about tossing Nevin's clothes in with his own when he did the laundry. Now, Nevin pulled on a pair of jeans—and one of Colin's T-shirts.

"Sweeney Todd?" Colin asked, grinning.

"My favorite musical." They'd watched the movie together three times, Colin singing along the whole time. Colin had hesitantly suggested they see a live performance—there was one scheduled for June—and Nevin had cautiously admitted it was a possibility.

Colin opted for a Captain America shirt. Once he was dressed, he fed Legolas while Nevin refilled the water bowl. They ventured outside to where Julie was parked in a perfectly legal spot.

As they drove east and over the river, Colin hummed. Nevin was abashed to realize he recognized the song—from one of Colin's Disney films—and he even knew a few of the lyrics. Jesus. When he'd first met Mrs. Ruskin's bow-tied landlord, he never would have predicted that five months later he'd be in a car with that landlord, on his way to certain doom.

All right, perhaps doom was overstating things a bit. Nevin willed his hands to loosen on the steering wheel before he cracked it. "How are your projects going?" he asked, hoping Colin would ignore the strain in his voice.

"Well. The crews have already begun on the Clinton houses. Things will go a little slow because of weather and the holidays, but spring's a better time to sell anyway. Let me know any time you want to take a peek."

Nevin shot him a glance. "Planning a repeat of last time, Collie?"

"Always a possibility. Although really, I prefer you in my bed. Less dry cleaning afterward." He reached over to give Nevin's thigh a light stroke.

"What about that place in Northwest?"

"Bob and Ivan's? We close next week. They said they want to throw a little party to celebrate. Some of the Bright Hope people will be invited, and Bob and Ivan's friends. Would you go?" The hesitance in Colin's voice made Nevin's chest hurt.

"I.... Maybe. If I can stop being a complete fucking pussy."

"You're not," Colin assured him. "You're more of a tomcat. And you have a few weeks to think about it, anyway. Bob says he wants to wait until after Thanksgiving. My mission in the meantime is to see if I can convince them to let us do some work on the parts of the house they're not living in. Their heating bills are ridiculous, and I'm worried about the roof. I think Bob and Ivan will go for it if I point out that reno work means a steady stream of hot construction guys to look at."

They were quiet for several minutes, Colin's hand warm on Nevin's leg. Then Colin chuckled. "Where are we going—Idaho?"

"Almost there."

"You could have taken the Banfield. It would have been faster. Oh. You didn't want faster."

"Almost there."

Colin patted him. "Not quite going to Troutdale, huh? Some weekend when the weather's decent, we could go to Hood River, find a cozy little B and B."

Nevin had never stayed at a B and B, and the idea was surprisingly attractive. He imagined curling up with Colin in an antique bed, the kind you needed a step stool to get onto—and pretending the rest of the world didn't exist. "What about Legolas?" he asked.

"He'll be fine," Colin said, laughing. "He can last for one night without us. If it's longer than that, Miranda and Hannah could come over to feed him."

Nevin tried not to be shaken by Colin's careless use of *us*—as if the cat needed Nevin too. "Germy likes to hike out that way. I could ask him for some good trails. If that's not too—"

"I can manage hiking," Colin said a bit tersely.

"Then I'll ask him."

"When I was a kid, we used to go there for picnics. I liked to stop at Bonneville Dam to see the fish ladders. Did you ever do that?"

When Nevin shook his head, Colin squeezed his leg.

It was just past five, so the restaurant parking lot was nearly empty. "Mexican?" Colin asked as Nevin pulled into a spot near the door.

"You object?"

"Nope. I like Mexican."

"It's kind of a dump, but the food's great. And cheap. I washed dishes here for a year or two when I was in college, and even after I quit, the Solorios used to give me a discount." The Solorios had retired a few years ago, but their daughter and her husband ran the place now, and Nevin still ate there when he was in the neighborhood.

As soon as they stepped inside, Gabi Reyes called a greeting from the back of the dining room, where she was setting a table. "Nevin! We haven't seen you in forever."

"Sorry. Been spending a lot of time on the west side lately."

Her gaze settled on Colin. "That's not Ford," she teased.

"My friend Colin." *Friend.* That was an acceptable word, right? Accurate, not too scary, yet not too distancing.

Colin seemed satisfied with it, anyway. "Hi," he said to Gabi.

"You guys sit wherever," she said, smiling. "You want a menu too, Nevin, or just one for your friend?"

"Make it three."

Colin opened his mouth, no doubt to ask who was joining them, but then the front door opened and Ford walked in. He waved at Gabi but didn't even bother greeting Nevin—his focus was on Colin instead, a little smile playing at the corners of his mouth.

Nevin took a deep breath and dove in. "Collie, this asshole is Ford Ott. Ford, meet Colin."

An enormous grin appeared on Colin's face and he launched himself at Ford with enough enthusiasm that it looked as if Ford had to brace himself. "Oh my God," Colin said, crushing Ford in a hug. "It's so good to finally meet you."

Ford hugged him back and laughed. He was still chuckling as they sat down at their table, Colin next to Nevin and across from Ford. Gabi brought them menus, but Colin and Ford ignored them and instead stared at each other, each sizing the other up. Nevin wondered what they saw. A nerdy guy with an expensive jacket and a tattooed bald man who looked like a thug?

"You're not what I expected," Ford finally said.

Undaunted, Colin asked, "What *did* you expect? Did he even tell you I existed?"

"Yeah. But only after I accused him of picking up a drug habit. He's been so mellow lately."

Colin snorted. "Yeah, that's Nev. Mr. Laid-Back."

When Ford guffawed and started a story about one of Nevin's tantrums, Nevin realized this was going to work. Yes, they were going to gang up on him, but he could handle that. Hell, he might be able to urge Katie onto his side, and that would be fun. Nevin had plenty of embarrassing Ford stories to share. In any case Colin wasn't going to treat Ford like hired help, and Ford was acting as if he and Colin were already best pals.

Fuck. They were both good people. Why had Nevin expected the worst from them? He was the only one who'd misbehaved, hiding Colin in the closet and keeping his brother almost entirely in the dark.

The conversation stayed lively over burritos, tacos, and carne asada. Nevin had told Ford very little about Colin—male, thirty, in construction—and Ford seemed genuinely fascinated when Colin started talking about the old houses he was working on. For his part Colin asked a lot of questions about Ford's landscaping business. "Would you be interested in taking on some commercial work? Totally redoing the front and back yards for our projects?"

Ford shook his head. "You don't have to hire me just because I'm Nevin's family."

"We Westwoods are firm believers in nepotism—I work for my dad, after all. But anyway, we've been looking for someone who's willing to do something a little more creative than junipers and bark dust. Look, you don't need to decide now. Think it over and we can talk about it another time."

Ford looked pleased. He could use the extra business, especially in winter. But Nevin wanted to jump into the conversation and ask them what would happen to this cozy professional relationship when his personal relationship with Colin blew up. Then again, Colin and Ford were grown-ups who would probably handle the situation maturely. Damn them.

They didn't linger long after their meal was done because Ford and Katie were going to a movie. Out in the parking lot, it was Ford's turn to initiate a hug with Colin, which was a bit of a shock to Nevin. Ford wasn't usually the touchy-feely type, and after he pulled away, he maintained eye contact with Colin. "I don't know how you and Nevin decided to give this a try, but I sure am glad you did. He needed someone to tame him."

"I don't want to tame him," Colin protested. "I like him prickly."

Ford laughed. "You got a point. He wouldn't be Nevin if he turned all soft and sentimental. But maybe you can settle him a little. That'd be good."

Colin glanced at Nevin with a smile. "He's nice to my cat. Beyond that, I just want us to make each other happy."

"Nervy Nevin happy—yeah, that sounds good to me."

"Fuck off, Four-Door," Nevin muttered.

When Nevin and Colin got into Julie, Nevin didn't start the engine right away. After a moment or two, Colin put his hand on Nevin's thigh. "Thank you. That's the nicest thing you could have done for me."

"Buying you tacos?"

"You know that's not what I mean."

Nevin looked down at Colin's hand, the shape of it indistinct in the dark car. "I introduced you to my brother and didn't die."

"Nope. We all survived. I like him. I see why you guys are so close. He's funny and he's... solid, isn't he?"

"As a fucking rock."

An enormous burst of air escaped Nevin's lungs, as if he'd been holding his breath for a very long time. "Is your dad going to be pissed over the landscaping thing?"

"No. He'll understand that it's worth paying a little extra to get plantings that aren't incredibly boring. It all adds value. You know what? He's even coming around on the rehab thing. He saw the plans for one of the Clinton houses the other day and almost admitted I was right."

Although Nevin smiled, he didn't reply. He didn't start the car either, and Colin seemed content to sit there in the dark, watching the inside of the windshield fog over.

"I think maybe I might survive meeting your family," Nevin said at last.

Colin didn't jump and shout, but he did grab Nevin's hand. "Yeah?"

"Probably."

"So how do you want to arrange the showdown? We can do casual or…." He bit his lip, as if the rest was too hard to say.

"Or?" Nevin prompted.

"Thanksgiving's coming up."

For most of his childhood, Nevin had ignored the holiday. Many of his foster parents had done the same or had at least been content when he'd spent the day in a bedroom, away from the real family. A few times he'd been in group homes or similar institutions, and on those occasions there had been dry turkey turned cold, canned green beans, stale rolls, and apple pie that tasted like soggy cardboard. And no real reason to give thanks. More recently he and Ford sometimes spent the holiday together—at a decent restaurant, since neither of them cooked. Or Rhoda would invite them to her house, where she'd gather an eclectic mix of friends, relatives, and strays. This year Ford was doing Thanksgiving with Katie's people. Nevin hadn't given his own plans any thought.

"I can't decide whether that's better or worse than brunch," he said.

Colin answered promptly. "Better. We argue at brunch. Friendly arguments, but…. On Thanksgiving, though, everyone eats too much to bicker. And God, Mom and Dad can cook!"

"Not the servants?"

Colin poked him. "Asshat."

Laughing, Nevin made a decision. "Fine. Thanksgiving it is. If I don't end up having a fucking nervous breakdown first."

EXACTLY A week before Thanksgiving, Nevin was walking by Frankl's office when he caught Jeremy Cox's name. Frankl wasn't as prone to gossip as most cops, and he didn't sound happy. Nevin entered the office without knocking and glared until Frankl hung up his phone. "What the fuck were you talking about?" Nevin demanded.

"Not your case."

"What case?" Nevin stomped closer to Frankl's chair. "What's going on with Jeremy?"

Frankl was one of the few people who refused to back down from Nevin. Now Frankl peered up at him, his eyes even sadder than usual. "He's landed in some trouble."

An unusual emotion flooded Nevin—guilt. He'd been so busy acting like a giddy schoolgirl with Colin that he'd neglected Jeremy. It had been some time since they'd met up for coffee or a run. He covered his self-disgust and discomfort by grabbing a chair, scooting it close to Frankl's, and sitting down with a scowl. "What's wrong?"

A blue ballpoint pen sat on Frankl's desk. He picked it up and clicked it a number of times, until Nevin was just about ready to grab the fucking thing and impale him with it. Then Frankl sighed and set the pen down again. "You remember his ex, right?"

"Donny? Yeah, I remember that steaming pile of shit. What the fuck did he—"

"He's dead."

Nevin blinked. The news shouldn't have been such a shock, considering the source. Frankl was a homicide detective after all. But still, Nevin had known the guy. And he'd seen that Jeremy had genuinely loved him, not that Donny deserved it. He drank, he was a shitty cop, and he cheated on Jeremy. "Jesus. Does Jeremy know?"

Frankl snorted. "Yeah, he knows. Because whoever murdered Donny also trashed Jeremy's apartment."

"Why?"

"Donny paid him a visit the day before he got killed."

"That son of a *bitch*! It's been, what? Five, six years? Goddammit, tell me Germy wasn't so hard up that he considered seeing him again." If so, Nevin would go beat some sense into him. Well, once the big guy stopped grieving.

But Frankl shook his head. "Nah. Donny showed up in bad shape—somebody had beat him. Jeremy patched him up, gave him cash, and sent him on his way. Somebody found Donny floating in the river the next day—shot in the back before he was dumped. We figure whoever did it thinks Donny left something at Jeremy's place."

"What?"

"Who the hell knows?" Frankl looked like he was considering playing with the pen again, but instead he removed a package of breath mints from his desk drawer, popped one in his mouth, and held the roll out to Nevin, who shook his head impatiently. After returning the package to the drawer, Frankl sighed. "Whoever it was, they tossed Jeremy's place pretty good. He's gonna have to stay elsewhere for a while."

"Fuck." Nevin gave a thought to offering his place. But he had only the one bedroom, and his couch wasn't comfortable enough to sleep on. Jeremy had other good friends—Rhoda, for instance. "You have any leads on the case?"

"We have some ideas. Not enough to make anything stick yet. Meantime, I've been telling Jeremy to watch his back." He barked a humorless laugh. "For a minute I thought his new boyfriend had something to do with it. But now I'm pretty sure not."

Well, hell if Frankl wasn't full of surprises this afternoon. "Germy Cox has a new boyfriend?"

"Yup."

"Not another scumbucket like Donny?" Nevin wasn't going to be respectful to a man who managed to screw Jeremy over even in death.

"I don't think so."

Nevin couldn't pull any additional information out of Frankl and decided it was better to go to the source. Besides, he wanted to make sure Jeremy was doing all right. If anyone could weather a run of bad luck, it was Jeremy Cox, but Nevin figured he ought to make sure. He called Jeremy, found out he was staying in the Marriott by the river, and arranged to meet him there at six.

After work, Nevin changed into sweats and jogged the half mile to the hotel. Jeremy waited for him on the sidewalk outside the lobby. He was big and handsome and grinning like someone whose life wasn't falling apart. Nevin decided Jeremy needed a good run more than an interrogation, so with little preamble, they took off.

Night had already fallen before Nevin left work, so it was difficult to see some of the details of their surroundings as they ran. Still, about three miles into their run, Nevin realized that he kept seeing the same car—a gray Toyota. It followed them at a distance, and sometimes it wasn't visible at all, but it kept reappearing as he and Jeremy zigzagged through town.

As they stood again on the sidewalk outside the hotel, trying to catch their breath, the Toyota drove by. "Did you notice—" Nevin began.

"That gray Toyota? Yep. I was a cop too, you know."

"He's been following us since—"

"Since we began. I know. I saw him the other day too. He's not especially sneaky."

There wasn't much Nevin could do about it. He didn't even have his gun on him. And Jeremy shrugged the whole thing off as though it was no big fucking deal. Then he changed the subject completely, grinning at Nevin and giving his shoulder a quick squeeze.

"Thanks for the run. Join me at Rhoda's next week?"

Shit. It should have occurred to Nevin that this might come up. "Nah. I, uh, got plans."

"Don't tell me you have to work. Avoiding crappy shifts is supposed to be one of the benefits of moving off patrol."

Nevin pretended to find the hotel sign fascinating. "I'm going somewhere."

"Somewhere?"

"Dinner." When Jeremy just waited, eyebrows raised, Nevin snarled. "Nosy fucker, aren't you? I'm invited to dinner at a fancy-ass house in the hills. I have to wear a fucking suit. And then I have to pretend like I'm goddamn civilized because I'm meeting the parents. All right? Satisfied now, asshole?"

Jeremy beamed like a man who'd just won the lottery. "Whose parents?"

God. If he said it out loud, it made the whole thing true, didn't it? He'd avoided asking about Jeremy's new boyfriend out of fear of falling into this exact discussion. He kicked the sidewalk. "This... this guy. Colin. He's fruity as a nutcake and he prances around with his twatty graduate degree and his fancy-schmancy everything, and the only reason I can stand to be near him is he's got a spectacular ass and he's hung like goddamn Pegasus." He glanced up at Jeremy, scowled, and looked away. "And he's also a pretty good guy," he muttered.

"Way to go, Nev. Mazel tov."

It was a funny thing. Here was Jeremy Cox with a murdered ex, a damaged home, and a suspicious car tailing him. But he looked genuinely happy just because Nevin had admitted he was seeing someone. The whole situation with Colin was weird and alien and just not something Nevin had ever pictured for himself. Yet it made Jeremy happy. And Nevin? Fuck. Maybe he was feeling happy too.

CHAPTER TWENTY

"AND DON'T forget to bring—"

"The pies and wine. I know, Mom." Although those were Colin's usual contributions to Thanksgiving dinner and he'd never once forgotten them, his mom always called to remind him. He didn't take it personally. He knew she also reminded Miranda to bring the candied sweet potatoes, and on Thanksgiving Day itself, she reminded his dad to baste the turkey every thirty minutes. One year for Christmas, his dad bought her a T-shirt that said *Control Freak* in red-rhinestoned letters. She'd worn it proudly.

"I'm really looking forward to meeting him," she said.

Colin glanced at Nevin, who sat on the couch with Legolas in his lap, both of them seemingly at peace. "He's special," Colin said loudly enough for Nevin to hear. Without even looking up, Nevin flipped him off, making Colin laugh. "I gotta go, Mom. We'll see you tomorrow."

"That woman keeps you on a short fucking leash," Nevin said as Colin plopped back onto the couch.

"Yep. It doesn't bother me, though." He knew it was her way of showing she cared. "Hey, Nev?"

Nevin grunted. An old episode of *Law & Order* was on the TV, mostly so Nevin could make fun of it, which Colin found more entertaining than the show itself.

Maybe this wasn't the best time to raise the subject, when Nevin was already stressed about the following day, but with some subjects, there was no good time. "Have you ever tried to find out what happened to your mother?"

"No," said Nevin, turning his head to look at Colin with flat eyes.

"You could, though, right? You're a cop, so you could access stuff."

"I don't fucking care what happened to that bitch. She left, good-bye, the end. She's irrelevant."

They both knew that wasn't true. Nevin's mother had left him with scars deeper than the one on Colin's chest. But Colin had been thinking about her over the past weeks. "Has it ever occurred to you that maybe she abandoned you because she cared about you?"

"Yeah, that's exactly what a loving mother does."

"Her life was pretty screwed-up, though, right? Drugs and stuff?"

"And stuff," Nevin echoed darkly.

"What if she realized she wasn't going to escape and was just dragging you down with her? Maybe she even tried to be your mom for a while. I mean, she kept you for three years. I bet that wasn't easy. But at some point, it just gets to be too much, so she walks away. She must have known the system would take you in."

Nevin's jaw worked. "And the system was such a tender fucking parent."

"Yeah, I know." Colin reached over to stroke Legolas and saw a bit of Nevin's tenseness release, just as if he were the one being petted. "I know it sucked, and I know you fought really hard just to survive. But would you have been better off if she stuck around?"

After a long silence, Nevin answered. "Dunno. But dammit, that doesn't make what she did all right!"

"No, it doesn't. I'm just saying that you shouldn't assume she didn't love you. You're…. Let's face it, Nev. You're a pretty loveable guy." When Nevin made a face as if doubting Colin's sanity, Colin smiled. "You are. Ford loves you. I love you, Nevin." Then he held his breath, waiting for the explosion.

But the explosion never came. Instead Nevin shook his head. "I don't know how you put up with me, Collie. Don't understand what you fucking see in me."

"You're strong. God, you're *so* strong. But when we're together, you're not afraid to let me be strong too. You're passionate, and I don't just mean about sex, although that part's fantastic too. You're funny. You want me to do what I care about, not what's going to make the most money. You don't settle for what's comfortable and easy. You have an energy to you, a vibration. When I'm with you, I feel like I can accomplish anything I want."

It was an unrehearsed speech, but every word was true. And there was more. The way Colin could trust Nevin completely. The way Nevin made even the most boring things interesting. The way just thinking about Nevin made his heart beat faster. "Legolas likes you," he added. "And he has excellent taste."

Nevin hung his head, eyes closed. When he looked up again, his mouth was set. "I can't say it. Don't know if I'll ever—"

"It's okay. They're only words. Actions speak louder, right? You're here in my home, where you've spent most of your free time for weeks. You introduced me to your brother, and you're willing to face my family. Trent used to say those three words, but they didn't mean anything."

"Douche bag," Nevin said automatically.

"Yeah. Anyway, I'm not sitting here pining away because you can't say the magic words. I'm not a princess in a tower."

"Wasn't it the prince who needed the magic words? Before his fucking flower died? The beast."

Colin laughed. "I *love* that you know Disney plots now."

"Jesus. Yeah, I know Disney plots and the difference between Star Trek and Star Wars, and I know how Harry fucking Potter got rid of Voldemort. Thanks to you, I know what a hobbit is and that it's a bad fucking idea to wear the One Ring, even if it does make you invisible. You bring me joy, okay? You bring me joy, and that's all I can fucking—" His voice broke and he turned away.

They made it to the bed and made love spooned together, Colin deep inside Nevin's body and stroking Nevin's soft parted lips. It wasn't earth-moving, and no fireworks exploded, yet Colin wouldn't have traded those moments for anything.

BY THE middle of the afternoon on Thursday, Colin was seriously considering giving Nevin his second blowjob of the day. He had provided the first when they woke up. After that they went for a run, Nevin slowing his pace to Colin's. They showered upon their return and spent a couple of hours dozing under the fleece blanket on the couch. But as the day wore on, Nevin grew increasingly jumpy, to the point that he paced the length of the loft like a caged beast.

"You don't have to do this," Colin pointed out for the umpteenth time. "Nobody wants to torture you."

"You promised your parents."

"We can tell them you're not feeling well. They'll understand. I'll make popcorn and we can watch *Cabaret* and *Hairspray*."

"I'm not some pansy-ass fuckmuppet who goes back on his promises. Just…. Fuck." Nevin stomped off to the bedroom, where he stripped off his clothes. Just before Colin could pounce on him for some nice, calming sex, Nevin grabbed his suit from Colin's closet and began getting dressed. Colin shrugged and started undressing.

Nevin was just finishing with his suit buttons when his phone rang. He answered with a barked "Ng." After he listened for a moment, his face went grim and pale. "Yeah, yeah, okay. I'm on my way."

He disconnected, then stared at Colin, his expression stricken.

"Oh God, what is it?" Colin asked. Had something happened to Ford?

"Germ—Jeremy Cox. He's been kidnapped."

Colin could only blink in shock.

Nevin hurried past him but then stopped and turned around. "I have to go. Jeremy's new boyfriend—he's the one who called it in—Frankl says he thinks the guy may start falling apart. I need to get over there and—"

"Go. It's okay."

"Thanksgiving…."

"Is less important than this."

After two jerky nods, Nevin grabbed him for a savage kiss. "I'm sorry, Collie. Thank you for understanding."

"Just keep in touch if you can. And please—stay safe."

Nevin nodded once more before heading toward the door.

Colin wanted to ask a thousand questions, beginning with who had kidnapped Jeremy and why. But his focus was mainly on whether Nevin was going to be in danger, and he knew Nevin didn't need to hear that right now. So Colin watched him put on dress shoes and a coat, and he grabbed him just before he left. "Be careful."

"I'm so sorry, Collie. I really—"

"Shh." Colin laid a finger over Nevin's lips and repeated the important thing. "Just be careful."

COLIN REMEMBERED the pies and the wine, but he arrived at his parents' house feeling as if he were missing something important. Which he was, of course. Miranda met him in the entryway and took the wine bottles from him. "Mom and Dad are—" She stopped. "Where is he?"

"He can't come."

"Colin Oscar Westwood, you look like crap! Did this guy dump you? On Thanksgiving? Because I'm going to—"

"He didn't dump me. He…. Let's go find Mom and Dad. I don't want to keep repeating the story."

Grumbling, she followed him into the kitchen, where their dad was fussing over cranberry sauce while their mom arranged rolls in a basket. Voices carried from the living room—aunts, uncles, and cousins watching a football game, most likely. He heard Hannah laughing with one of the younger cousins. He put on his bravest smile and faced his immediate family. "Nevin's not coming," he announced. Then, before Nevin could be unjustly accused of anything, Colin continued. "He got called in to work. A friend of his has been kidnapped."

"Kidnapped!" his dad exclaimed. "By whom?"

"I don't know yet. I don't have any details. I'm going to keep my phone nearby at dinner, though. Just in case."

His mom came over and gazed searchingly into his face. "Are you all right, honey?"

"I'm not the one who was kidnapped, Mom. I'm fine. A little worried, and I'm disappointed you don't get to meet him, but that's all."

Although she clearly wanted to say more, she didn't. That was a win.

Soon afterward, everyone gathered in the dining room. A few of the more clueless people asked about Trent, but Miranda gained points by steering the conversation into the more turbulent waters of politics. Everyone left Colin alone, instead squabbling loudly about who was likely to end up on the following year's presidential ticket.

Colin's phone buzzed in his pocket just as his dad was distributing turkey. Colin gave him an apologetic look before ducking into the kitchen.

No news on J. I'm at his bf's place, drinking tea. Safe.

Can I help? Colin sent back.

No. Fuck. J's bf, Qay? A goddamn mess. I don't blame him.

Neither did Colin. And it gave him a weird sense of pride to know *his* boyfriend was there, doing whatever he could to give moral support. *I still love you.*

Dope, Nevin texted. Colin grinned.

Although the meal smelled wonderful and doubtless tasted even better, Colin ate little. He wasn't as worried about Nevin's safety anymore, but that didn't mean he wasn't concerned. What if something awful happened to Jeremy? Nevin didn't have many friends, and he'd be devastated.

A couple of hours later, as everyone lounged in a tryptophan stupor in the living room, Colin's phone buzzed again. This time it was a call, so he hurried to his old bedroom to answer. "What's happening?" he demanded.

"They found him. He's alive but really banged up. Those motherfuckers tortured him!" Despite the anger, Nevin sounded exhausted.

"Why?" asked Colin.

"Some stupid shit having to do with Jeremy's ex. I don't know. There's never a good reason for this kind of crap."

"Will he be all right?"

"Dunno. He's in surgery now."

Shit. "How's his boyfriend?"

"Qay?" Nevin huffed audibly. "He used to be a junkie, so he can't even numb himself with a couple stiff shots. I gotta say, though, he's holding it together surprisingly well. If something like this happened to you...."

"It won't."

Neither of them spoke for a bit, but that was all right. Colin figured Nevin just needed to know he was there. Meanwhile, Colin paced his room. His posters were gone, the walls long since repainted, but his old bed remained, along with his dresser and desk and chair. The house contained more bedrooms than his parents needed, so it wasn't a great surprise that they hadn't repurposed this one. Still, it felt a little as though they wanted to preserve it, to keep a place for him in case he returned. The idea both upset and soothed him in equal measures.

"I'll let you get back to your holiday," Nevin said.

"I can talk to you."

"No. Look, I'm gonna stick around until we learn more. I'll call you then."

"Okay. Nev? Will you come over to my place after? Please?"

Another silence. Then, "Okay."

When Colin returned to the living room, his mom drew him aside. "What's going on, honey?"

"They found Nevin's friend, but he's not in good shape."

"Oh no!"

"Yeah, I didn't ask for any details. He's in surgery, and Nev's being moral support for the boyfriend."

She stroked his cheek. "Are you okay?"

"Mom, I've never even met Jeremy. I wish I could be there to... support Nevin's supporting, I guess. But he's got this. And I'll be there for him when he gets home." The last word was out of his mouth before he realized the implications. He winced.

"You've been seeing a lot of each other. He's important to you."

"He is."

She looked searchingly into his eyes. "But he's commitment shy?"

"He has issues. Jeez, so do I. Mine are different, is all."

"I just don't want to see you get hurt, sweetheart."

"I know you don't. But here's the thing. He's always been completely up-front with me about what he can and can't handle, so it's not like he's leading me on. He's doing his best. Until he got that call today, he was ready to come here, and for him... I think he'd rather be shot at. But he was going to do it."

Something exciting must have happened in the football game, because the assembled audience erupted into noise. His mom ignored them, concentrating on Colin instead. "I'm not trying to criticize him. I'll wait until I meet him for that." She grinned briefly. "But no matter how hard he's trying or how understanding you are, if it doesn't work out...."

"I *know*, Mom. I'm taking a risk. It's about time I tried that, don't you think? I'd rather have a broken heart than spend my life swaddled in emotional Bubble Wrap."

After a thoughtful pause, she nodded. "You're right. And I know you're not fourteen years old anymore. But that doesn't mean I can stop worrying. I'm still your mother."

He gave her a quick hug. "I know you love me. How about if you help me pack up some leftovers so Nevin can eat later?"

"Done."

NEVIN SHOWED up late, ragged and exhausted. But he'd texted earlier, so Colin knew that Jeremy was going to be all right and that Qay wasn't completely freaking out.

"Is everyone safe now?" Colin asked as he helped remove Nevin's coat.

"Yeah. Two of the fucknuggets are dead, and the others are going to spend the rest of their miserable lives in prison." He stood passively, allowing Colin to remove his suit jacket and shirt. "And Qay proved his mettle. If I'd met him before, I might have had my doubts. Germy's had shitty taste in men. This one's a keeper, though. High maintenance, but worth it."

"That's good." Colin unfastened Nevin's belt and slacks, then pushed them down to Nevin's feet. He and Nevin tangled awkwardly for a moment as Colin struggled to remove Nevin's shoes, but eventually Nevin was undressed except for underwear and socks. Colin towed him to the couch and gently pushed him down before draping him with the fleece blanket.

"I'm going to heat you up some dinner."

Slumping against the cushions, Nevin yawned. "Parker brought me some food. Rhoda's son."

Colin was glad to hear that. "How long ago?"

"Dunno." Another yawn. "A while."

"Do you want to eat again? It's Thanksgiving. You should be uncomfortably full."

Nevin smiled sleepily at him. "Sure. Thanks."

While he was at it, Colin reheated a plate for himself too. Nevin made appreciative noises while he ate. "'S good," he said through a mouthful of stuffing.

"Better when it's not nuked, but yeah."

"I'm sorry I missed—"

"Don't."

"You're not angry with me?" Nevin frowned.

"Why would I be angry? *You* didn't kidnap Jeremy. You're a good friend, Nev. The kind people can count on."

Nevin blinked in confusion, as if he'd never thought of himself as that kind of person. Colin chuckled. "C'mon. Finish up and come to bed."

"Too tired to ravish you. Jesus, I'm getting old. Never thought I'd be too wiped to fuck."

Twenty minutes later they lay spooned in bed with Legolas perched on the pillow beside Nevin's head. Nevin shifted restlessly until Colin wrapped his arms around him, at which point Nevin settled at once.

"Are there leftovers for tomorrow?" Nevin asked.

"Yep. Turkey and cranberry sauce sandwiches for lunch."

"Mmm. Did you have a nice time with your family?"

"Sure."

"Collie?"

Colin made an interrogative noise as he yawned.

"I'm thankful for you."

Chapter Twenty-One

December 2015

Colin was a goddamn saint. He didn't bitch about the missed Thanksgiving dinner and didn't ask Nevin to make up for it in any way. He didn't even push to reschedule a parental meet and greet, although Nevin was certain that would be coming soon enough. And then, just when things were running smoothly again, it was Jeremy's turn to call in a panic. Apparently Qay had relapsed and then taken a runner, and Jeremy was frantic to find him.

"I'll make sure all the gorillas keep an eye out for him," Nevin promised. He'd also warn them to go easy. As far as he knew, Qay hadn't broken any laws, and the last thing they needed to do was spook him. On the other hand, Nevin wasn't feeling optimistic about the results of the search. Personal experience had taught him how easy it was for someone to disappear.

He spent most of the following days visiting dive bars and talking to junkies and drug dealers but finding no sign of Qay. In between those forays, he and Rhoda teamed up to keep Jeremy from making himself sick with worry. Nevin didn't see much of Colin. And Colin didn't complain about that either.

On a Sunday two weeks before Christmas, Nevin finally managed a few free hours. He headed immediately to Colin's loft, where man and cat greeted him enthusiastically.

"Promise me," Nevin said over take-out Thai, "that you will never rabbit like that."

"Come on. I'm probably the least likely person on the planet to run away from home."

"Still. When you leave—"

Colin reached across the table and grabbed his hand. "I'm not leaving."

Nevin thought about Colin's history with the douche bag. "But what about if you *want* to leave? Will you just stick around, sick to death of me but too nice to hurt my precious fucking feelings?"

"I'm not a doormat. But unless you do something monumentally stupid, I won't want to leave. Luckily you're a pretty smart guy."

"Huh." Maybe Nevin would eventually stop being a fuckwad who needed constant reassurance, but he wasn't there yet. Colin seemed cheerful, though, as if he were willing to stroke Nevin's ego until the fucking apocalypse. But then, maybe he got something out of being the strong one in the relationship. He certainly enjoyed taking charge when they had sex. Hell, Nevin enjoyed that too.

Colin smiled sunnily at him. "So. Christmas is almost here."

"Yeah." Shit. That meant Nevin had to get him a present, and he didn't have much experience at that sort of thing. He and Ford bought each other dinner to celebrate things, and nobody else had ever been close enough for Nevin to worry about. What the fuck were you supposed to get your boyfriend when he was richer than you—and didn't seem to want much in the way of material shit?

"My parents are having a gala."

"What?"

"A gala."

"What the fuck are you talking about?" Nevin had heard the term before, but he didn't understand how it related to Colin's parents.

"They rent a space—this year it's a gallery a couple of blocks from here—and hire caterers and musicians. They invite everyone—all their friends and everyone they know from work. Everyone dresses up. It's fun. And the best part? They collect donations for a charity." He smiled widely. "This year it's going to be Bright Hope."

"Manny could always use extra cash."

"Last year they collected for an animal shelter. They got over a hundred thousand dollars."

"Holy crap!" Nevin narrowed his eyes. "But what does this have to do with me?"

"I can't wait to see how amazing you look in a tuxedo."

A FEW days later, Jeremy flew to Kansas and was reunited with Qay and, apparently, the two of them saw the goddamn light. They returned to Portland, shacked up at Jeremy's place, and emerged over the following days only for groceries.

"I'm so happy for them," Colin announced as he and Nevin lay in bed on Sunday morning.

"You don't even know them. And it's not one of your stupid movies with the happily ever afters. Qay's still got a monkey on his back and enough baggage to make me look well-adjusted. Germy's still got a hero complex."

"But they've survived a crisis and they're working together. That's sweet. Some people *do* get happy endings, you know."

"I'll give you a happy ending," said Nevin, giving Colin's cock a few strokes. He'd been thinking more and more lately about how he wanted that thing inside him without a latex barrier, and how he'd love to do the same to Colin. He'd never barebacked, not even once. Maybe he'd talk to Colin after the holidays about getting tested. Hey—that could be his Christmas present to Colin. Ho ho ho.

Colin whimpered, pressing his groin into Nevin's hand. But then he retreated slightly. "What happened to pancakes for breakfast?"

"Pancakes? You're thinking about pancakes when you can have this?" Nevin grabbed Colin's hand and placed it on his own cock. Maybe it wasn't as big as Colin's, but it did the job.

"Hmm, but I had that last night. I haven't had pancakes for—" Colin squawked as Nevin quickly flipped on top of him. An enthusiastic kiss stopped the squawk, and Colin parried with a double-handed squeeze of Nevin's ass. Just as Colin started to arch his hips upward, Nevin fluttered his fingers under Colin's arm. Colin was wonderfully ticklish.

They wrestled and groped, and their laughter was just starting to turn to moans when Nevin's phone rang.

"If that's Germy or Qay, they can fuck themselves upside down," he muttered.

But it was Frankl. "Double homicide," he said without preamble.

"Mother Mary's tits. Why are you calling to tell me this?"

"Because you know the vics."

Horrible images flashed through Nevin's brain—Jeremy and Qay, Ford and Katie, Rhoda and Parker. Broken and bloody. "Who?" he rasped.

"Bob and Ivan Thomas."

AT LEAST Frankl didn't insist they go to the station. He met them at a Starbucks instead, without Blake. He sat across the round wooden table, his hound-dog eyes grave. Colin was as pale as marble except for his eyes, which were swollen and red.

"Tell me what happened," demanded Nevin.

But Frankl shook his head. "I need a statement from Mr. Westwood first."

"Fuck that. Since Friday night, the only time Colin's been out of my sight was when one of us was using the john."

Frankl shifted in his seat. "I'm not asking for an alibi, Ng. At this point Mr. Westwood isn't a suspect."

"But—"

"It's fine," Colin interrupted. "Go ahead and ask whatever you need to, Detective."

After a curt nod, Frankl pulled out his notebook and a pen. "You were acquainted with Bob and Ivan Thomas?"

The questioning lasted for nearly half an hour, even though Colin clearly had little valuable information. Frankl was fishing, goddammit, which meant he didn't have a fucking clue who'd killed them or why.

Nevin had finished his second coffee by the time Frankl put the notebook away. "Your turn. What happened?" Nevin demanded.

"A friend dropped by their house this morning with breakfast and got concerned when nobody answered the bell. She called 911. Responding officers found the front door closed but unlocked and the decedents in the kitchen. Judging by rigor, I'd estimate time of death was yesterday afternoon."

Although Colin had managed to go even paler, he asked a question in a quiet voice. "How did they die?"

"Somebody tried to make this look like a murder-suicide. The larger man was strangled and the other one was asphyxiated with a plastic bag over his head."

"They wouldn't do that! They were enjoying life, and Ivan would never—"

"I said somebody *tried*. That somebody did a piss-poor job of it."

"How so?" Nevin asked.

"Half-eaten food on the table, for one thing. Nobody decides to do this in the middle of a meal. And it looks as if the one man's hands were severely arthritic. I doubt he had the grip strength to strangle anyone."

When Colin dropped his head, Nevin reached over to give his shoulder a squeeze. "What else you got?" Nevin asked.

"Not much. No forced entry. Techs are still sweeping the scene, and Blake's with them. We should have preliminary autopsy results in the morning."

"And that's it?"

"Mostly. That friend of the Thomases mentioned they had a housecleaner, and the name rang a bell, so I looked him up. He's the same guy who cleaned Mrs. Ruskin's house." He retrieved his notebook and took a quick glance at something he'd written. "A Jerry Griffin. Do you know him, Mr. Westwood?"

Colin slowly shook his head. "Mrs. Ruskin mentioned a cleaning service a few times, but only in passing." He frowned. "But usually she had me over shortly after the service came. My visits were... social occasions for her."

"It's probably just a coincidence," Frankl said thoughtfully. "But Griffin's got a couple old priors—some drug charges from the nineties—so we'll look into him."

"Keep me in the loop?" Nevin asked.

After a brief hesitation, Frankl nodded. "You too," he said with a significant glance at Colin.

After Frankl was gone, Colin remained at the table, his cup of cooled decaf cradled in his palms. "They were really nice people," he whispered.

"I know." Nevin had met them only once, when Colin had brought him along on one of his visits. Bob and Ivan had cooed over them like teenagers at a fan con. They'd shared some of their photos too—drag queens, people in sixties hairdos, venues long since closed and turned into something else. They were a bit over-the-top, maybe, but Nevin had liked them. He'd been happy at how clearly taken they were with his boy.

"They didn't even get the chance to celebrate the sale of their house. Why would someone do this?"

"We'll find out."

Colin didn't say anything, but his stare spoke volumes. *The way you found out who killed Mrs. Ruskin and Roger Grey?*

"You should go home," Nevin said, thinking of the calming virtues of petting Legolas.

"I knew them. Just like I knew.... God, what if this is my fault?"

"How could it be your fault? You were kind to these people, Collie. You went out of your way to bring some happiness into their lives. That has nothing to do with them being murdered."

Colin shook his head miserably. "But it's a pretty big coincidence, isn't it? I mean, if they'd all dropped dead of natural causes, okay. None of them were young and they all had health issues. But none were natural causes."

Nevin wanted to reassure him but didn't have the words and wasn't willing to lie. Sure, murders happened. But elderly white people weren't the usual victims, and the deaths typically weren't so mysterious. Killers generally knew their victims, yet no one among these people's acquaintances seemed likely suspects.

Unless, of course, there were acquaintances the bureau didn't know about. In fact, that seemed likely. In all three cases, there was no sign of anyone breaking into the victims' homes. And in Grey's case, there was that mysterious arm in the ATM surveillance video. Then there was the housecleaner, but Nevin had seen Grey's apartment and doubted very much that Grey had anyone tidying up his place.

It was possible the same perp was responsible for all the murders—a chilling idea. But fuck! Nothing tied them together except Colin.

"Collie?"

"Hmm."

An idea was floating somewhere in Nevin's head, but he couldn't quite grasp it. "How'd you get started with Bright Hope?"

To his surprise, Colin laughed softly. "Mrs. Ruskin."

"What?"

"A couple months before she died, she told me she'd always been attracted to women but never did anything about it. I was the only person she ever told. That's sad—staying in the closet for eighty-something years."

It was, but that wasn't important at the moment. "And?" Nevin prompted.

"Since she was lonely, I thought maybe she might enjoy meeting some other people like her."

"Octogenarian lesbians."

Another small chuckle. "Right. Um, not an easy demographic to track down. But I'd heard of Bright Hope—our company gave them some donations. I told Mrs. Ruskin about them, but I don't know if she ever contacted Manuel. It wasn't a very comfortable subject for her. After she died, I started volunteering there."

Then it wasn't just Colin who tied these cases together. That was a relief. Nevin needed to have a little chat with Manuel, it seemed.

But not now. The dead were already at rest, but Colin needed comforting.

"Come home," Nevin coaxed, wrapping his hand around Colin's and pulling him gently to his feet.

BACK AT Colin's loft, they checked on Legolas, who was curled up near a heating vent. He gave them the evil eye for disturbing his sleep, then ignored them.

"Get into bed," Nevin ordered Colin.

"It's two in the afternoon. I have to—"

"Bed."

For once, Colin let Nevin boss him around. He threw his clothes carelessly onto the floor, leaving on only his boxer briefs, and crawled under the blankets. He lay curled on his side, eyes wide open and blank. Nevin briefly considered calling Colin's parents. Surely his mother would be eager to comfort him. But no, goddammit! Right now, Colin was *his*. His lover, his friend, his responsibility.

"I'll be right back."

Colin didn't respond.

Nevin walked into the kitchen and spent a minute or two standing helplessly. His chaotic upbringing meant he'd never learned to cook properly. When he was poor and living on his own, he'd survived mostly on ramen and sandwiches, and nowadays he did takeout and frozen dinners. But Colin hadn't eaten anything all day, and going to a restaurant was out of the question. Nevin didn't even want to leave him long enough to run out for something.

Fine, goddammit. He could handle this. Hadn't he promised pancakes?

He found pancake mix in a cupboard, a bowl and frying pan in another, and milk, butter, and eggs in the fridge. Muttering to himself, he read the instructions on the box.

He dropped most of the eggshells into the first batch, then made a goopy mess trying to fish them out. He dumped that disaster into the garbage disposal, wiped the counter, and tried again. The second time, he poured mix too carelessly, resulting in a choking cloud of powder and another mess all over the counter and floor. By then Legolas had awakened and wandered over, watching from a safe distance and looking amused.

"Yeah? So why don't *you* make pancakes, mousebreath?"

Legolas licked his paw.

On the third try, Nevin managed to get the batter mixed to what he hoped was the right consistency. But his triumph was short-lived, because he soon discovered he was incapable of pancake flipping. They twisted and splattered and glorped, and the results were half-burned and half-raw.

And now he was out of eggs.

"Fuck it," he told the cat. Colin could eat toast instead.

When Nevin entered the bedroom, Colin glanced at him, froze, and began to giggle.

"What?" Nevin demanded, secretly pleased to see Colin momentarily happy. He sat on the mattress beside him.

Colin reached up and plucked something from Nevin's hair, then held it in a palm for inspection. It was a little ball of dried pancake batter. A quick run of fingers across his scalp revealed several similar bits of debris.

"And you have flour here." Colin gently poked the tip of Nevin's nose. "And here." That time, he brushed a finger over Nevin's cheekbone. "You look like you had a fight with the Swedish chef."

"Who?"

"Eersh kabish gabork kabish kadoo?"

"What?"

"Never mind," Colin said. "You made me food?"

Nevin looked doubtfully at the toast, which was slightly burned. "Of a sort."

Colin pulled himself to a seated position and grabbed a piece from the plate on Nevin's lap. He crunched through it quickly, then started on another. "How about you?"

"I already ate."

Colin's expression showed his awareness of Nevin's lie, but he didn't push the point. He just chewed, his gaze fixed solidly on Nevin's. God, Nevin would do anything to erase the sadness from those eyes. He waited for Colin to finish eating, then set the plate aside and leaned in for a butter-flavored kiss.

It was a truth Nevin learned long ago—the closer death comes, the more precious life seems. Over and over again, human beings celebrate survival and refute mortality with the most life-affirming act of all. Sex.

He'd done it himself over the years. A day spent tearing through traffic with sirens wailing, or hoping some drug-crazed fuckwit wasn't too quick on the trigger. A night spent naked, sweaty, plunging into someone else's body—for pleasure rather than pain. Once he'd even fucked another cop, a situation he normally avoided. Both new to the bureau, they'd spent an evening doing triage for victims of a flophouse fire. Still reeking of smoke, they'd gone off shift, driven to the other officer's apartment, got sloppy drunk, and screwed until their bodies gave out.

Nevin knew the need for human contact after the grim reaper paid a visit.

He pulled back from the kiss to find Colin flushed and breathing heavily, his pupils dark against the pale blue of his irises.

"Nev," Colin started.

"Shh."

Nevin stood and slowly undressed. He wasn't teasing but was instead gradually drawing in Colin's focus the way an angler might pull in a struggling fish. He was successful too, because by the time all Nevin's clothes were off, Colin was reaching for him. Nevin reached back.

It wasn't fucking. It was trailing hands and questing tongues, quivering bodies and rising moans. It was the scent of Colin strong in Nevin's nose—toast and sleep-sweat and sex and shampoo—and the taste of him filling Nevin's mouth. It was Colin lost to everything but what they were doing together, his head thrown back and Nevin's name tumbling from his mouth. And after their climaxes washed over them like warm waves, it was lying huddled in each other's arms, feeling the glory of bare skin against skin. "It's making love," Nevin said.

"Huh?" Colin had been dozing already.

Shit. "I love you. There. Happy now?"

Colin's eyes flew open. The smile spread slowly until it was so wide Nevin thought it might just wrap around Colin's head, and then where the hell would they be?

"Happy now," Colin whispered. He squeezed Nevin more tightly. "You know that abandonment issue you have?"

"Yeah."

"I thought you were afraid of everyone leaving you. I was wrong."

Nevin's heart raced, but it was strong and could withstand the strain. "Yeah, Sigmund?"

"What you're really afraid of is *you* leaving everyone else."

Nevin flinched. He started to pull away, but Colin held him fast.

"You don't have to go anywhere, Nev. You're not your mother or any of those people who let you down when you were a kid. You're better than any of them. Steady and tough and good to the bone."

Colin believed what he was saying. He was a man who saw rainbows where everyone else saw nothing but spilled oil. But he was smart too. Maybe he was right.

Nevin nodded. "I'm staying here until we find the killers."

"In my arms?"

"In your loft, dolt. We both still have to go to work, but at night I'm here with you." He knew that wasn't enough—death in its many forms could strike anytime. Murderers. TriMet buses. A heart betraying its owner. But he'd do what he could. "I need a safe spot for Julie."

"We own the building. I think we can manage a parking spot for you somehow."

All right. That wasn't so bad. Nevin's head hadn't exploded. But then Colin opened his mouth, and Nevin *knew* what was coming next. It was like one of those nightmares where you couldn't stop yourself from walking around the corner and encountering the horrible monster.

"Why not stay for good?" Colin asked.

And *bam*! There it was.

Only instead of slavering fangs and blood-drenched claws, the monster turned out to have bed-tossed curls, soft blue eyes, and a tentative smile. And he wasn't so horrible, was he? He was… handsome. And sweet. And beloved.

Fuck.

"Okay."

"Okay?"

"I'm not going to fucking say it again."

The corners of Colin's eyes crinkled. "Nap first. Then you can help me clear some space in the closet."

And God help him, that's exactly what they did.

CHAPTER TWENTY-TWO

COLIN WAS right—Nevin looked amazing in a tuxedo. So amazing that Colin was tempted to strip him right out of it and lick him like a Popsicle. Nevin would probably be all in favor of that plan. But Colin's parents were expecting them, and his mom had run out of patience about meeting the man who was shacking up with her son.

"You're getting ideas," Nevin said, narrow-eyed.

"Just thinking we'd better get out of here before Legolas covers us in fur." True, but Nevin probably sensed what *else* Colin was thinking. Which was that he ought to find more excuses to stuff Nevin into a tux. Like a wedding, for instance.

But okay, small steps. Look how far Nevin had come—much farther than he'd expected of himself. The least Colin could do was give him time and space.

"Let's go," said Nevin. And when he put on his long wool overcoat, he managed the impossible—he looked even more gorgeous. Except that his face was set in the grim, determined lines of a man about to face a firing squad.

"Drink as much as you want tonight," Colin said. "I can drive us home."

"You think I'm better behaved when I'm wasted?"

"I think you're a perfect gentleman all the time. Come on."

The gala was only a short distance from the loft, but cold rain sluiced from the sky. Despite umbrellas, they were both wet by the time they reached Julie. "Why can't you live in a building with underground parking?" Nevin groused as he started the engine.

"We can move if you want. We can—"

"No."

Colin smiled. Even though Nevin had moved his things in only a few days earlier, he was falling in love with the loft and not hiding it very well.

A pair of young men waited outside the gallery, protected by a tent walkway leading from the street to the door. As soon as Nevin pulled to the curb, one of them trotted over with an ear-to-ear grin. Nevin and Colin got out of the car, and Nevin handed the kid the keys and a twenty-dollar bill. "If she comes back with a dent or scratch, I'm hauling you off to jail, and you're spending Christmas in the company of Tiny Tuiasosopo and Pitbull Jones."

Smile undimmed, the kid gave Julie a loving pat. "I'll take very good care of her, sir."

As they walked inside, Nevin scowled. "I've lost my edge. Punk wasn't even scared."

"He was terrified," Colin said, squeezing Nevin's hand. "Also, Tiny Tu—Tui—uh...."

"Tuiasosopo. Busted him years ago on a theft charge. Dude was so big he wouldn't fit in the back of my squad car. We had to call in someone with an SUV to haul him away. Wonder whatever happened to him."

"Ah, the good old days."

A smiling young woman in the foyer took their coats and gave them claim checks. A few guests stood around in ball gowns and tuxedos, but they barely glanced at Nevin and Colin. Christmas music jangled behind a set of closed double doors.

Colin took Nevin's arm. "Courage."

"Today is a good day to die," muttered Nevin, who had been persuaded lately to watch some *Star Trek*. He seemed to have a special fondness for Worf. Colin had bought him a Klingon-emblazoned coffee mug for Christmas, already wrapped and hidden in Colin's office downtown.

As soon as they entered the main room, Colin's mother descended on them. She must have been lying in wait. "You look beautiful, Mo—" Colin began, but she swept past him to envelop a startled Nevin in an embrace.

"It's wonderful to finally meet you!" she exclaimed. In her high heels, she was the same height as him.

Dignity slightly rumpled, Nevin managed to extricate himself. "It's nice to meet you, Mrs. West—"

"Oh, please! I'm Paula." She took a step back and surveyed them both. "And aren't the two of you as handsome as can be!"

Although Nevin probably wouldn't bolt, Colin took his hand, just in case. "It's a good turnout this year."

"It is. We already have forty thousand in pledges for Bright Hope and the evening's hardly started. Mr. Ceja will be so pleased when he returns."

Nevin mumbled something unintelligible. He'd been trying to get hold of Manuel since the Thomases were murdered, but apparently he and his husband were off on a cruise, incommunicado.

Paula placed a hand on Nevin's shoulder. "Really, I'm so glad you could make it. I'm looking forward to getting to know you. Fizzy's been really closemouthed about you."

Nevin's eyebrows shot up and a wicked smile appeared. "Fizzy?"

Oh God.

Colin tried to tug Nevin away, but Nevin stood fast, his head tilted slightly. "Fizzy?" he repeated.

Paula grinned. Jesus. She was doing this on *purpose*. Could a grown man disown his mother? "Colin used to be obsessed by the *My Little Pony* movie, and—"

"I was four years old!"

"—and his favorite character was Fizzy. She's a unicorn. We used to—" Something jangled on stage, catching her attention and making her frown. She patted Nevin. "You boys go get something to eat before you collapse. We'll talk later." She hurried away.

Nevin tried hard to look innocent and failed completely. "Fizzy?" he said for the third time.

"Four. I was *four*."

"But you identified with a sparkly magic unicorn named Fizzy."

"I told you nobody was surprised I turned out gay."

Cackling, Nevin followed him to the buffet table.

The food was amazing, and Colin ate more than he should have and was pleased when Nevin chowed down too. Neither of them drank anything alcoholic, even though Colin repeated his offer to drive. Or heck, for another twenty bucks they could get one of the valets to drive them home. People from work came up to them, Colin introduced them to Nevin, and gradually Nevin relaxed. He stiffened up again when Colin's father came over, but Harold was in a jolly mood and overflowing with dad jokes, and soon Nevin was snorting with laughter.

Of course, the next member of the family to wander over was Miranda, but she was too sloshed for anyone to take seriously. Apparently Hannah had decided to skip this year's festivities and hang out with her father instead, and Miranda was drowning her sorrows in pomegranate martinis.

"Think she'll remember meeting me?" Nevin asked after she stumbled off to the bathroom.

"Doubtful. She's normally not...."

"Got it. Your family is funny."

He seemed to mean that in a positive way, so Colin smiled. "And you've decided this crowd isn't quite as scary as a jailhouse full of gangbangers."

"Maybe."

When the band began to play "Merry Christmas, Baby," Nevin looked up at him. "Dance?"

"Yeah."

"I lead."

"Fair enough."

Colin wasn't a great dancer, but that was fine. It was nice just to lean against Nevin, feeling those strong arms wrapped around him, smelling his aftershave. They stayed together for several more songs; then Nevin shocked him by asking Paula to dance, leaving Colin grinning on the sidelines.

"He's good," said his dad, who'd appeared at Colin's elbow. "And very handsome. I'm glad I don't have to worry about him stealing your mother."

Colin snorted. "Worry away, Dad. He's bi."

"Ah. Well, I take it you've captured his heart thoroughly enough that I'm safe."

"I think I have." And that was a warm, wonderful feeling indeed.

Word got around that Nevin was a police detective, which made him a minor celebrity in a room full of property developers and lawyers. They wanted to hear his stories, and he seemed to enjoy having an audience. Although Colin had promised Nevin they could leave early, they were still there when most of the guests were gone. Miranda had ridden home with a friend and an impending hangover, the band had packed up, and the caterers were busily packaging the remaining food. Colin's parents usually donated the leftovers to homeless shelters or nursing homes.

Colin had his arm around Nevin, who snuggled close. Harold and Paula stood across from them, his arm around her waist.

"I think it was a success this year," Paula said, looking around with satisfaction.

"A hundred grand is pretty fucking suc—" Nevin stumbled over his words. "Um, sorry."

"I'm a lawyer, Nevin. I've heard the word before."

He laughed. "I'll bet you have." He and Paula had hit it off, dancing several times and, judging by their expressions, sharing secrets about Colin. Although Colin was horrified to guess what kinds of stories his mother might have shared—and oh God, at one point she'd said something about showing Nevin baby pictures—in the end he was grateful to see Nevin enjoying himself. And his parents enjoying Nevin. A little embarrassment—okay, a lot of embarrassment—was a small price to pay for that.

Colin yawned suddenly and jaw-crackingly. "Up past your bedtime," Nevin said. "Let's go see if that little twit was good to Julie."

Paula nodded approvingly—at the bedtime part, probably. "Thank you for taking care of Colin."

Nevin glanced at Colin, then turned to Paula. "With all due respect, Fizzy can take care of himself. He does a damned good job of it, in fact."

"Yes, he does. But it never hurts to have someone who cares about us look after us." She crooked her head to smile warmly at Harold, who leaned down to kiss her.

Colin shook his head. "Ew. Okay, on that note, we're out of here."

But Paula held out her hand. "Nevin? I'm glad you have Colin to take care of you."

Nevin looked down at his shoes, and when he raised his head, his eyes glittered. "Me too."

After a round of discussions about plans for Christmas—dinner for everyone at Paula and Harold's house—and a few fond hugs, Nevin and Colin made their way to the exit.

"I like them," Nevin said quietly as they walked. "I used to think they'd be stuck-up assholes, but they're…."

"Occasionally annoying, sometimes mortifying, but always pretty wonderful. And Nev? When you feel up to it, my family's your family too."

Instead of running away, Nevin smiled.

ON CHRISTMAS Day, Paula carried out her threats and dug out the old photo albums. Hundreds of pictures of Colin as an infant, a toddler, a dorky little kid, a gawky teen. If seeing so many pictures made Nevin sad—he didn't have a single childhood photo of himself—he didn't show it. He actually cooed over Colin in diapers and laughed at him fast asleep in a high chair, face covered in squash. He critiqued Colin's fashion sense. When he saw a shot of Colin standing near Trent at a Christmas gala, he snorted and said, "Douche bag."

"Exactly," Paula agreed.

The only photos that made Nevin unhappy were the ones of Colin in the hospital. There were a lot of them. In some of them, Colin was an infant, hands balled tightly and a zillion tubes and wires sticking out of him. In others he was older, sitting in a bed with rails and clutching stuffed animals and comic books. In one he was a young teenager. A few acne bumps on his face, a fresh pink scar on his chest.

"That's a fuck-ton of pain for a kid to go through."

Colin shrugged. That had been the way things were. "Lots of people have painful childhoods," he said. He hadn't told his parents many details of Nevin's past, figuring those weren't his stories to tell. But Harold and Paula weren't stupid. They'd most likely guessed the main points. "But I think sometimes it makes for stronger adults."

Nevin also turned out to have an unexpected gift for relating to teenagers. Instead of sulking with her phone, Hannah ended up hanging on Nevin's every word. Colin didn't know which she enjoyed more—his stories or his swearing. Miranda was obviously besotted, too, mainly because Nevin was entertaining Hannah so well.

At one point Colin went to the kitchen to get some water, and Miranda followed him. "Hannah hasn't been laughing much since Russell and I split up," she said. "Today she is."

"Well, it's Christmas."

"It's your boyfriend. He's a charmer."

Colin grinned. "He charms the pants off of me."

"He's nothing like Trent. Or… who was that guy you dated before Trent?"

Colin wrinkled his nose. "Cameron." Also a rich kid, now a plastic surgeon in Seattle.

"Yeah, him. But Nevin's sui generis."

"Is that Latin for *incredibly hot*?" Colin teased.

Miranda swatted him lightly. "Unique. In a class by himself."

Loud laughter carried through from the living room—Nevin's mixed with Hannah's, Paula's, and Harold's. "That's him," Colin agreed.

"He is also incredibly hot, though. I don't know how to say that in Latin."

Family tradition called for opening presents late on Christmas Day, although nobody remembered why. Generally the gifts weren't extravagant, although exceptions were made. Hannah squeed over hers— the latest iPhone, which, unlike her old one, had an intact screen. Colin got some new DVDs from his family and, from Nevin, an autographed photo of Orlando Bloom in his Legolas costume.

"No!" Colin said, hugging the frame to his chest. "Where did you get this?"

"My source is top secret."

In addition to the Worf mug, Colin got Nevin a bow tie. The fabric was imprinted with images of yellow police tape, and Nevin laughed so hard that he had to drink some water to recover.

Colin's parents got Nevin a present as well. It wasn't anything big— just a nice set of drawing pencils—but it made him smile and duck his head like a shy child. It was a lovely holiday, sweet and filled with joy.

And thanks to Colin's stupidity, it was very nearly their last.

CHAPTER TWENTY-THREE

WHILE THE holidays were a slow time for real estate, they were extra busy for cops. According to Nevin, it was due to families spending so much time together, combined with stress and drinking. Everyone started arguing and then beating up on one another. So while Nevin worked long hours and came home exhausted, Colin had time on his hands.

On the Wednesday after Christmas, he spent the morning and a good chunk of the afternoon cleaning. He could have made a whole new cat by gluing together all the fur he swept up. As he was tidying the living room, he accidentally knocked over a stack of papers and discovered a sketch Nevin had recently completed. Nevin liked to draw while they watched movies together, and this one captured the inside of their loft, with Leg curled up in an armchair in the corner near the bookshelves. It was the first time Colin had seen Nevin draw something living instead of just vehicles and structures. Whereas Nevin had used firm strokes for the room and furniture, there was something tentative about the lines of the cat, something heartbreakingly sweet.

"This belongs on the wall," Colin informed Legolas, who yawned in agreement.

After a bit of searching, Colin found a cardboard poster tube tucked in the back of a closet. He carefully rolled the drawing and slipped it inside, donned his boots and jacket, and headed out into the rain.

The frame shop was only a few blocks away, and there was a short line at the counter. The holidays were probably a busy time for framers. Just as the clerk began to ring up the lady in front of him, Colin's phone buzzed. He juggled the poster tube so he could answer. "Hello?"

"Hey, Colin. It's Crystal. From Bright Hope? Happy holidays!"

"Thanks. To you too."

"So, Manuel's eating midnight chocolate buffets somewhere in the Caribbean, and I'm kinda in charge while he's gone. I'm calling to ask you a favor."

"Oh. Okay." The lady in front of him pulled out her credit card.

"We have a new client who really needs someone to visit him. I'll give you his info and you can—"

"I can't. I'm sorry." Feeling guilty, he hunched his shoulders.

"Yeah, I know it's a crazy time of year, but this poor old guy's all alone for the holidays. If you could just stop in really quickly, that'd be great."

"I wish I could. But I think it's best if I stay away until, uh, this thing with the murders is cleared up." He'd tried to keep his voice quiet, but the lady in front of him turned to stare. He smiled at her, but she didn't smile back.

Crystal was silent for a moment. When she spoke again, she sounded subdued. "Does this mean you're not volunteering for us anymore?"

"I'd like to, but I'm going to have to step back for a while."

Casting a glare his way, the lady gathered her things and left. Colin stepped up to the counter with an apologetic look at the clerk. "I'm sorry. I have to go, Crystal."

"If you're done volunteering, there's paperwork you need to do."

He wasn't really *done*—he hoped to pick it up again once he was assured he wasn't somehow bringing death to his clients. But with impatient people in line behind him and the clerk waiting, Colin didn't want to argue. "Fine. I—"

"I'll send it to you."

"Fine. I really gotta go. Bye."

She said a curt good-bye and disconnected.

"I am so sorry," Colin said to the clerk, a skinny guy with Buddy Holly glasses and a waxed mustache.

"No problem, man. What can I do for you?"

It took some time for Colin to choose a mat and frame, but finally he was satisfied. He paid, left the sketch with the clerk, and headed out. It was nearly dinnertime, the sun already set and rush-hour traffic clogging the streets. He hadn't heard from Nevin, who usually texted before leaving work. Another long day for him. Well, at least Colin could feed him decently. On the way home, he detoured to his favorite Lebanese place and ordered a small feast to go.

"A little party tonight?" asked the owner, smiling at him.

"Nope. Just a hungry boyfriend."

She laughed. "Well, the way to a man's heart *is* through his stomach. I'm going to add some baklava and kanafeh to your bag so you'll have something sweet and sticky to share."

Colin grinned as he walked home, imagining some creative ways he and Nevin could eat those desserts. They'd have to shower afterward, but that was fun too.

When he reached the loft, he put the food in the fridge. Legolas reminded him it was dinnertime, so Colin poured some kibble before going into the bedroom to change. He'd been wearing sweats and a tee, as seemed appropriate for housecleaning, but it would be nice to dress up a little for dinner—even if it was just reheated takeout. He put on jeans that Nevin said showed off his ass especially well, a pale pink shirt, and a blue plaid bow tie.

As he was walking back into the main room, planning to watch some TV, the buzzer sounded. Puzzled, he loped to the intercom. "Hello?"

"Mr. Westwood?"

"Yes."

"I'm Darren—uh, Crystal's boyfriend. From Bright Hope. She has some stuff you need to sign."

When Crystal had said she'd send him paperwork, Colin assumed she meant by mail. Either she was pissed off he wouldn't volunteer and wanted to get rid of him fast or, more charitably, she was eager to clear her desk before taking some time off for New Year's. Either way, it was easier to sign than to argue about it. "Okay. Come on up." He pushed the button to open the lock.

He answered the knock less than a minute later. Darren reminded him immediately of Ford—muscular, shaved head, tattoos peeking past the collar of his T-shirt. But whereas Ford had the type of brown eyes that always sparkled with good humor, Darren looked wary. He peered over Colin's shoulder into the apartment. "Sorry, uh, to bother you."

"It's fine. Come on in."

Intending to find a solid surface for signing, Colin led him to the dining table. "Hang on and I'll find a pen." He rooted around in a kitchen drawer until he found one, then rejoined Darren at the table.

Darren reached into his jacket for the papers—and pulled out a gun.

A weapon pointed at his chest was so unexpected that at first Colin could only gape blankly. Then his heart began to pound and his knees went weak. He grabbed a chair back for support.

"Don't move!" Darren barked.

All the pieces fell into place at once, and Colin moaned at his own idiocy. "You killed—"

"Where is he? That cop?"

"I don't know—"

Darren waved the handgun a bit. "Crystal saw that picture in the newspaper the other day. You and that cop together at some fancy-ass shindig. I know you faggots are a couple. Now where the fuck is he?"

Trying to ignore his rising panic and racing heart, Colin frantically considered his options. He could keep his mouth shut, in which case it seemed likely that Darren would shoot him. That was bad enough, but soon Nevin would arrive home, not expecting a murderer in his home. And if Darren pulled the trigger before Nevin could even get his own gun out.... No. Not acceptable.

"He's at work."

"Call him. Tell him to come. But if you even hint that I'm here, I'm gonna shoot you in the fucking stomach and watch you die real slow."

911. He could call 911. But when he pulled out his phone and unlocked the screen, Darren stomped so close that the muzzle nearly touched Colin. "Show me. I wanna see who you're dialing."

Shit. It was hard to get through his contacts with his hands shaking so badly, but eventually Colin managed to get to the Ns. He tapped Nevin's number. Seemingly satisfied, Darren moved away. He kept the gun pointed at Colin, but his attention wandered to the loft's contents. Colin stepped back from him even farther.

"What's up, Collie?"

Colin could barely hear him through the blood roaring in his ears. "Are you on your way home?"

"In— What the fuck's the matter?"

A guy is in our loft with a gun. He's already killed four people, and he's waiting for you. They had an entire lexicon of double entendres, but they hadn't developed a code for this situation.

"Colin?" Nevin's voice went tight and urgent.

Darren had found Colin's wallet on the counter and was rifling through it, the gun held tightly in one hand. But he silently snarled at Colin.

"Are you coming home now, Nevin?"

"Jesus Christ in a basket, Col. What in the ever-living fuck— Is it your heart?"

"No. Drive carefully." And that was the best code he could manage. Nevin hadn't driven to work that morning. Since the loft was less than two miles from his office, he ran to work unless the weather was truly foul. And God, Colin needed to warn him of the ambush, but his heart was trying to burst from his chest, and his brain was creaking to a halt, and he was just that weak, prancing little fairy who couldn't stand up for himself, who never did anything worthwhile, who—

No.

"Colin!" Nevin was screaming into the phone now. Colin could picture him, eyes flashing, white teeth sharp, his free hand balled into a fist. And God, Colin loved him so much. Nevin was… precious. Sui generis. Someone worth saving.

"I love you," Colin said calmly. "And you're worth this."

Darren growled, dropped the wallet, and pointed the gun at Colin. Nevin screamed Colin's name. And Colin said, "Crystal's boyfriend wants to kill us."

The gunshot was deafening as it echoed off the brick walls, and the bullet hit Colin in the torso, sending him stumbling backward. It didn't exactly hurt, though. He felt the impact, the heat, but not the sharp, tugging pain of a healing scalpel wound. Maybe dying would be easy, like sinking under anesthetic.

The phone tumbled from Colin's nerveless fingers. He thought he heard Nevin calling him, but maybe that was only echoes.

Darren must have pulled the trigger again, because behind Colin a lamp exploded. Glass fragments flew into his back—and *that* hurt, bright and prickly. He staggered forward, and Darren ran at him. Colin's heart thumped loud enough to bring the building down. Which beat would be the last?

An orange-and-white streak shot out from under the couch and attached itself to Darren's leg. Darren yowled and Colin fell against him, knocking them both to the floor and skittering the gun across the polished wood. Darren and Colin both scrabbled for it, and maybe Darren had an advantage because he wasn't dying, but Colin was on top. And Legolas, brave Legolas, clawed at Darren's face.

Crawling, Colin got to the gun first. Darren tried to yank it from him, but Colin clenched his bloody hand around the grip. *Now* his chest was agony, each breath a screaming torture, but it was far too late to care about that. He put a blood-slick finger on the trigger, did his best to point the muzzle at Darren, and pulled.

Chapter Twenty-Four

NEVIN COMMANDEERED the squad car from the nearest gorilla and, lights flashing and sirens blaring, drove at speeds that would have horrified Colin. He couldn't drive fast for long, though, because traffic was heavy as he fought his way across downtown. He wished he had a military tank that could simply roll over all the fucking cars in his way.

More sirens screamed around him. He hoped he'd had the presence of mind to yell the right address before he took off.

He came to a screeching halt in the red zone, where Colin used to yell about Nevin's illegal parking. Crowds had gathered on the sidewalk, people gaping up at the building. A couple of uniformed officers waited there too. Nevin pushed his way through to the door, entered the lobby, and willed his hand to remain steady so he could key in the numbers for the security door. A troop thundered in after him. He'd never been so happy to be surrounded by a sea of blue uniforms.

They didn't take the elevator but instead raced up three flights of stairs. Thank the fucking gods Nevin was in good shape—a lot of the gorillas gasped and wheezed behind him.

Colin's door—*their* door—was closed, and apart from the police bureau contingent, the hallway was empty. The neighbors either weren't home yet or were cowering inside. Proper procedure said he should approach with caution. Fuck proper procedure.

Nevin drew his gun and opened the door.

Two bodies lay bleeding on the floor. One of them—fuck, one of them was missing a good part of his head. But thank Jesus and all the apostles, *that* body didn't matter. The one that mattered appeared to be intact, although it was facedown and unmoving.

"Colin!" Nevin collapsed beside him. His first thought was irrational—*no need to get tested now, not when I'm fucking bathing in his blood anyway*—but then his training kicked in. He gently rolled Colin over. Blood fucking everywhere, gallons and gallons of it, but Colin was breathing. God, he was breathing.

"Paramedics!" Nevin screamed, even as he ripped open Colin's shirt. Fresh ribbons of scarlet streamed from a small hole in Colin's chest, not far from the scar. Nevin pressed his hand to the wound and did his best to keep the life inside.

HAROLD HAD brought him coffee.

That was how royally fucked-up things were—Colin was in surgery, life hanging in the balance, and his father had brought Nevin coffee. Nevin tried to drink it, but his throat wasn't working right. All he could do was sit on the hospital chair and try to hold it together. Harold and Paula huddled nearby.

Goddammit. They could send people into space, so why couldn't they make a hospital chair that wasn't a fucking torture device?

Someone tapped Nevin's shoulder, startling him so badly that he almost reached for his gun. "Fuck!" he yelled into Frankl's implacable face. At least nobody shushed him.

"We need to talk."

"We can fucking well talk here because I'm not fucking moving."

Frankl nodded and sat beside him. "How's he doing?" he asked quietly.

"Surgery. But he's going to be all right because I told the doctor if he *wasn't* all right, I'm going to reach into her goddamn throat and pull out her lungs."

"Making homicidal threats is always an effective technique for receiving top medical care."

Nevin sagged. "Maybe I didn't put it quite like that." He couldn't remember clearly. Everything was a blur—chasing the ambulance to the hospital in a squad car, calling Colin's parents, and then waiting. Just fucking waiting. At some point he'd washed the blood off his hands and someone had given him a clean T-shirt to replace the stained button-down, but he didn't remember those bits either.

"The perp's dead and we've secured the victim's apartment," Frankl said.

"My apartment too."

"Okay. It's going to need some cleaning...."

Nevin shook his head. None of that mattered.

Frankl cleared his throat. "The officers at the scene told me the perp was—"

"Crystal. She works for Bright Hope. That son of a bitch was her boyfriend."

"Yeah, we got that. She's in custody and talking to Blake already."

Lovely. Nevin rubbed his temples and tried to kick his brain into gear. He was a cop, dammit, and a good one. He knew how to think through these cases. "Ruskin, Grey, the Thomases... that was them too." He remembered something Manny had mentioned to him once, about how Crystal was struggling financially. "My bet is Crystal's boyfriend was shaking the victims for cash. When they ran out or threatened to tell someone, he got rid of the problem."

"That fits what she's said so far. She's blaming him, which is handy since he's in the morgue, but he had to get the information from her."

Killing over money. Nevin had known real poverty, the kind that came with no food in his belly and no roof over his head, but even then, he'd never have hurt anyone just to line his pockets. "Why'd he go after Colin? Just to get to me? Why?" He should have learned by now that there was no logic to violence.

"We don't know yet. But Crystal has already admitted she spoke to Colin today. She claims she was just asking him to do some volunteer work and he refused, but we all know that's bullshit. Something else went down."

"He told her no," Nevin mused. "And she realized we were getting close to making them, so they panicked." Maybe another story would come out in the end, but his gut told him he was close.

Frankl tugged his own ear. "You were first on scene, so technically I need a statement from you. But the uniforms were right behind you—I don't think they missed anything. You and I can talk later. After he's doing well." He jerked his chin toward the door to surgery. "And Ng? Take care of yourself. You want me to call Jeremy Cox?"

"No. I'm fine." Jeremy was still tucked away with Qay. Ford was on vacation with Katie—his first in years, their first together—and Nevin wasn't going to interrupt that just so he could have a shoulder to cry on.

Frankl stood, clapped Nevin's back, and walked away.

A few minutes later, Paula sat beside him. She was grim-faced and dry-eyed. It occurred to Nevin that this wasn't the first time she'd sat vigil for Colin.

"He's so fucking brave," Nevin said. "He saved me. He knew that fucktard was going to try to shoot me and he—"

"I know. He's strong, Nevin. The strongest person I know."

"Yeah."

"And he knows you're worth saving." She smiled at him. "I think so too, honey. Besides, you brought the cavalry and put your hand to his bleeding body. Didn't you save him right back?"

She didn't hate him. Neither did Harold. Their baby boy was possibly dying, but they were comforting Nevin. And something else occurred to him. When the shit had hit the big industrial-size fan, Colin hadn't abandoned him; he'd been willing to give up his own life to rescue Nevin. And Nevin? He hadn't run away either.

Although worry still made his chest tight and head ache, he discovered something new within himself. It was warm and comfortable and sweet. Holy fucking mother of God. It was optimism.

Now it was all in Colin's hands. Or, more accurately, his heart. All he had to do was live.

THE SURGEON was exhausted, but she smiled at the Westwoods and Nevin. "He is going to be fine."

The three of them exhaled in unison.

"The bullet?" Nevin asked.

"It bounced around his ribs but did remarkably little damage. He will need some rest and time to heal, but that is all."

"What about his heart?" asked Paula.

The surgeon grinned. "Strong and uninjured." Then she squinted at Nevin. "Didn't I see you recently? You were here for another of my patients. Mr. Cox?"

"I've been bad luck lately."

"Or good luck, since both survived. How is Mr. Cox doing?"

"None of us can peel his boyfriend away from him long enough to tell."

She laughed. The Westwoods had a few questions for her, but Nevin had already heard the important shit. The rest would take care of itself.

After the surgeon left, Paula turned to him. "Go home and get some sleep."

"But Collie—"

"Will be in recovery for a long time. Get some rest, then by morning you'll be fresh and ready to sit at his bedside." She scrunched up her mouth. "When he gets released, he'll need someone to take care of him. We can bring him home—"

"No. I'll do it at our place."

"Good." She rested a hand on his arm. "He'll be happier at home with you."

NEVIN WAS going to owe a thank-you to the techs, or maybe to the gorillas. Somebody had done a credible job of cleaning the loft. They'd swept up the broken lamp, scrubbed away most of the blood, and gotten rid of the miscellaneous crime-scene debris. He even discovered that somebody had filled the fridge with an array of Subway sandwiches—though he suspected the boxes of Lebanese food had been Colin's work.

Legolas meowed, and Nevin picked him up to scratch behind his ears. "He'll be okay, mousebreath. A couple of days. Then the two of you can spend all the time you want lying on your asses and watching Judy Garland." He was about to add more kibble to the cat's dish when he noticed flecks of dried blood on the orange fur. Concerned, he prodded Leg but found no signs of injury.

"Good. Collie would pitch a fit if anything happened to you."

Although he wasn't especially hungry, Nevin ate some tabbouleh and falafel. Then he showered, rinsing away the dried fear sweat and the last vestiges of Colin's blood. He climbed between sheets that smelled of Colin and hugged Colin's pillow close. And then, with surprising ease, he fell asleep.

COLIN'S SKIN was nearly as pale as the hospital sheets, but his grip on Nevin's hand was strong. Nevin had been keeping watch at his bedside for the past few days, leaving only long enough for meals, quick showers, and changes of clothes. And to feed Legolas. But this was the first day Colin seemed fully lucid and even restless. "The doc says maybe I can go home day after tomorrow."

"Are you sure?" Nevin asked. "You're not—"

"I'm sure. I hate hospitals, Nev. They smell weird, the gowns are stupid, and people wake you up a zillion times every night."

"All right."

Colin smiled. "Really? You're not going to argue with me or even swear a little? Maybe I ought to have them come over and check you out too."

"Asshole."

"There's the Nevin I know and love." Then his expression grew troubled. "Shit! Legolas! God, I forgot about him."

"He's fine. I think he misses you, but he's fine. This morning I opened a can of tuna to help him drown his sorrows."

"Good." Colin shook his head. "He's a hero, actually."

"How so?"

"When Darren was coming after me, Leg attacked him. I've heard of dogs protecting their people, but I didn't think a cat would."

"Jesus Christ." Nevin used his free hand to smooth a curl away from Colin's forehead. "What can I say, Fizzy? You inspire loyalty in man and beast. But how are you doing?"

"I told you. The doctor said—"

"I don't mean physically." Shit. He didn't want to have this discussion, but he couldn't avoid it forever. Not with Colin gazing at him trustfully. "Collie, when a cop shoots someone, the bureau puts him on leave for a while. Makes him talk to a shrink."

"Have you ever killed anyone?"

"No."

The tiniest grin flashed across Colin's face. "Who would have suspected my body count would be higher than yours? Look, I'm sorry that guy's dead, but I'm not sorry I shot him. He was— God, he was a serial killer, wasn't he? And he would have murdered you too. So I don't need therapy over it. I'm perfectly at peace with what I did."

Nevin knew better but decided he could press the point later. He closed his eyes and gathered his thoughts before opening them again. "Thank you."

"For what?"

"You took a fucking bullet for me."

"You'd have done the same for me," Colin said confidently.

That was true. And as Nevin sat there, looking down at his lover, he knew that if a man was worth dying for, he sure as hell was worth living for. "It's better than a bullet," he mumbled.

"What?"

God, Colin was adorable with his face scrunched up in confusion. And Nevin might as well take the full plunge, seeing as he was already in way over his head.

"Permanency," Nevin said. "New word for me. Also commitment, dedication, and, um, steadfastness."

"They have me on drugs, Nev. I have no idea what you're talking about."

Still holding Colin's hand, Nevin knelt at the bedside. "So maybe it was you who rescued me from that ivory tower. I think it's time for our ever after."

"Ever?" asked Colin, his eyes sparkling.

"Ever."

"You're real romantic under all those prickles, aren't you? A regular—"

Nevin silenced him with a kiss.

EPILOGUE

June 2016

"WERE THE cuffs too tight?" Colin held Nevin's wrists away from the shower stream so he could examine them.

"Nope. Just exactly tight enough."

"God, the way you looked, chained up and begging...." Colin held a hand to his chest, covering part of the old scar and all of the new. "I'm surprised my heart could take it."

"Your heart can take anything."

Colin pulled Nevin flush against him, clutching Nevin's ass firmly. That part of Nevin's body was a little sore, but in a good way. Just a twinge to remind him what he and Colin had been up to all afternoon. What they'd be up to again if they didn't focus on getting showered and dressed.

"We're going to be late," Nevin warned.

"They can wait."

"And when we walk in there, they'll know exactly why." Not that Nevin gave a shit. Hell, he'd trumpet it to the entire city, if anyone cared. He'd tattoo it across his ass: *Colin was here.*

But Colin sighed. "Yeah, okay. I guess we should get going. We can save something for tomorrow night. We've got forever, right?"

"And ever," Nevin agreed. The admission infused him with calm rather than panic. This thing he had with Colin, it was real and good and rock-solid.

They dried off and got dressed. Colin filled Legolas's dish while Nevin petted Leg and reminded him, for the thousandth time, that he was the best goddamn cat in the history of the fucking universe. Judging by his expression, Leg placidly agreed.

The weather had been glorious all day, so it was a bit of a shame they'd spent it indoors. But Nevin regretted nothing, and he enjoyed the warm sun as they walked to the parking lot. When they reached Julie, he tossed the keys to Colin and veered to the passenger side.

"You're letting me drive your car?" Colin asked.

"Treat her nicely." Nevin was still riding an endorphin high and thought it would be nice to sit back and relax.

But as they crawled east over the Burnside Bridge, he scowled. "I said treat her nicely, not like your great-grandma. That pedal on the right is the gas."

Colin just grinned and patted Nevin's knee.

When they reached their destination, they argued over where to park. A perfectly good loading zone sat empty right in front of P-Town—and nobody got deliveries on a Saturday night—but Colin flat-out refused to pull into that spot. He circled the block a few times before finding a place on a side street. When he got out of the car, he stopped on the sidewalk to stare at the nearest house.

"What are you thinking?" Nevin asked, although he already knew the answer.

"This place could use some TLC."

It could. Gray paint peeled from the siding, the roofing pitched and curved like foothills, and the second-floor windows were cracked. The neglected front porch displayed warped floorboards and a rail with missing slats. More weeds than grass sprouted in the front yard.

"There's no For Sale sign," Nevin pointed out.

"I know. But with home values going up like they are, sometimes people will consider an offer out of the blue. Might be worth a shot, anyway. It could be a nice house." He took a photo of the front, then tucked his phone away.

Nevin smiled as they walked hand in hand down the block. Colin had been keeping very busy with work, but he took such obvious joy in it that even his parents had noticed. He went off to the office every morning singing and came home to serenade Nevin some more. His happiness was a balm when Nevin's day had been stressful—which was often.

P-Town was always busy on Saturday nights. But this time it was full of people they knew, because Rhoda had reserved the entire place for them. And yes, everyone accurately guessed why they were late, because as soon as Colin and Nevin entered, knowing cheers and laughter resounded from the crowd. Colin blushed adorably, but Nevin just leered.

A pair of guitarists—regulars at the café—strummed on the little stage, while the heady scents of coffee and baked goods permeated the room. Looking cute in a floral dress and beribboned pigtails, Ptolemy waved from behind the counter.

Rhoda reached them first and had bosomy hugs for both of them. She'd met Colin in January, soon after he got out of the hospital, and had predictably taken to him at once. Nevin suspected she had to restrain herself from pinching Colin's cheeks. "I still can't believe you captured him," she said to Colin.

"Captured, maybe, but I won't try to tame him."

"I'm not a fucking tiger," Nevin grumbled. But he was secretly pleased by their conversation—it made him feel powerful and wanted. And made him think of a new game he and Colin might try in the bedroom one of these days. Where in Portland could you buy a pith helmet?

Rhoda hugged him again. "Mazel tov. I'm so happy for you guys." Then she released them to a steady stream of well-wishers.

During one of his few moments alone—on a trip back from the bathroom—Nevin paused for a good look at the room. Tables had been moved aside, and some people were dancing. Katie and Ford swayed in each other's arms, and although she didn't yet look as if she'd swallowed a beach ball, her belly made a noticeable bump between them. She was radiant and beautiful and all the things expectant mothers were supposed to be, and Ford hadn't stopped smiling for months. Near them, Colin's niece Hannah danced with a cousin, and Harold and Paula were doing a credible two-step.

At a table in the corner, Parker was deep in conversation with Manny and Manny's husband. At another, Jeremy and Qay sat with Frankl and his wife, all of them laughing heartily at something Qay was saying. The rest of the café was filled with people Nevin and Colin knew— relatives, friends, and a few coworkers. All of them happy, all of them there expressly to celebrate what Colin and Nevin had made together.

And there was Colin himself, standing with his aunt and Miranda, a glass of iced tea in his hand. He looked boyish and handsome in chino shorts, a pale blue shirt, suspenders, and—of course—a red bow tie. He might have been listening to whatever his aunt was saying, but he was looking at Nevin, his expression full of love and joy. His eyes said the same thing as Nevin's heart: *Hey! That man over there—he's* mine.

Even though everyone would see one another again the following day, the party lasted late. Colin was yawning when he hugged Rhoda good-bye. "God, we still have to pack," he complained to Nevin as they turned the corner. After the ceremony, they were going to throw a couple of suitcases into Julie and slowly make their way down the Coast Highway, with overnight stops in Newport and Mendocino before a couple of weeks in San Francisco and Big Sur.

"Don't bother. I want you naked most of the time anyway."

Moving quickly, Colin pushed him back against the brick building and pressed his own body close. "You know, we could just elope." His words tickled Nevin's ear.

Nevin chuckled. "And disappoint your mother? I don't think so." Tomorrow afternoon, three hundred people would gather at Harold's golf club to hear Colin and Nevin exchange vows.

"I'll tell Mom too bad. She's not the one getting married."

"You made me buy that fucking tuxedo."

"And you can wear it again to the Christmas gala. Every year. Or," Colin added, dropping to a hoarse whisper and pushing forward with his hips, "wear it just for me."

Ah, but two could play this game, and Nevin was a pro. He kneaded Colin's ass and nibbled his ear, making Colin shudder. "Don't want to disappoint *you*. Remember? Chocolate-dipped strawberries, Etta James, and the B-52s, just like you always dreamed of."

"Yeah. It's going to be nice. But here's the thing, Nev. When I was a kid, I dreamed about getting married. But now I know it's just another party. The important part? The part I'm really excited about? That's *being* married. To you. That's my dream come true."

Nevin had been an abandoned child, a punk with nothing but fists and attitude. He'd risen above that shit to become a man—one who helped the underdogs and made a difference in the world. But now, with Colin, he was more than that. He was a happy man, a loved man, a man who was going to marry the strongest heart in creation. He was a man with dreams that came true.

"What are you groaning about, Nev?"

"My life has turned into a Judy Garland song."

Colin laughed and kissed his cheek. "C'mon. I'll sing it to you on the way home."

"Screw that. We'll sing it together."

KIM FIELDING is very pleased every time someone calls her eclectic. Her books have won Rainbow Awards and span a variety of genres. She has migrated back and forth across the western two-thirds of the United States and currently lives in California, where she long ago ran out of bookshelf space. She's a university professor who dreams of being able to travel and write full-time. She also dreams of having two perfectly behaved children, a husband who isn't obsessed with football, and a house that cleans itself. Some dreams are more easily obtained than others.

Blogs: kfieldingwrites.com and www.goodreads.com/author/show/4105707.Kim_Fielding/blog
Facebook: www.facebook.com/KFieldingWrites
E-mail: kim@kfieldingwrites.com
Twitter: @KFieldingWrites

LOVE CAN'T CONQUER

KIM FIELDING

A Love Can't Novel

Bullied as a child in small-town Kansas, Jeremy Cox ultimately escaped to Portland, Oregon. Now in his forties, he's an urban park ranger who does his best to rescue runaways and other street people. His ex-boyfriend, Donny—lost to drinking and drugs six years earlier—appears on his doorstep and inadvertently drags Jeremy into danger. As if dealing with Donny's issues doesn't cause enough turmoil, Jeremy meets a fascinating but enigmatic man who carries more than his fair share of problems.

Qayin Hill has almost nothing but skeletons in his closet and demons in his head. A former addict who struggles with anxiety and depression, Qay doesn't know which of his secrets to reveal to Jeremy—or how to react when Jeremy wants to save him from himself.

Despite the pasts that continue to haunt them, Jeremy and Qay find passion, friendship, and a tentative hope for the future. Now they need to decide whether love is truly a powerful thing or if, despite the old adage, love can't conquer all.

www.dreamspinnerpress.com

Carter Evans is founder and editor-in-chief of *Astounding!*—a formerly popular spec fiction magazine currently in its death throes. Not only can he do nothing to save it, but stuck in a rathole apartment with few interpersonal connections, he can't seem to do much to rescue his future either. And certainly all the booze isn't helping. He snaps when he receives yet another terrible story submission from the mysterious writer J. Harper—and in a drunken haze, Carter sends Harper a rejection letter he soon regrets.

J. Harper turns out to be John Harper, a sweet man who resembles a '50s movie star and claims to be an extraterrestrial. Despite John's delusions, Carter's apology quickly turns into something more as the two lonely men find a powerful connection. Inexplicably drawn to John, Carter invites him along on a road trip. But as they travel, Carter is in for some big surprises, some major heartbreak… and just maybe the promise of a good future after all.

www.dreamspinnerpress.com

It's time for Austin Beier to grow up. His car is falling apart, his roommates are less than ideal, and he's just been fired for the umpteenth time. His love life hasn't evolved past bathroom hookups at his favorite clubs. Forced to borrow money from his father yet again, Austin is walloped by an epiphany—he needs someone to mentor him into maturity. And who better to teach him how to be an adult than Ben, his father's office manager? Cute in a nerdy sort of way and only a few years older than Austin, Ben is a master of organization and responsibility. But as he gets to know Ben better, Austin learns that whether you're eight or twenty-eight, growing up is never easy.

www.dreamspinnerpress.com

THE PILLAR

KIM FIELDING

During his youth, orphaned thief Faris was flogged at the pillar in the town square and left to die. But a kind old man saved him, gave him a home, and taught him a profession. Now Faris is the herbalist for the town of Zidar, taking care of the injured and ill. He remains lonely, haunted by his past, and insecure about how his community views him. One night, despite his reluctance, he saves a dying slave from the pillar.

A former soldier, Boro has spent the last decade as a brutalized slave. Herbs and ointment can heal his physical wounds, but both men carry scars that run deep. Bound by the constraints of law and social class in 15th century Bosnia, Faris and Boro must overcome powerful enemies to protect the fragile happiness they've found.

www.dreamspinnerpress.com

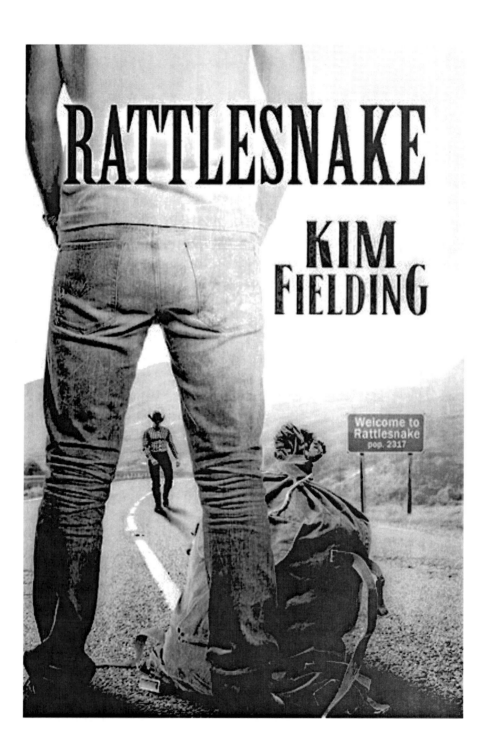

A drifter since his teens, Jimmy Dorsett has no home and no hope. What he does have is a duffel bag, a lot of stories, and a junker car. Then one cold desert night he picks up a hitchhiker and ends up with something more: a letter from a dying man to the son he hasn't seen in years.

On a quest to deliver the letter, Jimmy travels to Rattlesnake, a small town nestled in the foothills of the California Sierras. The centerpiece of the town is the Rattlesnake Inn, where the bartender is handsome former cowboy Shane Little. Sparks fly, and when Jimmy's car gives up the ghost, Shane gets him a job as handyman at the inn.

Both within the community of Rattlesnake and in Shane's arms, Jimmy finds an unaccustomed peace. But it can't be a lasting thing. The open road continues to call, and surely Shane—a strong, proud man with a painful past and a difficult present—deserves better than a lying vagabond who can't stay put for long.

www.dreamspinnerpress.com

Running Blind

KIM FIELDING   VENONA KEYES

Kyle Green is on top of the world. He and Matt have been together for ten years, and—as the voice of Ecos, the wildly popular anime character—Kyle is treated like a rock star in anime circles. But in an instant, a stroke leaves him blind. When photographer Matt gets the opportunity of a lifetime, Kyle reexamines their relationship, discovers it has been a safety net rather than a true romance, and sets Matt free to pursue his dream. Kyle's life and career as he knew them are gone, and he must now find the courage and creativity to draft a new plan.

After being away for fifteen years, Seth Caplan comes home to Chicago to care for his mother and to partner with a small start-up tech company. He and Kyle meet after Kyle's collision with a child's sidewalk toy, and they hit it off. Kyle wants to get back into running, and Seth becomes his guide. As they get to know each other, they start seeing each other beyond their three-times-a-week runs. But Seth's revelation of the dark reason why he left his career in California sends the relationship into a tailspin and leaves both men running blind.

www.dreamspinnerpress.com

CPSIA information can be obtained
at www.ICGtesting.com
Printed in the USA
LVOW10s1711220318
570811LV00013B/933/P